PRAISE FOR K.M. SOE.
THE WORLD OF NO

New York Blade be~~stseller~~
Washington Blade bestseller

One of the 10 Best Gay Novels of the year as selected by Amazon.com

A Selection of the InSight Out Book Club
A Selection of the QPB Book Club

"A stunning debut novel. While the setting is impeccably established, this is no nostalgic romp through tacky pop culture. Beneath the polyester veneer lies a work of uncommon craftsmanship which successfully chronicles the torrential turmoils seething within a thirteen-year-old as his life takes a sudden, dramatic change. Through Robin, Soehnlein explores a number of issues and dilemmas which readers of all ages will find relevant. Raw and painful (but in a good way), *The World of Normal Boys* may have to be put down several times, but you'll soon find yourself picking it up again to discover what happens."
—*Southern Voice*

"A gay teen's coming-of-age tale with a nostalgic twist, *The World of Normal Boys* captures a familiar world where conformists are rewarded, and anyone different is tormented. Soehnlein is at his best when describing scenes in which Robin's confusion runs up against the cultish homoerotic behavior of boys. By articulating the feeling of danger so well, Soehnlein sheds light on the threat of self-expression and discovery that must haunt many gay teenagers. It's easy to get hooked on the plot of *The World of Normal Boys.*"
—*The Hartford Courant* (Hartford, Connecticut)

"Every once in a while a book comes along that grabs you, pulls you in, and—even after you've finished the last page—refuses to let go. Such a book is *The World of Normal Boys*. Flawless in its physical and emotional detail, the story of Robin MacKenzie is one boy's spiritual awakening—funny, heartbreaking, but most of all, *real*—familiar to anyone who has ever dared to dream about the world beyond their front door."
—William J. Mann, author of *The Biograph Girl*
and *The Men From the Boys*

"Wonderful . . . a well-written tale."

—*After Dark* (Chicago)

More Outstanding Praise for
K.M. SOEHNLEIN and *THE WORLD OF NORMAL BOYS*

". . . captures that queasy, terrifying adolescent period of questioning sexuality."

—The Washington Blade

"Soehnlein's astonishing, heartfelt tale of growing up different in the suburbs is as vivid and fascinating as a page from a high school year-book. The seventies unfurl here like a polyester shirt: sexy, ugly, utterly unsuitable to the demands of childhood. For everyone who was ever picked on in their youth, here is comfort, revenge and understanding."

—Stacy Richter, author of My Date With Satan

"Compulsively readable . . . Because his characters are so engaging and his observations so acute, [Soehnlein's] story is a welcome addition to the canon. In Robin, Soehnlien has given us a character ready to handle anything the world throws at him."

—The Lambda Book Report

"Soehnlein skillfully depicts the background era of the late 1970s. He sensitively portrays Robin's awakening homosexuality and is especially effective when detailing the family dynamics."

—The Plain Dealer (Cleveland)

"*The World of Normal Boys* is so richly evocative of the year in which it is set, 1978, that the novel will have special meaning for those readers old enough to remember such scary ephemera as the Bee Gees, *Saturday Night Fever,* feathered hair and powder blue leisure suits. *The World of Normal Boys* is often so true to life in its recollection of the bittersweet conundrums of adolescent queer love that it will prove painful for some readers. Others will be elated to revisit a time in life when emotions were never so vivid or held greater promise. Either way, readers will not fail to be moved by this engaging story of spiritual and mental awakening."

—San Francisco Frontiers

THE
WORLD OF
NORMAL BOYS

THE
WORLD OF
NORMAL BOYS

A NOVEL

K.M. SOEHNLEIN

Kensington Books
http://www.kensingtonbooks.com

The author gratefully acknowledges the following publishers for permission to reprint the following lyrics:

"Last Dance." Words and music by Paul Jabara.
Copyright © 1977 Management III Music (BMI) and Olga Music (BMI). Worldwide rights for Management III Music and Olga Music administered by Cherry River Music Co.
International copyright secured. All rights reserved.

"(You Make Me Feel) Mighty Real" written by Wirrick James Tip and James Sylvester. Permission granted by Sequins at Noon Music and Spirit Two Music.

"Horses" written by Patti Smith. Permission granted by Codikow, Carroll, Guido & Groffman, LLP

"Just What I Needed," by Ric Ocasek © 1978 Lido Music, Inc.
Used with permission.

"Staying Alive" © 1978 Careers-BMG Music Publishing, Inc. (BMI)/Gibb Brothers Music (BMI). All rights reserved. Used by permission.

"How Deep Is Your Love" © 1977 Careers-BMG Music Publishing, Inc. (BMI)/Gibb Brothers Music (BMI). All rights reserved. Used by permission.

"Touch Me." Words and music by The Doors. Copyright © 1969 Doors Music Co. Copyright renewed. All rights reserved. Used by permission.

"Riders on the Storm." Words and music by The Doors. Copyright © 1971 Doors Music Co. Copyright renewed. All rights reserved. Used by permission.

KENSINGTON BOOKS are published by

Kensington Publishing Corp.
850 Third Avenue
New York, NY 10022

Copyright © 2000 by K.M. Soehnlein

All Kensington titles, imprints and distributed lines are available at special quantity discounts for bulk purchases for sales promotion, premiums, fund raising, educational or institutional use.

Special book excerpts or customized printings can also be created to fit specific needs. For details, write or phone the office of the Kensington Special Sales Manager: Kensington Publishing Corp., 850 Third Avenue, New York, NY 10022. Attn. Special Sales Department. Phone: 1-800-221-2647.

Kensington and the K logo Reg. U.S. Pat. & TM Off.

ISBN 1-57566-661-8

First Hardcover Printing: September, 2000
First Trade Paperback Printing: August 2001
10 9 8 7 6 5

Printed in the United States of America

This book is dedicated to
my friend Dave Hickey
and my father, Karl Soehnlein.

Acknowledgments

The readers of the earliest drafts of this novel instilled a faith that sustained me through a long writing process. I happily offer my gratitude to these friends and colleagues, who were there from the start: Maria Maggenti, Dave Hickey, Gary Rosen, Robert Kaplan, Sonia Stamm, Christine Murray, John Vlahides, Alexander Chee, Alan Klein, Michelle Carter and Fenton Johnson. Similarly, at crucial moments throughout the years, Kevin Clarke, Joel Perez, and Barney Stein each made an invaluable difference.

For advice and encouragement along the way, I thank Kenny Fries, Stuart Gaffney, Daven Gee, Garland Richard Kyle, Roberta Maggenti, Eric McNatt, Andy Moore, Michael Nesline, Jim Provenzano, Sarah Schulman, Michaelangelo Signorile, Mark Taylor, Trismegista Taylor, Jake Torrens, and Jack Walsh.

My agent, Jandy Nelson, has worked tirelessly on my behalf, greeting each challenge with enthusiasm, intelligence and determination. John Scognamiglio at Kensington Books has been a thoughtful, attentive and accessible editor. My deepest thanks also to the Creative Writing Department at San Francisco State University, my former coworkers at Film Arts Foundation, and my beloved playmates and coconspirators in the World of the Cubby.

Finally, I am indebted to my family for encouraging a writer in their midst. My mother, from whom I inherited "the gift of the gab," died before I began working on this book but remains a constant guiding force. My father, my sisters and their partners, and my grandparents have offered support in countless ways. They have made this possible, and for them, I gladly make one thing clear: this is a work of fiction.

Chapter One

Maybe this is the moment when his teenage years begin. An envelope arrives in the mail addressed to him from Greenlawn High School. Inside is a computer-printed schedule of classes. Robin MacKenzie. Freshman. Fall, 1978. He has been assigned to teachers, placed in a homeroom. His social security number sits in the upper right corner, emphasizing the specter of faceless authority. Someone, some system of decision making, has organized his next nine months into fifty-minute periods, and here is his notification. This is what you will learn. This is when you will eat. This is when you go home to your family at 135 Bergen Avenue. This is how you will live your life, Robin MacKenzie.

He has climbed out his bedroom window, onto the roof that covers the kitchen and back door below, with a pile of college-ruled spiral-bound notebooks purchased earlier that day at Woolworth's. His transistor radio is tuned to WABC, just now starting up ABBA's new song "Take a Chance on Me." He bobs from his shoulders, trying to harmonize, but his voice—revolting against him all the time lately—fails to hit a high note, collapsing into an ugly squawk, a bird being choked. He looks past the garage at the end of his buckled driveway and into the next yard, the Spicers' yard, wondering if Victoria has returned from her summer visit with her cousins in Pennsylvania. He needs to compare schedules with her, to find out how many classes they'll be in together; he needs to talk to her about high school.

The Spicers' lawn is a perfect spring green, stretching out from the cement patio and redwood picnic set to a neatly trimmed hedge that separates it from his family's weedy plot. The Spicers' graystone house rises up like a small mansion: slate-tile roof, royal blue shutters, and white curtains in every window. Only one thing upsets the serenity: a rebuilt '69 Camaro jacked up in the driveway, surrounded by tools and oil spots; Victoria's brother, Todd, has been repairing the engine all summer long, since he turned seventeen and got his license.

He's there now, Todd Spicer, rolling under the hood—all but his blue jeans and work boots disappearing from view—and then back out again, sitting up to swig from a paper bag stashed behind a toolbox. His sleeveless T-shirt is smeared with a greasy handprint; his arms tense up into lean ridges as he tries to make things fit into place. Even from his perch on the roof, two yard lengths away, Robin can tell the repairs are not going well, can feel Todd emitting frustration. When the hood slams violently, he knows the afternoon has been a failure.

Todd lights up a cigarette, raises his eyes. Pins Robin in his sights.

Caught staring, Robin blushes, embarrassment jetting up his neck, saturating his ears. He waves—what else can he do?—hoping the gesture reads as casual, just friendly, not eager. He knows—the way you just know how you're supposed to act—that he shouldn't pay this kind of attention to Todd.

Todd exhales and yells up to him, "What're you looking at, Girly Underwear?"

Girly Underwear. Todd picked the name just for him. Robin has a clear memory of when it started: he was seven, Todd eleven. Todd was circling around the yard on his dirt bike while Robin and Victoria were acting out plays they had made up; without warning, Todd zoomed in to swat Robin on the butt. Having done it once, he did it again, and again. Then he pushed it further, grabbed the elastic band of Robin's underwear and tugged up. His underwear that day—to his unending regret— was tinted pink; his mother had let something bleed in the wash. From then on it was, "Hey, Girly Underwear, watch your back," "Hey, Girly Underwear, how's it hanging?"

When he was seven or eight "Girly Underwear" could make him cry. It let Todd strip him down; it was all his weaknesses rolled up in one. He'd look at himself in the mirror: the sweep of his eyelashes, the swell of his lower lip, the curve of the bones around his eyes. His face was *girly.* Not like Todd's face: behind Todd's eyes was a storehouse of secret knowledge—how to be cool, to be tough, to get what you want. And the tone of Todd's voice, the weight of his stare when he called out the words—it was the way a guy teases a girl, an insult that shudders like a flirtation. It used to terrify Robin. But now, after years of it—years of watching Todd, thinking about Todd—now "Girly Underwear" leaves Robin feeling less assaulted than unnerved, as if enveloped in a nameless wish—a wish like wanting to leave Greenlawn and move across the river to New York City—something you can long for all you want, though there's no guarantee you're ever going to get it. Sometimes, "Girly Underwear" echoes later in his daydreams as a command, Todd's order that Robin strip off his clothes. Sometimes, in private, with his clothes off in front of the bathroom mirror, he wonders how his body compares to Todd's, wonders what Todd's body looks like naked.

On this late-summer day, the name and the disturbing longing associated with it evoke only anger. Maybe it's the safe distance between Todd's backyard and Robin's roof that emboldens him. Maybe it's the computer-printed class schedule he's clutching in one hand, reminding him that a week from now he'll be in high school just like Todd, that he's no longer some little kid to be picked on at will. Maybe it's just ABBA telling him to take a chance. When Todd yells, "Hey, Girly Underwear," Robin gives him the finger. "Fuck you," he yells back. "That's not my name."

Robin picks up his stuff and retreats through his bedroom window, his pulse thumping at this rare display of nerve. He glances back once before pulling down the blind: Todd is still looking his way, smiling, half a smile really. He sees Robin and nods. He might, Robin lets himself believe, be impressed.

Lying on his bed, Robin opens one of his new notebooks. High school. The hallways will be filled with boys, the speeding train of their conversation echoing off metal lockers. He thinks about popular boys from middle school, the jocks, boys whose names everyone knows. Their presence is inescapable, their actions gossiped about, their dating patterns speculated on by lesser beings like him and Victoria Spicer during late-night phone marathons. Popular boys are like TV stars: you don't have to know them to have opinions about them. You can spend your time imagining how they will react to something you've said out loud in class, or something you're wearing, when in fact they don't even know you exist.

On the top of a page he writes: TAKE SOME CHANCES.

Must make an effort to make friends with guys
Should get into a fight to prove myself
Should find a sport to play
Get a girlfriend
Tell jokes in class—people like that
Have not yet learned to smoke (buy cigarettes)
Should stop making it so easy for other people telling me what to do, etc.

The list pours out effortlessly, his handwriting uncontrolled, the tip of his ballpoint pen chiseling the soft paper. It's all so obvious—it's everything that he *doesn't* do. Everything normal. At the bottom of the page he writes, "Pick one to do everyday!" and underlines it twice.

The next day Victoria gets back from her cousins. Robin is mowing the Feeneys' lawn, another lawn in a summer of lawns he has taken on at three dollars a pop. He wears his work clothes—cutoff shorts and Keds and tube socks, all licked with mint-colored grass stains. Victoria is a gusher of stories about her Pennsylvania trip: the excursion to Hershey Park, the raft ride down the Delaware, the trip to the Colonial hot spots of Philadelphia. Her return is not the reunion he'd looked forward to: for months, he's been pushing the mower around the neighborhood, with just a couple of trips to New York City with his mother to break up the monotony, while she's been hanging out at a swim club, going to parties, letting some guy named Frank stick his hand under her bikini top. By the end of the afternoon he has nothing to say to her. She has her high school schedule to show him, but it yields only disappointment— they have no classes together. Without warning he jerks the starter cable for the mower. The clamor swallows up Victoria's voice and seals him into his own bubble of envy. Watching her strut away in her new pink satin jacket, like some tough-girl out of *Grease,* he can predict she'll fit right in at Greenlawn High. Hands in pockets, shoulders back, Gloria Vanderbilt jeans accentuating her developing body, she looks like she's getting away from him.

Todd is staring across the hedge. "Hey—"
    "Don't say it," Robin interrupts.
    "What?" All innocence in Todd's voice.
    "You know. Don't call me that name anymore." He pushes the lawn mower back into the garage. Speaking to Todd like that, telling him what to do, gives him the jitters—something bad is bound to follow.
    Todd is still standing there when Robin walks out of the garage. "All right, cool out, man. Robin."
    Robin. Not "Girly Underwear." It isn't quite an apology, but he relaxes a little. He looks Todd in the eyes.
    "So," Todd says, shifting his gaze away. "So, you wanna cut my lawn for me?"
    "I thought your mother had a *landscaper.*"

"That faggot quit, and now my father wants me to do it."

Robin shrugs his shoulders. "I charge three dollars."

Todd shakes his head. "No, see the idea is like this: *you* cut the lawn, and I give you a break on calling you—you know, *that name.*"

His face is so sure of itself, Robin thinks. He sputters out, "Like I can believe you? I'm not *stupid,* Todd. I'll cut your lawn, and then you'll just go ahead and call me whatever name you want."

Todd moves a step closer, lowers his voice. "That's the risk you take. That's what life is about, man. Especially in high school. Taking risks. Don't ya think?"

Robin stares in amazement. Has Todd been reading his notebook? Or is he just reading his mind? "I don't know."

Todd's face falls. "Man, I'm not getting any money from my Dad for doing it, so I can't pay you. How about if I give you a jay?"

"A what?"

"You know." He pinches his thumb and middle finger and mimics inhaling.

Robin gets the reference. "I don't think so." He turns to walk away, but Todd is suddenly through the hedge, right there at his back.

"Think about it," Todd says, and swats him on the ass.

Each step across the lawn, back to his house, he feels that pull. That magnetic thing Todd sends out like he's an evil Jedi Knight wielding The Force. The smell of cut grass and gasoline on his fingers, and Todd's voice echoing back at him. "Think about it." How weird to have Todd making some strange deal with him, Todd wanting him to take a chance.

His mother had taken him to R-rated movies a couple of times—usually on their City Day, when they take the bus into New York, just the two of them—but she outright refused to let him see *Saturday Night Fever.*

"Gratuitous," she pronounced its violence and sexual content, though she hadn't seen it herself. Robin suspected her objection arose from her dislike of John Travolta, whom Robin had become fascinated with ever since *Grease;* no, it went back even further, to *Welcome Back, Kotter,* a show everyone Robin's age had watched devoutly when it first premiered, but which Dorothy blamed for inflicting base expressions into her children's conversation: "Up your nose with a rubber hose," "Get off my case, toilet face." *Saturday Night Fever* elicited from Dorothy more than one harangue about disco and polyester and John Travolta, all of which Robin couldn't get enough of.

Robin reads that night in the Living section of the Bergen *Record* that the studio has announced *Saturday Night Fever* will be reissued as a PG. Robin is all resentment: a PG version! They're going to cut all the good parts! He checks the movie timetable: the R-rated version is still playing at the Old Tappan Drive-In. Someone has to take him to see this version before it is pulled. Someone seventeen or older.

The plan comes to him the next day, when the roar of an engine from the Spicers' yard catches his attention. Todd's Camaro is fixed! Todd could take him to see *Saturday Night Fever,* and in exchange, Robin can mow the Spicers' lawn for Todd. Forget about the "Girly Underwear" reprieve, Robin reasons, there is no way to make it stick. He brings the plan to Victoria, prepared to have to talk her into it, knowing how much she hates spending any time with her brother, but it takes no effort at all. She wants to see the R-rated version as much as he does. Apparently *Frank* had seen it, and it was one of his favorites.

Todd's reaction: "No fucking way I'm taking you to some sucky disco movie."

Robin: "We'll pay for our own tickets."

Victoria: "You don't even have to watch it. You can bring a date and make out in the backseat."

That part hadn't been Robin's idea, but it seemed to tip the scales for Todd.

The Camaro rushes from the end of Mill Pond Road, slicing open the afternoon quiet. Robin raises his face from the green of the lawn to meet the speed in the air. Sunlight on the glass and chrome, a blur of black metallic paint, the skid of rubber as Todd torpedoes into the driveway. Victoria protests the display—the noise, the skidmarks, the plume of gray exhaust. Todd struts out, lording over everything he sees.

Robin is mesmerized. This sweetens the deal, Todd eyeing the lawn, nodding approval at his work, shaking his hand. "OK, buddy. Looks like I'm taking you to the disco movie." *Buddy.* Robin wishing that it would be just the two of them, no Victoria, no date for Todd. *Robin and Todd,* he whispers to himself. *Buddies.*

When Mrs. Spicer gets home, she rewards Todd with a kiss on the forehead for his yard work. Robin takes note: how easily Todd accepts this undue praise. How he gloats.

It's been a long time since he prayed to God. He's never been led to believe that praying was particularly important. His father's obscure

Protestant background, combined with a few years of his mother's half-hearted stabs at raising them Catholic—the showy display of First Communion, the endless hours of Sunday School—have all added up to a lot of nothing. They've become what his grandmother, Nana Rena, refers to as "A&P Catholics"—"ashes and palms," people who go to church when they can bring home something to show for it. Even on those occasions when he sits through mass at St. Bartholomew's, Robin prefers silence over talking to God. Why would he expect anything from a Heavenly Father when he rarely asks for anything of his earthly father? If he needs something, he turns to his mother.

But now he has a secret to keep from her, and so he finds himself, without quite planning it, lying in bed, eyes raised upward, his hand moving into the Sign of the Cross. It is the night before *Saturday Night Fever.* He whispers out loud, "God, make it go OK."

Across the room, in the other bed, his younger brother sits up. "What'd you say?"

"Nothing."

"You said something to God," Jackson persists, a mocking amusement in his voice. Persistence is one of Jackson's trademarks. Unlike Robin, who tends to walk away from conflict, Jackson grabs hold and forces the issue. It's only one of their differences. In a new situation, Robin hangs back and observes, while Jackson gravitates impulsively toward the center, harnesses energy, and quickly begins spinning trouble. He laughs easier, has more friends—more *guy* friends; he is rambunctious where Robin is tentative. Jackson's half of their room gleams with brassy Little League trophies, Star Wars action figures, a colorful array of baseball caps lined up on his dresser; Robin has postcards bought at museum gift stores, a short stack of Broadway cast albums at the foot of his bed, scrapbooks stuffed with ticket stubs and matchbook covers collected on his trips to the city. The room's only shared territory is a nightstand between the twin beds, lined with Hardy Boys books that they've both read, Robin first, Jackson several years later.

When they were young, both in elementary school, they could play together and have fun; the two of them, with their sister Ruby—between them in age—could spend hours drawing pictures or creating elaborate plays to be enacted in the backyard or basement. Gradually this shifted; Jackson shifted away from them. Now he only liked games that could be won; now he shows up at the house with a group of friends, who divide up into teams and shout their way through competition, all along making fun of the slowpokes and spazzes.

"Dear God: This is Robin MacKenzie," Jackson squawks. *"Please make me not be such a jerkface."* He forces out a belly laugh for emphasis.

In silence, Robin amends his prayer. "And, God, could you please make something bad happen to Jackson?"

Maybe prayers are answered: Robin tells his mother he's going with Victoria to see *Grease* again, and she consents, as long as it's the early show, as long as he'll be home in time to get some rest before the first day of high school. And then, at the last minute, Todd's date cancels.

The girl collecting money at the Old Tappan Drive-In, who can't possibly be seventeen herself, drones at Todd, "You of age?"

"No, actually, I'm twelve. These are my parents."

"We'll keep an eye on him," Robin chimes in.

"You two are a regular comedy team," Victoria says, unimpressed.

During the previews, Todd lights up a joint. Robin leans across Victoria, who sits between them on the front seat, so he can study Todd's technique: inhale from the base of the neck, tighten your stomach to hold in the smoke. It looks like a special gesture known only to high school kids, like a secret handshake.

"What are you doing?" Victoria demands. Todd ignores her. "Todd, you could get arrested."

"You could get arrested for being so ugly," Todd growls, smoke leaking out his nostrils.

Victoria pokes into Robin's side. "Snack bar." She pushes him out of the car. "I can't believe you, Todd."

"What's the matter, didn't *Frank* ever get you high?"

"No, he doesn't do drugs. Anyway, this is like a *totally public* place."

Robin's eyes are on Todd, who's stretching backward, joint propped between his lips, arms reaching upward. His T-shirt rises, revealing the chalky skin along his waist, a seam of hair laid out like a spear from his belly button to the top of his jeans, where it fans out and disappears. No sign of an elastic band under his jeans. Robin feels his throat go dry: *Todd isn't wearing underwear.*

Victoria says, "When we get back, that better be gone."

Todd catches Robin's stare and floats the joint toward him. "There's plenty to share."

"I'll wait here," Robin blurts out. He watches Victoria's jaw drop and adds quickly, "I don't want to miss any of the movie."

Her surprise dissolves, replaced by betrayal. She slaps her hands against her thighs and trots huffily through the parked cars.

Just the two of them on the front seat. Robin and Todd. Todd and Robin. If it weren't for the scratchy soundtrack being piped into the car he's sure Todd could hear the nervous thump of his pulse. He usually tries to avoid being alone with Todd at all costs, a preemptive strategy for dodging harassment. *What was I thinking? I'm so stupid.* Robin stares through the windshield, fixing his gaze on the big screen, but all Todd says is, "My sister's a bitch," and passes him the joint. Robin studies it, pinched inside the teeth of a metal roach clip, the rounded orange tip like the butt of a firefly.

"My parents . . ." Robin mutters by way of refusal.

"Your parents drink, right?"

"My mother drinks wine and my father drinks whiskey." White wine and Seagrams, always in the house—he just takes this for granted.

Todd recites: "Man made booze. God made grass. Who do you trust?"

"What's that supposed to mean?"

"I saw it on a T-shirt at that head shop in Hillsdale. Makes sense, don't you think?" He leans closer, lowers his voice. "I told you, man: life is about taking risks."

Robin nods, saturated with new understanding. *Risk.* It's more than just a list of things to do—it's a whole way of life, a ride off the map. Todd's calm confidence expands until it's a safety net stretched out beneath them. Robin imagines the two of them as high school buddies— running into Todd in the courtyard, smoking pot between classes. "What the hell," he says, taking the joint.

The first surprise is the paper, damp with Todd's saliva, on his lips— the intimacy of it, like using the same toothbrush. Heat coils under his nose. He tries to copy Todd's approach, deeply drawing in the smoke, but his body rejects it. A stinging cloud explodes from his throat.

"Virgin," Todd mocks, slapping him on the back.

Robin is still coughing when Victoria returns with buttered popcorn, Raisinettes, and a single large soda. "Move it," she tells him with a shove. "All potheads on that side of the car." Her eyes comb over Robin; he guesses she's checking for signs that he's high. Maybe he is—when she waves her hand in front of her face, fussily clearing away the smoke, he bursts into laughter.

Todd sinks down behind the steering wheel, arms crossed, dopey smile stretching. His knuckles graze the fleecy hair on Robin's forearm.

Their hips are at the edge of pressing together. Robin glances into Todd's lap, still astonished at the idea that Todd is not wearing underwear. The folds of Todd's jeans offer some abstract sense of the shapes beneath, just enough to make Robin nervous. *Cut it out,* he admonishes himself. *Jesus.*

From the opening moments, when "Stayin' Alive" cranks up on the soundtrack and Travolta struts down the streets of Brooklyn, Todd is mouthing off. "Fuck, look at this fag." He asks Robin in disbelief, "You actually like this?"

It's the music Robin can't resist. He knows every beat of the soundtrack. To finally see the movie is like meeting his destiny, as if by playing the album on his parents' stereo all year long, he has conjured up this very moment. He realizes there's something uncool about the Bee Gees' high-pitched voices, but he feels like he understands the *need* in the lyrics: *I've been kicked around since I was born . . . I'm going nowhere, somebody help me, somebody help me, yeah.*

Todd pulls a Budweiser from under his seat, guzzles from it, and hands it to Robin. The can is slick with condensation. Robin takes in a mouthful, lets the fizz rub his burning throat.

"Oh, great," Victoria sneers.

"I'm thirsty," Robin rationalizes.

"I'll just tell that to your mother when you're totally wasted."

"Do you want some?" he asks, trying to appease.

Todd retrieves the beer, his fingers covering Robin's in the transfer. He sinks down farther in the seat, widening his legs. His thigh slaps Robin's and stays there. Robin closes his eyes and absorbs the contact into his skin before he pulls away. His heart is pushing blood straight up to his skull, pounding at his temples relentlessly. His dick—he realizes with alarm—is trying to get hard. This happens in school all the time; he's learned to always carry a book with him so he can cover himself if necessary. He crosses his hands in his lap, petrified Todd will notice.

He loses track of the movie's plot, simple as it is, and supporting characters blur into each other. The actress who plays the *love interest* is annoying—why would anyone spend so much time chasing after her? Even Travolta seems tarnished to Robin, who starts comparing him with Todd—the two of them in a battle for coolness, which Todd, through his Force-level disdain for every aspect of the movie, is easily winning. Concentration disintegrates. Blame it on the beer, which Todd keeps offering him (which he keeps accepting); on Todd's secondhand

cigarette and pot smoke, which Robin sucks from the air experimen-
tally; on being caught in the crossfire of Todd and Victoria's steady bickering, which persists even after Victoria finally relents and has a beer
herself. Blame it most of all on two hours' worth of Todd fidgeting at his
side—Todd's leg/arm/hip again and again meeting his own—and on his
own obstinate hard-on, impervious to any mental picture (bugs under a
rock, his grandmother's cooking, the bloody crucifix above the altar at
St. Bart's) he calls forth to banish it.

Only near the end, when the movie climaxes in a series of eruptions—
a big fistfight, a girl getting gangbanged in the back of a car, a guy falling
off the Verrazano-Narrows Bridge—does Todd seem at all involved in it.
And then Robin gets drawn in deeper, too. He remembers that some of
these scenes are going to be cut out of the new PG version, that he's
lucky to get what he wanted. The final scene has the Brooklyn boy moving out, and moving *up*, to life in Manhattan. It's perfect: he gets away
from his family, his lousy job, the mean streets of Brooklyn. The whole
night is perfect—well, not completely; Victoria is annoyed with him. But
Todd—Todd offers to drive him to school in the morning.

Nearly every window in the house is glowing as he makes his way from
the Spicers' yard to his own; he's mashing a wad of grape Bubblicious
between his teeth, extinguishing his beer breath in the sugary perfume.
As he pushes open the screen door, a whine of protest is rising up from
Jackson, who stands in the center of the kitchen, fists clenched at his
side.

"What's the problem?" his father, wearing the shorts and tank top he
jogs in every night, is asking.

His mother flashes what looks like a glare of accusation. "He owns a
very nice pair of gray trousers from Penney's—"

"It's a prison uniform," Jackson whines.

"I'll say it one more time," Dorothy announces, "for the benefit of
everyone involved." Here her eyes meet Robin with a quick scan from
head to toe; he shuffles guiltily, imagining his transgressions spelled out
on his T-shirt in iron-on letters. "I am taking a picture tomorrow morning, and I would like my children to look presentable. Allow me this *one*
motherly indulgence. After tomorrow you can go to school in your underwear for all I care."

Clark appeals to Jackson. "Be a sport, wear what your mother wants
you to wear. It's no big deal."

"I'll be the only nerd in the whole sixth grade in *dress* pants," Jackson says, dropping cross-legged onto the floor in front of the oven.

Robin fakes a kick toward Jackson. "Get up, Rover. No dogs allowed." Jackson grabs his leg and pulls, knocking Robin off balance. He reaches for the counter to keep from falling. "Cut it out!"

"Jackson, leave your brother alone," Dorothy commands, which only makes it worse for Robin: needing his mother's protection against his little brother. He pulls his foot free and slides away.

In the midst of the scuffle, their sister, Ruby, flutters into the kitchen. Her hair frames her face in golden tubes, carefully sculpted with her curling iron, and she's wearing a new white jumper and a gauzy flowered scarf tied tight around her neck. The steam of splashed perfume surrounds her—Love's Baby Soft, Robin guesses, or maybe Jontue; all the girls at school smell like this. She stands in the doorway, hands on hips, ready for attention.

"Hey, who's this beautiful princess?" Clark asks, right on cue.

A proud smile on Ruby's lightly glossed lips. "Do I look like a seventh grader?" She skips toward her father—and then lurches violently forward over Jackson's suddenly outstretched leg. She falls to her knees and skids across the linoleum to Robin. Her face is stricken; the impact of the fall hasn't yet sunk in.

An expectant pause, followed by the eruption of voices.

Jackson: "It was an accident!"

Robin: "You retard." He looks at Ruby, whose shock is giving way to misery; at each of her eyelids, a puddle hovers. "You're OK, Ruby. Really. Don't cry."

Jackson: "It's not my fault you're a spaz!"

Ruby, brushing a dingy smudge at each knee: "You got my pants dirty! What am I supposed to wear tomorrow?"

Dorothy: "I'll throw them in the machine tonight. They'll be good as new by morning."

Clark, yanking Jackson to his feet: "Accident my elbow! Get the heck up to your room!"

Robin: "You should make him apologize."

Clark: "Robin, keep quiet."

Jackson: "Yeah, shut up."

Robin grits his teeth, not wanting this uproar to turn against him. He's newly aware of his intoxication, realizes how all those swigs of beer and secondhand puffs of pot have added up, a recipe for confusion.

Ruby rubs furiously at her stained pants. "I have nothing else to wear!"

"Don't get too worked up about it, Ruby," Dorothy urges. "Clothes come clean."

"I'm not going to school if there's a stain on it. This *sucks.*" Ruby spins on her heels, treading heavily from the room.

"Spoken like a true princess," Dorothy mutters, finishing off her wine.

Clark joins Robin and Dorothy at the table. "Doesn't this happen every year right before school?"

Under the stained-glass lamp hanging by a chain over the table, Robin sees the exhaustion marked on his parents' faces: bags under their eyes, shadows thickening their brows. Frustration snakes around their ankles like horror-movie smoke. Robin studies a triangular sweat stain dried into the front of his father's tank top. Strange, he thinks, the way men sweat so much more than women—as if the heat under their skin can't be contained. He looks away from his father, bothered by this thought.

"I am utterly wiped out," Dorothy sighs. She stands up and stretches her arms over her head. Robin watches as the motion transforms her: the unfastened sleeves of her sapphire-blue blouse slide down her smooth arms, her honey-colored hair—the same color as his—falls away from her face and the skin on her neck pulls taut before relaxing into a faint pinkness. He blushes when she catches him staring.

She takes a step closer to him and narrows her gaze. "Were you and Victoria smoking in the movie theater?"

He rolls his eyes, trying to display the annoyance of someone falsely accused. "No."

Her nose is in his hair, an arm on his shoulder to keep him still. "*Someone* was smoking."

"No, it was just"—he fumbles for an excuse, and the sentence completes itself almost against his will—"Todd."

"Todd Spicer, the blemish on the neighborhood?"

"What are you doing hanging around him?" Clark asks. "That kid's nothing but trouble."

Instinctively, his glance shifts out the window in the direction of the Spicers' house. He makes a note to conceal the fact that Todd, and not Mrs. Spicer, as Dorothy expects, will be driving him and Victoria to school in the morning. "Todd just gave us a ride home. He's cool," Robin offers casually.

Dorothy shoots him a look as if he just told her he'd packed his bags and would be leaving home on the next bus. "Cool? Have you been watching too much TV lately? What's that character's name—the Fonz? Look, Robin, you don't need any *cool* friends. The cool kids in your high school years are always the ones who go nowhere fast. My brother Stan was cool as ice when he was Todd Spicer's age."

"What does that have to do with anything?" Robin asks—wanting to defend Todd against the comparison. Todd could *never* grow up to be like Uncle Stan—loudmouthed, ill tempered, full of prickly, conversation-killing opinions. Could he?

"Robin, you're being difficult. You're sounding like . . . a *teen*ager."

"Duh, I *am* a teenager."

Dorothy presses her fingers to her temples. "I need an Anacin."

Clark stands up and moves to the door, turning to wink at Robin. "Hope you had a good date with Victoria."

"It wasn't a *date.*"

"She's looking very pretty these days."

"Oh, did I tell you, we're getting married next week?" Now *his* head is starting to ache.

"OK, OK, forget I said anything." Clark waves himself from the room.

Robin whips his head around to Dorothy. "God, I hate when he says that. He knows she's not my girlfriend. I'm immature enough to have a girl just be a *friend,* you know."

"You mean *mature,* dear. Not *im*mature."

"That's what I said."

"No, that's not what you said."

"I know what I said, Mom. I'm the one who said it."

Dorothy glares at him. "When you make a mistake you ought to be big enough to admit it."

Robin kicks back his chair and stands up. He raises his voice. "Why are you all of a sudden on my case?"

"You *really* are watching too much television," she says angrily. "'On my case.' Is that another thing from the Fonz?"

"It happens to be from *Welcome Back, Kotter,*" Robin barks back.

"Another wellspring of culture." Dorothy points a finger at Robin, her voice raised. "This is your notice: there will be far less TV watching now that school is starting."

Robin begins walking from the room, twisting sideways as he steps past her. "I could care less."

As he makes his way across the living room floor, his mother shouts, "The phrase is, I *couldn't* care less." He stamps his feet on every step toward his bedroom. His mother's irritated shout follows him, echoing through the house. "Did you hear me, Robin? I *couldn't* care less."

A half hour later, Robin is sitting on the roof outside his bedroom window—his head pounding as he comes down off the high of the drive-in and the buzzing chaos in the kitchen. He stares across the lawn to the Spicers' house. On the top floor, a gable juts out, with a dormer window that leads to the attic. Todd has claimed this space for his bedroom. Robin tries to discern Todd in the shadows swimming behind the curtains.

"Mind if I join you?"

He jumps at the sound of his father's voice. Clark's already making his way onto the roof, squeezing his lanky frame through Robin's bedroom window. Robin doesn't answer the question, because he *does* mind. He minds very much when anyone, even Jackson, climbs out onto this little patch of shingles. It's like having someone break into his clubhouse.

"Tight squeeze," Clark says, landing awkwardly on the roof. "Good thing I'm jogging. Working off that spare tire." He pats his stomach, a gentle curve under his tank top. "Yessiree, Buck."

Yessiree, Buck—it's right up there with "accident, my elbow." Where does his father come up with this stuff? And what's he doing out here anyway? Robin stares straight ahead; the less he says, the sooner his father will leave.

"Thirty-seven years old, sitting at a desk all day. Walking to the train was about the most exercise—"

"Jogging's boring," Robin interrupts. "Just the same thing over and over."

"You have to admit, it's getting very popular. When your uncle Stan and I are out at the track the place is packed. There's plenty of teenagers there, too. You should come along."

Robin rolls his eyes. Is that what this is about? Cornering him on the roof for an athletic pep talk? "Maybe you can get Jackson to jog with you," he says, effectively stalling the conversation. The easiest way to derail his father's expectations is to shift them onto Jackson. It's always been this way. Robin only lasted a year in Cub Scouts before it became clear to everyone involved that it wasn't for him; the only thing worse than his father's silent disappointment was the prospect of another season of Pinewood Derbies and Wilderness Camp-o-rees. Jackson does all that stuff willingly. And Robin sees the way Jackson brings out something vibrant in his father: they're hosing down the car in the driveway and next thing you know there's a swell of playful shouting and a water fight going on. Or they're watching a Giants game on TV and tossing popcorn in the air for some last minute touchdown, or wrestling in the backyard as if they're *both* eleven years old. Every now and then Clark still tosses a ball Robin's way, at which point Robin tosses it to Jackson and leaves.

Clark clears his throat. "OK, look. Forget what I said before. In the kitchen. About Victoria. That was just teasing, but now you're mad." Robin bites his lower lip and doesn't reply. Clark continues, quickly. "Serves me right, butting in like that. That's the kind of stuff you don't need, I know. I know, I know. My father was pushing girlfriends at me for years before I was interested, and here I am doing the same thing to you and you're only fourteen!"

"I'm thirteen," Robin says.

"I didn't really get serious about girls until your mother. Or just before your mother." He slaps the heel of his palm hard against his forehead. "Geez."

Robin smiles despite himself. "Don't hurt yourself."

"No, this is important. You're going off to *high* school tomorrow. So, you know, just as a reminder—if you have any questions, the man-to-man type, just ask. I know you and your mother are closer, but feel free, don't be shy—" He pauses. "So what do you say?"

What am I *supposed* to say? Robin wonders. A tinge of panic sends his leg bouncing. He is keenly aware of his father's impatient breathing, his father next to him, just *waiting*. Robin finally blurts out, "I know about the facts of life. That's what they teach us in health."

"Oh, of course, right. That's great." Clark falls silent; Robin can't be sure if his father is relieved or disappointed to close the discussion. After a moment, Clark says, "I'd like to get a bigger house," with such certainty it seems to be the solution to all his worries. "If we had a bigger house you could have your own room. A young man should have his own room. I've been meaning to build the swimming pool, too, but maybe we should just knock down the living room wall and build an extra bedroom into the backyard." He opens his arms wide, as if the land below stretched out for acres.

Robin nods, trying to keep up. "Jackson probably wants a swimming pool more than he wants his own room," he says, but his father keeps talking, almost over his words.

"When you're young you don't really know what you'll need when you're older, or even who you'll be. My father used to tell me, if you want to be a man at night, you have to be a man in the morning. I didn't realize he meant six A.M., every morning, on the train, off to work. You probably don't know this, but I didn't *expect* to be in sales. I liked *science* in school. I wanted to work for the space program. I never thought I'd have a teenage son—I just thought about having *little* kids, if I even thought about it at all. Not kids with growing pains."

Clark drops his head in his hands. Robin is speechless with discomfort. It's like one of those moments when his father comes out of the bathroom and the ripe stench of his shit floats out into the hallway after him—you want to ignore it, but it's right there in your face. You can only *pretend* to ignore it, just like he can only pretend his father isn't slipping into some kind of—what's it called?—*midlife crisis* before his eyes.

"Uh, I'll be OK, Dad," he says at last.

"Yeah, you will. You'll be a lady-killer, and a big success. All in good time." He rises, brushing dirt from his bare legs. Robin's eyes glance at his father's running shorts, bunched up to reveal the lopsided package of his genitals. Does his father wear underwear under those shorts? Maybe, Robin thinks with some discomfort, maybe he wears one of those supporter things—a jock strap. It's embarrassing to think about his father this way, even though that's kind of what his father was referring to: his *thing. If you have any questions about your* thing, *you can ask me, man to man.* Without thinking, he moves his eyes back to Todd's window, where a faint purple glow radiates. When he looks back at his father, their eyes meet, and his father sighs almost imperceptibly before disappearing into the house.

When he finally climbs back into his room, the lights are out, and Jackson is sleeping. Under his blanket, Robin shimmies off his pajama pants and his underwear; then he pulls the pajamas back on. The synthetic material is slippery against his ass and his dick, which makes him feel exposed and daring. Is this why Todd doesn't wear underwear, for this sensation, this freedom?

Lying awake, replaying the night's events in his mind, he pushes down the covers and raises up his shirt. His fingertips trail feathery across his belly. The skin along his ribs shudders with pleasure. He liked seeing that strip of hair on Todd's stomach, but he likes the smoothness on himself. He feels his dick stretch and stiffen. With a glance to Jackson's bed to make sure he's really sleeping, Robin reaches under his waistband. His fingers close around his dick as if he's giving it a handshake. Does Todd do this, touch himself this way? He must—all boys do, according to what he read in the "Ask Beth" advice column in the *Record*. It occurs to him suddenly that each *accidental* contact between him and Todd in the car was instigated *by* Todd; it was Robin who retreated every time. Was this some new game Todd was playing, a more crafty version of calling him names? Why else would Todd have done it? He doesn't answer his own question; instead he rubs himself more insistently, until the friction burns so sweetly that he has to stop. He wants to keep going, but it feels like trouble.

He is sitting in the Greased Lightnin', the '57 Thunderbird that John Travolta soups up and drives to victory in *Grease*. Travolta is tensed and focused behind the wheel, and Robin sits next to him, sits on his lap—no, he's *behind* him, in the backseat, his hands braided into Travolta's lacquered hair. He keeps shifting, but Travolta stays in place. The speedometer escalates. *Where are you taking me?* he asks, or he thinks he asks—he's not sure. A siren blares at his back, a squad car giving chase. Todd speeds up the car. *Todd* is driving, not John Travolta. Todd's driving so recklessly Robin's body rattles.

Gulping in air, hands over his head, fingers scratching at the headboard—he's awake. Awake and alarmed: *I did something wrong.* He rolls on his side, and then he feels it—warm goop like rubber cement in his tangled pubic hair.

Morning rays push through the blue corduroy curtains, the light thick and cloudy, like something you should skim, like pool water. Jackson's bed is empty, thank God. He pulls the covers over his head and sniffs deeply. It's a pool smell, chlorine, with the weight of some other damp thing: moss, soggy bread, an old washcloth. He touches it, licks his finger. Slimy, sweet, bitter—all of that. He knows what this is. *Nocturnal emissions,* they called it in health class. *Wet dreams.* He remembers Travolta, the car, the vibrations of the ride. The sirens. He squeezes his eyes shut as if in defeat.

At least this morning Jackson, with his acute, bratty radar, his relentless teasing, is already up. Robin wipes himself with a T-shirt, pulls on some pants, strips the sheets quickly. It's two flights down to the washing machine. Arms full, he heads to the stairs.

"I want to talk to you about last night—" His mother, emerging in a blast of humidity from the bathroom, toweling her hair, is addressing him. "It's one thing for me to have an occasional cigarette, but I don't want you to get any ideas—what are you doing?"

"Just doing some wash," he says with a wide, false smile, as if this is normal.

"Robin, I cleaned those two days ago." She moves forward, peering at the soiled bundle, prepared, he realizes, to take it from his hands.

He clutches the sheets tighter, wanting to trap the smell, keep his secret. His skin is heating up. A split-second image: Travolta's face—or is it Todd's?—laughing at his predicament.

"Mom," he says in the firmest voice he can muster. "They need to be cleaned. Trust me." Her face is blank for a moment before something registers. Then she blushes, too.

"Oh, well, go ahead, sure. Just throw them in the washer, and I'll put them in the dryer later. We have to get you ready for school." She turns away hurriedly, muttering something—scolding herself?—and closing the bedroom door behind her.

A panicky jolt: today's the first day of high school. He'd been so focused on his dream, he'd forgotten. His first wet dream. He's been waiting for this, a plunge into the world of puberty, of sex. A couple of years ago, Victoria had been waiting for her first period, and she let him know as soon as it happened. He feels only the pressure to conceal. If he told someone, they'd ask about the dream, and what could he say? There were no girls in it, just him and Travolta and Todd and the police. All his life police have crowded his dreams, and he always wakes sure of his own guilt. It stays with him each minute of the day, a slight burning flame in the back of his mind. Unseen, constant as a pilot light.

He takes to the stairs quickly, dragging his mess to the basement, wanting to be free of it.

Sitting in the backseat of the Camaro, Robin finds Todd's eyes in the rearview mirror. Todd flashes him a sly smile and says, "This morning is the traditional first-doob-of-the-year party in the courtyard, Robin. You gotta be there." Todd pretends to smoke a joint and "passes" it to him. When they get to the parking lot, Todd fakes a punch to Robin's chest and winks at him before he leaves.

None of this escapes Victoria's attention. "So are you two supposed to be *friends* now?" she challenges.

"It's just a new way for him to bother me," Robin says dismissively—though, in fact, he's not bothered; he feels triumphant. Not once did Todd call him *that name*.

Chapter Two

EXPECTATIONS. REALITY.

Mr. Cortez writes each word on the blackboard, then draws a vertical line separating them. "What kind of things have people told you about high school? These are your *expectations*. What did you find when you got here? That's *reality*." This is group guidance, the last class of Robin's first day of school, a class provided just for freshmen: "a rap session" was how Cortez, his guidance counselor, had described it when Robin met him last spring for orientation. Cortez is a young Puerto Rican guy with a mustache and curly hair. He wears Frye boots and tells the students, "Expectations and reality don't always match up. That can be a really bad trip. That's why we try to keep the lines of communication open and not get hung up."

Robin's own gloomy expectations for the day have largely been met. Every class begins the same: nervously waiting for seats to be assigned. He longs to sit in the back, or along the windows—somewhere inconspicuous—but the tyranny of alphabetical order always leaves him smack dab in the middle, an "M" surrounded on all sides, third row across, third row back, like some obnoxious center square on *Hollywood Squares*—like *Paul Lynde,* except he wasn't even as funny as Paul Lynde. (He remembers a question from the show: "Betty Ford said *it* was her second greatest pleasure in life. What was *it?*" Paul Lynde: "Sucking on a rum cake.")

All the guys in his classes have longer hair than they did last year. They look like teenagers now—taller, wider necks, deeper voices. There are three acceptable ways to dress: sports team logos (for the jocks), concert T-shirts (the scums), and plaid shirts with snaps instead of buttons (the brains). Robin's in a polyester patterned thing, brown and gold and white, and snug fitting, chocolate brown dress pants that he really likes—though after looking around at what everyone else is wearing, he starts to think he might like them too much.

Humiliations great and small greet him every class period. In English, the guy in the seat in front of him, Jay Lunger, announced, "Your name is gonna be *Ears*." Jay was bigger than him by a couple of inches and had no problem saying whatever he wanted. When Robin tried to laugh off the insult, Jay said, "It's not that funny. You're walking around like you got half a plate on each side-a your head." For the following forty-five minutes Robin examined every pair of ears in the room: how far they stuck out, how long they were, if the lobes were attached or not. Between periods he checked himself out in the bathroom mirror, turning his head from side to side. His ears weren't *that* big, he reasoned, they just curved out at the top, like fins on a classic car. He decided he'd have to grow his hair longer anyway, just in case he was wrong.

In phys. ed. they played kickball, and when he was up, he swung his foot and missed the ball entirely. "Never heard of anyone getting a strike in *kickball*," Billy Danniman, standing on deck, sneered. In algebra, he wound up in the seat behind Diane Jernigan, who gloated to him about how *psyched* she was that she and Victoria had so many classes together, while he seethed with envy: *Diane Jernigan, that bitch, last year she got a whole bunch of girls to gang up on me because I said I hated Kiss.* At lunch, he took his place at a table with a kid from his neighborhood named Gerald and Gerald's friends, who passed the hour talking about an upcoming *Star Trek* convention they were all *really stoked* about. He spent most of the period surveilling the cafeteria for someone else to sit with tomorrow; there was his lab partner from science, George Lincoln, but George was black, and the black kids all sat together at three tables on the far end of the cafeteria.

The one class he was looking forward to was art—he'd been told that freshmen learn how to develop film and print photographs, which he's always wanted to do. There was no mention of this, however, from Miss Blasio, who used up the class drilling them on which solvents counteract which kinds of paint. Miss Blasio was six feet tall, with brown hair halfway down her back and long, red-painted fingernails. Robin became mesmerized by the way she regularly let a thick ribbon of hair fall in front of one shoulder, then, with a purposeful toss of her head and the back of her hand, flipped it behind her again. It was hypnotic—hair sliding around the left shoulder, then *flip*; then around the right shoulder, *flip*. He timed it—one flip about every four minutes. Every ten minutes or so she gathered the whole mop of it in the back, made a ponytail in her fists, and then let go. *Whoosh*. Next to Miss Blasio's name in his notebook he wrote "a.k.a. Cher."

Already group guidance is an improvement on the day. The chairs are in a circle, and Cortez has instructed them to sit anywhere they want while they rap about *expectations* versus *reality*:

"School sucks."

"I hate it when people make fun of me for liking school."

"I'm sick of all these uptight teachers telling me what to do."

"I'm a Christian, and I find it very hard to feel comfortable because kids act like that's not cool."

Cortez writes, "Expectation: We're all in this together. Reality: Conflicting values."

Robin gets the nerve up to raise his hand. "I was told that we'd be doing *photography*, you know, in art, but she didn't even mention it."

Cortez nods. "We can check into that. Who's your teacher?"

"Miss Blasio," he says, then rolls his eyes and adds, *"Cher."*

A few big laughs from around the circle. His face turns red—embarrassed, until the satisfaction of having told a successful joke settles in. He even dares an imitation of Miss Blasio's hair toss—*flip, flip*—which grabs a few more approving chuckles from his classmates. Cortez himself breaks into a wide grin, though some sense of propriety prevents him from actually laughing at a teacher's expense.

Robin remembers his list of Chances: one of them was to tell jokes in class. This is the first victory of his high school life. For a few hours, it erases all of the day's defeats.

A well-placed sarcastic comment, out of earshot of his teachers but loud enough for those in the desks around him to hear, becomes Robin's sole release—the one chance he successfully takes again and again, until it isn't chancy at all, until it is one of the few times that he doesn't shrink from the sound of his own voice. Mornings are gloomier since Victoria's proclaimed that she is no longer accepting rides to school from her brother—"I'm not gonna sit around and wait for him to get busted for drugs," she announces to Robin—thereby effectively cutting off Robin's access to Todd. Most days, he gets home from school and for no reason he can articulate is so lethargic and exhausted that all he can do is collapse in front of the TV. He disappears into the heated storylines of *General Hospital* and *The Edge of Night* until his mother gets home from her part-time job at the Greenlawn Public Library. Fatigue takes root in his joints—from his knees to his jaw, as if he's been holding himself stiff for hours. When his mother asks him how the day went, he scavenges for something he can tell her, something she would *appreciate*. He doesn't tell her Billy Danniman called him a fag in gym class after he dropped a fly ball; she would only urge him *not to dwell on it.* He leaves out the disappointment of yet another awkward, on-the-fly conversation with Victoria—the only kind of interaction they seem to have anymore; his mother would simply remind him that his future is far away from Greenlawn and that *adolescent friendships are never the important ones in life.* He certainly doesn't tell her when the best thing that happened all day was Todd sending a halfhearted "Yo" his way as they passed in the hall (leading to a kind of hopeful reverie on Robin's part that yes, in fact, he and Todd might actually hang out sometime). So instead he tells her what he's reading in English because this delights her most of all. Dorothy rereads for herself whatever he's been assigned so that they can talk in detail about the story. Books—*stories*—are what his mother appreciates above all else.

One day toward the end of September, Dorothy lets Robin miss school. He's been waiting for this: their City Day, one of the days every few months when they disappear from Greenlawn together. They've been doing this for years, dressing up in their most stylish clothes and traveling by bus through New Jersey towns that bleed together unremarkably, onto the Turnpike, where the first views of the New York skyline are revealed, and into the eerie glow of the Lincoln Tunnel. They hurry through the crowds at the Port Authority Bus Terminal into one of the Checker Cabs that line Eighth Avenue like chariots for visiting royalty.

Robin gives instructions to the cab driver—"Take us to the Museum of Modern Art, on 53rd Street between Fifth Avenue and Avenue of the Americas"—and Dorothy tips generously, her bracelets jangling as she pulls bills from her purse. She is most animated on these days, an enthusiastic tour guide, telling Robin about her adventures in the city in the early '60s, when she graduated from Smith College and found work as a secretary at a publishing company. She tells him about the well-dressed crowds strolling Times Square at 2 A.M., about drunken authors at book parties, about the handsome men who courted her over coffee at the Automat. She shows him the apartment on West Twenty-Third Street where she and Clark first lived after they were married, where Robin spent the first four years of his life. She tells him things on these trips that he never hears her telling anyone else—punctuating the details with dramatic exhalations from her Pall Malls—which leaves him feeling un-common, a coconspirator, the keeper of secret myths.

And her stories change: today she mentions a surprise appearance by Miles Davis at the Five Spot in 1963; the last time she told this story it was Sonny Rollins in 1962. Robin used to correct her, but Dorothy only laughed off the inconsistencies. Now he has come to welcome the way her stories shift; it is the excitement of them, and not the facts, that he values. She encourages him to make up stories of his own. A woman in sunglasses and a fur coat hurries past the park bench in Washington Square where they are sipping coffee. "Who is she," Dorothy asks, "and what is she up to?"

Robin takes a moment to think, and a tale tumbles forth: she is a jet-setting fashion model who dances all night at Studio 54, but deep down she's miserable, she's spent all her money on champagne and caviar and cocaine; now she's broke, all she has left is that fur coat, and she'll be trading that in at the Ritz Thrift Shop any day now. It feels like ESP when he does this, but instead of reading someone else's mind, he's tun-ing in to transmissions from some alien part of his own, where ideas are always buzzing, where static can be translated into stories.

The tragedy of the City Day is always the aftermath, when he sits across from Ruby at the dinner table and absorbs her jealousy at having been left behind, or argues with Jackson about why a symphony at Lincoln Center is more interesting, more *relevant*, than a playoff game at Yankee Stadium. Even his mother loses her sheen in the days that fol-low, as she returns to shopping at the A&P and telling his father to re-move his feet from the coffee table and correcting Robin's language whenever, God help him, he slips into slang like some common New Jersey teenager.

A Sunday night at the beginning of October: Clark is dragging Dorothy to a World Series party with Uncle Stan and Aunt Corinne. As Robin watches his mother glide down the stairs wearing a new pantsuit that he helped her accessorize—rhinestone post-earrings, a Diane von Fursten-burg scarf, a bronze leather bag and matching shoes—it becomes clear how unpleasant this night will be for her. Stan berates her for keeping them waiting, and Clark fumbles to apologize on her behalf. Even Corinne has shown up in a Yankee cap, spirited and enthusiastic for the big game. Robin admires his mother for not displaying false excitement, for letting her style set her apart; still he can't help notice in her departure a dread that they share. This party is like a grown-up version of gym class.

His cousin Larry has been deposited at their house, placed with Ruby and Jackson under Robin's care, though Robin quickly retreats to his room with the paperback copy of *East of Eden* he's been assigned for English class. His mother once took him to see the movie at the Thalia in New York, and now every page is charged with the electric image of James Dean. Robin lies facedown on the bed, skipping ahead until he gets to Cal's scenes; he hears James Dean speaking for Cal, murmuring his pain and rebellion. It gives him a boner, which he grinds distractedly into the sheets as he reads.

An hour later, when a sharp, burning stink wafts under his door, he heads downstairs to investigate, carrying the book in front of his fly to hide the evidence.

The living room is hazy with smoke; the game is on TV but no one is watching it. In the kitchen, Jackson stands on a chair in his underwear, trying to push open the skylight over the sink. Larry, in his underwear, too, is clutching his ribs and faking an uncontrollable coughing fit.

"What the hell?" Robin demands.

"We torched the Rice Krispie Treats," Jackson says.

"You're supposed to put them in the fridge," Robin admonishes, "not the oven."

"Shut up, Susie Homemaker," Larry snorts. Jackson begins laughing and loses his balance in the chair. Larry gives him an extra shove, which knocks him into the sink; his elbow hits the faucet and the water pours out onto his belly. When he stands up his underwear is soaked.

"Ah-ha," Larry says. "Couldn't hold it in."

There are few people Robin dislikes more than his cousin. Even though Larry's a year younger, he always manages to intimidate Robin. Larry has a Bowery Boy's face: eyes forever moving into a squint, nose scrunched up as if he's been forced to do something he hates, mouth in a sneer. Proud of his farts, quick with his insults, endlessly pulling pranks—of all the put-downs Robin's learned from his mother, the one that suits Larry best is *primitive*. Worst of all is his influence on Jackson. Most of the time Robin thinks of Jackson as simply the pest in the next bed, the loudmouth never out of earshot, a nuisance no worse or better than bad weather. But Larry drags Jackson behind closed doors, and after much giggling and half-whispered plotting they emerge with a new campaign of terror laid out. They bellow dirty jokes they don't necessarily understand and laugh too loudly at them. They taunt Robin. Put

Jackson alongside Larry and it's as though the monster has grown a second head.

"Don't expect me to clean this mess up," Robin says, and leaves the kitchen, opening a window to air out the room.

Ten minutes later, Robin is roused from his reading again, this time by Ruby's squeals. He runs to the hall and sees Jackson and Larry darting out of her bedroom naked. "Streakers!" Ruby shrieks in horror.

Robin freezes for a moment—stunned at the flash of skin—and then, feeling that it is his duty as the oldest one to impose some order, calls out, "You guys, cut it out."

Larry and Jackson stop at the top of the stairs. Side by side, hands in the air, they shake from the hips. "Freddy and Petey on parade!" Larry yells.

Robin looks at their dicks slapping to and fro. Jackson's is just a little boy's pud, no bigger than his pinky, but Larry's is already developing, taking on a fullness that looks like his own. Larry pinches two of his fingers around it and gives it a shake. "Squirt, squirt," he says mockingly, staring Robin in the eyes, his gaze a dare, not just defiant but belittling. Robin turns his eyes away from them, red faced, and yells, "I said cut it out."

"Oh, we're scared." Larry smirks and then takes off downstairs after Jackson.

Robin charges after them, unsure what else to do. His confusion escalates as they race through the living room, the dining room, the kitchen—their bared flesh in this setting is doubly disturbing. Larry's daring makes Robin feel timid; the way he just flaunted himself in front of Robin feels like a personal insult, a knowing "gotcha" for which Robin must now retaliate.

Jackson disappears through the basement door. Larry turns around and spits out, "No girls allowed," slamming the door behind him.

The aftermath of the Rice Krispie Treats is strewn across the countertop. Robin grabs the metal mixing bowl, smeared with sugary goo, the spoon, the box of cereal, and the charred baking pan. He throws open the door. At the bottom of the dark stairway, he can make out two crouched figures. Before they have a chance to move from their hiding place he hurls everything at them. A surprised yelp rises up from Jackson. Larry just laughs like a gleeful gnome. Robin storms away, frustrated that he missed his main target.

Every door has its own particular voice. The *chunk-chunk* of the car being exited in the driveway, the squawk of the screen door arcing wide, the metallic turn of the front door's loose knob, the sweep its lower edge makes on the hall carpet. From his bed Robin follows the path of his parents' return, hears their muffled speech, the heaving pad of their feet on the rug. Something's not quite right: he can hear Aunt Corinne with them, moving toward the basement (the airy fling of that door familiar, too). She's calling for Larry. Robin gets up and goes to the top of the stairs.

"Mom?"

His mother lies wilted over his father's shoulder. He's trying to maneuver her up the stairs. Behind them Corinne is placing Dorothy's purse on an end table and motioning for Larry, who's standing in his shorts and T-shirt. "What's the big idea?" he asks sleepily, but Corinne shushes him.

"Will you be OK, Clark?" she asks.

"Yeah, that's me, the OK Kid," his father says flatly.

Corinne pauses before moving. "I'm sure Stan didn't mean anything. I think Dottie just took it wrong."

" 'Course," Clark says, not meeting her eyes.

Robin feels himself tensing up. Uncle Stan insulted his mother? She got drunk because of it? "What did he say?" he blurts out.

"Never mind," Clark says. "Give me a hand here."

"Why do I gotta go?" Larry complains, but Corinne just pushes him out the door.

Robin steps to his parents. "Your mother outdid herself tonight," Clark says. Dorothy's sagging face seems to have been loosened from its bones. Robin wipes a thread of spittle from her chin. "Let's get her upstairs," Clark says. "She's gonna give me a dislocated shoulder."

Clark swings Dorothy upward, and Robin hooks himself under her free arm. He drags the weight behind him, one step at a time. "What happened?" he asks again, a growing sense of outrage and fear knotting in his belly. Did it have something to do with her outfit? Did his mother feel overdressed and out of place? Is it his fault for encouraging her to dress as she would on one of their City Days?

Clark guides them to the bathroom. "She's going to need another stop at the trough." They position her on the floor in front of the toilet. In the sudden bright light, the bathroom's grime rises to prominence. The toilet rim where Clark places Dorothy's hands is marked by pale yellow splashes and a couple of stuck pubic hairs. Robin runs a cloth under cold water and presses it to his mother's face.

She stirs at the contact, sliding forward and bonking her skull on the upturned seat. "Oh, it's you," she slurs.

The sloppiness of her speech fills him with pity. "Hi, Mom." He wipes the cloth across her forehead tenderly.

"Come on, Dottie," Clark says, "Let's take care of business and get you to bed." Robin can smell alcohol on his father's breath, too, though he shows no signs of losing his composure.

Dorothy remains motionless. A sweet noise hums from the back of her throat, the gurgle of an infant. "This is taking too long," Clark says. He reaches around and pries Dorothy's mouth wide. Robin watches in horror as one of Clark's fingers disappears inside.

"You're hurting her," he protests, as his mother gags, the tendons in her neck tightening.

"I've done this before," Clark whispers solemnly. He wiggles his finger and then pulls it out just in time to release a funnel of clear vomit.

Jackson is suddenly there in the doorway, wide-eyed. "Holy barf bag!" he exclaims. Robin spins around and glares at him.

Clark speaks without looking at him, "Why don't you go back to sleep, kiddo?"

Dorothy heaves again and sends out another splash. "Ladies and gentlemen, welcome to Puke-o-rama," Jackson announces.

"Dad, could you tell Howard Cosell his services are not needed?" Robin says.

"Where'd Larry go?" Jackson asks.

Robin says, "We put him out with the trash."

Clark slaps his hand on his thigh. "Can you guys just put the sibling rivalry on hold? Jackson, go to your room. Robin, wipe Mom's face again."

"Oh sure, Robin gets to have all the fun," Jackson says before splitting.

"We're gonna lift you now, Mom, OK?" Robin says softly into her ear, but she does not respond.

"She's out again," Clark says. Robin can hear the disgust in his father's voice. He feels it, too, but not for her. His mother this far out of control—this just can't be her fault. Someone else is to blame.

"I saw Mom do the Technicolor yawn." Jackson's voice is an excited whisper in the dark. Robin stares up from his bed to a crack in the ceiling.

"Don't talk about your own mother that way," Robin says.

"Oh, give me a break. That was a pisser."

"I'm sick and tired of your attitude."

Jackson breaks out into laughter. "Why do you do that?"

"What?"

"Talk like Mom. *I'm sick and tired of your attitude.*"

The words sting. Robin rolls on his side, faces the wall. "You don't understand anything the way *I* do."

"All I know is nobody wants some kid their own age talking like their dumb mother. Why do you think Larry's always bothering you? You *ask* for it, Robin."

Robin feels his eyes watering. Maybe Jackson's right. Maybe he does provoke the trouble that finds him. But how could he explain to Jackson the look that Larry gave him when he wagged his dick at Robin, the way he knew Robin was staring at his dick, the way he turned it against him? How can he explain himself to Jackson when they don't even seem to speak the same language?

He finally speaks of the only thing he understands: his idea of the far-off future. "I'm going to move to the city one day and live in a penthouse, and all of this will be some funny thing in the past if I even remember that much of it."

"Yeah, right. You and Mom can move off together and talk to each other like a couple of old ladies and drink until you puke." Suddenly he throws back the covers. "I gotta take Petey for a pee."

"You have a name for your dick?"

"Yeah, me and Larry. His is Freddy."

"That's disgusting."

"No, it's not. It's funny. What's your problem?"

He shuts his eyes so tight that neon bleeds into the blackness. He doesn't understand how this works. Larry and Jackson get naked and name their dicks, but when Larry sees him staring at "Freddy," it's a bad thing. He says a little prayer. *God, give me a new life. This one isn't working for me.* He waits for a merciful bolt of lightning to strike his brain, to offer him some clue as to how it all works, this whole world of normal boys.

Chapter Three

The next day, after school, he goes to a place that he has been warned against. At the east end of the reservoir, where he regularly rides his bike on Sunday afternoons, is an unpaved road. You'd hardly notice it driving a car; its entrance is a sharp right turn past some high trees just where the main road loops left. At school Robin has overheard kids mention a hidden pond at the end of that road—they call it the Ice Pond and talk about it as a place where every illicit thing happens, a place where adults don't venture. Robin mentioned it once to his mother, who dismissed it as local lore: "Oh, just another one of those fabled lovers' lanes."

"You should *hear* the stories about what goes on there," Robin told her, immediately regretting the wondrous tone of his voice.

"What's the big interest?" she asked, staring suspiciously.

"No biggie."

"I suggest you stay away. I'm sure it's positively seedy. Soused-up, hormonal bullies trying to impress their girlfriends."

The story that Robin cannot forget, that compels him this early October afternoon to steer his ten-speed impulsively down the road toward the Ice Pond, was whispered just a few days before, in the locker room after his phys. ed. class. Donny Meier and Seth Carter were talking about a contest: the two of them and a couple others drinking beer and then trying to knock the cans off a stump with the force of their piss. Donny saying, "That was really fucked up," and Seth saying, "We should do it again, for a goof," and Donny agreeing, "Yeah, we gotta get Danniman to come along again. He'll probably put a hole through the can." And then they both laughed, and Seth said, "Long Dong Danniman," and Donny said, "Aw, man, that's fucked up."

Robin usually ignores locker room conversations. He can rarely find a way into the back-and-forth of them, the language and rhythm that boys his age all seem to understand instinctively. He does not give himself a reason that this one is different, but simply lets the picture form: the boys, their pants around their ankles, the elastic bands of their underwear tugged beneath their dicks. He hears the air split by the hissing streams, the ruffle of piss on dry leaves, the *ping* as cans are struck and topple. Donny Meier's laughing mouth, and Seth Carter's brown bangs feathered across his excited eyes, and Billy "Long Dong" Danniman with *it* in his hand. He lets this picture form and then, when he gets to what he most wants to see, snaps it off guiltily.

He speeds toward the pond as if outrunning a pursuing authority. The dirt road is just wide enough for a car to get through, with crisscrossing tire treads layered deep. In the stillness of the woods, his bike's chain is loud as a motor. The wheels kick up pebbles and stiff clumps of dirt that smack him in the back—each nick almost pleasurable, a small hardship to reinforce the adventure of this unplanned ride.

He reaches a clearing strewn with litter: empty beer containers, mangled newspapers, cast off, soiled clothing. No cars—he is relieved, and vaguely disappointed. He dismounts, sets his bike on its kickstand in the soft, trodden earth and follows the edge of the pond toward a place where granite boulders are piled as high as his shoulders. In the charred remnants of a campfire, a piece of ripped, colored foil gleams among the cigarette butts, the word "Trojan" embossed upon it. He's only ever heard of Trojans; he scans the ground for what was once inside this wrapper, not sure exactly what a rubber even looks like. Seeing nothing that fits the description, he pockets the wrapper, a souvenir of his visit.

Water laps at the silty shore; crows squawk from treetops. All else is silence. Robin removes his shoes and socks, lets his feet dangle from a rock into the pond. The water isn't icy at all—it's warm, soothing. He hikes up his pants and glides in to his ankles, the pond's bottom soft as mashed potatoes. Do the kids who hang out here ever go swimming? He conjures up late-night skinny-dipping parties, the sexual laughter of older teenagers, a bonfire glowing upon wet bodies and aluminum beer cans and foil Trojan wrappers. Todd Spicer might come to a party like that.

He is gripped by the sudden, terrifying notion that someone is watching, but scanning the pond's perimeter, he sees no one. Not a soul. The rarity of this solitude makes him giddy—when is he ever completely alone? And then, before even comprehending the action, he is back on shore, impulsively tugging off his clothes. He wades into the water, naked, mud squishing up through his toes. He holds his balance and keeps walking, pausing, with a gasp, when his balls hit the water's surface. He doesn't want to get his hair wet—doesn't think he could explain it to his mother later—but he lowers himself down to his shoulders.

He touches his dick under the water, grabs it between his fingers, wiggles until it stiffens. He hops up and down, careful at first not to slip, and feels his hardness cutting through the water. A quick fear of a fish biting him there makes him stop, and then he laughs at the thought—*Yeah, right, like Jaws lives in the Ice Pond.* He laughs out loud, his laughter surrounding him, free and unleashed. The sound fills the air for a few moments—all he can allow himself before fear of discovery closes in again.

He makes his way back to the shore, hiding himself behind the boulders, and shakes himself off like a dog. His dick is still hard—with his hand he presses it against his belly, then looks around again, expecting *someone* to be nearby. He is still alone; he rubs himself some more, letting the warmth build underneath his palm until it travels through his body. He keeps at it until the friction is too much and just as he thinks he should stop—*What am I doing? Someone might drive up*—he finds he is so weak against his own will that he can't not continue. He looks at the mud streaking down his legs and the beer cans around his feet, he thinks of the pissing contest, Donny and Seth and Long Dong Danniman—longer than himself, longer than this thing in his hand— their pissing contest happened *right here,* at the Ice Pond. They stood side by side, as he's seen them in the locker room, pissing next to each other the way he and Jackson have done at home, crossing streams into the toilet. He sees himself doing that with Todd Spicer—standing right here, feet planted in the garbage and the Trojans, their streams crossing, the two of them with their things in their hands, Todd without underwear, just his skin and his bushy hair under his open fly and his hand shaking out the piss, his strong hands, his arms with their definite muscles, shaking the piss out of his thing right next to Robin, making him shiver and gasp—Robin is gasping, he is standing but it feels like falling, falling through thick humid air. He braces his back against the rocks behind him and watches the pink tip of his dick open up and shoot out something that is not piss. It lands on the garbage at his feet—a wet, white shower on the char-black ashes.

He has a moment of stunned disbelief that he let this happen, out here where anyone could see. Sweat trickles down his ribs. He breathes deep, he feels as if he hasn't breathed for hours, that time has bent around him. Disbelief gives way to shame: he hurries back into his clothes and onto his bike, his untucked shirt flapping as he pedals away.

On the dirt road a car is approaching, a guy at the wheel, a girl snuggling up next to him. Robin panics—just a few minutes earlier and they would have seen him!—and loses his grip on the handlebars, skidding to the side, his wheel grinding into a spindly bush. The driver stares at him quizzically as he passes. Robin snaps a branch from his spokes and continues his escape, all the way home imagining that guy and girl discovering his white goop on the ground amid the garbage. He imagines that they could read the splatter like tea leaves and discern what he was thinking while it happened. They could chase him down and have him arrested for being a pervert in public.

All that is left is the embarrassment of returning with a secret. The leaves above him are shiny with diamonds of light breaking through, the sun falling lower in the sky, stretching across the front yard as he turns into the driveway. He's rehearsing a quick speech for his mother, something designed to spare him too much explanation—*I rode into town to play Asteroids*—when he recognizes Uncle Stan's car in the driveway.

As he swings open the screen door, his mother stands at the counter, an oven mitt on one hand and a glass of wine in the other.

Stan's voice carries above the clamor of the nightly news from the living room TV set. "Come on, Dottie. If it's ready, let me have a piece now."

Dorothy faces Robin, but raises her voice loud enough to carry to the living room. "I *thought* your uncle came over to apologize for his boorish behavior last night, but he seems to be doing nothing but barking orders."

"I'm hungry," Stan says.

"Well, if your son wasn't keeping my son out playing through dinnertime, maybe we'd be able to sit down and eat." She turns off the oven and leaves a tray of lasagna on the stove. "And where have *you* been?"

"Nowhere. Just riding my bike." A chill moves along his skin, and he wonders if he'll catch a cold from having been naked in the water. Or if maybe he did something bad to himself by touching his thing like that.

Dorothy flicks her head to the side in exasperation and throws up her hands, sloshing liquid over the lip of her glass. "Fine, everyone just run around and *play* while I try to get dinner ready. Don't offer any help. *Fine.*"

"Where's Ruby?" he asks.

"I sent her out to fetch Larry and Jackson. I think they're at the playground." She glances at the clock on the stove. "She should have been back already."

Smelling the lasagna, Robin realizes how hungry he is. "Well, if it's done, maybe we should just start."

Dorothy sighs at last and gulps down a mouthful of wine. Robin watches her throat move above the soft depression between her collarbones. Her chest is flush. He has a flash from the night before—her skin was ghostly white then, her face a morbid contortion as the vomit dripped from her lips. "Do you still feel sick?"

"Just fed up," she says. "I'm trying to make dinner and no one's around. Your father's coming home late. Here, bring your uncle some dinner and let him eat in there by himself. What do I care anyway?" She takes off her apron and picks up her purse. "I'm going to have a cigarette."

"Really?" He's stunned—smoking at home! He's only ever seen her smoke in the city.

She pulls her Pall Malls from her purse and walks to the screen door. "Everyone else is doing what they want."

Robin follows her with his eyes; through the screen door, she looks grainy, like a newspaper photo. Taking a drag of her cigarette, she raises her nearly empty wineglass and calls out, "Clark MacKenzie, you poor excuse for a family man, where the hell are you?"

Robin carries the lasagna and a fork to his uncle. "I'm so hungry I could eat a pigeon at a Chinese restaurant," Stan says, spearing the fork into the pasta before Robin's fully let go of the plate.

Robin's own appetite seems to have instantly disappeared. "Where's Aunt Corinne tonight?"

"She's at one-a those meetings again, getting brainwashed into selling vitamins," his uncle blurts out angrily. "There's a load of quackery if I ever heard of it. Not to mention a conspiracy to undermine the American family farmer."

Robin scowls. Uncle Stan is always putting Aunt Corinne down. For years, she was sort of quiet, almost mopey at times. If you asked her for anything she complained that everyone took from her and no one gave back—the way his mother sounded a minute ago. But lately she's been in a better mood. She's started selling vitamins, and it seemed to make her happy to have something to do besides wait on Stan and Larry. She'd even begun wearing streaks of pink and purple blush on her cheeks. "For contour," she told Robin, "to thin out the face."

Robin has come to like his aunt; he feels the need to come to her defense. "I read in *Time* magazine that researchers are discovering vitamins and other nutrients are more important than anyone ever knew." It was actually his mother who read the article and told him about it, and as he parrots back her words he worries about Jackson's accusation that he talks too much like her.

"Well, if you look at who's selling vitamins, it's all Jews. Like that guy Goldberg who got my wife hooked. You get all the nutrients you need if you eat three square meals a day. My mother never took vitamins and she's a hundred years old and big as a house."

The fact that Stan is actually his mother's brother, that they were created by the same chemistry, is always a difficult leap for Robin's imagination to make; he tends to think of his uncle as a weird neighbor who shows up for a free dinner from time to time. He tries to picture his mother and Stan growing up in the same house—Nana's old place on Route 7, near Northampton. Robin can still remember it, back when Grampa Leo was alive: the front porch with the broken railing, the dusty pantry under the staircase, where you could hide and jump out at someone to scare them, those smelly chicken coops in the backyard with the crusty turds along the edge. Dorothy tells a story about Stan as a child, peeing into the coop and a chicken taking a nip at his wiener. It is one of the few stories he has heard his mother tell about their childhood.

He squints his eyes at Stan, looking for a physical resemblance at the very least. The nose, maybe: it's a good nose, really, not too big but definitely not a pug like Larry's. And the cheekbones have that same curve as on his mother's face, enough to create a decent smile without looking like a chipmunk. He could even imagine that Stan was a handsome guy before he grew up and his stomach bloated from too much beer and his face got rubbery around the jaw.

He watches the lasagna piling up behind Stan's thin lips, mush shoveled in upon mush, suddenly fascinated by the grotesqueness of it all.

"Your mother just doesn't know how to get it right," he is saying as he chews, "with the spices and everything. I tell you, I'm a lucky SOB, having a mother who cooks for a living. Only time I ever see my wife in the kitchen is when she's raiding the fridge. Women today, terrible cooks."

"Aunt Corinne makes that Jell-O cake for my birthday. *That's* pretty good," Robin says. "With the different colors and the Cool Whip holding it together."

"Yeah, you and that Jell-O cake. Damn thing would fall apart after one bite. I'd say, 'Corinne, how 'bout a pumpkin pie,' and she'd say, 'I'm making Jell-O cake. It's Robin's favorite.' If it wasn't for you and that Jell-O cake I might have had a decent dessert once and a while."

Robin decides he has had enough and begins to stand. He spits out a phrase he has heard his mother say a thousand times, whenever he or his brother and sister complain too much: "I didn't know I caused you so much grief."

Stan drops his fork and leans forward. "Sit down, Robin," he commands. "Let's have a talk."

Robin buckles under the authority in Stan's eyes and lowers himself onto a chair.

"You, Robin, are the kind of kid who's been mollycoddled all his life and thinks he's better than everyone else. I knew a kid like you when I was growing up. Dodo Scanlon. Donald, but we called him Dodo. Which is funny, now that I think about it, 'cause a dodo is a bird, and you're named after a bird, so there's something to it."

"Dodo *Scan*lon?" Dorothy is suddenly in the doorway, her voice trembling. "Dodo Scanlon was a little genius whose life became the ninth circle of hell thanks to you. You and that bunch of greasers you associated with! Stan, you just don't know when to stop—"

Stan interrupts, his voice smug. "At least I know when to stop *drinking.*"

"You bastard." A curtain of silent tension descends upon the room. Robin's head is spinning; it feels as if he's on a playground, waiting for the punches to fly. He wants to speak up, to help his mother, but before he comes up with anything to say or do, Dorothy's gaze meets his. "I think," she says, "you should go fetch your brother and sister."

Summer has made one last defiant appearance. The evening air is warm, the streets bruised with orange light punching through the empty oaks. Robin heads toward the playground. He makes a path between the sidewalk and the curb, kicking up leaves as he goes. The ones on top are dry and crisp and flutter to his side; beneath these, a slick layer has already been flattened into the dying grass.

He walks down Bergen Avenue, where he has lived for nine of the thirteen years of his life, past the Delatores' and the Feeneys', past the house where Mr. Kelly, whose wife died last year, lives, past Mrs. Lueger, who is sweeping her cement stoop as she does every night before her husband comes home from work. Robin waves to Mrs. Lueger out of habit, and she waves back without a word. He watches her turn her gaze across the hedge, trying to catch a look at the young couple next door, who are laughing over a flaming hibachi at the back of their driveway. Robin doesn't know their names; they are new to the block. Everyone refers to them as The Hippies. They have friends who ride motorcycles. A few days before, Robin heard Mrs. Feeney announce that she is sure the couple *smoke dope,* to which Mrs. Delatore responded: "They're probably *growing* it back there." There has been a lot of talk about drugs lately; in group guidance, Robin has sat through several films depicting teenagers who were "slipped a mickey" and wind up throwing themselves from open windows or losing their minds into a trippy haze of colors and wild sounds; even the ones who try to return to regular lives are always at the mercy of acid flashbacks.

He turns left onto Hopkins, crosses Kickmer and then Whalen and then Tully. The streets of Greenlawn are all named for local men killed in wars. Every year the names are read at the Memorial Day rally in the park. He turns down Lester, takes it to the end, where the woods begin. There is a broken concrete path that cuts between the old oaks and winds into the playground behind Crossroads Elementary.

The school is an orderly brick building, one story high with a flat roof, tucked between the street and the woods. He has spent more time in this building—kindergarten through sixth grade—than any place except home, but in the three years since he's gone to school here everything, he realizes, has changed. The building is so small. The windows are low to the ground, the doors, painted green, look quaint, like doors on a clubhouse. Crude, construction paper goblins and witches and pumpkins are taped to the windows. He remembers creating such things himself. *It* didn't change, he realizes. *I* changed. He sticks his hands in his pockets and fingers the sharp foil edge of the Trojan wrapper. He is unexpectedly struck by the notion that he was a *child* here, that he is not a child, not in the same way. He wonders, how did this happen? I didn't plan for it.

The sun is now quite low in the sky, a blood red disk licking the tops of trees and houses. Across the playground, almost in silhouette, is the slide. With the asphalt ground, its two legs form a triangle: on one side the ascending ladder, on the other the metal trough. Ruby is in a dress on the tiny platform at the top, gripping the handrails, Jackson stands at the base of the ladder, and Larry leans upward from the mouth of the chute, yelling, "Ruby MacKenzie, slide on down!" As Robin gets closer he can see that Larry is wagging his tongue at her and wiggling his butt in the air like an excited puppy ready to pounce.

Ruby pivots to climb back down the ladder, but Jackson, at the bottom, is an obstacle to her escape. "Come on, Ruby," he says. "Time's a-wastin'."

"I mean it," she says.

"No way," Jackson says. "Only one way up, only one way down."

Larry lets out a "Woo-hoo!"

Robin calls across the playground, "You guys." And then louder when they don't respond, "It's suppertime."

"Move it, Ruby," Jackson says, then steps onto the ladder.

"No fair," Ruby yells. "Get off!" Jackson takes another step. Ruby sees Robin approaching. She calls to him, "Make him cut it out."

"Jackson, get off," Robin says.

So many years of recess on this playground have imprinted certain rules in Robin's head, and one of the first ones is that you can't get on the ladder until the person before you slides down. The ease with which Jackson dismisses this concept angers Robin, not because he cares about the rule so much but because Jackson cares about it not at all. He is nagged by Jackson's carefree attitude, more so by the way it intimidates him.

"Get out of the way, Larry," Robin says.

"Shut up. I'm not doing anything."

Jackson is now halfway up the ladder. Robin reaches up and swats his leg. "Jackson, get off." But Jackson continues his climb, one step at a time. Then Larry, on the other end of the slide, begins walking up. The metal is too smooth for his shoes to get a grip so he drops to his belly and begins slithering up toward the top.

Ruby yells, "I'll jump over the side. I mean it."

"No, no, don't jump," Larry snarls, continuing his upward slither. "Let me rescue you." He is about halfway to her, his chest at the point where the slide bulges.

"We're eating dinner, cut it out," Robin says. "Get off the ladder, Jackson. Cut it out, Larry."

He hates the sound of his own voice. He knows that they won't listen to him. He makes another grab for Jackson, which sends Jackson scampering to the top. Jackson pauses long enough to smirk at Robin and wave his fists above his shoulders, like a weightlifter flexing his muscles.

Robin's exasperation is at its limit, and he does something he doesn't want to do—something he thinks is exactly what Jackson wants him to do, which makes it even worse—he gets on the ladder himself. He scurries up the steps and reaches out for Jackson's leg. Jackson hops up one final rung, forcing himself onto the landing right next to Ruby. He circles his arm around her neck and hisses back toward Robin. "One false move and she's dead."

Ruby shrieks. From the other side, Larry grabs her by the ankles and she shrieks again. Robin thinks they might really push Ruby off. He improvises a karate chop into Jackson's shinbone. Jackson yelps and loosens his grip enough for Ruby to free herself. She squats down and pounds her fists into Larry's head.

"Everyone go down the slide," Robin yells. "Now!" He hears the command in his words—his voice at last has some authority to it—but he knows it is too late. Ruby is twisting out of Larry's grip and leaning back into Jackson, and Robin is trying to hold Jackson in place and reach toward Ruby at the same time, and then Ruby and Robin are both squeezing Jackson between them. Disorientation overwhelms him—the sky is darkening above and the pavement blurs way down below and the four of them, somewhere in the center of it all, compress tighter in struggle. No one is speaking, their throats release only grunts. Robin grabs the denim of Jackson's pants in his fist and feels him wriggling away, feels the material pull across his fingernails, senses the intent in Jackson's escape. He tightens his fist but now there is nothing to hold, he senses Jackson lurching away from him, away from all of them. Robin makes a lunge at Jackson, and then Jackson is being pulled upward, his legs rising, his body slipping across the metal curve of the railing, arcing into the wide empty dusk. Jackson is flying.

There is a gasp. Then a sucking whoosh. Then a collision, a stone split open.

Stillness.

Robin looks at Ruby, at her amazed eyes, her mouth straining against silence. He looks at Larry, who is sliding backwards on his belly. He looks into the air where he last saw Jackson. The only place left to look is down.

*   *   *

The wrinkled red and blue stripes of Jackson's shirt, the *back* of his shirt.

A curve of skin—Jackson's neck, very white against the ground.

His face in profile, an open eye, the shell of his ear.

His legs are stretched apart from each other. It is all twisted up, it is not making sense to Robin.

Larry is there, down below. Larry breathing loud, his breath is a chain pulling sounds back into the night—cars moving in the street and crickets chirping and a distant door slamming shut. Larry shoves Jackson's shoulder and Jackson's torso rolls sideways but his head stays the same. There is a terrible new noise: the sound of knuckles cracking. Not knuckles. Jackson's neck.

"Get up," Larry says. And then louder: "Get up!"

"Stop!" Ruby cries out. "You're hurting him!" She slides down to the ground.

Alone on the platform Robin's confusion dissolves, and he grasps at last what has happened. He begins the climb down the ladder, but each step seems to take an eternity so he leaps out, into the air where Jackson just flew. For a moment he believes he'll hurt himself, and then he obeys an instinct that says *bend your knees for the landing.* His feet smack, his knees rush into his armpits, his palms screech along the blacktop. The ground burns into his skin.

Larry is repeating, "Get up, get up," and Ruby is yelling, "Leave him alone," and finally Robin speaks in a hollow voice. He says, "Be quiet." And they are.

Larry runs away. Ruby runs away. Robin calls after them, "Go tell somebody what we did."

It is just the two of them on the playground for a long time.

This much registers: Jackson is breathing. Robin kneels next to him, watching his body inflate and subside. He brushes his fingertips along the back of Jackson's neck. The spine is not right, he can tell from the way the skin pulls. He says aloud the words he has heard on TV shows: *It'll be all right. Hang in there. You can make it.* He says, *Don't die,* and then thinks, No more Jackson. No more dragging him home for dinner. No more having to apologize to strangers for Jackson saying the wrong thing. No more Jackson bouncing around on his bed practicing new curse words. They'll plant a cherry blossom tree in front of the school like they did for that girl who had leukemia. They'll write about this in the *Community News.* They'll ask me questions.

He is sure he will be blamed.

He wonders if an unconscious person can read minds. He thinks, Can you hear me? Blink if you can hear me, Jackson.

A wet ribbon of blood draws from Jackson's mouth, inching along the ground. Robin dips his index finger into the tip of the stream and it pools around the nail. He puts this finger in his mouth—the taste of a nosebleed. A grain of stone from the playground floor is mixed in with the blood, he pushes it between the tip of his tongue and the back of his teeth. He remembers his own jump to the pavement, checks his hands. There is blood there, too.

It'll be all right. Hang in there. You can make it. Don't die. A faint groan travels up from somewhere inside of Jackson. A sob through mucus. His breaths continue, eerie. Wind moving through a cave.

The pavement pushes up into Robin's knees. He feels it. The hard ground is everything, there is nothing else beneath. No soil, no tangled roots, no Indian bones, no fossils, no magma, no core of the earth. He could not dig down to China. The earth is nothing more than a solid slab of playground.

He puts his fingers in Jackson's hair, lifts his hand, lets the hair drop back against the skull.

"Don't touch him!" Dorothy is screaming from the car window. She is speeding onto the playground. The vibrations of the auto reach him first, then the headlights. Jackson looks sicker in the blinding glow. The car seems to roll even after Dorothy jumps out of it. She is hurtling toward them. The place is filled with new smells—exhaust fumes, scorched tires, the tobacco and wine on Dorothy's breath.

The ambulance siren cries into the night.

They wait in the hospital, sitting on chairs covered in fuzzy brown material that scratches Robin's legs and ass through his pants. They entered through the emergency room and then into intensive care. There is a nursing station nearby where the sounds of muffled phone calls can be heard. The sheer amount of activity in the building—two car accidents, a heart attack and Jackson all within the same hour—shrinks the walls around them. Nurses appear from around corners and out of doorways and pass by on their way somewhere else. Robin follows everyone with his eyes.

Jackson is being operated on. A specialist has been called in from New York City. The first time Robin sees a doctor in aqua blue scrubs, face mask and a shower cap he thinks, *That must be the specialist.* On *General Hospital,* doctors wear long white coats, their full hair combed neatly. Then he sees another man dressed like this, going a different direction. Later, another. He doesn't know who anyone is, which ones might have seen his brother's body, which ones might know the story of the fall. He had tried to explain to his mother in the car but she only listened for a few minutes before making him stop. He tries to picture the surgery. He thinks of a game he owned a couple of years back called "Operation." A cartoon body with tiny removable body parts. *Take out wrenched ankle,* the card said. If you touched the skin with the tweezers the game honked at you.

He sits on a chair next to his mother, who clutches his hand in hers. Across from them, Ruby is laying her head in Clark's lap. She hardly blinks, as if she might be sleeping with her eyes open. His father is crying. He has been crying the entire time, not making a sound, wiping his wet cheeks again and again. Robin is amazed by this sight. He wants to ask questions, but those tears are what keeps him quiet. He looks so handsome, Robin thinks. They both look like new people, so beautiful and serious in their tragic faces.

A man dressed all in white is there suddenly. He is young, with a helmet of blow-dried hair and dark bars on his sleeves. "Mr. and Mrs. MacKenzie," he says in a delicate voice.

His father says, "Yes, Doctor?"

The man smiles. "Oh, I'm the nurse," he says. "Dr. Glade would like to speak with you. Come with me."

Robin gets up to go along, but his mother motions for him to stay. "Watch your sister for a minute."

"Where are you going?"

Dorothy holds her finger to her lips. "Shhh . . ."

The man who is a nurse smiles at Robin. As they walk away, Robin hears a siren from down the hallway, toward the parking lot. He imagines that they have left him and Ruby behind to be arrested by the police. You killed your brother, they will accuse. You have the right to remain silent.

The nurse returns and comes over to them. "You must be Robin and Ruby," he says. "I'm Harold." Ruby sits up. Robin nods, fearful.

"I hear you got a little scratched up, too," Harold says to Robin. "Let's see." Robin turns his palms face up and lays them on Harold's outstretched hands, which are warm, a little callused. His own palms are streaked with cuts, some already scabs. There is a film of blacktop powder embedded in his skin. "Why don't we clean things up a bit?" He motions for them to come with him.

Ruby crosses her arms in front of her. "I'll wait here," she says.

"Let's stick together, OK?" Harold says. He reaches in his pocket and pulls out hard candies wrapped in cellophane. They each refuse.

"I'm staying here for my mom and dad," Ruby says.

"Come on, Ruby," Robin pleads.

"No!"

Robin thinks of her at the top of the slide, trapped between Jackson and Larry. He thinks none of this would have happened if she had just slid down into Larry and kicked him. "Don't act like a baby," he snaps.

She bursts into loud sobs—her body instantly convulsing. Harold motions to an older woman in white at the nursing station. "Would you keep an eye on Ruby while I clean out Robin's cuts?" Harold asks.

Ruby's stare implores Robin to stay, but he feels the sudden urge for an escape. He follows Harold toward an examining room. "I'll be right back," he says, and Ruby heaves herself into the lap of the other nurse. "Good girl," the nurse says. She reaches into her pocket and pulls out a hard candy wrapped in cellophane.

The examination room is cold and bright with a black window facing the parking lot. Harold pats his hand on an examination table. The paper crinkles as it gives in to Robin's weight.

Robin's hands sting under the antiseptic; he squeezes shut his eyes and bites down on his teeth. Harold is talking about something but Robin doesn't hear the words. When the bandages have been taped down, he looks up and Harold is smiling.

"How come you have stripes on your uniform?" Robin asks him.

"They give these to the male nurses to identify us."

"Why? Don't they already know that you're a guy?" Robin asks, and Harold laughs. It seems like a real laugh, a laugh that they share.

"Any other questions?" Harold says, lifting him back to his feet.

"Yeah, about a million. Like, about my brother . . ."

Harold pauses, wiping off his instrument table. He sighs. "I'll take you back out to your parents."

When he comes back into the waiting area Dorothy is there. "Your father took Ruby home," she says. "I need a cigarette." It is the most she's said to him since they got here.

She walks him out to the parking lot and is lighting up before the automatic doors swing closed behind them. Neither of them has a coat, and the temperature has dropped, so they hurry to the car and sit inside with the heat on and the windows cracked to let out the smoke.

"Jackson is not doing well. He suffered a neck injury."

"He's going to live?"

"So it seems." Robin watches her to try to understand what this means, but she is silent for a while. She inhales. She exhales. Smoke hits the windshield and then flattens out around her. In the momentary glow from the ember, he sees the lines at the corner of her eyes, around her lips, across her forehead. She doesn't look beautiful now.

She says, "I want you to tell your sister this is not her fault."

He doesn't say anything, and then she says, "She told me it was her fault and I don't want her thinking that way."

"I'll tell her."

"And I want you to tell Larry it is not his fault."

"OK." He says this less quickly.

"It's not anyone's fault," Dorothy says, as if convincing herself. "It's not . . . it's just something that makes no sense."

"OK."

"I need you to be strong for me, Robin. You're so much stronger than the others."

"I guess."

"You are. You are. This is going to be difficult." She puts out her cigarette in the ashtray, stubs it over and over until every speck of flame is extinguished. Then she pinches the butt between her fingers and throws it through the crack in her window.

"Is Dad mad?" Robin asks.

"He's very concerned," she says.

"Very concerned?"

"Yes, dear. He's waiting to see—"

"—If Jackson's going to die."

Dorothy leans back in the seat, focuses her eyes into the rearview mirror. She pokes at the corner of her eye as if flecking something painful from it. She says, "I don't think it's that bad. We don't know how bad it is."

He hears her impatience with him, which makes her words less convincing. It makes him angry with her, and when he speaks again there is spite in his voice. "He could have brain damage or turn into a vegetable or a retard with a crooked body spilling his food on the floor and shitting in his pants."

"Good Lord, Robin, enough! We don't know. We'll just have to wait and see." It sounds like an order.

He asks, "Are you mad at me?"

"No, of course not. Of course not." Long pause. "Of course not."

"I wish Jackson didn't go up that slide," he says.

She is silent.

"I wish I didn't go up after him," he says. "I thought they were going to push Ruby off."

More silence.

He asks, "Is this God's will?"

Dorothy leans forward and sighs in exasperation. She says, "Robin, I said I want you to be strong."

"OK," he says. He thinks, I have never been that in my life, ever.

In the dark Jackson's empty bed is a gaping hole, a vacuum. Robin stands next to it staring, unblinking. The blanket ripples, as if covering boiling liquid. He holds his breath, throws back the cover, steps back in fear. The sheets are flat and still, pictures of superheroes frozen in action. He crawls onto them and sniffs Jackson's smells: gassy and dirty and a hint of syrup. He gets up again and smoothes everything back in place.

His parents take turns at the hospital all night, coming and going in shifts. Robin does not want sleep. Downstairs his father sobs in waves, Robin feels them through his feet. His mother paces back and forth between the living room and the kitchen. The fridge swings open again and again, he knows she is getting drunk on white wine. He goes to the window, needs air, his throat is dry. His hands are itching under the bandages, it hurts to push up the sash.

There's a piece of rock stuck way back in his throat, rotating its sharp edges. He coughs. He keeps coughing until his mother comes upstairs.

"Have a little of this." She tilts the glass to his lips. It's sweet and bitter—perfect. "Try to sleep, Robin."

"I will."

She kisses him good night on the lips and he pushes his face into hers until their noses mash and she pulls away. "Give me more wine," he says. He finishes it off, a couple of gulps.

He dreams he is a woman with scarlet flowers in her hair. A woman in a dress with pieces of glass stitched into the wool. His sister letting the hem out, him tripping on the edge, cuts on his feet. When he wakes he is on the floor. He gets up to pee like any other night and then remembers the whole day. In the bathroom he tries to force out vomit, his finger down his throat. Just a few sour burps. He rips the bandages off his hands. The skin beneath is whiter, edged by a thin, gummy line from the tape. Back in bed he dreams again. Sharp-fanged dogs snapping in the air in front of him. His fingers weaving through their rough coats, grabbing on, tearing off chunks of hairy flesh. Running. The pitch of sirens.

Chapter Four

His eyes open, then shut against the bright assault. He hears his name, wags his head to shake off sleep. Even through his eyelids, he can tell the room is holding too much light. Again, a voice. Ruby's.

"Nana Rena's here," she says.

Robin pulls his arms down from above his head—his sleeping position—and props himself up on one elbow. He breathes deep before making the effort of opening his eyes again. A pain somewhere below the back of his neck clamps against his shoulder. He jerks to a sitting position to relieve the pressure, rubs his hand where it hurts. The room looks like a black-and-white photo, all the color sucked out by the sunlight.

Ruby is sitting upright on the edge of Jackson's bed, watching him. Her heels are kicking backward into the bedspread and the metal frame beneath. Her uncombed hair is straining against a couple of crudely placed barrettes. "We don't have to go to school today," she says.

"What time is it?"

"It's lunch," she says. "Nana wants you to get up and eat something. Mom and Dad are at the hospital." He feels instantly annoyed to have been left behind, but also something else—some vague relief.

She says, "Do you feel like eating olive loaf? That's what Nana's making. Olive loaf sandwiches."

He groans and drops his head into his palms, presses his fingertips into his face. "What's going on with Jackson?" he mutters, filling his cupped hands with his moist, sour breath.

"Uh . . . uh . . . I don't know." Her heels thud faster into the bedframe.

"What do you mean you don't know?" he says, then wishes he didn't because when he looks up her face is a guilt-stricken mask.

"I don't *know*," she says. Her voice nearly cracks and her face seems to be growing flatter as she tries to hold back tears or a wail or something.

"OK, sorry," he says. "Sorry." Her face relaxes a little. He presses his fingers deep into the gristly shoulder muscle, still aching. He senses another, more familiar pressure in his lap, realizes he's woken with a boner, realizes he has to pee badly. He wants Ruby to leave, but except for her swinging legs, she isn't moving. She's staring past his face at something. "You were doing it again," she says. "Picking at the paint in your sleep."

He looks behind at his headboard. A jagged circular patch the size of a dinner plate has been scratched into the blue-black woodgrain varnish. The exposed spot is smooth and pale like hard plastic, and certainly bigger than the last time he took note of it. He scans his fingernails and sees the telltale dark filings embedded there. His father has yelled at him about this but he doesn't know what to do about it, he can't very well control what he does in his sleep.

"You were doing it when I came in here," Ruby says. Her face holds a certain fascination in the midst of everything else it's telegraphing—the guilt, the anticipation—which pisses him off.

"Yeah, well." He almost says, *At least I don't wet my bed*—which was Ruby's problem for years—but something tells him that's the wrong attitude to take with her under the circumstances. Then he remembers his conversation with his mother in the car. He sucks another heavy intake of air and says, "You know, it's not your fault." The words don't come out as comforting as they were supposed to.

Her face freezes again. "What?"

"You know"—he nods his head toward Jackson's pillow—"what happened."

"I know." Her eyes move inside their sockets as if she's trying to remember something she's been told. "Umm . . . it was an accident."

"That's right." He nods vigorously, and she mirrors the gesture, matching him nod for nod. This seems to do the trick. Ruby hops to the floor, turns around, and smoothes out the spot where she had been sitting. "See you downstairs," she says as she exits.

He tears off the covers and makes a dash for the bathroom. He taps his toes on the cold tile until his bladder lets go and he pisses for what seems like forever. The releasing of it actually hurts. At the first sense of his muscles relaxing, it's as though the air in the room begins to stir, blowing back at him the noisy memories of the day before. "Goddamn it," he says, suddenly finding himself on the top of the slide, looking down at Jackson's striped shirt. "Fuck fuck fuck fuck fuck."

Ruby is sitting at the kitchen table, studying the flat sandwich on her plate with a degree of scrutiny intense even for her. As far as Robin can tell it's just the usual pink meat on white bread with a yellow smear of butter—the way she always has it—though Ruby's lifted off the top slice of bread and is poking at the insides, dropping her head close for a good sniff. When she looks up at him, her eyes bug out a little; it's that guilty look he saw upstairs in his bedroom. The feeling that the two of them are accomplices in a crime against their brother is so strong it takes all his concentration not to think about it, which he knows doesn't make very much sense: thinking hard about what you want to forget. With her wounded stare focused on him, Ruby looks like something stuffed with too much of something else, as though she might literally burst open. Robin has a sudden flash that this is the face Ruby will be wearing all the time now, and he feels angry again, wishing she could just play it cool the way they're supposed to, at least until someone tells them what is going on.

Across the room, at the counter, is their grandmother, her broad back to them, her doughy elbows poking into the air. She is building a pile of sandwiches like the one on Ruby's plate.

"Robin's here," Ruby announces.

"And it's a good thing, too, with enough food to feed an army of boys twice his size," Nana Rena says.

Robin hasn't seen his grandmother since the summer, at a family picnic at her house in Massachusetts. The sight of her, the sound of her peculiar accent—that funny Polish roughness mixed in with the twangy New England vowels—is an instant comfort. She's the first person, the first *anything*, he's seen since the playground that looks and sounds exactly the way it's supposed to. She's wearing her "around the house" wig today—the plainer, grayer of the two she has—and her green dress, the one with the hundreds of faded blue flowers printed onto it. In the past Robin and Ruby and Jackson have joked about Nana Rena's wardrobe, about the three ugly dresses she wears in regular rotation, but today the sight of this dress couldn't be more welcome.

She turns around slowly, balancing herself carefully in a series of steps that allows her weight to shift in increments. Robin's never seen her pivot from the waist; in fact he isn't sure that under her big square frocks she actually has a waist. He thinks of his mother's joke: "It's easier to jump over Nana Rena than walk around her."

"Well I'd like to say good morning," she says, "but you couldn't find enough good to kick your boots at today."

He walks to her open arms and lets himself be clasped into the meat of her, her thick fingers combing through his hair. He smells her predictable smells, the battle between cooking and cleansers, the heaviness of age in her breath. He lets himself stay there against her for a lot longer than usual. Only when his eyelids begin to dampen does he pull back.

"Did you drive all the way down here?"

"Since the crack of dawn," Nana says, arranging a sandwich and some potato chips on a plate. "I had to fight for a day off, if you can believe. As if those girls couldn't go a day without me. The world is full of places that need kitchen help and full of bosses who give you a darn day off, and if Smith College won't let me out when my own grandson is at death's door—" She cuts herself off suddenly.

"Mom said Jackson's not going to die," Robin says.

Nana Rena moves her hand swiftly through the air in front of her face and chest, a blur that Robin recognizes as her abbreviated Sign of the Cross. He knows what the next thing out of her mouth will be—"P.G.," which means, "Please, God." She hands him the plate she's been fixing. He stares at the food and can't decide if he is very hungry or if it will make him sick. Nana Rena says, "I don't know what the doctors are telling her today but when I was over there this morning, there wasn't anyone breaking out the champagne."

Against his better judgment Robin finds himself looking back over to Ruby, to see what her reaction to these words will be. Her frightened, guilt-stricken face has given way to something more focused and intent, and she opens her mouth to ask a question. "What about a guardian angel?"

"You mean for Jackson?" Robin asks, surprised.

"Well everyone has one. Nana, doesn't everyone have one?"

Nana Rena nods without a great deal of force and says, "You just say your prayers, young lady, and you'll get all the guarding you need."

Ruby looks off into the air, her gaze fixed on nothing in particular. "Can you pray to a guardian angel or does it have to be to God directly?"

Nana puts her hands on her hips and pauses for a moment. "If there's any doubt, you should go right to the top."

"What do I do? Just ask God to make him better?"

"What *else* would you do?" Robin asks, impatient with this discussion. It's like being in school and one kid keeps asking all the questions, tying up the whole class, and you can't figure out why the teacher just doesn't tell him to shut up.

"There are other prayers, you know," Ruby says. "You know, real prayers like 'Hail Mary' and that stuff."

"Anything will do," Nana says. "These days, anything will do for the Catholics. We didn't used to have it so easy; you used to *work* for your grace. When I think about how many rosaries I've said—"

"I think a guardian angel might be more friendly than God," Ruby says hopefully.

Robin slaps his sandwich to the plate. "We don't even go to church anymore," he says to Ruby. "So what makes you think you know so much about it? Since Jackson's first communion, we never even go."

"So? I can pray if I want to. It's a free country."

Nana speaks up. "Your mother has to live with herself for that. I won't take the blame. Eighteen years bringing my children to church every Sunday. I did my part." As she speaks, she repeatedly squirts a mist of blue, all-purpose cleanser from a bottle. She bends into her work, her arm militantly arcing a dishcloth across the countertop. "Of course, things are on the up and up now that we've got one of *us* in the Vatican." A delighted smile takes hold of her; Nana has treated the recent appointment of the first Polish pope as a kind of modern-day miracle.

Robin bites into his sandwich and stops listening. He likes everything about his grandmother but her unwavering belief. If he prayed to God right now would Jackson get better? If he prays to God and Jackson doesn't get better what would that prove? Flashes of going to mass: people mumbling lengthy, memorized prayers, standing, sitting, kneeling like robots, the priest trying to convince everyone (even himself?) about the lessons in the Bible. Lessons thousands of years old! What did the Bible have to say about guys like Larry, who bullied and hurt people and got away with it? What did it have to say about high school? Or wet dreams, or Todd Spicer, or thinking about boys the way you're supposed to think about girls?

He shakes his head to clear his thoughts, hating the fact that one piece of confusion inevitably leads to another: that thought he just had about boys—about liking boys instead of girls—that was a thought he'd never quite made into a sentence before, with a beginning, a middle and an end, even in his head. He concentrates on chewing his sandwich, on the way the slippery meat with the smooth flecks of green olives and pimentos sliced into it wads up into the bread between his teeth. Salt and sweet on his tongue. A lump going down his throat into his belly. A beginning, a middle, and an end. Communion never had any taste at all.

A car is coming up the driveway. Ruby runs to the window and then returns to the kitchen. "It's Aunt Corinne," she says. "I think she brought food."

Nana Rena checks her wig with her hands, rocking the hairpiece from side to side until she judges it just right. "Well, don't leave them waiting out there, Ruby. Go on. Let them in."

Ruby remains in place. "She's with Larry," she says, her face blanking out again.

The doorbell's *ding-dong-ding* chimes around them. "Go on, Ruby," Nana Rena repeats.

Robin understands that Ruby doesn't want to see Larry. He stands up dramatically, both hands on the table, hissing an exasperated take-charge sigh. *"I'll* get it."

Corinne's face is the picture of pity—neck tilting to the side, lips pursed in a frown, eyes glossy and blinking. The softness under her chin is rippled into itself. Her hair is pulled back into a single ponytail, with plastic combs above her ears keeping it all flat and shiny. Robin can detect none of the goofiness he saw Sunday night, when she was dressed up in her World Series outfit.

She holds a Corningware dish covered with its own fitted plastic lid. "I made that one I know you like: green beans and cream of mushroom? Larry's got the dried onion rings."

"Thanks. I'll take it." Flat heat settles on his palms. Larry is standing behind her, nearly hidden, looking over his shoulder at . . . what? Robin follows his glance for a moment—Corinne's tan Vega parked halfway up the drive, the row of hedges between his place and the Delatores', a yellowed copy of the *Community News* at the curb. He quickly gathers that Larry is probably staring at anything but him.

"Hey," Robin says to Larry. Their eyes hold for a moment, and Robin imagines that the wide, empty look he sees there could just be another version of what he and Ruby are feeling. But then Larry squints and curls his lip in a way that makes Robin feel as if he's just been told to shut up.

"Here," Larry says, dropping a red-and-blue can on top of the casserole. Robin tilts his right hand up to keep the onion rings from rolling off as Larry shoves his way inside.

Nana Rena and Aunt Corinne hug each other. "You're looking good, Mother. That's a very nice dress. And how are things at Smith?"

"Except for the Hitler I work for, just fine, just fine. We've got a lovely crop of girls in this year's house. They know how to be ladies at the dinner table. I think the unrest of the past few years is over and done."

Corinne laughs, "Oh, you know, young people and their self-expression."

"The time comes to settle down—that's the truth. Have your fun and settle down. Of course, Dottie's fun came after she left Smith. She didn't get to be so wild, what with me working there."

Robin leaves the two women to their small talk. Larry follows him to the kitchen, maintaining his hands-in-pockets silence.

"Where's Ruby?" he asks finally.

Robin looks around. "I don't know. She was just here."

Larry absorbs this information without a word. Robin goes back to the table to munch on some potato chips. The clock says 1:30. He's already wondering how long they'll stay.

"So you been to the hospital?"

"Last night, but I didn't see Jackson."

"He's pretty messed up?"

"What do you think? He took a bad fall."

Larry stares at him, his face set in a challenge. "I don't know about you, but I think he jumped. I mean, he went *over* the bar."

Robin studies Larry's face to figure out how serious he's being. "No way," he says. "He got knocked off."

"Bullcrap," Larry says. "He was always doing that shit: jumping out of trees and running in front of cars and all. He's crazy."

Jackson does have that streak to him. Robin remembers the time they went to Howe Caverns in upstate New York and Jackson, who was about five at the time, sneaked off the trail and got lost somewhere deep inside the damp, unlit corners. When the guide found him he was high up on a ledge; he said he'd been playing Tom Sawyer. But something about this doesn't seem right. "If he jumped, he wouldn't have landed on his head," he says. "Maybe he would've broke his leg or something."

"Well, it's not *my* fault," Larry says, grabbing a fistful of chips from Robin's plate, shoving half of them into his mouth.

"Yeah, that's what my *mother* said," Robin says, watching as the chips turn into golden mulch between Larry's lips, remembering Stan devouring lasagna the night before. "She told me I'm supposed to tell you that it's not your fault." He sours his voice so that Larry understands that he's repeating something he doesn't believe.

Larry lowers his voice. "Listen to this: just say he jumped. Otherwise they'll try to pin it on us. I'm telling you, we should stick together."

"You're mental," Robin says, but he finds something powerful, self-protective, in Larry's words.

Larry pulls a carton of milk from the fridge. "What's this 'two percent' mean?" he asks. "Is it skim?"

"It's for people on a diet," Robin says. "Like my mother."

Larry pours some in a glass. "I should give some to my mother. All she ever talks about is Weight Watchers." He raises the pitch of his voice. "'Myrna said I can eat anything I want as long as it's in small portions.' I said, 'Yeah, Mom, except some of us around here are already skinny.'"

"You're a growing boy," Robin says, putting on his own fake-mother voice.

"That's right," Larry says and chugs the milk. He wipes his mouth on his jacket sleeve and then leans closer to Robin. "I'm growing hair near my dick," he says, his voice lowered. "Wanna see?"

Robin looks away and then back. Larry's holding out his jeans from the waist with his thumb. He raises his eyebrows twice. Robin shrugs, then leans forward. Larry takes a step toward him, then another, then unhooks his thumb and bops Robin's nose with it.

"I bet you do!" He howls contemptuously.

"You *re*ject!" Robin hisses. He grabs Larry's shirt with one hand and tosses him aside, harder than he thought he could, into the countertop. Larry's elbow sends the casserole skidding into Nana's plate of sandwiches.

Corinne's voice from the living room: "What's going on in there?"

"Cool out, man," Larry demands.

"I'm going up to my room," Robin says.

"Hey, man," Larry says. "Remember, we gotta stick together. And tell your sister, too!"

Corinne is suddenly there in the doorway. "Tell your sister what?" she asks.

"Nothing," Larry says.

Robin looks from mother to son and back again. "Yeah, nothing. Just, you know, hope she's doing OK."

Corinne smiles. "Well, Robin, you can tell her that from me, too. We've got to get going now. Tell your mother I'll call later. Maybe we'll stop by tonight with Stan."

"Sure." Robin follows them back to the living room, where Nana Rena is holding out Corinne's coat.

"Maybe there'll be some good news, P.G.," she says.

Larry gives Robin a punch on the shoulder as he heads toward the front door. "Later, man." He adds a final nod—a reminder of the new game plan.

In his room with the door closed, Robin replays the scene with Larry over in his mind. He slams his fists into the bed—enraged at how Larry just *gets* to him every time. What if Larry's right? What if there is trouble ahead for all of them and they really ought to blame it on Jackson? No one would question that Jackson gets himself into trouble over and over again. Why should this thing be any different? Still, the image that remains from the day before is of Larry turning Jackson over on the ground, the noise of Jackson's bones cracking. Whose fault was *that*?

Jackson's just got to get better, he's just got to be all right and then none of this will be a problem. Robin hasn't been able to think about this with any outcome except Jackson dying or Jackson being retarded, but maybe . . . maybe the doctors will figure something out. They're doctors after all. That's what they're supposed to do. And why haven't his parents called? He wishes now that they had woken him up this morning and taken him along. Then he wouldn't have had to deal with any of this . . . Ruby being weird, and Larry being . . .

He lays on his back and pushes down his pants. He's got hair growing around his dick, too—seems like more every day. Each one is curvy and long. They start in one direction, then twist around like question marks. Darker than on his head or legs, more like the few brownish hairs starting to poke out from his armpits. He wishes he did get a look at Larry's, and Larry knew it, too. That's the worst of it. He wishes he got to see Larry again like on Sunday night, naked and shaking it around. He wants to compare, and he wants to know if Larry knows how to jerk it off like he's discovered. It feels perverted to think this way, but he starts getting hard, pushing his penis up toward his belly, tangling it up with his pubic hair. He lets the heat of his hand increase the stiffness. He does this until he can't think of anything else, all the pressures of the world lining up behind this one pressure from the core of his body: shuddery, rough, soundless. He closes his eyes and concentrates on himself, just himself getting crazier and stronger at the same time, stronger than anyone, definitely stronger and tougher and bigger than Larry.

Nana Rena is sleeping on the couch in the living room, her feet, mis-shapen from years of serving meals to rich college girls, propped on a pillow. Ruby crouches on the carpet. A sketchbook she's been drawing in rests open on the floor, a shock of black and red streaked across it. The TV glows blue-gray from the wall, the volume low, a soap opera sending out images of intrigue and heartache.

When the phone rings, both Ruby and Nana Rena stir, but Robin leaps to his feet first, dashing to the kitchen. "Hello?"

"Hey, champ." A very deep man's voice, almost no emotion.

"Dad?"

An attempt at an offended chuckle. "Who'd you think?"

"You sounded different."

Ruby's at his side, waiting.

"Well, it's been a rough day." Quick sigh. "You holding down the fort?"

Out of the corner of his eye, Robin catches Nana Rena making her way drowsily into the kitchen. "Is that your mother?" she asks. Her wig has slid backward and sideways; wispy white strands poke out at the ears. She shuffles closer to him to take the phone.

He steps away, stretches the cord toward the basement door, and curls more tightly into it. "Wait, Dad. What'd you say?"

"Listen, we're going to hang around for a couple more hours. They've just done some tests and we want to wait for the results." A pause, a sniffle. "So your mother and I will be here for a while. Waiting."

"What kind of tests?"

"Oh, you know, to . . . uh . . . assess the situation. The brain and all that." There's a kind of a choke that gets covered up, a hand over the receiver. Somewhere back there Robin guesses the tears are starting again. He hands off the phone to Nana Rena.

"Hello? Hello?" She has raised her voice as she always does on the phone, forever living in the old days of weak, staticky connections. "Clark?"

Ruby is curling her sketchbook into a tight tube with both hands. "What did he say?" she asks Robin.

"They're doing tests."

"What tests?"

"How should I know?" Now his voice is raised.

Nana Rena is waving at both of them, trying to quiet them down. "Dottie? Dottie, what have you got to tell me?" Robin tries to read her face, which reveals only her attentiveness. She nods as she listens, interjects "Mm-hmm" and "Yah" every few seconds, her eyes cast downward.

When Robin senses the conversation winding down, he says, "Let me talk."

She hands the phone to him with the receiver covered up. "Now don't trouble her," she commands.

Robin grabs the phone and stretches the cord past the basement door, closing himself into the darkness. "Mom?"

"Hello, darling. How are you holding up?" He immediately wishes he were with her.

"Fine, you know. I mean, I'm really bored here."

"Yes, well, the waiting will do that. But it's best for you to be there for now, with your sister."

"She's kind of bugging me."

"Robin, honey, please. I need you to—"

He cuts her off. "I know, I know. So I told her what you said, about it's not her fault."

"That's very good of you."

"And I told Larry, so, you know, mission accomplished. So what are these tests?"

"Modern medicine. More tests than you ever imagined." She says this lightly. He can feel her needing him to take on this same tone but he remains quiet. After a tiny cough she says, "I don't want to upset you, Robin."

"I'm already upset."

"I know, honey. I know. It's just a bunch of complicated medical hoohah. They have to scan the brain to see how well he's responding."

"Did Jackson's brain get smooshed when he fell?" He pictures a mass of scarlet jelly in his brother's head, bone chunks and brain matter suspended within.

Another sigh. "It's the spine, the point at which the spine enters the brain. There's a question about motor skills."

"Oh, yeah, that." He's not sure what this means exactly but waits until she continues.

"There are different parts of the brain that do different things and some of them don't seem to be working right and some of them they can't really tell, so the tests will continue until we know everything we can."

The operator's voice intrudes suddenly: nasal, impersonal, looking for more money.

"Oh, Christ," Dorothy says. "Clark? Give me another nickel."

There's a knocking on the door behind Robin. It's Ruby. "I want to talk to her, too."

"Hold your haystacks," he shouts and pounds back.

In his ear, he hears the metallic drop of the coin. "What's going on? Are you still there?" Dorothy asks.

"Can I come to the hospital?" he asks her.

"Maybe tomorrow."

"This sucks."

"Robin, I'm going to get off the phone now. I can't have you come here. It's just too chaotic. Why don't you do some reading or help your Nana cook dinner?"

"Yeah, right."

"Put your sister on the phone and say good-bye, OK?"

He is silent. Along the gray staircase, he can see the lines of wood paneling, line after line like jail bars. His father put up the paneling himself. Robin and Jackson held it in place while his father hammered in skinny nails and the smooth board shuddered under their palms. He recalls laughing with Jackson, the two of them sharing a joke at their father's expense. The memory confuses him.

"Robin? I love you, dear."

"Yeah, me, too." He stands up and kicks back the door. Ruby gasps. The afternoon sun is shining through a window into his eyes.

"You almost hit me!"

He holds out the phone. "Here." He walks past her, past Nana Rena and the humming refrigerator, out the back door to his bicycle.

Pedaling fast in the fading afternoon sun, Robin is unsure which streets to take to the hospital. He cuts down Schrader and Lewis, which takes him past the shop where his father bought him his bike last winter, past the Episcopal church and the Italian delicatessen. It's eerie being outside again, because the world is the same as always, yet in some way unfamiliar, slightly shifted, askew. As he speeds by on his bike certain details rise up and surprise him: the sharp angle of the church roof, the gnarly twists of low-hanging tree branches, the broken concrete of sidewalks he's walked a hundred times but never before studied. He passes a couple of houses where kids he goes to school with live, expecting faces at the window, eyes following his flight. He wonders if the word has gotten out, if people he'll see in school when he goes back (tomorrow? next week?) will know about the accident. They *must* know. He can't imagine that something he's spent every minute thinking about isn't already common knowledge. What will they think? They'll know he caused it all, they're readying their accusations, it's only a matter of time. As he comes to a halt at a stop sign, a police car drives across his path, and when the officer in the passenger seat stares his way, he feels his insides tighten up. It's all in slow motion: the officer's dark glasses and beaked nose, a finger adjusting the brim of the cap. A touch of breath on the inside of the window. The muffled squawk of the police radio.

Robin drops all his weight on the pedals; he passes the library, where his mother would be working today, moves toward the center of town. He slaloms around the trunk end of cars pulling out of parking spaces. Up ahead, the siren of the nightly commuter train—the one his father usually rides home from the city—blankets every other sound. Red lights flash at the edge of the tracks. Cars obediently slow down and pedestrians freeze at the corner, but Robin doesn't want to break his momentum. He gauges that he has enough time to get across the train tracks before the wobbly black-and-white warning arms drop. Someone shouts for him to stop as he moves toward the tracks, his wheels slamming over the steel ties, his pelvis vibrating. The train bellows, its dagger of light widening. He sucks in his breath, lowers his head and races under the second descending arm. The train rumbles behind him, squealing to a stretched-out halt at the depot.

"Are you outta your mind?" A woman in a trench coat, her hair piled under a scarf, a briefcase in her hand: she looks familiar. A teller at the bank where he has his Christmas Club? The mother of someone from school? She keeps her disapproving eyes on him. Keep moving, he tells himself.

On Tappan Boulevard, the cars rush past his left side in a continuous, menacing whoosh. He keeps his eyes low, measuring the pace of the traffic by the red taillights ahead of him. Every vehicle pumps the fear of the chase into him, each rumbling auto a possible accident—maybe the last sound he'll hear before being knocked to the pavement. *Maybe I am out of my mind.* The glare of oncoming cars has quickened the darkening of the sky. It's the same spooky half-light that surrounded him as he approached the slide last night. He wants to shake it from his head but he can still feel every angry step he took up the ladder. What happened up there? He can't make any more sense of it now than he did yesterday: the heat coming off Jackson and Ruby and Larry locked in their struggle, the dull steel railing and chute, the final crazy impression of Jackson flying away. Not jumping, not falling, *flying*.

At the intersection of Tappan Boulevard and Washington Road he finally stops. Three smaller streets spread out from the two main avenues and drivers are nosing past each other in six different directions. He needs to cross, can't figure out how. The sensation that an accident is waiting to happen takes over—every car that turns without signaling seems to have his name written on it. For the first time since leaving his house he thinks it was wrong of him to take this trip, that if he gets hurt on his way to see Jackson it would be the absolute worst thing possible, not even for his own injuries but for the proof that he is foolish and can't take care of himself, much less anyone else. He considers going back but remembers the stifling anxiety of the long afternoon and decides instead to cut through the Shell station at his right. He pedals up a hill that he thinks might get him to the hospital. The traffic here is just as heavy, but the road is only one lane in either direction. There might be a safer chance to cross up ahead.

He's not familiar with this end of town. There's a shopping plaza with a big hardware store he's visited once or twice with his father, and the only Chinese takeout place for miles, the one Uncle Stan insists uses pigeon meat in the chicken dishes. Beyond that, he's not sure. He keeps moving forward, until the road narrows a bit and the streetlights are less frequent, the houses are smaller and less packed together. In the distance he can see the bright perimeter of a cemetery, a row of gravestones glowing behind a chain link fence and then the impenetrable darkness beyond. It's so obviously ghostly he snickers a panicky laugh, no way he's going to ride any closer to *that*. He cuts sharply to the left, enough distance between him and the nearest approaching car to get him across Green and onto a side street he hopes will lead him back on course.

His thighs are starting to ache, and the underside of his butt where he didn't even know he had muscles. A persistent itch is circling across his scabbed palms. He slows down a bit to catch his breath and feels the air against his sweaty face. His ears ring before they adjust to the noises fading behind him. Gentler sounds make their way in: the click of a car door, a couple of voices from someone's front stoop, some muffled TV dialogue drifting from an open window.

A car starts up in a driveway, he glimpses the back of a black man's head in the orange interior light. Farther down he sees a couple of small figures chasing each other across their lawn, black kids, younger than himself, and a woman, also black, taking out her trash. She squints her eyes at him and watches as he passes by. A sign above a mechanic's shop on a corner: Marble Road Auto Body. *Marble Road:* his first reaction is disbelief, that this place really exists beyond the fearsome stories he's heard—like the one Larry told him about a gang of black girls who jumped a white girl walking down Marble Road and wedged a miniature-golf pencil up her ass. He had an image in his head of high rise apartment buildings, gangs of young men hanging out, and funk music blasting from big cars, like a miniature Harlem, or the opening credits on *Good Times.* But this place is so quiet, and not even quiet enough to be scary. It's just another part of Greenlawn. The only thing that strikes him as really different is the road, which is more cracked, and weedy at the curb. The streets in his neighborhood get paved every year.

He turns at the next intersection for no reason at all, just full of doubt, needing to change directions. His bike chinks and rattles over the broken-up macadam. Some lights up ahead: a baseball field, a few cars parked at the edge of the glow. Two girls and two boys on the hood, one of them smoking. A bass line thumping lightly under their conversation. A face turns toward him, a halo of light on slicked down, straightened hair. A girl's voice: "Hey? Who's that?"

Another girl: "It's a white boy."

A guy's voice, duller: "Some white boy got lost."

"Ooo." This from one of the girls.

"Hey, where you going, boy?"

For a split second, he thinks about asking for directions but his feet impulsively push harder on the pedals—an impulse so old he doesn't think he's ever not had it. He rides away, away from a taunt he can't comprehend and the tail end of bored laughter. And now it seems like he's been riding for hours, and he's wondering if he's going anywhere at all.

Chapter Five

He makes it to a road that he recognizes, running beneath a vast slope of dead, flattened grass. Surrounded by chain link at the top is a mansion, a gray silhouette against the sky, that's been uninhabited for years and is rumored to be haunted. In the winter kids sleigh all the way down from the fence, though it's dangerous because you have to turn sharply at the bottom or wind up in the line of traffic. Up ahead are two more landmarks: the Dairy Queen, where he and Victoria used to hang out before she went away for the summer, and beyond that the town dump, where he's accompanied his father with bottles and newspapers for recycling. A CLOSED UNTIL APRIL sign is nailed to the front of the Dairy Queen.

The parking lot is lit up but empty—except for a van parked near the back, which seems suspicious to him. He wheels his bike toward the pay phone. He's got some change in his pocket but isn't sure who to call. Nana Rena, by now mad with worry? Maybe Uncle Stan is back at the house. She'll send him out looking; everyone will be pissed off. As he rounds the corner of the low building he's startled by a noise.

A boy his age is sitting on the ground, his head tilted back against the wall. Robin can see dried blood around the boy's nostrils, little clay-colored flakes on the white stretch of his upper lip. He's wearing a baseball cap; dark hair pokes out around his ears and neck. His ears are the perfect kind of ears, delicate and flat, the right size for his thin face. Robin's seen this guy before, in school.

"What's up?" Robin says, digging into his pocket for a dime.

The boy stares at him, startled. His face is sad or angry or something that sends out a warning. He wipes the bloodstain from under his nose with the cuff of his flannel shirt.

Robin puts a dime into the slot. No dial tone. He flicks the coin-return lever but gets nothing back.

"It doesn't work," the boy mutters.

"Oh," Robin says, and then just stands there. "The hospital's not far from here?"

The boys squints up at him. "I don't need no fucking hospital."

"No, I mean for me."

"What's wrong with you? You sick?"

"No, my brother is. He's . . . hurt."

The boy shoots a quick look toward the van at the back of the lot. Robin sees some motion in the trees behind the vehicle, makes out the blurry figure of a man stooped over, picking something up. Then the boy stands up, dusts off the seat of his jeans, and speaks. "I know who you are."

Now Robin recognizes him from phys. ed.: the other kid hanging out at the top of the bleachers, trying to avoid the Skins vs. Shirts punchball game. "Yeah, yeah, I remember. Gym class. Pintack? Fourth period?"

"I fuckin' hate that guy," the boy spits out. "Fuckin' asshole jock. He fuckin' hates me and I hate him back."

Robin nods, happy for something in common. "Yeah, I can't stand him. He acts so tough and gets everyone all riled up about all those stupid games and—"

"Yeah, I know about you," he interrupts.

Robin tries to figure out what he means—does he know him from somewhere besides gym class?

The boy starts walking away toward the van, muttering, "Shit." He's caught sight of the man back by the van, who has emerged from the woods, carrying a plastic garbage bag stuffed full. He's also in a flannel shirt, jeans, and a cap: the logo is General Motors. He's not very tall but there's something instantly mean about him. He clears a big gob from his throat and spits against the gravel. When he looks their way he drops the bag.

"Get the fuck over here," he yells.

Robin watches Scott take his time. There, he's remembered the boy's name: Scott Schatz. He's one of those kids no one pays any attention to, though Robin's always been curious about him. How has Scott managed to sit out the same games as Robin but avoid the kind of name calling Robin has put up with?

"I got another bag back there," the man says to Scott. "Go get it." Robin can't figure out what's going on back there. Is this man barking orders Scott's father? His mind races: a dead body in the bag, a pile of drugs, something illegal. One too many weird possibilities. *Just get out of here.* He's pretty sure that there's a turn somewhere not too far down the road that would curve him back toward Tappan Boulevard. Pretty sure, but not positive, and his instincts have been off all night. And then Scott turns back to him and lifts up his index finger as if to say, Wait one minute, and there's something in his eyes, not quite comforting, but friendly in a simple way, for which Robin feels instantly grateful. So he decides to wait. Maybe Scott will give him directions after he does whatever it is being demanded of him. He takes a deep, steadying breath and leans his bike on its kickstand.

The man at the van has opened a beer and is swigging it down. Scott returns from the woods, dragging another full bag with both hands. He struggles to lift it into the back of the van until the man gets impatient and does it for him, shoving Scott out of the way. Then they talk for a minute in very low voices, glancing back his way. Finally Scott waves Robin over.

The man asks in a slurry voice, "You going to the hospital?"

"Yeah," Robin answers timidly.

"What the hell you doing over here?"

"I got lost. I wound up driving around Marble Road."

"Hah!" The man spits again. "You're lucky you didn't get the shit kicked outta you." He chugs his beer.

Scott rolls his eyes and frowns. "Shut up, Dad. You don't know what you're talking about." *Dad,* Robin thinks. This scary guy *is* Scott's father.

Scott looks at Robin. "We practically *live* on Marble Road."

"Practically ain't the same as actually," Mr. Schatz says. He crushes the empty can in his hand and chucks it at Scott. "Throw your bike in the back."

"You don't have to. I mean, you could just tell me how to get there."

Scott reaches out and grabs his handle bars. "It's not that close, man." Together they lift the bike in the van. The front wheel falls on one of the bags and the insides let out a tinny crunch.

"Don't you rip those goddamn things," Mr. Schatz says, "or you'll be carrying cans to the drop off one by one between your fucking teeth."

"Shut up, we're not ripping nothing," Scott says. "C'mon," he says to Robin and climbs in. Robin props himself at Scott's side. Scott reaches across him, the tail of his oversize wool shirt brushing prickly against Robin's arm, and shuts the door. It's dark as a cave.

Mr. Schatz starts up the motor. Rock-and-roll music jangles the air. Robin thinks it must be Elvis, but he's never been able to tell any of those '50s singers apart. The air inside grows stuffy very quickly, filled with the stench coming from the empty cans: moldy beer, rotting sugar. Then there's sharp burning of a match and a cloud of smoke from Mr. Schatz's cigarette. Scott calls out to his father, "Hey, pass the smokes back."

Mr. Schatz ignores him. Scott picks up a can and hurls it into the dash. "C'mon, give 'em over."

"You better calm down, motherfucker, or you're gonna get it."

Scott rubs his nose self-consciously. "A little late for that," he mutters.

Robin nods and says, "Guess so," which is all he can come up with. He hasn't been hit by his father since he got a spanking at age six for who knows why—he can't even imagine getting a bloody nose from him. Scott acts as if it's not such a big deal, but with his eyes adjusting to the darkness, Robin can again make out that sad-angry combination he first saw on Scott's face.

Scott stamps his feet on the metal floor a couple of time. "Cigarettes, man!" he yells over the doo-wop harmonies.

"You're too young to smoke," Mr. Schatz yells back, but in the tone of voice that sounds like he doesn't really care. A pack of Winstons comes flying back at them and bounces off the spokes of Robin's bike.

Scott squints at him. "You don't smoke probably."

"I've smoked my mother's cigarettes plenty." A lie: only once or twice, with mostly unpleasant results.

"You can have a drag of mine. I don't want you hacking to death."

Robin forces a laugh. "OK, that's fuckin' cool," he says. He thinks he should say things like "fuckin' cool" with Scott.

Scott pulls a match from his pocket and lights one. Even with all the hardness in his expression, Scott has a face that Robin thinks of as cute, which is just one more thing for him to be nervous about. He's glad when the match goes out. Scott takes a drag and coughs a little himself. "They're getting rid of the bottle bill next month, so we're getting everything we can now," he explains.

"That's a good idea," Robin says, taking the cigarette from Scott's fingers.

"It's a fuckin' hassle is what it is. Every fuckin' night for a fuckin' week."

Mr. Schatz yells from the front, "Don't you start that shit again."

Scott pulls his cap over his eyes and then drops his fist into the bag. Another groan of aluminum. Robin brings the cigarette to his mouth and sucks in. For a second it's just warm, and then it's like something is trapped in his throat and he can't breathe. He tries not to cough, which only makes it worse. He can't see or hear anything for what seems like forever. There's a slap on his back, flat and hard, Scott's hand. He pats him a few times until the coughing stops, lets his hand rest there until Robin calms down.

"Sorry," Robin says.

Scott takes the cigarette back and drags in on it. "It's a bad fuckin' habit anyway."

"Warning: Smoking may be hazardous to your health," Robin recites.

"Yeah, just like parents."

Robin shakes his head. "I feel a little dizzy."

Scott moves over. "You wanna rest?"

"OK." He pivots so they're side by side, shoulder blades wedged between the bent edge of plastic-covered cans, Scott blowing smoke above them like a chimney.

"So your name is Robin, right?"

"Uh-huh. And you're Scott?"

"Bingo."

Robin can feel his heartbeat speeding up. It always surprises him when anyone knows his name, even though he knows everyone's name at school: these little mental files he has going all the time, gathering information, mapping out the terrain around him. Is Scott that kind of person, too? Or has he just heard someone picking on him in the locker room?

"So what's with your brother?"

"He fell, maybe broke his neck."

"No way! Older brother?"

"Younger." He hesitates: how much should he say? But then Scott says in a very genuine voice, "That really sucks," which opens up the floodgates. "There was this whole fucked up thing yesterday. He fell off the slide at this playground near my house, when I was up there with him. Me and him and my sister and my cousin, Larry, who's a pain in the ass—we were all up at the top together and then, I don't know, next thing he was on the ground, knocked out."

"He broke his neck? Doesn't seem like it's tall enough."

Robin considers this. How tall was the slide? Six feet, seven? Seemed tall as a house yesterday but obviously that's not right. "I guess it doesn't make much sense."

"Welcome to the fucking world."

Robin reaches for the cigarette and takes another drag, not very deep. This one goes down smoother. He speaks as he coughs out smoke again. "Larry says Jackson jumped off, but I think I might have done it, me and my sister, pushing."

Scott reaches across and takes the cigarette back. He taps his fist on Robin's chest. "Don't get heavy about it, man. He'll be all right."

Robin wipes his eyes, which are watering from the cigarette smoke, though he wonders if Scott thinks he's crying. He manages to croak, "Yeah, sure, thanks," when the van makes a sharp turn and comes to a stop.

Scott crawls to the door and swings it wide, revealing the stadium glow of the hospital grounds, green lawns sparkling under the mist of concealed night sprinklers. Robin strains under the weight of the bike until Scott helps him with it. "So, thanks again."

"Yeah, later." Scott pulls a hand from his pocket and sticks it into the air between them. They shake, locking their eyes on each other. "See you in Jockville," Scott says.

"Yeah, I guess I have to go back to school tomorrow."

"I'm usually out by the wall in the back, near the breezeway. You know, before homeroom, if you wanna hang in the morning. I don't know if it's your crowd, probably not, all the burnouts." He shrugs. "Whatever."

"OK, maybe." Robin's always made a point of avoiding that area— it's definitely not his crowd, it's more of Todd Spicer's crowd—but Scott's invitation seems worth considering.

Mr. Schatz guns the engine for emphasis. Ride or no ride, Robin hates the man. How could anyone punch their own kid bloody, especially someone as nice as Scott? As Scott closes himself back in, Robin is afraid for him, for the long night ahead, picking up other people's castoffs to make money for that old bully. Peeling back onto Tappan and blasting out fumes, the rusty brown van is an eyesore. Robin waves, though Scott obviously can't see him.

And then he's alone again. The air coats his exposed skin like a damp rag. Every piece of his body feels weak: stiff knuckles, burning thighs, cold, sooty nose. He hasn't eaten for hours but thinks he might throw up if he did. It's as if he's been tricked by a few minutes of sort-of friend-ship into forgetting how terrible everything else is.

The residue of tobacco is on his fingertips, a smell like hot chocolate or burned popcorn. He'll have to find a sink inside before he sees his parents.

The longer he stands there looking up at the building he's been trying to get to all night long, the more he feels responsible for this entire situation. He should not go inside; he should not even show his face in public. Another TV-movie sentiment forms in his head, a voice like a prayer: *Let him live and I'll die instead.* But then he thinks of his mother's instructions: *Be strong.* Is it "strong" to want to die so that Jackson can live, or is that the weakest thought of all?

When his foot lands on the big gray entrance mat, the glass and silver doors swing apart with such silent speed he feels as if he is under their control. The hospital lobby is barren, with none of the confusing activity of the emergency room the night before, and only the dimmest tremble of music in the air. Everything here is bright and angled: square, flame-orange couches without pillows, magazines inert on shiny end tables, checkerboard floor tiles waxed to a bluish gleam. His sneakers squeak with every step. On each wall hangs a many-colored mural depicting doctors and nurses and families on the mend: a man in a white lab coat rests his big hand on the shoulder of a boy whose arm sports a bulky cast; a woman holds her sleeping infant up to an approving nurse. The faces beam but to Robin they are menacing: the heads have a crude, rectangular shape to them, the bodies are stiff and cardboard flat. With his knees still wobbly and his head pounding from the ride, he feels like an alien form of life—one that sweats and throbs and does not smile. At the far end of this room is a Formica counter, where an old lady is staring intently at a single sheet of paper. She is wearing a white tunic but no cap, and Robin isn't sure if she is a nurse or just dressed to look like one.

He stops a few feet from the counter. "Excuse me," he says. "I'm here to see my brother."

She continues gazing at her paper until Robin thinks he should speak up again, and louder, and then with an unexpected flick she slaps the paper down on the counter. "Unbelievable," she says, walking around the counter. She is wearing pale blue pants stretched tight across her wide backside. "Visiting hours are over, son," she barks. "Wait over there. I'll be right back after I talk to someone about this." She points to a couch, not the nearest one, which makes little sense to Robin, but her face is stern and so he moves toward it. She narrows her eyes as if she has finally taken a close look at him. "And wipe your nose. Cripes, what's a kid your age doing here on a school night?"

He doesn't have to answer her because she's gone down a corridor.

The doors swing open at the other end of the lobby and a couple enters. Before they get too close, Robin makes a quick decision and turns down a hallway. A sign near an elevator bank reads: INTENSIVE CARE, 2ND FLOOR WEST. He pushes the UP arrow and gets inside the silvery compartment. The ride to the second floor takes much longer than it seems like it should. His head spins. He imagines getting stuck between floors.

When the doors open a man stands in front of him—it's Harold, the nurse from last night. Robin lowers his head and tries to pass by, but Harold recognizes him.

"Oh, hi," Robin says, his voice deliberately casual.

"Oh, hi," Harold repeats with a tinge of sarcasm. "Just strolling around, huh?"

"My brother's room is on this floor," Robin says.

"Yes, I know. I was just there. Come with me." Harold drops his arm across Robin's shoulder and they walk together. "Must have been a pretty tough day."

"Well, I didn't go to school or anything."

"Did you walk here?"

"I rode my bike. It's not very far."

Harold looks down at him as if he knows Robin's lying but is going to play along with it a little longer. "You know, your brother's really not up for visitors."

"My parents have been visiting all day."

"Yeah, they're still here. Down in the cafeteria at the moment, I think."

"Well, I'll just go and take a look at Jackson."

"Robin," Harold says, stopping and turning Robin so that they're face-to-face, "your grandmother called half an hour ago. Everyone's been worried about you."

Robin feels suddenly defensive. "It's a free country. I can see my own brother if I want to."

"Look, I'll take you there, but I'm warning you, it's not pretty. OK?" Harold's face is serious now, and it frightens Robin. "He's hooked up to a bunch of tubes and there are machines around the bed and he's not really . . . awake. He's not going to look like what you expect."

Robin manages a nonchalant shrug. "I can take it."

Harold guides him to the open doorway. "I'll wait outside."

Robin peers into the room, which is lit only by a single fluorescent light above Jackson's bed, and wants to cry immediately. It's kind of like Harold described, with the tubes and machines and all, but somehow, when Robin formed that picture in his head, he didn't imagine Jackson in the middle of it. Jackson's head is propped up by a neck brace, half obscured by a pillow squishing in around his flattened hair. Bags of clear liquid hang from poles; stringy tubes snake toward Jackson's body and disappear under yellow strips of tape against his skin. His face is swollen as if filled with too much blood, his eyes are closed, and his mouth is open at one side and sticky with drool.

"Jackson?" he whispers. The room is silent except for a calm beep from one of the machines. He steps closer. The sheets across Jackson's chest rise and fall. "Jackson?" He touches the edge of the bed and has the urge to shake it, to wake Jackson up. "I rode my bike here," he says. "I got lost or I would have been here sooner. I got lost on Marble Road—you believe that?"

Someone clears their throat behind him, but when he turns around it's not Harold in the doorway, it's his mother. She's nearly in silhouette, the bright corridor behind her absent of detail.

"You stubborn child," she says, her voice raspy, weary. "I told you to stay home."

"I was going crazy at home. Why'd I have to stay there?" He backs up a step and bumps into a chair, which rubs sharply along the floor. The noise panics him, as if he might have broken something important, and he quickly sets the chair back in place.

She walks into the room and curls her arms around him; his face gets pushed against her breasts; he is enveloped by the smell of cigarettes and powdery sweat. Just as he wants to pull himself free he is yanked away, fingers digging into his arm.

His father's blue-gray eyes stare at him, the skin on his forehead pinched, his lower lip quivering angrily.

"Hey," Robin says. "You're hurting me."

"What the fuck are you trying to prove?" Clark says. Robin has never heard his father say "fuck" before and he can't stop himself from smiling. The pressure from Clark's grasp increases. "Do you think this is a game?"

"Clark, don't," Dorothy says, pulling Robin back toward her.

"Don't you tell me *don't*," Clark says to her. He tugs Robin again. "I've got enough on my mind without having to worry about this one.

What the hell is wrong with you, Robin? When we tell you to stay home, we mean, stay the fuck home."

"Let go," Robin says, shaking his arm against the stiffness of Clark's grip. He looks past his parents at Harold, who is standing in the hall staring at his feet.

"Clark, enough. Please," Dorothy's voice is an urgent whisper.

"*I've* had enough," Clark says.

"He just wanted to see his brother, Clark. You're overreacting."

"Leave me alone!" Robin yells. Clark pulls harder on his arm until Robin is ripped from Dorothy, then spins him toward Jackson's bed.

Clark's voice is steel. "Take a good look, OK. That's your brother. He's had an operation. They've put a pin in his neck to realign his spine. There's been nerve damage. They don't know yet if there's been brain damage. There's a lump the size of a baseball on the side of his head. One of his ribs was poking into his kidney. He's got a fracture in his arm. You wanted to know? You wanted to see? Now you know."

"Why are you yelling at me?" Robin snaps back. He starts to say, "It's not my fault," but he's not sure about that, he's only sure he shouldn't say it. Clark stares at him for a moment and then looks back at the bed. His shoulders drop. He lets go of Robin.

The machine attached to Jackson beeps in time, oblivious to them all. Robin feels his own heart beating faster than the machine. He almost imagines a grin on Jackson's blank face, laughing at their argument, laughing at Robin in trouble.

Dorothy whispers, "Clark? Please, no more of this."

Clark shoots another look at Robin—Robin can still see the anger but now there's no strength behind it, as if his father is melting in front of him. Clark mutters, "I've had it. I'm getting out of here. I'll meet you at the car." He pushes past Robin and Dorothy. Robin hears his father ask Harold if he can see the doctor once more. He hears their footsteps as they walk away. Somewhere in the hallway a wheel on a moving cart squeaks.

Dorothy puts her hands on Robin's shoulders and brings him back into her. She rests her cheek against his ear.

"Mom—" is all he can say and then he shuts his eyes so tight he sees red and green.

"Shhh," she says, tightening her grip around him. "You don't have to say anything, sweetie." Robin's legs are shaking. The tighter his mother holds him, the more he feels like he will collapse without her.

* * *

They get to the parking lot before Clark. Robin unlocks his bike and they wedge as much of it in the trunk as they can. The front wheel hangs over the bumper like a monster trying to crawl out. They wait in the front seat with the engine running, a fumey smell wafting up from below their legs.

The hospital doors whoosh open. The woman who was at the front desk when Robin first walked in hurries out. Her lips are moving, and she shakes her head side to side as if arguing with someone. Suddenly she stops and rummages through her purse, pulling out a pack of cigarettes, which she throws into a trash can. She shakes her fist at the building. Dorothy bursts out laughing.

"Who is *she?*" she asks.

"She's the old bag at the front desk," Robin says. "She was kinda rude to me."

"But what's her *story?*" Dorothy asks with a sidelong glance to Robin.

"Oh," he says and thinks for a moment. The woman reaches her car, a big economy sedan with a dent in the back door. She kicks the front tire before she gets in. Robin smiles and says, "She's got a house full of screaming kids waiting at home for her. All of them from different husbands. All of her husbands have left her and she's miserable."

"Hmm," Dorothy says. "Hard to believe she ever got a man at all with a crazy disposition like that." Her voice has picked up some amusement, and Robin is encouraged.

"Well, once upon a time she was a very beautiful rich girl in New York," he says. "That kind that has a big party when they turn eighteen."

"Oh, a *deb*utante. I always wondered what happens to debutantes after the glitter fades."

"Just one bad marriage after another, all of them want her for the money and then one day she winds up talking to herself—"

"—At a hospital in New Jersey, no less," Dorothy says. She flicks lint off her coat. "All roads lead to New Jersey for the lonely hearted."

Robin senses the weariness creeping back into his mother's voice, so he picks up speed. "But see, first she lived for a long time in Paris, where she had a mansion on a hill by a cathedral and a view of the Eiffel Tower. And then the troubles started. Her kids were ungrateful and spent all her money. And none of the husbands would stick around; they had French mistresses they took to little cafes along the Sane River."

"The *Seine,*" Dorothy corrects.

"Yeah, the one Gene Kelly dances along in the movie. What was that movie called? We watched it on TV that time?"

Dorothy's expression freezes. "There's your father."

"An American in Paris, right?"

"Let's give him some peace and quiet."

Robin slumps down in the seat and sits on his hands.

Clark makes his way to the car with his head down. He gets in and shifts into gear with hardly a pause. As they pull out of the parking lot he says, "So Dr. Glade is pleased with the operation after all."

"Really?" Dorothy asks. Robin catches the surprise in her voice. "There's something new?"

"Just that his blood pressure is back up, and there's an indication that the kidney damage is less than they thought." He sighs and shakes his head. "They want to do that new scan tomorrow—the CAT scan."

"So we'll know for sure then," Dorothy says.

"There's no 'for sure' at this point," Clark says. "But there's nothing more for us to do there tonight." He rests his hand on Dorothy's leg. "I'm about to pass out. I can't think straight."

"We'll all be better off at home for a little while," Dorothy says.

Robin watches his mother put her hand on his father's. Neither of them says anything to him. As they turn onto Tappan, the picture of Jackson in the hospital room forms again—Robin tries to imagine a pin in Jackson's spine, or a rib puncturing his kidney. He sees damaged nerves like frayed ropes under his brother's skin. If Jackson was in the car with them right now, he'd be pulling some rowdy stunt in the back seat or blabbing about something he saw on TV, driving them all crazy; for the first time ever, Robin finds himself longing for Jackson's obnoxious, noisy presence. He leans his arm into the car door, pushing against it to stop the tingles where his father's fingers had pressed so strongly. He stares through his window as they pass through town, all of the stores closed, all of the lights dimmed. He pretends he's not in this car, he pretends he's riding on a bus next to strangers who are talking about something that's none of his business.

Four of them sit at the kitchen table picking through leftover olive loaf sandwiches and string bean casserole with dried onion rings. Robin watches his mother, his father, and Uncle Stan struggle to talk around Jackson's condition; they talk about the weather, the Yankees' World Series victory, the latest scandal in the Carter administration, a report on the news about teenagers doing cocaine. The conversation keeps shifting gears and then stalling. Stan tries to juice up the conversation with his generalizations and pronouncements, but Clark and Dorothy don't take the bait. Dorothy refills her wineglass several times, and Clark seems to be sleeping with his eyes open.

Robin feels something burdensome about the fact that he is the one person at this table related to everyone else by blood, that he might be the only one among them who can see them all clearly because something inside of him is a piece of something inside of the rest of them. When his father starts crying again, Stan shoots Clark a look of such pity that Robin decides he has to get away. He announces he's going to bed.

"Not in your room, you're not," Stan says. "Ruby and Nana are in there."

"What do you mean?" Robin asks.

"Something about keeping Jackson's bed safe from demons," Stan says casually, as if it makes sense, though Robin can't think of anything crazier he's heard all day.

He looks at his mother. She twists her mouth as if preparing to explain. Robin says, "You let her sleep in Jackson's bed?"

"Just for tonight. She's so upset, and she wanted to be in the same room as Nana."

"What do you mean, 'keeping away demons?'" Robin asks.

Dorothy says quickly, "She's been praying with Nana all night, and she got it in her head that she can make Jackson better if she . . . I don't know, sends out a *message* that his bed is being kept warm." Dorothy frowns as if she knows this explanation makes little sense.

"So I'm supposed to sleep in Ruby's room?" he asks.

Clark speaks up firmly, dabbing his cheeks. "Robin, don't make a stink about it."

Robin sinks into his chair, his face burning. A silent tension stretches through the room. I wish I could read minds, Robin thinks.

Stan says suddenly, "Hey, Dottie, remember that time Dad fell off the roof? The old drunk."

"Oh, God that was awful. I was thinking about that today."

"We thought he was a goner, but he got better." Stan gets up and pulls a can of Budweiser from the refrigerator, which Robin thinks Stan must have bought himself, since there's never any beer in the house. Stan doesn't return to his seat, and his gaze rests on the far wall, as if he needs to stand up and concentrate to bring these memories forth. "For a while we were home alone all the time, Mother at the hospital every day. We stayed up all night planning on running away to Canada, remember that?"

"We did?" Now Dorothy stands up as well, moving to the sink and running water over dirty dishes.

Robin asks, "Should I do those for you, Mom?"

Dorothy doesn't answer him. Her brow is furrowed. "Stan, I don't think it happened that way."

"Sure, we were going to be runaways."

"What was I thinking?" Dorothy asks. "That I was going to take care of *you*? We were what, about seven and eight years old?"

"We figured Mother couldn't take care of us since she was so preoccupied with him in the hospital."

"Ha!" Dorothy exclaims with a force that surprises Robin. "We were probably just looking for a good reason to get away. Mother was such a taskmaster. When I think of how much laundry I did, and by hand." She turns to Robin. "No washer-dryer set back then, no dishwasher, none of that at all."

"We used to stick together, you and me," Stan says, still not looking at Dorothy.

Dorothy frowns into the sink. "That was a long time ago."

Robin sits fascinated, listening to this pieced-together tale, sensing how impossible it is for the two of them to really talk to each other. This is more information than he's ever heard about his mother's relationship with her brother, and it's just a peep. The door to their past is only slightly ajar, and he senses his mother is ready to slam it shut again.

Stan guzzles from his beer can. He wipes his mouth with his sleeve as he speaks. "I'll tell you one thing. If Dad had died that time, we'd of all been spared a lot of crap. It only got worse after that."

"Stan, that's morbid," Dorothy says, but her voice is too weary to really convey disapproval. "Don't let Mother hear you talking that way."

"Ah, she's used to it. She knows I couldn't stand the bastard. The louse. If I had a buck for every time he belted me . . ."

She moves the dishes around in the sink, not speaking.

"Come on, Dottie. You feel the same way."

Robin can no longer hold back his curiosity. "Do you, Mom? Did Grampa Leo belt you, too?"

From his silent corner of the table, Clark speaks up. "Robin, give your mother a break, would you?"

"I'm just asking a question."

"That's enough!" Clark is resolute in his anger.

"I don't think about my father very much," Dorothy says with finality. She turns off the water and rubs her hands on a towel. "Some things are better forgotten."

Robin picks at the casserole congealing on his plate. He looks at the empty beer cans, at the wine bottle his mother keeps reaching for. In group guidance, Mr. Cortez said that alcoholism gets passed down from generation to generation. Grampa Leo was a drunk—should he be worrying about his mother?

Clark pushes himself up from the table. "I can't keep my head on straight anymore."

"I'll walk upstairs with you, Clark," Stan says. "I've got some ideas about Jackson that I want to run past you. Physical therapy stuff. There's this guy I know who's selling equipment, very state-of-the-art stuff. I'll tell you a little about it." He continues talking as they leave the room.

Dorothy returns to the table, to her wineglass. "Why don't you turn in, too, Robin? I'm just going to drink myself to sleep down here."

Sitting on Ruby's bed, unable to sleep, Robin hovers on the verge of a torrent of weeping. It feels like an itch around the edges of his eyes, like muscles knotted up under his cheekbones. But he stops himself from letting go—being strong means not crying. But not crying makes him seem like an unfeeling creep—he should cry out loud, wake the whole house so that everyone will know he feels sad about what's happened to Jackson. The fact that he can't makes him wonder if he is secretly happy Jackson is in danger. The thought spooks him; his skin tightens across his back. It can't be true—sure, Jackson has always been a pest, but how could he be happy to see him in the state he is?

A memory surfaces: family vacation in Washington, DC—a walk along the Tidal Basin; Robin lifting Jackson on his shoulders, Jackson plucking cherry blossoms, handing them back to Robin; the two of them presenting the pink bouquets to Dorothy and Ruby with a victorious flourish. It was explicitly forbidden behavior, and soon enough a park ranger was upon them. Clark was contrite, and reprimanded his sons for the benefit of the man in uniform—though later he took them all out for hot fudge sundaes, and they laughed together about the MacKenzie family's scrape with the law.

Why haven't there been more days like this, with Jackson? Did they share the blame for their deficient brotherhood? Or was it just him, lacking an ingredient necessary to play his part? If this was TV, they'd be in and out of adventures on a weekly basis. He thinks of *The Brady Bunch, The Partridge Family,* the Bradfords on *Eight is Enough.* Older brothers are forever bothered by younger brothers; that annoyance is just part of the deal. But on TV they manage to work it out: the younger brother needs guidance only the older one can provide, or the older one gets in over his head and the younger saves the day with a clever, last-minute brainstorm. Every time he has wished Jackson could just be out of the way—even a passing, half-conscious thought like *I wish I had my own bedroom*—stares back at him now, accusing him, mocking him.

Next to Ruby's bed is a lamp in the shape of a ballerina: a knee-length pink tutu thick with white ruffles, a serene face dotted with lavender on each cheek. The frilly shade rises out of a column behind her neck. He flicks it on, looks around Ruby's room. On the floor near the bed is the sketchbook she was drawing in this afternoon. The first few pages are very carefully shaded, every color as close to real as possible, pictures of trees and boats drawn inside the lines. He flips the pages, looking for a blank one, thinking if he can't sleep maybe he'll draw something himself, but he stops suddenly and snickers out loud. This page has two children in front of a house—their faces are purple and their arms are red and their clothes are just scrawls of darkness. "God, Ruby," he says out loud, "didn't know you could do modern art." Each page that follows is the same: the faces bright red and magenta, the hair and clothes forest green and black and that shade of brown called burnt sienna. Every page is a little bit crazier, darker, with a steadily decreasing attempt at naturalism. The last one is entirely covered in black with *Jackson* written across the top in red. He tries to think of Ruby drawing in the book this afternoon; she had been so quiet, but the pictures are wild. If he hadn't seen her sitting calmly at the foot of the couch, with Nana Rena dozing above her and the soap opera music warbling from the TV, he'd think she'd been throwing a temper tantrum while she drew this.

He closes the book and slides it under the bed. The wind outside the window is curling around the trees, the whole night is beginning to frighten him. He does not want to sleep in this room.

He tugs a blanket off the bed and wraps it around him and makes his way downstairs. When they were little, they'd play a game: Robin would drape a long blanket around him and pretend to be a bride with a long train attached to her dress, and Ruby and Jackson would creep along behind, hiding under the trailing material until they were "discovered," at which point a chase would ensue. They would do this over and over, sometimes for hours, acting the same scene, laughing every time. The fun was in the discovery—sometimes they would trip him, sometimes rip the blanket off, sometimes jump out and yell, "Boo!" Sometimes he would just run very briskly "to the altar" and unmask them. Thinking of it now, Robin picks up speed through the living room so that the blanket flutters along, just above the surface of the carpet. He zips around the coffee table and into the dining room all the way to the window that looks out on the backyard.

Todd Spicer's bedroom light is on, a bluish rectangle through the trees. Robin tries to discern if the gray form he sees is actually Todd or some piece of furniture. He thinks of the binoculars his father keeps in his workroom in the basement—the ones he brought on their trip to Cape Cod a couple of years ago, where they tried to spot whales in the ocean. If Uncle Stan wasn't in the basement, Robin could go down there right now and get the binoculars. What if Todd had binoculars too and caught him looking? The idea of it sends a shiver through him: if Todd caught him looking, that would mean Todd was looking too, which is as scary as it is exciting.

He lets the blanket fall to the floor and sits on the couch in the living room. Nana Rena has left a row of votive candles burning on an end table in front of their school pictures. Jackson's picture has been pushed closest to the front. *P.G. make him better,* Robin thinks. He doesn't know what Nana expects from burning candles and prayers.

"Robin?"

He jumps.

"I'm sorry, honey. I didn't mean to startle you." It's his mother, coming in from the kitchen.

"I couldn't sleep," he says guiltily.

"I fell asleep at the kitchen table," Dorothy says groggily, smoothing down her hair. "I was just sitting alone in the dark and the house was so quiet—well, next thing I know it's two A.M." She turns toward the mirror at the bottom of the stairs, across from the couch, and looks disapprovingly at her reflection. Her blouse hangs crookedly from her shoulders, the tail of it untucked. She pivots on her stocking feet. "Nothing like a good catastrophe to make you look like hell," she says.

Dorothy sits down next to him on the couch, rippling the cushions beneath him. He thinks about how heavy she is compared to him, looks down at his arms and sees his skinny wrists and fingers like delicate claws. Her breath has the unpleasant smell of a musky cork. His own skin is still vaguely clammy on his back and around his balls from the bike ride. The candles cast a glow on the two of them, and the rest of the room shakes in the shadows.

"Those candles are creepy," he says.

"Well, maybe Nana's got a connection or two we could use right about now."

"Yeah, P.G.," Robin says and smiles at her. She smiles back and rests her hand on his shoulder and they sit like that for a moment, quietly.

"I'm sorry I got everyone worried," he says. "You know, with the bike ride and all."

"It was a bit too much excitement for the day."

"Now Dad's mad at me," Robin says.

"He's just upset."

"He doesn't have to take it out on me." He wonders if his father would be crying nonstop if it was him in the hospital instead. A stab of something unpleasant hits him—jealousy? Is that the problem? Does he wish for something in common with his father, the bond that has been so natural for Jackson and Clark, a closeness that has always eluded him? "Does Dad think it's my fault? Will you ask him if he thinks it's my fault?"

"No, I will absolutely not ask him that." The admonishment in her voice surprises him. "Robin, I asked you to be strong."

"I don't know what that means!" He hates that his voice sounds sulky, but he doesn't know how else to convey his confusion to her.

"It means that you have to be a son to your father. Help him out if he needs it. Don't pester him with your every question."

"You usually want me to ask questions," he mutters.

"Well, don't ask questions I can't answer. In fact, don't ask any right now because I don't have any answers."

She pulls him to her, and he leans stiffly against her body. Her hand strokes his hair, but it does not comfort him. Her impatience feels like a betrayal. It confounds him more deeply than his father's anger.

Chapter Six

He wakes up the next morning disoriented and aroused. It takes a few lengthy seconds to figure out that he is in the living room. He sits up and pulls the blanket around him, peers across the room so that he can see the clock over the dining room table. 8:15. No one woke him up, maybe they really don't care if he goes to school or not. The sky is pale and bright through the crack in the living room curtains. A crow caws outside. A flash of a dream image comes to him: he is running past a house with a broken front porch toward a swimming pool with no water; he slides down into the deep end and talks to a boy—it was *Scott*, that kid from gym class in the van last night. What happened? His dick is half hard, and the dream of Scott is part of that. He leans back into the couch and closes his eyes again, trying in vain to remember more.

He shakes his head, loosens a few long strands of hair stuck to his face. The dream is gone except for the picture of Scott. He reaches down and puts his fingertips on his underwear, squeezes his butt muscles so that his dick bobs against the fabric. A couple of seconds of this—bob, bob, bob—and he stops, not wanting to be caught touching himself in the middle of the living room.

Upstairs, Ruby is stepping out of the bathroom. She's wearing a dark dress he hasn't seen on her since some night they all went out to a restaurant, probably six months ago.

"Are you going to school?" he asks her.

"No. Mom said I don't have to."

Robin's bedroom door opens and Nana Rena emerges, sliding a coat over one of her familiar dresses. "If it isn't Rip Van Winkle," she says.

"How come no one woke me up?" Robin asks. "Where's Mom?"

"Your mother was poking and prodding every ten minutes with not a blink out of you; I would have thought you were dead and buri—" She flinches and cuts herself off with a wave of her hand. Robin bites on his lower lip at the word *dead* and at the blush on Nana's cheeks after she caught herself saying it. *Dead* is not a word he thinks anyone is going to throw around in a joking way right now. Nana says, "Your mother is at the hospital. Your father is taking us to eight-thirty mass. Come on, Ruby. The house of the Lord awaits."

As they walk down the stairs, he hears Ruby saying, "I don't wanna sit on the side with the bloody Jesus on the wall."

He slips into one of his favorite shirts—shiny and synthetic, with photos of a Parisian cafe repeated across the material—and a pair of white pants that look like jeans even though they are made of polyester. At the last minute he removes the pants long enough to take off his underwear; when he puts them back on, he studies the way the shape of his dick reveals itself under the fabric. Before he can debate whether or not this is OK, or why he's even thought of it today of all days, he grabs his Trapper Keeper binder and *East of Eden* and heads downstairs.

His father stops him in the kitchen as he moves toward the back door. "I'm gonna go with Victoria," Robin tells him. He checks the clock in the shape of a teakettle over the table. 8:25. "She might have already left. I should hurry up."

Clark runs a hand through his hair. "I guess I should write you a note about yesterday." He slides his hand across the countertop, searching out a pen. He pulls a piece of letterhead from the junk drawer under the dishrack and chews on the pen before writing. "Your mother usually does this," he says as he writes. He crosses out a word or two and then finishes with the jagged scrawl of his signature.

"Thanks," Robin says, folding it in half.

"I'll see you this evening. Maybe I'll take you over to the hospital tonight." He holds Robin's stare and looks away, unsure. "We'll see."

"Great," Robin says, trying to sound appreciative but unable to read his father's expression—is Clark trying to say he's sorry for exploding last night, or is he still laying down the law, making sure Robin knows who's making these decisions?

Robin crosses through the hedge to the Spicers'. Victoria is walking out her back door as he gets there. He feels as if he hasn't seen her for weeks though it's only been a couple of days. He's wondering if it is possible she doesn't know about Jackson, but then she holds open her arms. "Oh, my God," she whimpers, pulling him into a hug. "I can't believe it." He wants to feel comforted by this but his books are poking into his ribs, so he pulls away. "You should have called me," Victoria says, "Why didn't you call me?"

He can't quite formulate an answer, can't explain to her that he couldn't tell anyone about Jackson's fall without feeling like he'd be setting up evidence against himself.

A horn honks. "Your mom won't mind taking me, right?" Robin asks.

"My mom's sick. I'm getting a ride from Ethan—you know, Todd's friend?" She puffs out her cheeks, an indication of how fat Ethan is, and smiles. Robin smiles back, glad to share the joke. She curls her hair over her ear. Her fingernails are painted pale blue. "C'mon," she says. "Hopefully it won't be too disgusting."

A smooth blue Chevy Malibu sits in the middle of the street. Ethan, in a denim jacket with a Harley Davidson logo on the sleeve, leans into the horn when he sees them.

"Cut the horn action!" Victoria barks. "My mother will kill you if the neighbors start complaining."

"Who's the dweeb?" Ethan asks, catching sight of Robin. Robin swallows but his mouth is dry. "*Groovy* shirt," Ethan says sarcastically.

"If you don't have anything nice to say," Victoria says, "stuff a Twinkie in your mouth."

Todd's head pops out above the roof of the car. "Hey, Robin," he calls out. "Big surprise."

"I couldn't get a ride from my father," he lies. He moves his books in front of his crotch, suddenly self-conscious about his underwear-free bulge.

"Get in, get in," Todd says calmly, jumping down to the street, his brown workboots slapping flat against the pavement.

"Man, we gotta *book*," Ethan says impatiently.

Todd holds open the back door and waves Robin toward it.

"What are you being so nice about?" Victoria asks suspiciously.

Todd goofs up his mouth. "I'm just a little crazy sometimes. I get the urge to act *nice*. You ought to try it some time. You'll live longer if you're a nicer person."

"In that case you'll probably be dead before you finish high school."

Robin smiles at Todd's silly expression and slides in. Victoria follows and Todd slams the door forcefully behind her, squishing his face against her window and crossing his eyes grotesquely.

"In case you didn't notice," Victoria says in a bored tone of voice, "I'm ignoring you."

Todd gets in the front seat and the car peels out, throwing Robin into the side door.

"Don't speed," Victoria says. She turns to Robin. "What's the scoop with your baby bro?"

Todd turns his head to listen, and Robin catches the attentiveness in his eyes before looking down at his books. "You know, he got fucked up," he says, trying to formulate his answer in Todd's language.

"My mother heard it from Mrs. Delatore yesterday," Victoria says. "So is his neck broken? I mean, that's what *she* said."

"Hey, are you that kid who pushed his brother off the slide?" Ethan says excitedly.

Robin feels his face drain of blood. "Who said that?"

"Man, you are about as dumb as you are fat," Todd says.

Ethan slams on the brakes. "You wanna walk?"

Robin gets thrown forward, and his father's note slips off the top of his binder.

"What's that?" Victoria asks, scooping it up and reading it out loud. "'To whom it may concern—' God, doesn't he even know your teacher's name? 'Robin MacKenzie missed school yesterday because of a sudden, unfortunate situation at home. Please excuse him from classes. I can provide details if necessary.' Aren't there two c's in necessary?"

"No," Todd says and pulls the paper from her hand. "His name's printed on the top. 'Clark MacKenzie, Sales Analyst.' Mighty *professional* don't ya think?" Robin smirks—*professional* coming from Todd sounds like another word for *boring*. Todd hands him back the note and says, "He started to write 'tragic,' then crossed it out and wrote 'unfortunate.'"

"Jackson *fell*," Robin murmurs quietly, folding the note small enough to slide into his back pocket. "It was an accident."

Todd lights a cigarette and blows smoke out his open window. Robin watches the gesture, the way Todd's neck tenses when he sucks in, the way his lips keep the cigarette in place even as it looks like it might drop from his mouth.

"I heard he had an operation and he's in a coma," Victoria says, her voice sounding gossipy to Robin.

"He's not in a *coma*," he responds testily, though he wonders what a coma really looks like. Jackson in the bed last night, with those tubes and machines—maybe that *was* a coma. Wouldn't his parents have described it that way, though? Or is that one of the "details" his father will provide only "if necessary?"

"Well, can he talk?" Victoria asks.

"I don't think so," Robin says. "I mean, he's . . . I don't know." He isn't sure how to compress the information he has. He bites on the inside of his lip, understanding that no one has made the situation completely clear to him. "He's fucked up, that's all."

"Bummer," Todd says.

Ethan interrupts. "Hey, Spicer, you think we have time for doobage before homeroom?"

"Always time for that."

"Do you two have to flaunt what major delinquents you are in front of Robin?" Victoria says.

"Robin's cool," Todd says, smiling at him. "Right?"

"Sure," Robin says, pleased at the sound of it. *Cool.* "Hey, can I have a cigarette?"

"I can't believe you," Victoria protests. "I don't see you for like two days and now you're smoking."

"I smoke my mother's cigarettes," Robin says defensively.

Todd brings another cigarette to his mouth and lights it, passing it across the back seat. Robin's hand shakes as he takes it from Todd, meeting his stare. Todd's eyes: brown with pumpkin-gold flecks inside. He puts the filter to his lips, feels the trace of spit on the end, like with the roach at the drive-in. He remembers last night in the van with Scott and makes sure to blow out quickly enough to avoid burning his throat.

"Thanks," he says to Todd. Even a simple word is a struggle with so much concentration on not coughing.

"Anything I can do to corrupt the youth of America." Todd winks at him before turning his eyes back to the front seat. He reaches to the dashboard and pops in an eight track. A romantic rock piano spills from the speakers.

"*Bruuuuce!*" Ethan howls. "Jersey's own."

"I never get sick of this," Todd says.

Robin takes a few more puffs, not really liking the taste but liking the moment: the hungry sound of Springsteen's voice, Todd's lips moving with the music, the controlled sway in Todd's shoulders.

When they pull up in front of the school, Robin slides out of the seat after Victoria.

"Thanks for nothing," Victoria says, striding away.

"Ah, you can walk next time," Ethan shouts after her.

"There won't be a next time," she calls back.

Robin raises his eyebrows at Todd. "See ya."

Todd leans out the window to him. "You know, what happened to your brother . . ." His voice fades out as he exhales a stream of smoke. "If I was you, I'd just not think about it. It's too heavy, you know. You should get your mind off it—blast some music, get wasted." He pauses and raises his eyebrows. "Get laid."

"Yeah, sure, thanks," Robin sputters, trying to remain cool even as a blush rises in his neck and cheeks.

Todd nods intently at him. "Anytime." He flicks his cigarette out the window, then shakes another one from his pack of Marlboros and hands it to Robin. Robin stamps the first one out and puts the new one over his ear.

"You know, if I was you, I wouldn't even go in that place," Todd says with a look toward the school. Then he says, "Later," and Robin mouths back, "Yeah, later."

Ethan hits the gas and the car roars away. Robin stands in the smell of scorched rubber, trying to understand Todd's attention, fighting back the notion that Todd is actually his friend now, because how could that possibly be true after so many years of torment?

The morning crowd is noisy with chatter; Led Zeppelin blares from a radio. Robin catches a glimpse of a short guy in a baseball cap moving through the crowd toward the courtyard. Scott. He feels a nervous clutch in his stomach; an image from his dream last night—with Scott at the empty swimming pool—rears up in front of him. He thinks about trying to catch up with him—surprised at how much he'd rather be with Scott than Victoria at this moment—but a glance at the big clock on the face of the building reminds him it's almost time for homeroom.

"Are you coming?" Victoria calls to him. He runs to catch up with her. "God," she says, "my brother is so mental around you."

He pretends to shrug off her comment. "Todd was probably just making fun of me because he knows I don't know how to get high."

"God, what's he trying to prove anyway? I mean, you're *my* friend, not his." Victoria stops suddenly and looks at him. "But you play right into it, Robin."

Robin turns away from her penetrating gaze. "I do not."

"I can't believe you even like him."

"You just don't like him because he's your brother. I mean, Ruby and I are always bothering each other."

"Oh, my God," Victoria gasps, her mouth hanging open. "How is *Ruby?*"

Robin shrugs—he doesn't want to think about the state his sister is in: she's sketching psychotic pictures one day and racing off to church the next. He sees Ruby and Nana kneeling in the pew at St. Bart's: Ruby in her fancy dress, her skinny knees pressed into the plastic-covered footrest, her eyes searching the rafters for Jackson's guardian angel; Nana next to her, her body twice as wide, eyes closed, lips floating over mumbled prayers, rosary beads spilling from her thick fingers. Looking around the crowded school lawn now—kids hanging out, acting cool, pushing past each other, pushing into each other—Robin is bothered by the idea of his sister and grandmother in church, because maybe he should be there too, acting serious and holy, trying to convince God, whoever *He* is, that Jackson deserves to get better quick. "I guess she's OK," he says to Victoria.

"She must be *so* freaked out. She's the type that would probably feel guilty," Victoria says. "I bet *she* didn't go to school today, right?"

Robin hears something in Victoria's voice, sees something in her stance, the way she balances her books on her hip, the way she's twisting her lip as if she's suddenly condemning him for not being upset enough, or something—all of it makes him mad. "You don't know anything," he growls, and walks past her to the front doors.

"Where are you going?" Victoria demands. "What's your *deal?*"

Robin doesn't answer. He moves against the crowd, bumping and pushing his way in, wishing he'd chased after Scott when he'd had the chance.

He swings open the stained wooden door and the locker room explodes into his senses: boys' bodies lit from single bulbs on the concrete ceiling, the smell of armpits, sneakers and disinfectant, voices rising and falling between the vibrations of slamming steel. Robin makes his way to his own locker, past Seth Carter pulling his red gym shirt over his head. Robin nods but Seth just looks at him blankly and lets him by. Ever since he jerked off at the Ice Pond thinking about Seth's pissing contest, he's been nervous in Seth's presence, as if his imagination was flickering in his eyes like a dirty movie on a screen.

Robin sits on the bench, a heavy pile of books in his lap, trying to remember the combination to his lock. He looks up at the clock—11:30. Most of the day still ahead. He shouldn't have come to school. Every class so far has been a blur, no clearer than a dream. In English they were discussing *East of Eden* and he couldn't even follow the questions

Mrs. Tadesci was asking. She'd lectured about symbolism, about Cain and Abel and the book of Genesis—what did that have to do with James Dean?

He is fumbling with the numbers on the lock when he senses someone standing nearby. He looks up; it's Scott. Again, a snapshot of last night's dream forms—he and Scott squeezing together through a doorway—and disappears.

"What's going on with your brother?" Scott asks, bouncing on the toes of his Keds. His pants, which are too long, bunch up on the floor at his heels.

Robin feels a surprising flutter in his belly and looks away.

"Not too good, huh?" Scott asks.

"No. He looked really fucked up." Suddenly the details are pouring out of him. "He was hooked up to these machines and it made me think he was like Frankenstein or something, some kind of experiment. I mean, I knew it would look bad but then when I got there it was even worse and then my parents were mad at me because of me taking my bike there after they told me to stay home—"

Scott steps closer and interrupts. "I'm ditching. Pintack's outside setting up hurdles on the track. My fucking favorite."

"Yeah, right?" Robin groans. Last time they ran track, he could barely keep one foot in front of the other, worrying that he was running too much like a girl. "Where are you gonna go?"

"Town," Scott says. "Maybe to The Bird after that."

The Bird is the county park on the other side of Five Corners, at the end of Greenlawn Avenue. The name is short for "bird sanctuary;" once upon a time there was an aviary there, though the building has been empty for years. It's a place like the Ice Pond where teenage things are supposed to happen, a place Robin has never dared to go. "How are you getting there?"

"I dunno. Hitch, maybe."

Hitchhiking is another thing he's never done, another thing he's been too scared to do. He mutters, "Cool."

"So you wanna come?"

"Is anyone else going with you?"

"Fuck no. I'm pretty much a lone wolf, you know?"

The expression makes Robin smile—he thinks of *Call of the Wild*, of Scott traveling through the Arctic, beyond the bounds of civilization. "I probably shouldn't ditch," he says.

Scott looks disappointed for a moment, then seems to cover it up.

"Never mind," he says. "I gotta hit it before Pintack starts tooting his fucking whistle." He stands for another second, shifting his weight back and forth on his legs, his darting eyes hinting at the promise of escape.

From the next row Robin hears someone bragging about getting a blow job. He recognizes the deep voice—the infamous Long Dong Danniman. A voice responds, "I'd never kiss a chick who just had my dick in her mouth. No way." Another voice: "Ah, you probably suck your own." "Faggot." "Cocksucker." Jittery laughter.

"Man, I'm getting outta here," Scott says.

"Hold on," Robin says. "I'm coming. I got a cigarette I want to smoke anyway." He grabs the lock and spins the dial around—he remembers: 32, 8, 17. He feels a jolt of energy as he drops his books inside and clicks the door shut. Scott is in front of a mirror, his baseball cap pinched between his legs, running a long-handled comb through his hair. He watches Scott's shoulder bones rise and fall beneath a David Bowie concert T-shirt and a loose, unzipped sweatjacket; he lets his eyes drift to the curve of his ass inside tight, worn-down jeans. He sucks in his breath, tries to let his face slide into the same tough expression Scott wears so effortlessly.

They reach the door at the same time as the group of guys from the next row. "Man, I'm telling you, you gotta get some head," Long Dong Danniman is saying. Seth Carter, standing next to him, says, "Yeah, sure. The chicks're just knocking down my fucking door." Robin starts to step past Danniman and his friends, but Scott grabs his arm to let them go first.

Danniman gives Robin a withering look. "Nice shirt, girlie."

"Shut up," Robin whispers.

"Hey, girlie, you wanna give Seth someone to practice on?" Danniman teases, punching Seth in the arm.

"He's not my type," Robin mutters. The circle of boys seems to tighten around him.

"I guess she's shy," Danniman says and pushes Seth into Robin.

Robin and Seth shove each other away. Robin steps back into the wall.

"Cut the shit, man," Seth whines.

"Ah, you'd just be a snack anyway," Danniman says to Seth. He grabs his crotch and shakes his bulging red gym shorts at Robin. "This girlie probably wants a meal."

"Fuck you," Robin hisses, looking from Danniman's crotch to his eyes. Danniman takes a step closer to him, and then Scott steps in.

"Hey, man, he's cool. Just take a pill," Scott says. Robin is amazed as they all back away. Even though Scott looks like the runt of the litter, they listen to him. It's that face again, Robin thinks. There's something about Scott's face that tells you not to cross the line with him. There's something there no one wants to know too much about.

The gang moves past. Scott waits for the last of them to go before moving toward the door himself. "Come on, man. Are you coming or what?"

Robin follows him past the red-and-white Exit sign, away from the gymnasium, the squawking of sneakers on polished wood, the cacophony of boys' voices. It is only when he gets into the parking lot and he can breathe the outdoor air that he realizes his body has been trembling from the contact. He's never said, "Fuck you," to a bully before, and he's wondering if Scott's presence emboldened him, even before Scott stepped to his defense. Is this what it means to have a guy like Scott as a friend, that he might be able to avoid the traps set by guys like Danniman?

As he runs to catch up with Scott, away from school, away from the proscribed schedule of his life, he gets the sense that he is actually running *toward* something—toward something new, something risky.

"Don't you worry about some maniac picking you up?" Robin asks. Scott is walking backward, sticking his thumb out as cars approach.

"What could happen?" They are at the side of Hooper Avenue, beyond the point where the sidewalk ends in a trail of dirt and dead leaves, where the houses and lawns give way to oak and pine trees and the air is quiet and the sky is stretched wide through the branches ahead of them.

"What about murderers and those kind of people?"

Scott laughs. "I think you're paranoid, man."

"I read in *Time* magazine a story about serial killers." He snaps twigs beneath his shoes. "They always show up in small towns. You never hear about it in big cities. The more people around, the safer."

Scott shoots Robin a look of disbelief. "What about Son of Sam?"

"He's an exception."

"The Boston Strangler. Charles Manson?"

"What's your point, Scott?"

"All you ever hear about in cities is fucking crime. Especially New York. My father got mugged in New York last year. A couple of black guys with a fucking tool." He makes his thumb and forefinger into a gun and points it into Robin's chest.

"People in New Jersey always think New York is full of crime," Robin says knowingly. He folds Scott's index finger back toward him, surprising himself with the touch. "You just have to *act* like you belong. If you look like some stooge from New Jersey *of course* they're going to pick you out. New Yorkers are cool—*really* cool, not like New Jersey cool. Do you think Danniman would last ten minutes in New York without everyone knowing he wasn't some bridge-and-tunnel loser?"

Scott shrugs. "What makes you such an expert? You're a bridge-and-tunnel loser, too."

"For your information, I was born in New York, and I'm going to live there again someday. Plus, I go there all the time with my mother. She takes me to the theater and to museums and—" He pauses; Scott looks dubious.

"She ever take you to CBGB?" he challenges.

Robin frowns. "Oh, right. Like my mother's going to bring me to a rock music place on the Bowery."

Scott shrugs. "At least you know what it is. That's where I'd want to go, not to some stupid museum with my mother." He searches the road for cars, spits when he doesn't see anything. " 'Course, my mother doesn't get out much."

"What do you mean?"

"Nothing," he says quickly.

"She doesn't have a job?"

"She's just . . . she's kind of sick, so she's in a hospital."

"What kind of sick?" Robin asks.

Scott loops his finger next to his head, indicating craziness. Robin stops in his tracks, unsure if Scott is being truthful. Scott sees his quizzical look and turns away. "Never mind—forget I mentioned it."

A maroon Galaxie 500 convertible approaches and Scott sticks his thumb back out. The driver is a girl with a head of frizzy, mousy blond hair bouncing in the wind. She catches sight of them and hits the brakes. She is wearing sunglasses even though the sky is gray. "Don't you boys know that hitchhiking is against the law?"

Robin shrinks back but Scott stands firm, planting his hitchhiking hand in his front pocket. "What are you, a cop?" he challenges.

The girl laughs. She's maybe 21 or 22, and Robin thinks he has seen her before. Her lipstick is deep purple against frosty-white skin, and her fingers, curled around the steering wheel, taper to matching dabs of color at the nails. "A cop? *Please.* If you insult me like that there's no way you're getting a ride," she says. Her scoop-neck pink T-shirt reads *Foxy Lady* across the chest.

Scott turns away, as if he can't be bothered with negotiations, but Robin steps forward. "Can you take us into town?" he asks.

"Get in, boys."

The air is cold against their faces, and the car speakers roar with the kind of funky music he hears coming from the black kids' radios in the cafeteria. Robin taps his fingers on his knees. "What's the name of this group?" he asks her, as one song fades out.

"It's Parliament," she says, as if everyone should know this.

He remembers where he has seen her before—the music store in town. "You work at New Sounds, don't you?"

She pulls her glasses down and peers at him studiously. "Are you the kid always buying the Broadway records?"

"Yeah! That's me. I bought *The King and I, West Side Story* and *Cabaret*. But I haven't been in there for a while."

She breaks out into a big smile.

"We had a nickname for you. *Broadway Baby.*"

Scott busts out laughing from the backseat. "*Broadway Baby*. That's a pisser!"

Robin turns around and glares at him. "I like other music, too."

"Like what?"

"I like disco."

The girl tugs on the sleeve of his shimmery shirt. "I could have guessed *that,*" she says.

Scott is still laughing. Robin adds, "And I like some rock, too."

Scott puts his face in his hands. "Man, no one likes rock *and* disco."

"*And* show tunes," the girl says. "You like it all, huh?"

Robin squints his eyes at Scott. "I have a *lot* of interests. The problem with you is you haven't seen enough of the world to have an open mind." He hears his mother's voice in his words but he's glad it's there. He doesn't need this hassle from *Scott*.

"What do you know about my mind? You don't even know me," Scott says.

"Yeah, well, maybe I don't want to," Robin says. "You don't know me either."

"That's what you think," Scott mumbles.

"What'd you say?"

"I know more about you than you think." Scott closes his eyes and leans his head back against the vinyl upholstery.

Robin waits for more, wondering if Scott is bluffing or getting at something. Robin pulls the cigarette Todd gave him out of his shirt pocket and fingers it like a talisman. Scott remains silent, his silence like a little punishment. The problem with taking risks, Robin realizes, is that you don't know what you're getting into.

"I would have thought you two were bosom buddies," the girl says. She presses in the cigarette lighter. With a glance at her purse lying on the seat, she says to Robin, "Pull one out for me."

He finds a pack marked *Eve* in scripted letters; the cigarettes are longer and skinnier than the one he got from Todd. "These are neat," he says.

Scott speaks up again. "Bosom buddies. Yeah, right. We're just two rejects from gym class."

"Yeah," Robin says. *"Broadway Baby* and *Baby Burnout."* The lighter pops out and he brings it to the cigarette, which is hanging from his lips in as close an imitation of Todd Spicer as he can pull off. He coughs at the puff and turns around to pass it to Scott.

Scott leans forward and takes it from him. "Yeah, a couple of rejects," he repeats, smoke disappearing from his mouth into the wind racing past. He hands the cigarette back. "Man, don't pay any attention to me, OK? I'm just goofin' on ya."

Robin studies Scott's face. The apology seems real enough, but how can he be sure? He sighs and takes another drag. Each one gets easier. He feels Scott's knees pushing into the seat under his back and leans back into it. Maybe Scott *is* just some closed-minded kid he can never be friends with. But maybe not.

He watches the blur of trees at the side of road. His hair flies back. He feels exposed in this convertible, his decision to ditch announced to all of Greenlawn. He closes his eyes. *I'm leaving Greenlawn,* he thinks. *I'm on a magic carpet, and I don't know where I'm going.*

"I think I'm stoned," Robin says.

Scott laughs.

"No, I really think I'm stoned." Every time he turns his head, his thoughts need another moment to follow, as if his mind is having trouble keeping up. They are sitting on a concrete loft in the abandoned aviary at The Bird; Robin imagines that they're hiding in a spooky outlying building on a big estate, something in one of those British novels from a hundred years ago. The room is damp and shadowy. Metal bars line the walls below them, and all around lay stacks of cages, their sides bent and smashed by years of vandalism. The roof above them slants to a peak twenty feet above the floor. All of the windows are boarded up except for the one they climbed through after Scott bought the joint from a kid in the parking lot. The place is big enough to echo their conversation, but the air is thick with a dank, animal odor and the marijuana smoke they've been exhaling for the past ten minutes. Their feet dangle off the edge of the loft. He looks down past his feet at white birdshit splotches. The more of Scott's pot that he smokes, the more Robin considers moving back into the safety of a corner.

"How do you know when you're stoned?" Robin asks. "Is it when the way you usually think isn't the way you're thinking right now?"

Scott narrows his eyes at Robin, ruminating. Robin waits, expecting Scott to say something authoritative, and when what seems like ten minutes pass and still no sound comes out of him, they both bust out laughing. "That's so funny," Robin says. "How you didn't give me an answer, and I was waiting for one. That's the way everyone in the whole world always seems to me—I ask a question and I don't get an answer."

"You can't be stoned," Scott says. "No one gets stoned the first time they smoke."

"Did you?" Robin asks.

"Yes," Scott says, and breaks into laughter again.

They lie on their backs and stare at the rotting wood beams stretched across the ceiling. Robin is talking. He has been telling Scott everything about the accident, from Jackson baiting him into climbing up the slide, to his father's explosive anger in the hospital room, to Victoria's gossipy questions in the car. Scott is tapping his fingers on his stomach—his shirt pulled up from his waist—and the delicate patter of flesh against flesh, repeating itself throughout the story, provides a hypnotic beat beneath Robin's words. Scott interrupts every now and then to ask a question that only needs a yes or no answer but which sends Robin off into a fresh rush of revelation. When Scott asks, "So Jackson is *younger* than Ruby?" Robin tells him how Jackson is the only one of the three of them born in New Jersey, how Jackson stopped playing with him and Ruby when they were little, how he still likes Ruby better than Jackson even though she's been acting so religious lately. When Scott says, "You mean your father *never* hits you?" Robin explains how his father lets him go off with his mother to the city and never seems to care though Robin knows—he just *knows*—that his father doesn't like it. When Scott asks him who Uncle Stan is, Robin tells him about the World Series party, and how he thinks Stan drove his mother to drunkenness, and how Robin was stuck with Larry that night. He takes another hit off the joint and tells Scott about Larry running around naked and wagging his dick at him and how that bothered him because Larry was the one who was perverted but he wound up making Robin feel that way.

And then he gets quiet, having reached the stifling moment when he realizes that he's revealed more than he ever planned. Scott stops his tapping. The skylight on the other side of the roof is darker than when they got here, and it occurs to Robin that he's ditched more than just gym class. The hours he has spent with Scott lay themselves out like a chain, one link after the other, stretched long against the sky. "I should probably shut up for a while," he says, worried now that Scott has heard too much, that he could not possibly want to spend any more time with him.

"No, man, it's cool. I been listening."

"I probably sound like a big crybaby—"

"Nah."

"—or worse."

"I can tell you're pretty smart," Scott says. "I knew you were a brain. But I mean you have a way of thinking of things that's pretty fucking heavy." He rolls over on his stomach and reaches across Robin, who tenses up from the nearness. "Where's the roach, man? I want to get my money's worth." His hand brushes the ground at Robin's side.

The roach is still pressed between Robin's fingers; he lifts it into the air with a flourish. "Ta-da."

Scott lights a match and holds the flame near his face, waiting. Robin understands after a moment what to do: he lifts the roach to Scott's lips, surprised how steady he holds it, watching the concentration as Scott pulls in the smoke. The end of the joint is a tiny star burning orange, and Scott's face glows softly behind it.

Robin thinks Scott will move away from him, but he doesn't. In the closeness, Robin wonders what it would be like to kiss Scott, and then he *hears* himself wondering this and stamps out the thought. "You said something before, in the car—" His memories of the morning race to catch up with his words. "You said you *knew* things about me."

"I hung out in your neighborhood before."

"With who?"

"Doesn't matter."

"I've never seen you in my neighborhood. Only in gym," Robin says. "You're like the only other kid who isn't *into* it. I mean, I didn't know you were a burnout but I knew there was something about you, *different.*"

"That's right," Scott says. "I told you, I'm a lone wolf." He takes another puff.

"So how come I get all the shit from guys like Danniman and you don't?" Robin asks him. "Is it because of your face?"

"What the fuck's wrong with my face?"

"Nothing," Robin says quickly. "I mean, there's this expression you have."

"You *are* high, man. Danniman and those other guys won't fuck with me 'cause I sell them joints."

Robin stares in amazement. "You do? You deal?"

Scott smiles, almost with pride. "Sure. I buy it from upperclassmen at school for like fifty cents, or at The Bird—like that guy Socks I just scored from in the parking lot? Then I sell it back to Danniman or whoever for seventy-five cents or a dollar."

"Wow. Don't you worry about—"

"What? You're too uptight about that stuff."

"It could happen," Robin says defensively.

"Even if I got caught, what would happen? The state could take me away from my father for him being a bad parent, which would not fucking bother me one bit. I'd get set up with some rich family. Like yours."

Robin rolls his head to the side. "Yeah, right, we're just dripping with money."

"You got two cars in your driveway."

"How do you know?"

"You gotta have some household cash to have *two*. There's a gas shortage going on, man."

"You hung out in my neighborhood?" Robin tries to concentrate on the notion of Scott on Bergen Avenue, close enough to know how many cars his family has. He weaves his fingers into his hair, lifting, then letting it drop back against his ears. In the swimming-through-water of the high, words feel increasingly clumsy, but his gestures leave him fluttery, feeling almost graceful.

When he turns his head back to Scott, he sees that Scott has been watching him intently.

"You know, I don't need anybody anyway." Scott has lowered his voice, narrowed his eyes. "A lone wolf doesn't travel with the pack." He bends his head back and howls into the room. The sound collects in the eaves and returns to them, vibrating. Scott keeps his head back and Robin's skin shivers. He thinks it again: *I want to kiss Scott, right there on the neck.* There's a gauzy dreaminess to the wish that offers a split second of peace before giving way to pure, immobilizing panic.

"Yeah, it's true," Scott says. "I've been spying on you." He growls, then whips his head forward. Robin falls back to the concrete, trying to make the roof stop spinning, certain that Scott knows what he's thinking.

Without warning, Scott lifts one leg and throws it across him. Robin stifles a gasp as Scott sits down on his thighs, just below his crotch. "I'm the stoned lone wolf and I'm stalking through the jungle." He lowers his head again, his hair sways across Robin's chest. "The lone wolf spots a robin in the birdhouse and gets ideas."

Robin's dick is like a finger pushing almost painfully against his hip. He thinks maybe Scott can feel it, too. He thinks maybe Scott doesn't mind but he can't believe that, even with Scott's legs clamped against his, Scott's head bobbing dreamily in front of him, Scott's breath giving off heat against his shirt.

Scott growls again. He grabs Robin's arms and extends them over Robin's head. "The stoned wolf," he whispers. Robin stiffens from his head to his heels. The tremor of Scott's growling voice moves along Robin's body, into his shoulder, up against his neck—Scott's lips are on his neck, then off again, the growl moving against Robin's jawbone, his ear. Scott has caught him by surprise; a shaking has started in his legs and is moving up through his chest, into his throat, his lips. His body trills against the concrete. And then Scott is pushing against him, Scott's legs on top of his legs, Scott's crotch pressing his, Scott's boner prodding through his jeans into Robin. Scott's hair falls across Robin's lips. Robin lifts his head, opens his mouth to protest, and then Scott's lips are right there against his, and it all becomes clear to Robin: what he'd been wanting just moments ago is actually happening.

Robin raises his face and then, unsure what to do, bites Scott's lower lip. Scott's lips part, his mouth is a puddle of spit, their mouths are pressing wet into each other, tongues moving, circling, slippery, sloppy. Robin rushes the slick end of his tongue across Scott's, can feel the roughness of taste buds. Their breathing mixes up together, puffs of effort, Robin unable to tell what noise is his and what is Scott's. A chorus of *Oh my God oh my God* bellows in his skull. He hears a warning—*Someone will see us*—then he hears Todd's voice from that morning saying, *Get laid.* He pushes up and tastes Scott's smoky spit and he wants to tell Scott each of these thoughts, he wants Scott to say something back.

Scott pulls out of the kiss and slams harder into his crotch. Robin thrusts back and Scott pounds at him again, it's almost painful to Robin but he pushes back over and over until he is just counting the beats of this rhythm like a crude children's song—*bum-bah-bum-bah-bum*—forgetting about the voices in his head and what he wants to say, just trying to do whatever Scott is doing—for how long they do this, he doesn't know. The whole world is just the press of Scott against him and him trying to keep up. And then without warning the sound from Scott's mouth is not a growl but a gasp and his teeth clamp down on his lower lip. He stretches out, flat as an iron. Everything freezes.

Robin sucks in his breath as all of the tension from Scott's body disappears.

Scott collapses, then rolls off him. A slice of air hits Robin's knees, crotch, stomach, chest, neck—everywhere Scott was and now isn't.

In and out, quick, shallow, Robin's breath is all stunned gasping. He opens his eyes to a vast room deep in shadow and stinking like sour breath. His body is still shaking.

"I shot," Scott says.

"What?" Robin leans toward him, sees Scott lying on his back with his arm across his eyes.

"Did you?" Scott asks.

"Did I what?"

Scott peeks out from under his arm. He reaches his other hand out and pokes it into Robin's crotch as if he's testing a loaf of bread. "Did you come, man?"

Robin sticks his hand down his pants. The tip of his dick is sticky with goo but it's not the whole thing. He looks at Scott's lap, at the dark stain there. "No."

"Shit. I sure fucking did."

Robin doesn't know what to do. Is it over? He wants to kiss Scott again but Scott is sitting up now, unzipping his fly. His half-swollen dick flops out like a few inches of garden hose, hairs tangled in the glop. No underwear. He wipes himself with the hem of his T-shirt.

Robin presses his hand on his dick. He watches Scott trying to clean up. "Wow," Scott says, looking at him with a wide grin. "I really shot."

"Yeah," is all Robin can say. Is there something wrong with him for not shooting yet? Should he jerk it off right now or would Scott think that's too weird?

Scott looks around the room, then back at Robin's crotch. "Hurry up, man. We could get snagged or something."

Robin keeps pulling on it but each stroke feels less effective, not quite right, and not all like the feeling of a few minutes ago when he could feel Scott's breath on him. He tries to read Scott's face, tries to figure out what Scott thinks of him here with his unfinished business.

"Put out your hand," Scott says.

"What?"

"Give me your hand." Robin takes his hand off his dick and holds it toward Scott. Scott flips it over and spits into his palm. He raises his eyebrows. "Use that," he says. "I'll meet you outside. I don't want to get busted in here." And then he's scurrying over the edge of the loft, lowering himself from sight.

With Scott gone, the spell is broken, the plug pulled. A final silent shudder travels across his skin, and he shakes himself to be rid of it. A bead of sweat runs from his temple. His dick is going soft. He rubs his hand on the concrete, smearing Scott's spit. In the webby part between each finger, the smell is like lemon juice or spinach, like Scott's breath and his own spit and the herby trace of what they smoked. He listens as Scott's footsteps fade away. They were not caught. No one knows but him and Scott. He looks around for some evidence of what they did; nothing remains except a mucusy drop of Scott's goop on the floor.

The night air is cold, the sky silver. Scott stands, hands in pockets, at the edge of the creek running past the picnic tables. Robin approaches cautiously.

Scott looks at him, then away. "I got really fucked up on that weed," he says.

The water trickles quietly by. Scott picks up a rock and tosses it in. *Plink.* Robin leans back against an oak tree, rubs his sticky hand on the bark, which breaks apart like chalk. He shakes his hair, lets the faint breeze soothe him. His lips tingle. "I never did that before," he says quietly.

"That's cool," Scott says, still not looking at him.

He studies Scott's back, his untucked T-shirt, the hair hanging across his shoulders. He knows he can't touch him, though that's what he wants to do; if he could feel the temperature of Scott again, he could believe the two of them actually did what they just did. Already the noise of the world is intruding: an automobile skids to a stop in the parking lot, grinding loose dirt under the tires. In the distance the sound of end-of-the-day traffic at Five Corners collects into a whoosh.

"Don't make a big deal of it," Scott says, then turns and walks past him toward the parking lot, toward the entry road that leads back to town. Robin follows. The dark concrete of the aviary looms at their side.

Two girls wearing feather earrings and tight jeans and high-heeled sandals pass them, heading back toward the building he and Scott just left, gossiping to each other, their conversation peppered with swearing and laughter. Robin lowers his head as he moves by, smelling their sharp perfume, wondering what they might smell on him.

"So I'm gonna go that way," Scott says when they get to the edge of the park. He nods in the direction opposite town, the other way from Robin's home.

"I think I've got a whole lot of trouble waiting for me," Robin says, calculating the lost hours, the explanation he'll have to provide. He pictures his school books in his gym locker, untouched for most of the day.

"A shitload," Scott says.

"See you tomorrow?" Robin asks.

"Yeah. In fucking gym class."

"Maybe I'll try to find you before homeroom."

"OK," Scott says. "Later."

He watches Scott walk away, hoping he'll turn back and just wave at him. But Scott is walking fast, he doesn't check for cars when he gets to a curb, enters the intersection without looking. Robin hears a car horn, the screech of brakes—he runs toward the noise in a panic. Scott hops aside and the car slams to a stop, its chrome fender plowing over the crosswalk, the driver yelling a reprimand. Scott flashes his middle finger at the car and breaks into a run, disappearing downhill into the grainy evening. Robin loses sight of him in the twisted oak branches and pale streetlight. "Later," he says, pushing his hands in his pockets.

He turns and runs the opposite way, darting into the street, into the glow of an approaching car. He stops short on the solid yellow line in the center of the road, waiting for the oncoming traffic to pass, feeling the dangerous growl of speeding vehicles just inches from his body. The vibration of the road grumbles under his feet, up through his legs, into his body like a fever.

* * *

He has his story prepared, but it evaporates as he approaches the drive-way and sees only his mother's car. He remembers his father had wanted to take him to the hospital tonight, and his stomach tightens in appre-hension. Most of the lights are off. He reaches under the flower pot at the bottom of the stoop for the key but finds the door unlocked. Light spreads across the hall carpet from the living room. His mother is home. The stereo plays an aria, the one from *Tosca* she adores so much. "I have lived for only art and love" is the English translation. He brushes off his pants—white pants smeared with crud—and swallows and walks forward.

She is on the couch, gripping the edges of a *New Yorker*. Her hair is clipped up in the back. The floor lamp glows on the back of her neck and casts half her face into shadow. It occurs to him to walk up the stairs and ignore her, but her eyes are upon him immediately, cold and severe. He cannot think of a single thing to say. She shuts the magazine, folding it into one hand. With the other, she lifts her wineglass from the coffee table and drains the last mouthful. She rises and steps toward him, moving into silhouette and then into the glow of the votive candles, burning softly on the table at his side. Her eyes scrutinize him.

"I'm sorry," he says.

The magazine swings flat against the side of his face. He trips back-ward, has a moment to register the sting of the first swipe before a sec-ond and a third are upon him. The edge of the pages nick the soft skin under his ear. "Your apology means nothing to me," she says, her voice shrill, trembling. "You were sorry *last* night." She raises her arm again and he catches the next blow on his shoulder. He smells the stench from his armpit, which smells to him like Scott, which makes him feel dirty and self-protective all at once.

She lets the magazine drop to the floor and pulls him desperately to her. He lets her hug him, listens as she sniffles and her weight falls upon his shoulders. He holds her waist, steadying them both, sure he cannot support her, that they will collapse to the floor together.

"I *am* sorry," he says after a moment.

She pushes him away. "Shut up," she says, her throat choking on speech. "Don't lie to me, Robin." She wipes moisture from her eyes and stumbles to the couch.

Seeing her try to recover, Robin thinks he might cry, too. He rubs his hand along his neck, hot from the swatting she gave him.

Dorothy composes herself, blows her nose into a cocktail napkin, shakes the hair from her eyes. "Let me be clear, Robin. I don't really *want* to know where you've been because I'm sure it will only disappoint me, but you are going to tell me because I am your mother. I am your mother and you are going to tell me where you've been for"—she checks her wristwatch—"the past seven hours."

"I ditched gym," he says.

"That much was made known to me by Mr. Cortez. On the telephone." She stares at him. He has never seen her look at him this way, the way other people's mothers look at their teenage children, as if they are strangers. "Sit down," she says.

He sits on the arm of the chair across from her.

"Your pants are filthy," she says.

He retraces his steps with Scott, back to their locker room conversation. He selects the parts of the day that matter least, the things he can tell her. "I went into town," he says. "I got pizza and looked at magazines at Woolworth's and went to that antique store where you can watch old flip movies in the viewer. You know, the five cent ones."

"Nickelodeons."

"Yeah. We saw a funny one with Keester Cops."

"Key*stone.*"

"And then we went to the park."

"We?"

He slides down to the seat cushion. He looks at his fingers, rubs one hand with the other, wishing he could have washed before he got home.

"Me and Scott," he says. He is unsure how much to say, does not want to be trapped into saying everything.

"Were you drinking? I can tell you were smoking cigarettes. I can smell that on you." Her posture remains rigid, her eyes unblinking now that the tears have stopped.

"We had one," Robin says. "Scott found it."

"Who is Scott?"

"Scott Schatz. A kid from school."

"What kind of kid?"

"Just a *kid,* some kid in my gym class."

"One with enough *luck* to find a *cigarette* in the park."

"Exactly," Robin says, matching her sarcastic tone. "And nice enough to share it."

"Hooray for you, pumpkin. You've made a friend."

He slams his fist into the seat.

"Don't you have a temper tantrum, Robin," she hisses. "You have not *earned* a temper tantrum. So what else?"

"There's *nothing* else," He watches her refill her wineglass, hating the gurgling sound, the sound of his mother drinking *more*. He crosses his arms. "Where's Dad and the rest of them?" he asks.

"At the hospital. Where do you think?" He hangs his head guiltily. "When your father found out you left school unexcused, he hit the roof. He was ready to *hit* you."

"You did a pretty good job for him," he says, rubbing the side of his face for emphasis.

She bangs her wineglass on the table and raises her voice. "You're acting like a juvenile delinquent—what do you expect from me?"

"I left school 'cause I couldn't take it!" he blurts out. "It was worse than ever and nothing made sense and these guys in the locker room were calling me names. What was I supposed to do? Stick around and take it?"

"You should have come home. That's where you belong—not in the park like a common New Jersey greaseball. You should have *come home.*"

"I made a friend, you should be happy I have a friend. A *guy* friend." His voice trembles. He hears the truth and the lies in his words battering against each other and cannot contain the explosion of it. "Isn't that what everyone expects, for me to be more like a guy? Have *guy* friends? So you know what guys do? They ditch school and hitchhike and smoke and they don't run home to their mothers like a big crybaby."

Without expecting it, he has shattered a silence so ever-present, so *old*, he'd forgotten it was there. Up until third grade, he hadn't felt so separate. He'd played with guys and girls, moving between different circles during recess. And then, after some arrangement between the school and his parents, he'd been put up to fourth, and it wasn't ever the same. He was suddenly an interloper, a *brain*, spurned by new classmates whose social hierarchies were already cemented. He'd already dropped out of Cub Scouts, stopped going to Little League—moving up a grade severed the last link. There were still guys he could call friends if he wanted to—George Lincoln, his lab partner, Ricky Feeney from down the street, a shy kid who sits next to him in social studies, Gerald the Trekkie from the cafeteria—all of them contained by school hours, familiarity that starts at nine A.M. and ends at three. Only Victoria has been constant, someone to gab with for hours on the phone, to accompany him on bike rides to Dairy Queen, to watch *Grease* with a half dozen times, she singing Sandy's songs, he singing Rizzo's. A girl for a best friend.

"I'm taking Jackson fishing on Saturday," his father might say. "Why don't you come along? Bring a friend?"

"Victoria wouldn't like that," he'd reply, squashing the conversation. His father turning away, frustrated, baffled. The rest of it unspoken, rippling in waves.

Dorothy leaps up and walks to the mirror, addressing her image as she speaks. "This is an absurd discussion. Your brother is in the hospital, for God's sake, and I have to sit here and psychoanalyze *you*."

"Then don't psychoanalyze me!" he shouts. "Just leave me alone."

"This entire conversation has been at fever pitch, and I won't have it. My mother and I used to scream at each other all the time, I won't have it with my own children."

Robin sees the effect of the wine in her bleary eyes. He wants to turn the spotlight off himself, so he says, "I never heard Nana scream at you."

She returns to the table for her glass and paces across the floor. He hears her words slurring together as she picks up speed. "Because she doesn't anymore! When I was younger she was always drawing me into screaming matches. She's an incredibly aggressive woman. You wouldn't know that because she's mellowed with age. But she has spent her whole godforsaken life waiting on Smith girls, and when she came home, she had nothing but examples to give me. Emulate this one, avoid that one. This one's showing poor character, that one's going to be a lady. I never had a choice but to attend Smith; it was free and it was where my mother was going to have her day, with me as Exhibit A."

The speakers buzz with static; the aria has ended, and the needle is hissing against the center label, stuck in place. Robin gets up and flips it over, letting the music build again into a crescendo. He falls back on the couch, exhausted. He isn't sure why his mother is saying all this; is she still trying to get information from him about what he did today? What would she do if he told her what really happened? Would she tell his father? Would he be punished? He can't even guess what they'd do to him if he told the truth.

He wonders where Scott is right now, if he's being yelled at by his father and mother. Not his mother—he remembers Scott saying his mother was in a mental hospital.

Dorothy drops into a chair in the dining room, her back to Robin. She speaks with her face raised to the ceiling; she doesn't seem to notice him at all. "Even in New York, she demanded that I call her every Sunday morning. I was twenty-two years old and working at Scribner's,

I was an executive secretary to the vice president of public affairs, I was dating men and going to parties. I was doing everything I wanted to do and my mother was still nagging me about doing it better."

He gets up and sits across from her at the table. In the dim light he can see only a hint of her faraway expression. She laughs—the sound is almost cruel. "The only thing she ever approved of was my marrying your father. She had no choice, of course." She catches her breath and lowers her head. She reaches out and clutches one of Robin's hands. He is surprised by the strength of her grasp. "Robin, I'm upset. I shouldn't have struck you. Jackson's situation is driving me crazy. Do you understand that? I know you understand that, Robin—you *know* me."

He nods in agreement, though right now he doesn't think he knows her at all.

"Don't make it any worse for me. Don't disappear on your bike. Don't cut school. Don't pick fights with your sister." She is shaking his hand; their knuckles rap against the tabletop.

He wriggles free of her grip. "Don't drink so much wine," he says coolly. He takes her glass with him as he leaves the table. He rinses it out in the sink, dries it, places it in the cupboard methodically. He walks past her without a word and climbs the stairs, letting the music continue its dramatic rise and fall.

Later, tossing atop the flannel sheets on Ruby's bed, the blanket and bedspread crumpled at his feet, he wonders if he is ill. His eyelids are heavy and dry, each blink an irritant. He is exhausted but can't sleep. His father yelled and yelled when he got home, grabbed him by the shoulders and shook until Robin thought his neck might snap. Called him a jerk. Said he was an embarrassment. Told him he would be confined to the house except for school for the foreseeable future. His father is back at the hospital now but Uncle Stan is here. Robin can hear the distorted rumblings of the television in the living room, and the more urgent whisperings between his mother and Nana Rena from his parents' bedroom. He is sure they are all talking about him. He leans over the edge of the bed and spits a salty, gluey gob into the white garbage pail. His throat stings as if rubbed by sandpaper. He leans his head into the pillow and his ear throbs with the memory of his mother's slaps.

He is remembering Scott's face as a series of snapshots, frozen portraits: Scott in the locker room mirror; Scott in the backseat of the car, wind on his face; Scott's hair falling forward as he pushed his body into Robin. They were kissing—he has to remind himself of this simple fact:

it seems now as if it didn't happen, couldn't have happened. His face is hot to the touch. He runs the back of his hand along his mouth, pressing the delicate bones into the flesh of his lips, embarrassed for wanting Scott's mouth against him again, wondering if Scott will even speak to him again. Was he a bad kisser? Scott definitely knew how to kiss, he knew how to make it feel good. *He wanted to do it with me. He got me stoned and then he made me do sex.* He asks himself, *How do I know that was sex?*

His hand is in his pajama pants, and the images are taking over: not Scott, but Todd, Todd's eyes in the car that morning, Todd's hair falling into his face, Todd's body, bigger than Scott's, the arms stronger against his arms, the stiffness stronger against his legs. He sees Todd smiling, a smile that scares him; he feels his skin, his neck, his spine coil together into a tightening knot. Todd is shaking a fistful of his crotch like Danniman. Danniman is saying, "This girlie wants a meal," Robin is pinned against a locker room wall, and Long Dong Danniman is pushing him pushing him pushing him.

He buries his face in Ruby's pillow and lets the rush of wetness fill his cupped hands.

The clock says 11:15. He takes a chance, tiptoes downstairs. On TV, Johnny Carson is interviewing an actress in a tight dress. Johnny is raising his eyebrows, having just told an off-color joke, and the actress is laughing along uncomfortably. Uncle Stan looks up from the TV set and breaks off his own snickering to ask Robin where he thinks he's going.

"I have to call my friend Victoria," Robin says, not stopping.

"I think the phone's pretty much off limits to you right now, buster."

"I'm supposed to get a ride from her in the morning," Robin says, still moving toward the kitchen, but slowing his steps.

"Oh, yeah?" Stan responds in a challenging tone. Robin recognizes the start of an unbearable lecture. *Here we go,* he thinks, stopping, resting his hands on his hips. "Weren't you listening to your father? You're not getting rides from any of your hotshot friends anymore. A little taste of house arrest is the idea. Your *mother's* gonna take you to school." Stan folds his arms smugly across his belly.

"Well, then I have to tell Victoria before she goes to bed."

"She'll figure it out." Stan jerks his thumb toward the staircase. "Good night."

Robin rolls his eyes. "How long are you planning on hanging around here anyway, Uncle Stan? Don't you have to go to work?"

Stan glares at him. "If it's any-a your business, wiseguy, I'm taking a couple of days off. A guy's gotta stick by his family in times of trouble."

"What about Larry? *He's* your family."

"He's with his mother." Stan uncrosses his arms and throws them over his head, speaking while he stretches. "Anyway, I got some ideas about physical therapy for Jackson. Your father and I are gonna check out this new system a buddy-a mine's selling."

Robin frowns. "Yeah, right."

Stan picks at a fingernail while he continues. "It's very state-a the art stuff. I kid you not. When Jackson gets outta the hospital, it's gonna take the newest technology to get him back up to speed." He looks up, catching sight of Robin's dubious expression. "Between you and me, Robin, I'd-a bought you a beer for acting a little bit out of line today. 'Cept of course you made everyone worry, and that never works. But I've said it before, and I'll say it again: you're already too tied to Mama's apron strings. When all this stuff with your brother wears off, you oughtta get out there a little. I let Larry hang out, never hurt anyone. Never hurt me. In fact, I'd go so far to say that if you get some-a that stuff out of your system now, you'll be more prepared. You know, the real world don't have a lotta tolerance for smarty-pants types like you."

"Can I just make my phone call before she goes to bed?"

A big laugh on the TV captures Stan's attention. "Make it fast," he says.

Robin dials Victoria's number from memory and stretches the phone cord to the basement stairs.

On the second ring, he gets Mrs. Spicer's surprised voice.

"It's Robin MacKenzie. Is Victoria up still?" he says quickly.

"I usually don't let her take calls this late, Robin. Is everything all right?"

"Oh, you know. Could be better." He taps his bare toes on the stairs.

"Is there some news on your brother?"

"Maybe he's getting better. They're thinking about physical therapy." He cringes as he hears himself making Uncle Stan's plan sound like a solution.

"Tell your family our prayers are with him. We're all very concern—"

"Mrs. Spicer, would you mind getting Victoria? I really need to talk to her."

"Oh, all right. But don't keep her on long."

Nana Rena steps into the kitchen doorway. Her footfalls are slow and heavy. She isn't wearing a wig, and her scalp shines pink under the few wiry tendrils that shoot off in every direction. Her nightdress is an enormous swatch of plaid—something Robin vaguely remembers Dorothy giving her for Christmas.

"I thought we put you to bed hours ago," she says.

"I forgot I had to call Victoria."

"But it's past eleven!"

"Did you come down for a cup of tea?" he asks.

"Why should I be able to sleep any better than the rest of this clan?" she asks, balancing herself against a chair and studying him. "I can hardly believe the state of the lot of you. You off like a hooligan two days running. Your sister scared witless. Your father"—she shakes her head as if confronting the greatest tragedy of all—"well, *he* was fit to be tied. And isn't Dottie just worked into a tizzy, keeping me up for hours, telling me this is all *my* fault."

"Robin?" Victoria's breathy voice.

"Yeah, hold on," he says. "Don't hang up." He puts his hand over the receiver. "Nana, this is private." He closes himself in behind the basement door before she can register a protest.

"Hi, Victoria. Sorry. My Nana's talking my ear off," he whispers.

"I'm *really* glad you called," she says.

"You are?"

"I've just been bumming out all night. I was even crying, I swear. After school I was thinking about your brother and how this morning I was such a jerk in the car."

"That's OK," he says. He had nearly forgotten about the ride to school. It already seems days old.

Victoria keeps on. "It's just that Todd makes me crazy. I can't help it. He's so weird—"

"Look, Victoria," he interrupts. "I had a really big day. I have to talk to you about it. I just got in a big fight with my mother. I think she has a drinking problem."

"At first I just thought I shouldn't even *talk* to you. You walked *away* from me this morning without even saying good-bye. I mean, that's just *rude*. But then I thought it over, you know? I thought about it all *day*, and you and I have been friends for so long and you're really special and I don't ever want you to change."

He sighs, frustrated that she's doing all the talking. "I know," he says, trying to be patient. "We *have* been friends for so long." But he wants to ask why it feels so strained lately. High school has stolen the ease from their friendship. When the Spicers moved to the neighborhood seven years ago, he took Victoria in. He introduced her to other kids in their neighborhood and at Crossroads, made it easy for her to be the new girl; she rewarded him with her free time, her enthusiasm for his stories of the city, her willingness to participate, along with Ruby, in his after-school basement dramas.

It wasn't only shared interests, like *Grease* and gossip, that kept them glued together over the years. Sometimes they just hung out, doing homework, watching TV, listening to 45s in her bedroom. Before she went to her cousins' this summer, Victoria would join him on his lawn mowing jobs, sitting on a stoop as he crisscrossed the grass or, if he needed the help, trimming the edges with clippers. They'd spend the money on pizza and video games at Jerry's in town. The neighborhood ladies sometimes referred to them as *going steady,* but they'd just roll their eyes, understanding, without needing to say it, how stupid adults could be.

"I think we should stay friends," she says in a rush, "even if we make *other* friends."

He pictures the pout on her face as she twists the phone cord around her wrist like a bracelet. He knows the best way to reassure her is to launch into his story, to bring her back into his confidence. "OK," he says. "Listen—today was *major.* I cut school from fourth period on."

"You ditched?"

"Yeah, me and this kid Scott Schatz."

"Scott Schatz?" she gasps.

"You know him?"

"Yes," she snaps as if this should be obvious. Now he sees her hopping up on the counter next to the draining board, where she sits for hours on the phone every night. "Robin," she says with a dramatic pause, "he's such a *scum.*"

"I know he's a burnout," he says defensively. "But he's really nice. He really listened to me."

"No, I mean he's a *major* scum. He used to be friends with Todd."

"He used to be friends with Todd?" he repeats, his voice cracking in shock.

"Like, like two years ago, when Todd was a sophomore and Scott was in eighth grade. They were hanging out together all the time."

"How come I never saw him?"

"I don't know. He was at our house a lot."

"He didn't tell me he knew Todd," Robin says, more to himself than to her. He thinks of what Scott said: how he'd hung out in his neighborhood, how he knew about the two cars in his driveway.

"Well, they stopped being friends. I mean, Todd was older and going to high school and Scott was bugging him. He used to call up all the time and want to talk to Todd, and then he wouldn't say anything when Todd got on the phone."

"He doesn't talk much," Robin says. He can't quite absorb this, feels himself sinking under the notion that he is somehow the target of a conspiracy. "I can't believe he knows Todd."

"*I* can't believe you ditched school with him."

"That was only the beginning. We hitched a ride with this crazy girl who works at New Sounds. Then we hung out at The Bird and we smoked cigarettes and smoked pot."

"Robin, he'll turn you into a scum, too," Victoria says very seriously. He hears a sudden mechanical buzz from her end of the phone. "Sorry," she says. "I'm making a yogurt shake. Diane showed me how. Diane Jernigan? It's with this new frozen yogurt."

He's suddenly feeling like this call was a terrible idea. "I gotta go."

"Wait! You can't just start something—"

He sighs heavily. "We just got pizza and stuff and then when I got home my mother freaked out." He realizes he has been holding his breath, as if in suspense of what he might allow himself to say. It's a relief now not to tell her everything. "I might get detention. Maybe Scott will get it, too."

"Scums *never* get detention." She punctuates this pronouncement with a slurpy suck on her straw. "They always figure out how to talk their way out of it. Or they sign in and then don't stay, and the teachers never tell, or even if they tell the principal, what else can he do? Give you *more* detention?"

"They could suspend you."

"They tried that with Todd, but my father just went in there and said"—she deepens her voice—"'*If you keep this boy out of school he'll be on the streets even more. We can't keep him at home.*' And the principal was like"—she changes to another adult male voice—'*OK, but then it will be your responsibility to make him stop ditching.*'" She takes another slurp and resumes with her own perfectly satisfied voice. "And then my father just beat the shit out of Todd and he stopped cutting for a while and went to detention like he was supposed to."

"I remember that, when he was in detention for a month." A memory forms of those months: Todd's increasing presence in the yard, smoking cigarettes, fixing up motors. Robin peeks his head out the door to see if Nana is still there. Seeing no sign of her, he walks to the window. The light is on in Todd's room. Todd is probably sitting on his bed listening to rock music with no idea that Victoria is downstairs telling Robin things about him. I am a spy, he tells himself, figuring out secrets. "I can't believe Scott didn't mention Todd."

Victoria bangs something down on the counter—the sound might be her spoon or glass or maybe the blender itself. *"Todd, Scott.* Are you trying to turn into a scum, too?"

"I'm just having fun, Victoria. I'm taking *risks.*"

"Hey!"

Robin jumps and spins around. Uncle Stan gives him a long, authoritative gaze, nodding his head as if computing information. "What are you still doing on the phone?"

"Nothing."

"You got sixty seconds before I hang up for you," Stan says before strutting back to the TV.

Robin squeezes his fingers around the receiver. "Shit, I have to go," he says. "I'll see you in school."

"Wait," Victoria says, almost desperately. "I mean it, Robin. You're really special. Don't hang around Scott Schatz."

"God, Victoria, don't make a big deal of it. Good-bye." He hangs up before she can respond.

In the living room Robin kisses his grandmother good night and does his best to ignore Stan. He is halfway up the stairs when Stan calls out, "Anything you want to tell me, Robin?"

Robin spins around. It's almost surreal—Stan has spent so much time here that now he's trying to keep Robin in line. It's like having a third parent who is far worse than the first two. He answers sarcastically, "I was just telling Victoria how lucky I am to have an uncle who is so concerned about me."

"You better watch your mouth, kid," Stan growls, but a moment later he's fixating on the TV set, guffawing along with the studio audience. As he carries himself up the stairs, Robin is almost glad Stan is here. Stan is the one person in this house he can hate without feeling any guilt.

Chapter Seven

"I understand things are pretty touchy at home," Mr. Cortez is saying. He's sitting on the edge of his desk, working a loop of string into a cat's cradle. Robin watches his hands scissoring, transforming the geometry of the taut string. He thinks his guidance counselor might be trying to hypnotize him. "You want to talk about it?"

"Everything's messed up since my brother got hurt," Robin says.

"The hardest part is usually trying to make sense of it."

"My mother says it's just something that doesn't make sense. It was an accident."

"Well, she's right about that. But the thing to remember is that you'll still be affected by it." He pauses. Robin feels him trying to make every word sink in. He knows Mr. Cortez is a nice guy and is probably trying to be nice to him now, but he's suspicious. Cortez already told him he has detention for a week. Why should he trust him? Besides, he's been pulled out of gym to have this lecture, which means he won't get to see Scott, who is all he can think about.

"Why don't you tell me how it's affecting *you?*" Cortez prods.

"I don't know. It makes me confused, I guess."

"Confusion is a natural reaction. Is that why you ditched yesterday? Were you confused being back at school?"

"I hate gym. What's the point? It's not like I'm going to be an athlete. I don't even like sports, except maybe gymnastics. In seventh grade I took this gymnastics class after school." A dim memory surfaces: the terror of learning to backflip, the blindness, the risk.

"Unfortunately the government says you have to take phys. ed. So try not to get hung up on that one, Robin. I'm more interested in why you chose to cut the *rest* of the day."

"I'm sorry. I know better," Robin says, thinking he might get out of this if he just says the right thing. He studies the wall where Mr. Cortez has hung a couple of framed diplomas and a day-glo poster from some peace rally in 1969. He was definitely a flower child in the '60s, Robin thinks, which seems like something Cortez would be embarrassed to advertise. It's funny to think about—a guy who was once a hippie is now responsible for keeping him from acting up.

"Look, look," Cortez says, letting the string fall from his fingers into a snarled pile on his cluttered desk. "Let's not bullshit each other, OK?"

Adults cursing always seem ridiculous to Robin—like his father saying *fuck* at the hospital the other day. It doesn't come natural or something. He feels his smile breaking through, but he doesn't want to seem obnoxious, so he lowers his head contritely and murmurs, "OK."

"Tell me what's on your mind. From your gut." Cortez leans forward, resting his hand against his belly for emphasis. A silver ring on his wedding finger catches Robin's eye, its turquoise stone an otherworldly miniature egg. He looks at the desk, at a framed photo of a smiling young woman in a loose paisley-print dress, the colors vaguely faded. Her hair is sandy blond and ironed straight. She wears Indian jewelry but no makeup. Mrs. Cortez.

Robin asks him, "Don't you ever feel that talking to kids like me is just a waste of your time?"

"How would you characterize *kids like you?*"

"Kids who cut class, who should know better. All that stuff."

"Do you feel like you're wasting my time?"

It's confounding—Mr. Cortez has a question for every one of his. Robin runs his fingertips back and forth along the notebook in his lap, pressing a trace of friction onto his skin. "I think you're probably not enjoying this."

"It's part of the job, isn't it?"

Robin figures his own expression must show how little he believes Mr. Cortez's answer because Mr. Cortez lets out a chuckle. "OK, I said we wouldn't bullshit each other. The truth is, helping out kids like you is, for me, pretty *spiritual.*"

Robin wrinkles up his nose. "My grandmother is really religious. I should introduce you to her."

Mr. Cortez smiles knowingly—his smiles are starting to irritate Robin; the guy really does seem to be getting some little kick out of this. "I'll spare you the whole discussion of Eastern religion, which is important to me but which I know will sound pretty kooky to you. Let's just say that, in another life, I was someone very selfish who never took the time to do anything for anyone." He pauses, looks directly into Robin's eyes. "Do you catch my drift?"

"Are you talking about reincarnation?" Robin asks. It's something he read about in *Time*—people meditating and doing yoga and believing in past lives. His mother said it all started with the Beatles traveling to India.

"Sure, sure," Cortez says happily. "See, the thing is, if you load yourself up on good karma—good *deeds*—maybe next time around you won't have so much to account for."

"Next time around I hope I'm not in Greenlawn High."

"Everyone's got their own bag," Mr. Cortez says. "The point is, talking to you isn't a waste of time."

Robin looks out the window where Mr. Pintack, his gym teacher, is leading a single-file line of student joggers around the school perimeter. He can hear a muted whistle, which makes him wince. The sound of bogus authority. He cranes his neck, hoping Scott might slide into view, but there's no sign of him.

"*I* think it might be a waste of time to try and get through to me. I think I might be in my own world too much."

Mr. Cortez sits very still, his face frozen in concern. "Why don't you tell me about your world, Robin?"

His stomach glugs, a signal warning him he is about to be trapped in a revelation. He hugs his notebook defensively, wishing he hadn't said anything at all. Ever since he left Scott outside The Bird, he has felt consumed by what happened between them. In every conversation since— with his mother, Victoria, now Mr. Cortez—he finds himself wanting to explain what happened so that he might get a better explanation from someone else. But then he remembers that Scott said not to make a big deal about it, which seems to be the best way to handle it—though if it wasn't a big deal, Robin concludes, Scott wouldn't have said that.

"I have this way of seeing everything," he blurts out. Mr. Cortez is waiting, his eyes questioning. "I don't mean seeing like *thinking* about something, you know: *I see it this way.* I mean seeing like actually *looking* at the part of things that maybe other people don't see." He pauses; his own words make little sense to him; they exist on a separate parallel plane with his thoughts: thinking one thing, saying something else. He feels almost crazed with nervousness. "Like in gym class I don't *see* the ball when they're pitching it to me—I always strike out, and everyone thinks it's because I'm a wimp. Maybe I am a wimp. No, I mean, I just don't like sports, but that doesn't mean I'm a bad person. It's just that I don't *look* at the ball when they pitch to me. I, like, look at the way the air slices open when the ball moves through it, like in *The Ten Commandments* when the sea splits open, which is *freaky*. How can you hit a ball when you're looking at the place where the ball just *was?*"

Mr. Cortez shifts his position, inching himself a fraction closer to the edge of the desk. "Is that a scary feeling?"

"What?" His ears are burning hot.

"Not seeing what you need to see in order to participate in the game you're playing." Robin scrunches up his face. Mr. Cortez asks, "You follow?"

Robin can tell Mr. Cortez is not following *him*. "Who *cares* about the game? Of course I hate it when I get picked on for striking out, but the worst thing isn't even that they're picking on me—it's that I'm getting picked on for something so stupid." He leans back and slaps the notebook with his palms. "*Soft*ball. As if that has anything to do with my life."

Mr. Cortez raises his eyebrows; Robin wonders if he has impressed him or increased his skepticism. Cortez bows his head, holding his hand over his mouth. Robin can see the crown of his scalp, where the curls are thinner. "OK, let me see if I get this," Mr. Cortez says, which Robin immediately takes as a sign that he has more explaining to do. He checks the clock. This has been going on for twenty minutes. It could go on for quite a while.

"Could I go to the water fountain? My throat is really dry."

"I'll get you a cup from the cooler." Mr. Cortez slides off his desk; Robin's eyes catch his crotch bunching up with fabric and the shifting curves beneath. When he stands, the excess smoothes away. He watches the tension of Mr. Cortez's ass and the back of his thighs as he walks out the door; Mr. Cortez's legs are probably covered in tinier versions of the hairs on his head. He flushes with the guilt of staring, but Mr. Cortez's trousers are snug against his skin—he must know, Robin reasons, that people will look at him this way, imagining his body beneath the clothes. Does Mr. Cortez imagine that Robin would be looking, or does he only expect girls to look?

You are thinking about guys too much, he tells himself, with a mounting sense of terror. *You are turning into a major queer.*

"The question I have for you is," Mr. Cortez says, suddenly there again, handing a waxy paper drinking cup to Robin, "if you think of yourself as seeing the world differently from everyone else, do you think you can participate in the required activities of this school?" He shakes his head. "That probably sounds like I'm criticizing—let me try again. Is there any way to redeem your experiences here at Greenlawn High?" He frowns, then exclaims, "Is it all just a bum trip for you?"

Robin downs the water in one gulp, savoring the cool path of the liquid traveling to his stomach like in an X-ray film from health class. "I don't have much of a choice, right?"

Mr. Cortez reaches for a weighty book on his shelf. Robin can't make out the title. "There are other options," Mr. Cortez says, opening the cover and scanning the contents page with his finger. "There are private schools, schools with gifted programs that surpass what we can offer you here even in honors classes."

"Gifted? That sounds like *retarded* to me."

"No, no, it's the opposite." He pulls a pencil from under a stack of papers and writes something quickly on a yellow pad. "You're bright, Robin. No question about that. You were put up a grade when you were younger, if I'm not mistaken." He scans a form on his desk.

"They moved me up from third to fourth," Robin says, returning to last night's flash of heavy memory: the struggle of making all new friends after being singled out. Jimmy Woods saying, *We don't need no faggots in fourth grade.*

"Your grades have slipped since last year—especially in science and math—but you're bright."

"So I'm supposed to go to another school?" It's a thought both attractive and terrifying: no Long Dong Danniman, but no Scott either.

"We'd have to do some research," Mr. Cortez says, flipping pages. "I have a couple of ideas, schools that don't cost much but focus more on the humanities, a kind of precollege curriculum."

Robin never thinks about college. College is just something his father brings up when he's trying to impress other grown-ups about his children. "I don't know," he says.

"Let's give it some thought. I'll call your parents in for a conference."

"No!" Robin nearly shouts. "They've got other things on their minds right now. Don't bother them about me."

"We'll just have a little rap session, maybe all of us together."

"Oh, brother," Robin says under his breath.

"Hey, buddy," Mr. Cortez says, walking behind Robin and laying his hand on his shoulder. Robin inhales at the touch, shuts his eyes, sees a big canyon laid out in front of him for no reason he can understand: a yellow sky pressing down upon purple-brown rock formations, fading away to a cluttered, threatening horizon. A beautiful, eerie landscape. "Don't sweat it. This might be a good dialogue to have. Keep the options open." He squeezes Robin's shoulder and walks back around to where Robin can see the resolution on his face.

"OK," he says. "But tell them it was your idea, not mine."

"Absolutely."

"Promise? I'm already in enough trouble."

"I wouldn't lie to you, Robin. It's bad karma." He smiles and extends his hand. It takes Robin a beat to realize he's supposed to shake it. He reaches out. The grip is strong, the shake very man-to-man. Robin lets go first.

In the cafeteria, he takes a green plastic tray and slides it along the silver railing toward the steam trays, the cafeteria ladies with plastic caps and gloves, the shiny, wobbly puddings and fruit cups. The conversation with Cortez has left him dazed: somehow he escaped what felt like a very close call—a near revelation of what really happened with Scott yesterday—only to skid without warning into unknown territory. He feels tricked, conspired against. Did he really agree to consider private school? What kind of place would it be—a boarding school in New England filled with preppies who spoke through clenched jaws? Catholic school, classes taught by priests? Military academy? As much as he hates Greenlawn, every alternative seems awful. He understands what Nana means when she says, *The evil you know is better than the evil you don't know.*

The lady at the register frowns at him. "I said one-fifty."

"Give me a cookie," Robin says. He walks out of the line, staring at the unidentifiable brown stew sloshing on his plate against a soft pile of mashed potatoes.

"Hey, man, what's up?"

Scott is bouncing on his toes, staring intently at him.

"Hey, Scott." His mouth is suddenly as dry as toast.

"So let me guess," Scott says knowingly. "You got busted by Pintack."

"Umm, no, I never even saw Pintack," he says. "Mr. Cortez pulled me out of gym class. He told me I have detention for a week."

"Me, too, but no fucking way I'm going." He rips open a bag of

M&Ms and empties half of it into his mouth. Robin is sure that they are being stared at; anyone could tell that they're an odd pair—Robin in his orange-and-yellow-striped knit shirt, his school lunch piled neatly in front of him; Scott in the same dingy sweatjacket he wore the day before, the hood bunched up around his neck, looking like he's ready to ditch again. "You should just sign in and leave and then come back after an hour. That's what I always do."

"Who taught you that trick?" Robin asks, remembering what Victoria told him about Scott's friendship with Todd.

"I got a million of 'em." Scott picks the chocolate chip cookie off Robin's plate and takes a bite from it. "I'll see you later, man. If you want to cut, meet me outside the cafeteria before it starts."

"OK," he says eagerly, then is gripped by the image of his mother's angry face. "But wait. I can't. I mean . . . I just can't."

"It's easy. After you sign in, and *before* they make the seating chart, you go to the bathroom. They'll try to hassle you but they can't make you hold it in."

Scott grabs Robin's cookie again and breaks off a piece. He tosses it in the air; Robin watches his neck arch back and his mouth open up for the catch, remembers Scott's neck crushed against his shoulder, his mouth pressed wet against him. His dick starts getting hard; he lowers his tray to cover up.

Scott's eyes catch sight of something; his face pales a shade. Robin turns to check over his shoulder. Todd Spicer walks toward them, his arm draped over a girl. Robin has the sudden urge to flee. His conversation with Victoria last night speeds through his mind like an express train's whistle while everything that happens next plays out in terrible slow-motion. Todd notices Robin, and his face softens until he catches sight of Scott—then his expression turns steely, almost defensive. Robin understands that he is in the middle of something, but he doesn't understand what. Todd squeezes his girl tighter, holds Robin's gaze, and says, "Hey, Robin, how've you been?" in a tone that is downright chummy.

"I've been cool," Robin hears himself say as Todd ignores Scott and walks on by.

Robin can't make himself look at Scott; Todd's attention has stricken him with guilt, as though the two of them have ganged up against Scott.

Scott mutters, "Later," and slips between a row of crowded tables. Robin feebly calls his name, but Scott disappears out the door. Robin stares down at the unappetizing food on his tray, scoops the broken cookie off his plate, and dumps the rest of it in the garbage.

* * *

When the last bell rings Robin makes his way to his locker. He puts away his science book and takes out *East of Eden* and his social studies book and tries to remember what other homework he's supposed to be doing tonight. He stares at the darkness inside his locker, while the end-of-the-day buzz goes on around him. Detention looms, the cold, steely slam of lockers punctuating his dread. Just the sound of it is ominous: central detention. He's a freshman who hasn't been in trouble so far; he doesn't know what to expect. He imagines walking in to find that everyone is looking at him, glad that he's there, glad to see him brought down a notch. He's also not sure he's got enough nerve to cut out with Scott. Yesterday was more than enough trouble for a while, and he is supposed to go to the hospital after detention—if something went wrong and he wasn't waiting for his mother at four o'clock when she showed up . . . He shudders with the possibility that she'd slap him again.

The idea that he and Scott could get away together, maybe hang out for the hour before he has to rush back to get picked up by his mother in front of the school—when he thinks of that, he feels almost hungry. He's aware of his own brain working in ways it never used to: a switch has been flicked and he is now a stranger to himself—a stranger he has not yet decided he wants to be. He looks at one of the pictures taped to the inside of his locker: Natalie Wood as Maria in *West Side Story*. She's got a dreamy look on her face, thinking of the new guy in her life, the *wrong* guy, and more than ever he understands her. Right before the dance at the gym, right before she meets Tony, she complains because the dress she has to wear is white, too pure for such a big occasion. She pleads for a chance to taste what life has to offer; she wants to take risks. And then what she wants comes to her. He's been waiting for the future, too, for that first thrilling taste: the music slowing down, the kiss in delicious slow-motion, the colored lights a misty halo. Yesterday, with Scott at The Bird, he got a taste—but it was the taste of smoke and spit, the smell of musty concrete and birdshit. There was the seismic thrill of kissing but also the dismal silence that followed, the aloneness.

He checks a clock on the wall. It's one minute past three. He's supposed to be at the cafeteria for detention by 3:05, and has no desire to get there even a minute early. He ducks into a bathroom, empty inside except for a pair of legs in one toilet stall. He hears the paper unraveling, the weak little rip and the crinkling of someone wiping his butt—he feels perverted for listening. At the urinal he pretends to pee even though he doesn't have to. He flushes so that the other guy won't know that he's not peeing, though he feels doubly perverted for thinking that the other guy might be listening to him, too. Being in this silent bathroom with a strange guy isn't like being at home, peeing with Jackson at the same time.

The door opens and Scott enters, telegraphing his agitation. "What are you doing? We go to central to sign in first; *then* we go to the bathroom. And *then* ditch—that's the plan." He's bouncing on his toes impatiently. "Cortez isn't gonna cut us a lot of slack."

"Mr. *Cortez* is at detention?" Robin asks.

"Yeah, he's the monitor."

"Oh, great," Robin says, dropping his shoulders, defeated. "I can't cut if Cortez is the monitor. He *knows* me."

"That's bullshit, man. I knew you would cop out."

"I can't, Scott. I'll get in even more trouble." He hates this conflict. Strike one: Todd Spicer smiling at him and blowing right past Scott without a word. Strike two: he comes in the bathroom too early. Strike three: he refuses to cut detention.

The toilet flushes. The thick-necked jock who emerges from the stall is someone Robin recognizes from gym class, Greg something. He looks at the two of them like they are a joke.

Robin is intimidated by the sneer, but Scott snaps. "What are you looking at?"

"Couple-a losers," Greg says cockily, passing by the sinks without washing his hands. He stares them down as he leaves.

"Eat me," Scott barks. Robin waits for Greg to charge back in, but it doesn't happen. Scott makes it seem so easy, like these guys aren't bullies, just bothersome. "Look, man, you can play teacher's pet but no way am I staying there."

Robin squeezes his eyes tight for a moment, trying to think. "I can't." He hopes the plea in his voice will make Scott understand that it's out of his hands.

"I thought you were going to be cooler," Scott says flatly.

Robin tries one final call. "So do you want to hang out again sometime, maybe this weekend?" But Scott is gone. The pinewood door, gouged and scrawled upon, swings shut. Robin clenches his jaw to keep from shrieking, spins around, and sends the two books in his hands flying into the opposite wall. One *ka-booms* against the towel dispenser and falls to the floor, leaving behind a dent. In the mirror, he sees an unfamiliar mania in his eyes. His face looks like someone in the middle of a fight—only he's alone. He's angry with himself. He can't even be mad at Scott—why should Scott want to hang out with a mama's boy like him? Scott knows something he doesn't—how to pass through the world swiftly, how to get past every guy who calls you a loser and every teacher or guidance counselor who wants you to sign your name to your own punishment. What does he have to offer Scott?

He picks up his books and tucks them under his arm and heads for the cafeteria. He doesn't know what else to do. Scott is gone, and his mother is coming in an hour and she expects him to be here. She's going to take him to the hospital. He tries to clear out all thoughts of Scott and remember this one fact: Jackson is really sick, and that should be the only thing on his mind.

The hour goes by slowly. Robin tries to concentrate on his reading but he feels like he's being watched. There are a dozen other kids in there. Talking is not allowed. He sits at the end of a table, a few seats down from two black girls named Jocelyn and Monica who slide notes back and forth across the table when Mr. Cortez isn't looking. Jocelyn has a comb sticking out from the back of her trimmed afro. On her notebook, in big magic marker capital letters, she has written, *If you're not part of the solution you're part of the problem.* She catches him glancing over, reading the slogan, and puffs out her lips in a big frown that makes him think he must be part of the problem, whatever it is.

At the next table, facing him, is Seth Carter from his gym class. On the way in, Seth, who never has anything friendly to say to him, said, "I got busted cheating on my math exam. What did you do?"

"I ditched all day."

"Cool," Seth said, and for the first time Robin wondered if detention might actually gain him some respect. Robin watched Seth walk to a seat, watched his butt move. As Seth sat down Robin looked at his crotch, studied the movement underneath the denim, the soft curves among the folds.

Seth doodles on a paper bag book cover, writing the names of bands in fancy album cover designs: Led Zep, Yes, Blue Oyster Cult. The tip of his tongue edges out over his lower lip as he concentrates. Robin looks up at him every few minutes. Their eyes meet once and Robin freezes his face into a smile. Seth looks around, puzzled, as if Robin might be look-ing at someone else. Robin looks away to hide the flare of his desire and the embarrassment that seems so closely tied to it. He reminds himself that only yesterday Seth's friends were calling him "girlie" in the locker room.

At the end of the hour, he looks around for Scott in the hall, wondering why he hasn't shown up again, getting depressed by the idea that Scott is really mad at him and won't talk to him again. He makes his way to the front of the building, past the displayed senior class paintings, all of which look like visual tricks to make your eyes go dizzy—circles inside of circles, black-and-white checks that seem to vibrate on the canvas, lines in V formation that curve if you stare at them too intensely. His mother dismissed it all with a wave of her hand once. "I always knew Op Art was an illegitimate movement, and here's the proof: it can be imitated by any adolescent with a palette and a ruler."

Outside, the sky is a shimmery, cold purple. His mother is waiting in her car; she beeps when she sees him. The car stinks of cigarette smoke. Dorothy has her hair in a kerchief. Beneath her rabbit fur coat he can see that she's wearing jeans and a sweatshirt, as if she had hurried getting dressed.

"What have you been doing?" Robin asks her.

"Sleeping."

"During the day? Aren't we going to the hospital?"

"After dinner. I have a monstrous headache," she says. "I spent half the day arguing with your father, with my mother, with Stan, and I spent the other half sleeping. I nearly forgot to come get you."

As they pull away, Robin imagines the afternoon the way he would have wanted it: he ditches detention with Scott; his mother, meanwhile, oversleeps and so she never finds out that he wasn't here at four. He could be with Scott right now—maybe back at The Bird, maybe doing what they were doing last time. Then the rigid half of his mind interrupts: even if his mother had overslept, there's no way he would have known. He sees himself kissing Scott but not enjoying it, too full of worry to let it go far. He brings himself back to reality, to the quiet Greenlawn streets stretched outside the car, women and children raking leaves, a postal truck stopped at a corner mailbox. He sighs, lets his eyes glaze over. What good does it do to fantasize a scenario where you not only get what you want, but it comes risk-free? Life is never as perfect as you can make it in a daydream.

Nana Rena cooks them a big dinner—pot roast with potatoes and carrots and chunks of onions in a salty brown gravy, bread dumplings, peas with butter melted on top. Robin eats even though he isn't hungry, just to make Nana happy. He pretends he isn't listening to Uncle Stan, who is talking about how the country is headed for disaster under Jimmy Carter's "peanut-brained lack of leadership." Clark and Dorothy are strangely silent throughout; their eyes never meet. Robin guesses that whatever they were fighting about has yet to be resolved. After dinner, Ruby hugs Nana until she has to be pried off, and breaks into tears as Nana packs her bags and leaves. Then Clark makes them all wash up and get in the car.

The hospital is calm this evening. Dorothy leads the way, waving at the reception desk as she passes. Robin holds Ruby's hand as they walk down the corridor. She is silent, wide-eyed. It's her first time seeing Jackson, and he's worried that she'll freak out. Sweat coats their palms. Ruby holds a little bunch of hothouse carnations in her free hand. Dorothy grabs on to Clark's arm, but to Robin it reads as though *she* is trying to steady *him*. Clark's footsteps have a stumbly, exhausted quality.

Jackson looks the same as the last time as far as Robin can tell. Maybe a little less injured—as if the hospital staff has been doing a good job making him appear healthy, though not any more alive. It would be hard for Jackson to look alive in this condition, because Jackson alive is Jackson wild and moving and talking and driving you crazy. Anything short of that is abnormal.

A nurse is at Jackson's bedside. She turns and smiles tenderly at them as they enter. "He's being a very good boy," she says.

"Yes, well, the reports aren't getting any *worse,*" Dorothy responds dryly. The nurse's smile freezes, and the muscles in her face go tight as if she's trying to stay sympathetic despite Dorothy's bluntness. At times like this, Robin is so glad for his mother's ability to take the upper hand through simple disapproval. The hospital is supposed to be healing Jackson, not turning him into a well-scrubbed "good boy."

Clark crouches down next to Ruby. "Why don't you say something to him? I'm sure he'll hear it."

Ruby steps to the bedside and speaks in a strong voice, as if she's reciting from a podium. "I've been sleeping in your bed, Jackson. I hope you don't mind. I pray for you all the time. Nana does, too. I bet the angels are working on getting you better right now." Ruby speaks with an urgency none of them are used to.

"That's good," Clark says, laying his hand on her shoulder.

"I'm not done."

"OK, but not too much more, dear," Dorothy says.

Clark shoots Dorothy a scowl. "Leave her be."

Ruby lays the flowers on the bed. Her hands now free, she lays them on Jackson's stomach and prays. "Jesus, Sister Margarita said you loved the little children, so please make my brother better."

"Ruby, don't touch him, honey. You never know," Dorothy says.

Jackson's eyes are open but unresponsive. Robin can't remember if they had been shut last time. Would the nurse have opened them for some reason?

Ruby begins to sing "Jesus Loves Me," bowing her head solemnly. Robin feels spooked, and Dorothy's face is registering something close to shock.

Ruby raises her head when she is done, looking pleased with herself. "Sister Margarita sang that one at morning mass yesterday especially for Jackson."

"Very nice, Ruby," Dorothy says. Her voice reveals discomfort—they can all hear it.

"Mom," Ruby says, stung, "I'm serious."

"I know you are, dear, but I'm still getting used to your transformation. Your grandmother has made you so . . . devout."

Clark interrupts, "Ruby, this is wonderful. It's just what Jackson needs. We *all* need a little help during these times."

"I didn't say it wasn't wonderful," Dorothy says, the pitch of her voice rising.

"Dottie, just stay calm," Clark snaps back.

Robin moves closer to the bed, wishing he could just turn off his parents' squabbling, all the horrible tension that has surfaced. He struggles to say something, but the rising and falling of Jackson's chest and the bandages around his head and the glaze of his eyes leave him speechless. The force of what's happened to Jackson seems so strong and mysterious and menacing that he can't believe he has been thinking about so many other things over the past few days. He thinks about how he would feel if it was Scott in this bed right here, and *that* makes him want to cry—which makes him feel even worse than before. Worse about himself: the new, secret self none of them can see. He wonders if Jackson is in some psychic state, if he's really floating above the room and able to monitor their thoughts. He thinks, *Jackson, if you can read my mind, give me some signal, like an extra beep on that heartbeat machine.*

But nothing happens. Jackson isn't floating around like a coma spirit. He's a fragile mass of pale flesh tucked under a blanket, bony and small. Robin is sure that this is not going as well as the doctors want them to think. They say he's getting better, *stabilizing,* but Robin doesn't believe it. This world doesn't let everything turn out right. He thinks of all the books and movies where terrible things happen so that people can learn their lessons. But what good do those lessons do? Even in his favorite film, *West Side Story*—by the end, everyone has learned not to hate each other, but there's still a dead body in the middle of the screen.

During the week that follows, everyone falls into a hushed routine. Clark and Dorothy travel back and forth to the hospital. With Nana back in Massachusetts, Stan isn't around as much, and the house quiets down. Robin's mother and Mrs. Spicer take turns driving to school, while an awkward tension floats between him and Victoria. In gym, Scott hardly says a word to him, and the silence is unbearable, but they're never alone long enough for Robin to try to get him talking. A couple of days toward the end of the week, Scott doesn't show up at all. Robin looks up Scott's number in the phone book, but when he calls, Mr. Schatz answers gruffly and Robin hangs up before saying anything.

He's still sleeping in Ruby's room. She insists on occupying Jackson's bed, and he won't go back to his own bed as long as she is in there. She's become creepy, like a little witch cooking up spells. She buys a Miraculous Medal on a fake silver chain from Woolworth's and wears it around her neck. She's arranged all of Jackson's things into an altar on his dresser—his baseball mitt, his school books, his souvenir mug from their trip to Cape Cod—and keeps votive candles burning without end.

On Friday night, while everyone else is downstairs, Robin goes into his parents' bedroom and calls Victoria's number. A male voice answers.

"Todd?" Robin says, his voice cracking.

"No, this is his father." Before Robin can say anything else, Mr. Spicer is calling, "Todd, it's for you. One of your girlfriends."

Robin feels his throat go dry. Todd picks up the phone and says, "Debbie?"

Robin deepens his voice. "It's Robin."

"Robin?" Todd pauses and laughs. "He said it was—"

"I was calling for Victoria and he didn't even let me finish."

"That's pretty fucking funny," Todd says. "He thought you were my *girlfriend."* He sweetens his voice into a seductive whisper, "Hey, baby, whatcha doing this Saturday?" Robin titters nervously. "What's a-matter? Are you shy?"

Robin toys with the idea of playing along with this, but his voice cracks again when he tries to speak. "I'm not doing anything this Saturday."

"Well, just so happens there's a party going on," Todd whispers. "I was just thinking too bad I don't have anyone to go with."

Robin twirls the phone cord around his wrist. When he looks to the mirror over his mother's dresser, he has a flash of himself as a Hollywood actress, enshrined in her satiny *boudoir,* the camera tracking in for a close-up as she struggles to resist the dubious attention of a suitor. He lifts one of his mother's earrings—a jangly bit of costume jewelry— to the side of his face, and he silently mouths the words, *All right, if you insist.*

"You listening to me?"

Robin slaps the earring onto the dresser, fed up with this whole thing. "Yeah, I'm listening," he says, his voice petulant. "You're so funny I forgot to laugh."

"Seriously. You want to come?" The exaggerated gigolo voice is gone, replaced with his regular smooth talk, which Robin finds only slightly less gut churning. "You could come. It's at Maggio's. It's an open house, so anyone can come."

"I can't go to a party like that. I'm not part of that crowd." He waits for a reply, but now Todd is silent. Robin would kill to be able to read Todd's mind. "What would I say to my parents? They'll never let me go."

"I'll get you high. You want to get high, don't you?"

Somewhere, a voice is warning him that this is all a humiliating setup, but he takes a step forward anyway, saying, "I got high last week for the first time since we went to the drive-in."

"See? So it's time to do it again. *High* time, ha ha."

Robin slides to the floor, curling into a corner at the side of his mother's dressing table. He whispers, "Is this a joke?"

"If you don't want to, forget it. Just thought it would be fun. You know, with your brother all messed up, I just thought you'd want to get wasted, forget your troubles. But if you're not into it, I'll just get Victoria."

"No!" Robin says too strongly. "I mean, I don't really have to talk to her about anything important anyway." Was he imagining that Todd was being cruel when he was really just being sympathetic?

"I bet you'd be pretty funny on grass," Todd says warmly.

"It just made me talk a lot. Is that supposed to happen when you get high? I mean, I was a real blabbermouth."

"Really? What'd you talk about?"

"Just stuff."

"Who'd you talk to?"

He starts to say Scott's name, then remembers the looks that passed between Scott and Todd in the cafeteria. "Just some kid from school."

"Anyone I'd know?"

"No, just some kid in my gym class."

"I know some kids in your grade."

"If I go to this party," Robin says, changing the subject before Todd pushes it too far, "maybe I should just go over to your house and tell my parents I'm studying with Victoria."

"Just play it cool. Right, Robin?"

"Yeah, sure. Of course."

"This will be a pisser."

Robin hangs up without talking to Victoria. Maybe Todd is just being friendly. Maybe Robin's just gotten old enough for Todd to take him seriously. Maybe this is just natural: now that he's in high school he gets to go to high school parties. He looks at himself in the mirror, searching his face, his body, for some clue. What does Todd see when he looks at him?

He locks himself in the bathroom and pulls down his pants. His dick is hard. He spits on it, pumps it frantically with his eyes shut tight, his mind racing through a thousand jump cuts of Todd Spicer doing every sexy thing he can imagine: kissing him all over, licking his skin, lying on top of him, their boners pressed together like Scott showed him. He lets his fingers roam down to his balls, explores the shape of them, different pressures and frictions. Pushing on the ridge beneath his balls sends a warm current in either direction. His fingers travel back to his asshole. He spits into his hand, like Scott did, and pokes around down there until his middle finger slides in through the puckered entrance. In the strange, spongy warmth of it, he presses upward until he finds a spot that rockets an electric charge from the base of his dick to the base of his throat. It's like he's being hoisted into the air or pulled up a roller coaster's slope or driven into the wide blue sky by John Travolta at the end of *Grease*. His limbs rattle.

In the unexpected frenzy, he knocks his mother's hairspray off the vanity and it clanks loudly on the tiled floor. He reaches for the faucet, for a rush of water to cover up the clamor. In just a few seconds, he is on his tiptoes, gasping for air, aiming into the sink. The sensation is so strong he clamps shut his lips to stifle a howl.

His come sticks to the porcelain like rubber cement—he scrubs the streaks with his fingertips to wash it away, ashamed and overwhelmed by the ecstatic urges inside of him.

Chapter Eight

The big surprise is that the party is so tightly compressed, a hundred people bunched up like in a crowded theater lobby. Robin had imagined room to stroll, small gatherings of conversation, a makeshift dance floor in the living room. Instead, Maggio's house rumbles with rock music and noisy chatter and the chanting of drinking games. Most of the faces are familiar from the halls at school, but they're not people he ever talks to, and as he enters, he gets questioning stares thrown his way, the kind that remind him that there's a big difference between seventeen and thirteen, seniors and freshmen.

This house is bigger than his but not so different in its layout—the staircase goes right up from the front hallway, the living room opens into the dining room and the kitchen beyond. There are kids in the kitchen, up the stairs, on the couches. A group at the dining room table is bouncing a quarter into an empty glass. When the quarter misses, someone drinks. Everyone is very enthusiastic about this. Robin gets that the point is to do a lot of everything: talking, drinking, smoking. Making out, too. They're going at it everywhere. A boy on the couch has his hand inside a girl's shirt; both of them have closed their eyes. I'd close my eyes, too, Robin thinks, if I was doing *that* in the middle of this room.

He lets Todd clear a path, following him closely before the space fills in again. There's no other way to move around without risking shoving someone, pissing off an upperclassman. He's surprised how few people Todd talks to. There are nods here and there, but he doesn't stop for anyone. Todd slinks through the crowd as if leading them somewhere, though Robin can't figure out where that might be. Finally they get to the bathroom, where a metal keg rests in a tub filled with ice. It looks like something that washed ashore from a shipwreck—dented, scratched along its curved surface, the pump at the top like a periscope. Todd fills two plastic cups for them and then finds an empty section of the hallway where the idea, apparently, is to stand and lean.

"Pretty big scene," Todd says.

"Yeah," Robin agrees, sipping the beer. He doesn't like the taste but takes a big gulp anyway, then coughs a little on the foam.

"I don't usually deal with this party scene too much," Todd says. "I like to party, but I don't like *parties*, you know?"

"Sure," Robin says, trying to sort that out.

"I might not stay too long," Todd says, scanning the room through narrowed eyes.

Robin imitates Todd's stance—one foot on the wall behind him, his weight on the other leg. When he was getting ready for the party, Robin settled his panic about what to wear by trying to dress like Todd: he put on his most faded, worn blue jeans and a dark blue T-shirt with a New England Patriots logo ironed on the front—a shirt that Larry left at his house. The only problem is his jacket; he doesn't own a denim jacket like Todd's, and the closest thing he came up with was an old beige windbreaker that he's left unzipped because it's too tight in the shoulders. His mother frowned as he left the house, saying, "You look like you work in a gas station." She seemed to have believed his staying-up-late-at-Victoria's story, though he won't be sure until he gets home. He's trying to not think about his parents now, trying to not even care.

Todd pulls out two Marlboros. He lights his own and then lifts the flame to Robin's, locking eyes for a moment across the disposable lighter, a moment Robin immediately suffuses with significance and desire. It doesn't last, though; before he can settle on the secret meaning stored within the flick of Todd's Bic, Ethan is suddenly there, growling, *"Spicer!"* and landing a punch on Todd's shoulder. "Man, you said you'd be a no-show!"

Todd looks surprised. "I thought *you* weren't coming. What happened to your big night with what's-her-name?"

"Fuck her, man. She's a stuck-up twat. But we knew that, right?" He play punches Todd in the stomach again. Robin watches attentively, wondering if Ethan remembers him. Another guy named Tully joins them. He's short and stocky, smiling drunkenly, the long bangs of his messy hair covering half his face. He and Ethan talk quickly back and forth about what's-her-name, coming up with a stream of contradictory insults: slut and prude, bitch and tease. Robin strains to keep an agreeable expression on his face, though this is exactly the kind of boy talk that drives him crazy. He's having a hard time believing that either one of them has really been with a girl at all. Todd is still scanning the party, cool as ever, leaving Robin to wonder exactly what Todd is doing with these losers.

Ethan asks, "Who'd you come with, man?"

Todd tilts his head toward Robin. "I'm letting neighbor boy tag along," he says offhandedly. Ethan and Tully look blankly at him, finally registering his presence.

"I'm probably the only freshman here," Robin says.

"Which means you're candidate number one for getting fucked up and blowing chunks!" Ethan sends a fake punch his way. Robin flinches.

Todd smiles as if the idea pleases him. "Can't get him too shitfaced. We don't want to be on cleanup duty, you know?"

"Listen, let's get to my car and spark up. I'm not wasting it on this crowd."

"Definitely," Todd says.

Robin tries to keep up with the three older guys as they step back into the crowd, but quickly understands that this kind of navigating takes practice. A menacing guitar solo is blaring from a pair of enormous wood-paneled speakers. He feels his enthusiasm dropping with every step, hates the way Todd has gone from being his protector to acting like a pathetic follower trapped by his friends. He thinks he might just sneak out the back door and go home.

In the middle of the living room he is blocked by a couple of girls swaying to the music with their cigarettes held aloft. Behind them Robin sees a familiar face: Scott.

Scott doesn't see him. Scott's eyes are on Todd, whom he seems to be pursuing. Robin calls out Scott's name to no avail. He lunges past the swaying-cigarette girls, only to be cut off again.

"Are you Tracy's brother?"

He looks up at a girl with frizzy brown hair and a T-shirt reading *Virgin.* "No," he says, trying to move past.

"Oh, I thought you were Tracy's brother. She's got this younger brother who always parties with her." Her voice is unnaturally high-pitched.

"No, I'm nobody's younger brother," he says.

She stares blankly for a moment and then giggles. "That's so *funny.*"

He glances over her shoulder. Todd and his buddies are out the door, with Scott closing the gap a couple of paces behind. Robin sucks a mouthful from his plastic cup and leans against the wall, suddenly needing to put distance between himself and whatever confrontation might happen between Todd and Scott outside.

The self-proclaimed virgin is smiling at him over the lip of her beer. Her eyes and her eyeshadow are both green, and red rouge dots her cheekbones. She might be pretty, he thinks, if she toned down the makeup. She is waiting for him to say something else.

"I have a younger brother of my own," he says.

"I hope he isn't here!" she squeals.

"No. He's in the hospital."

"Really?" She frowns. "That's a depressing thing to say."

"I can't help it," Robin says, hoping she'll stop talking to him. "He's really messed up."

"Like does he have leukemia or something?"

"No."

"Good, because there's a lot of that going around. I keep hearing about these kids with leukemia. I mean, like two years ago I never even heard of leukemia. Now there's always a new kid with leukemia or something." Her voice pitches higher.

"Maybe it's because of pollution," he says without much energy. He inches to the side, hoping she'll get the hint.

"What do you mean?"

"Air pollution, water pollution. You know, *pollution*." He finishes off his cup with a gulp, holding the excess beer in his mouth until he can fit it all down his throat. The alcohol is a warm flood, vaporizing into his skull.

"I bet you're right, like we've just totally poisoned everything and now it's affecting little kids," she says. She reaches out and surprises him by wiping suds from his lower lip with her wrist. Powdery perfume invades his nostrils.

"Could be," he says. He takes a step forward, bumps into someone, hastily adjusts himself against the wall.

"That's so sad," the girl whines. "I have to stop talking about this or I could cry." She leans against the wall next to him and brushes her hand against his. "Too bad you're so young," she says quietly.

"I'm thirteen," he says.

"I went out with a freshman last month," she says. She rolls her head toward him and lowers her eyes.

Is this how it happens with girls? he hears himself thinking. *I could go for it—that would show everyone.* But there's no conviction to the thought, only a renewed urge to flee. He announces, "I have to find my friends outside. Wait here." Before she can respond, he pushes past her and forces his way toward the front door.

Todd and Scott are standing next to each other, forming a circle with Ethan and Tully near the hood of Todd's Camaro. A joint moves from one to the other. Robin crushes his empty cup in his hand and drops it on the lawn. He hears Scott talking rapid-fire as he gets closer.

"So, then I'm like, no way, Dad, I'm not doing this shit anymore. I fucking painted the garage last month, no way I'm painting the house. You know what a drag my old man is, he just doesn't quit. You know what I'm saying? Todd, remember that time he chased me down the fucking block just to beat my ass? Remember?"

Todd takes a long puff. "No." He doesn't look at Scott, and Robin sees on the faces of the older guys that Scott is talking too much, too frantically.

"Hey, guys," Robin says.

Scott spins around, his mouth agape.

"Robin, the boy blunder!" Ethan bellows. He slaps him on the back. "Pass the doob to junior, man."

"Thought we lost you," Todd says, patting him on the shoulder.

Robin takes the joint. "Hi, Scott," he says before inhaling.

Scott turns his stunned face away from Robin and resumes talking to Todd. "I'm like definitely not hanging out there for more than a year, you know? 'Cause like you told me that time, once I'm sixteen I can file a petition of the court or whatever? Remember, Todd, you told me that."

"Chill out, Scott," Todd quietly orders. He takes the joint from Robin again. "You guys know each other?"

Robin answers first. "Yeah."

Scott's face is some mix of confusion and contempt. "Sure," he says without much emphasis. Robin holds Scott's glance and then looks away. Scott hops up on the hood of the car and crosses his arms.

"We got the two freshman at the party in this crowd, man," Ethan says. "Not gonna make *us* look very cool."

"Not like you'd win some cool contest anyway," Todd says to Ethan.

"Aw, fuck you, Spicer. Tully, man, you notice Spicer is always hanging around with these little dweebs?"

"Maybe I'm just sick of my old friends," Todd says.

Tully's deep voice wanders out from behind his hair, "Give me that joint, Spicer. You're bogarting."

Ethan says, "You're one fucked-up stoner, Spicer—you know that?"

"Takes one to know one," Robin says to Ethan, the pot making him suddenly nervy.

Ethan flips him the finger. "Who asked you anyway, fag?"

Todd reaches out and shoves Ethan hard. "You're bugging me, man. You're *rude.*"

Robin backs away as Todd and Ethan glare at each other. Scott watches him intently, almost angrily. Scott's figured out Robin came here with Todd—Robin can see it in Scott's piercing glare.

Scott slides off the hood. "I'm going back inside," he says. "You want to come, Todd?"

"What for?"

Robin suddenly wants to get away from Todd and his crowd, wants to offer some explanation to Scott, though he doesn't know what that might be. "I'll come with you," he says to Scott.

Now it's Todd scowling at him.

"I have to go to the bathroom," Robin says, hoping the lie will be good enough for Todd.

"Maybe you can sniff out some pussy in there," Todd sneers.

Robin runs to catch up with Scott, who doesn't look back at him. When they get into the house, Scott says, "The bathroom is upstairs," and slips into the crowd before Robin can say anything.

The pot on top of the beer has hit hard. Robin wanders around for an hour, hoping to latch on to someone. Scott hasn't reappeared, and he's only seen Todd for a moment, passing through a doorway, whispering something to an obviously drunk girl. He's heard the expression "make-out party" before, but only now does he get the picture. At this point in the evening, almost no one remains uncoupled. Bodies drape across the furniture and press against the walls, heads moving feverishly, hands groping. The nonstop guitar rock that fills the air casts a hallucinatory pallor, numbing his discomfort, creating the illusion that he is floating, an invisible observer.

He squeezes himself onto the end of a couch, trying to ignore the entangled petting going on next to him. A hand falls on his arm; he expects Scott or Todd, but it's the girl in the Virgin T-shirt, several shades more wasted than before. "Hi!" she exclaims. "Where did you go?"

"I got stoned," he says.

She clasps his arm and moves her face close to his. "You blew me off," she whines.

As he is trying to remember what he had said to her, she puts her arm around his neck and pulls their faces together. Her lips mash his. His first thought: *I don't know how to do this.* It takes him a few startled moments to comprehend that, mechanically speaking, this is the same thing as kissing Scott, which he managed OK. He watches the girl, her eyes closed, her face a blur at the end of his nose; he looks past her ear to another squirming twosome—the girl's hands are planted on the guy's ass, which looks really sexy. Robin remembers Todd telling him to go get some pussy and decides this is his chance. He prods his tongue into her mouth and wiggles it around.

The kissing seems pointless pretty quickly—too hurried to be enjoyable and not leading anywhere. From some back corner of his mind he starts to form an argument about the stupidity of the whole thing: making out with this girl whose name he doesn't even know, when he might still be able to find Scott, whom he would really like to be kissing.

Robin pushes back from her, meeting her startled eyes. "I can't do this. I have too much on my mind."

"Like what?" She looks crestfallen.

He scrambles for an excuse. "I told you, my brother's in the hospital."

"You can't cure him tonight!"

He hops off the couch, and she stands up next to him, tucking in her shirt. He feels bad about this encounter—wishing she were Scott, using Jackson as an excuse to dump her—and he wants to get away. "You're really nice, but I have to go." He pecks her lips, hoping this is an appropriate sendoff.

She circles her arm around him, stumbles against his chest. "You're so cute," she purrs.

He pries her off. "I really have to go."

"Fucking freshmen," she mutters as he walks away.

He makes his way through the kitchen, bumping into people all the way. "Watch it," someone says, and when he doesn't look up, a hand shoots out and blocks his path. A guy in a varsity jacket with one arm around his girlfriend is glaring at him. "You just spilled my fucking beer."

"Sorry."

"You better be fucking sorry."

Robin takes a step backward. "I'm just buzzed, that's all. I didn't mean to."

"It's on your jacket," the girlfriend says, pointing to a darkening stain on the sleeve.

Robin reads the embroidered name over the chest pocket: Maggio. *Oh, great. It's his party. I'm so fucking lame.* He looks toward the hall, plotting an escape, when Todd's face appears in the doorway. Robin calls out his name.

"What's up?"

The guy narrows his eyes at Todd. "This little wimp just totaled my beer."

"Lay off, Maggio," Todd says. "I'll take care of it."

"Fuck you, Spicer. You gonna clean my jacket?"

"Take a pill, man," Todd says, pulling Robin away. When they get out the back door, Todd mutters, "Fucking jock."

"Thanks," Robin says. "I'm so klutzy sometimes."

Todd pats him on the head, squeezes fingers against his skull. "You're wasted, Girly Underwear."

The old insult, so soon after escaping Maggio's wrath, wrenches Robin from his momentary gratitude. He crosses his arms and turns away.

"What's your problem?" Todd challenges.

"I thought you weren't gonna call me that."

"Just a joke." A car curves from the street into the driveway, drenching them in yellow light. Todd spins away from it, throwing himself into silhouette. "I just saved your ass. Don't get on my case."

Robin shields his eyes, trying to read Todd's face. "I just hate it when people call me names." He exaggerates the pout he feels himself sinking into. "Especially my friends."

Todd grabs his arm again and pulls him farther into the backyard. "You want to go for a walk?" he says, his voice more hushed, more like his voice on the phone when he invited him here.

Robin agrees, letting himself be pulled along a few steps, liking the way Todd is paying attention to him again, feeling special. And then he thinks about Scott, wonders if this is what it was like when he was Todd's friend, which makes him stop guiltily in his tracks. "Wait. I never said good-bye to Scott."

Todd scowls. "He's passed out upstairs. He's a total beer lightweight."

"I should check if he's OK."

Todd grabs him by the shoulders and shakes him roughly. "Forget about Scott-fucking-Schatz, OK? He's a fucking pain in the ass, and a liar, too."

"OK, sorry," he says meekly, a little afraid of the force of Todd's grip.

Todd leads him through an opening in the fence at the back of the Maggios' property. They run across another yard while a dog barks from inside, winding up on a street that leads down to a dark golf course at the end, the Valley Ridge Country Club. They struggle drunkenly over the fence. A few ghostly lights spaced far apart throw the rolling green hills into spooky, shadowy patterns. He shivers in the cold and keeps pace with Todd.

"I've never been here before."

"My parents belong," Todd says. "They wanted me to caddie here, but I said *no fucking way.*"

When they get to a little slope over a pond, Todd drops to the ground. He lies on his back and stretches out. Robin watches the light catch the pale of his stomach as his jacket and shirt tug up, revealing, as far as he can tell, that Todd is once again without underwear. He wishes he'd remembered to not wear any tonight—that would have been perfect.

"Why don't you like him?" Robin asks, trying not to stare at Todd's flesh.

"Who?"

"Scott."

Todd shakes his head as if confronting an irresolvable problem—though Robin can't tell if the problem is Scott or the fact that Robin keeps talking about him. "He just drives me crazy, that's all."

"But you guys used to be friends. I *know* about that."

"Yeah, who told you?"

"Victoria."

"Don't listen to everything you hear, Robin. It's not usually the true story, you know?"

"So you weren't friends?"

"Forget about it."

"Me and him were going to be friends," Robin says, lying down next to Todd. He rests his face against the damp grass, which actually feels warmer than the air; lying down flat seems to reduce the intoxication, too. Crickets are chirping loudly. When he rolls over on his back, the black sky is flecked with stars.

"What about that girl you were with?" Robin asks.

"Man, you got a lot of questions." Todd grabs a clump of grass and throws it at him.

"I told you, when I get high I can't shut up." He giggles nervously. "Do you have a girlfriend?"

"No one serious. I mess around a lot."

"Why not? Don't you want a girlfriend?"

"Girls are a hassle."

"But everyone wants a girlfriend."

"No, everyone wants to fuck around. It's not the same thing." Todd stands up. "*You* don't have a fucking girlfriend, freshman."

Robin feels instantly defensive. "For your information, I was just making out with a girl. That girl in the Virgin T-shirt."

Todd shrugs as if he can't place her. "Where were you doing it? Did anyone see you?"

"Probably. We were on the couch. I mean, I was. She was next to the couch."

Todd leans down toward him, smiling in some combination of disbelief and titillation. "How far did you get?"

"I don't know."

"I'm gonna find out her name and fix you up with her," Todd says. "We'll get you hooked up."

"I don't even like her." Every time he speaks to Todd, he feels outsmarted, as if he can't possibly keep this conversation from somehow trapping him. He's never talked for so long with Todd, alone like this. Robin sits up and leans his head on his knees. The green ripples out in front of him like a low-pile carpet, bleeding in and out of focus.

In the distance, a faint bass line from the party is thumping; closer to them, night creatures buzz. Robin looks at Todd, who is studying him, his face unreadable. Then, in a sudden gesture, Todd pulls off his jacket and tugs his shirt over his head. A soft line of hair brushes across the shallow muscles in his chest. Robin watches in disbelief as Todd leans down and pulls off his shoes, and then starts unfastening his jeans.

"Let's go," he says, pointing toward the dark pond below them. "This'll be a total goof." He pulls off his pants, his dick bouncing as he dashes naked down the slope. Robin—eyes open in surprise—jumps to his feet as Todd bellyflops into the still water, then rises a moment later, cursing and rubbing his shoulder. "Shit! I forgot it's only like a foot deep. You gotta come in slowly."

"I'm not going in there!" Robin is immediately getting hard just watching this—he can't take his clothes off now; he doesn't want Todd to *see*.

"Get in here, Girly Underwear, or I'm throwing you in, clothes and all." Todd rises up, his naked body streaked with slime dragged up from underneath, and takes a few steps forward, arms extended like the monster in *Creature from the Black Lagoon.* His dick dangles out from the shadow of his groin.

"OK, OK, give me a minute." Robin fumbles with the zipper on his jacket. He feels the shakes taking over his body, same as when he was with Scott at The Bird. He tries to concentrate on something other than Todd's body—he thinks about that girl in the Virgin shirt, her garish makeup, her whiny voice—but it doesn't help. He's almost completely stiff. He turns around and lowers his pants, then his underwear. His dick springs free. Behind him the splashing has stopped.

"Close your eyes." Robin spins around, hands over his crotch, and charges down the slope. As he nears the water, he loses his footing and skids, flapping his arms to right himself. Then he's down, landing hard on his ass, sliding into the pond. The silty muck oozes up through his legs, around his balls. "Ow!"

Todd is crouched in front of him, looking between Robin's legs, wearing a grin as wide as his face—and before Robin can cover himself up again, Todd is chopping his arms into the pond, sending water in every direction. Robin strikes back, giggling as he tries to keep up, slapping and spitting dirty water though he can't really see his target; he gives it his best until it's clear he can't win. In the postfight stillness, Todd rises up again, looming above him as if he wants to be studied and appreciated—or so it seems to Robin, who thinks of statues in art books, naked men frozen in time. Todd is dripping from head to toe, dark dribbles of pond scum across his body, down around his half-hard, bobbing dick, around his balls—Robin is fascinated by his balls, which are really different than his own: they swing like small eggs suspended in a sac, stretching the skin down with them.

"You know what this reminds me of?" Todd asks, dropping back down into the water with a splash.

"What?" Robin asks, aware of how long he let his stare linger.

"*Zabriskie Point.* You ever seen that movie?"

"No."

"It's fucking mind blowing. It was playing at the midnight movie in Ridgewood a few years ago. It was rated R but I snuck in. There's this guy who kills a cop during a student riot. It's during the '60s, you know?"

"Yeah."

"And he steals this plane and flies over the desert and meets this girl." Todd flips onto his stomach. He's propped up on his elbows, his face near Robin's hip, his ass rising above the water like a flotation device. Robin positions his leg so Todd can't see his erection cutting up through the water.

"'Cause there's this scene, see, when him and this girl are in the desert and they're naked and having a fight with all this sand, throwing it at each other and stuff. So I was thinking about how, you know, having a waterfight and throwing sand—it's kind of the same thing."

Robin just stares, unable to respond, hoping Todd just keeps talking. The shakes are threatening to begin again. He rubs his arms along his shoulders to bring some warmth to his skin.

"This guy is really cool, you know?" Todd says. "Mark Frechette is the actor's name. I mean, if I could be any guy in the whole world I'd be this guy. He just does whatever he wants. I mean, he gets killed at the end, but mostly he just does what he wants. He's really studly, too, you know?"

Robin holds himself still, afraid to even nod because that would mean he was admitting he thought that a guy was studly, that he looked at guys that way. Even though Todd just said it, it could be a trick, because even sitting naked together in this water, even after Todd stood in front of him practically demanding to be looked at, it's too much to believe— Todd thinking about a guy *that way*. Robin asks in a nervous burst, "So what happens in the movie? After the sandfight?"

"They *do* it," Todd says. He pushes Robin flat on his back, then crawls toward him, grabbing one of his knees in each hand, pushing them apart. He slides his hands down Robin's legs and around to his ass, lifting him out of his muddy seat, raising his dick into the night air. Robin gasps, falling back on his hands for balance. Grains of silt rub between Todd's hands and his own thighs. Todd says, almost casually, as if he isn't even touching him, as if Robin's boner isn't sticking up in his face, "They just roll all over each other, and then all of a sudden there's like a hundred people in the desert, all these guys and girls, and some of them are in little orgy scenes, two guys on a girl or two girls with a guy, and they're all making it in the sand." He drops his head down between Robin's thighs. "Like if I was Mark Frechette, and you were that girl, Darla or whatever her name was, this is what we'd be doing in the desert. In that movie." His lips close in around Robin's dick. Robin feels the rush of it all the way up through him, all the way to his chattering teeth and down his arms to his wobbly wrists. The saliva mixing with pond water in Todd's mouth is like liquid polyester, like a smooth shirt being rubbed all over him. He gasps as Todd pulls him deeper into his throat; he can't believe that Todd is doing this, that his dick is *inside* Todd.

Todd lifts his head, mumbles instructions Robin can't quite make out, and pushes him out of the pond, up the slope. Todd's face is smudged with mud. His eyes are glazed over, eager, oblivious to anything else—it reminds Robin of his own face in the bathroom mirror while he's jerking off.

For a while, getting his dick sucked is more pleasurable than anything he's ever felt: lush, concentrated, far more intense than what he's done to himself. It feels like magic that Todd can do this—how could a tongue or lips turn his whole body inside out? He feels teeth, too, which almost hurts, but not really, it feels better than that, the way getting tickled is both fun and not fun at the same time. Momentum builds inside of him and then subsides again, or maybe he makes it stop so that he doesn't shoot in Todd's mouth. He can't really tell what he's doing versus what's being done to him, and after a while this not knowing turns his pleasure into anxiety, and he's not feeling anything. He's just looking around, watching out to see if anyone else is about to come stumbling down the golf course.

"Todd?" he whispers. "Wait a minute."

Todd's face is spaced out, trancey. Saliva drips from his lips. "What?"

"Someone might see."

"Shit." He climbs up on his knees, takes a dazed look around, then spits on his dick and starts pumping. He slips back into the trance, staring at Robin's dick. "You should see that movie."

Watching Todd like this, totally focused on making himself come, Robin drifts back into the thrill of it. Todd looks sexier than anyone he's ever seen. He looks *studly*. Instinctively, Robin reaches out, wanting to touch him.

Todd backs away. "No, don't." He puts his other hand under his balls and rubs. This a completely new Todd, an animal Todd; the usual Todd is disappearing into this pleasure more deeply with every blurred stroke—after a while he's not even looking at Robin. He's *gone*. He keeps at it until the motions slow and his body seizes up in a series of grunts and his dick fires out three stringy squirts that land soundlessly on Robin's leg.

"In two years I'm getting out of here. I'm going on the road," Todd says, his voice slurred with wasted exhaustion. They are lying on the grass, watching a green-white cloud blanket an incomplete moon.

Robin has gotten fully dressed but Todd is only in his jeans and T-shirt, his feet still bare. Robin had expected Todd to run away as soon as he came, the way Scott did, but here they are, talking.

"Where are you gonna go?" Robin asks, still jittery from the encounter. He hasn't come and his hard-on is pulsing in his pants. He shivers from the cold but now he doesn't mind it. He can't take his eyes off Todd. A Bee Gees song from *Saturday Night Fever* is stuck in his head: *How deep is your love? I really need to learn.*

"All over this country. Colorado. It's beautiful there. The Rocky Mountains are outstanding. And I'm going to New Mexico and Arizona and to Death Valley."

"I went to the Grand Canyon when I was little," Robin says encouragingly.

"The Grand Canyon is for tourists. I'm going to the cool places, with no families on vacations. There's a lot of room out there. You can just do what you want to do. And I'm going to California, too, the northern part. There's *fields* of pot growing there. I'm gonna set myself up with a cabin in the woods, and no one is gonna be on my case."

"I never thought about going to any of those places," Robin says, suddenly wondering why not. Todd's world is unlimited, he thinks. Todd has vision.

"What, are you going to spend your life in New Fucking Jersey?"

"No. I want to move to New York."

"New York sucks. Eight million people? No fucking way. Plus, it's way too close to home."

"It's where all the people go who appreciate art and culture."

Todd grunts, unimpressed. He sits up and pats the ground to find his socks.

"One day I'm going to have a big apartment with a view all the way down to the Statue of Liberty, and a good job. Like I'll work in a museum or something."

"Work in a museum? I never heard anyone say that before: *work in a museum.*"

"I want to move to the Village. That's where all the artists are."

Todd stops in midgesture, leaving a sock dangling off the end of his foot like something suddenly withered. *"Artists?"* he spits out. "You mean *homos.*"

Robin braces against the word. "No, I mean—"

"Those people are sick, man. They're a bunch of very messed-up people." His voice grows more agitated. "Perverts and sex maniacs and child molesters and guys who think they're really girls and big ugly women who look like men and stuff. Why would you want to go there?"

Robin looks down at the ground, feeling attacked. "I've never seen any perverts and sex maniacs."

"Oh, come on? You've never driven down the West Side Highway and seen those transvestite hookers by the underpass?"

"You're making it sound worse than it is," Robin protests. "Don't you think?"

"No, I *don't* think." Todd slams his sneaker into the grass. "Those people are nothing like you. They're *sick.*" He slams his sneaker again. "They parade around wearing dresses and leather and all that—I *saw* one of those parades once in the Village. I know what I'm talking about. You're the one who's full of it." One more slam and then he throws his sneaker across the green.

Robin scowls at him, speechless, not sure if he should argue or change the subject. He feels accused, but he's not sure if Todd's right or wrong.

Todd points his finger at Robin, which reminds him of Uncle Stan ranting that he was a mama's boy. "If you wanna go live there, fine with me. I don't give a fuck."

Robin backs away defensively. "You're the one talking about sex movies with orgies."

"That's different. Mark Frechette wasn't a pervert; he was a free-spirit. He was out on the road."

Their eyes lock on each other's, and this time Robin doesn't look away. Robin is thinking about the sex that just happened between them; the whole thing replays itself again in fast motion. Todd was sucking his dick, right here, just a few minutes ago. Now Todd's trying to use the Force on him, to hypnotize him into forgetting. Robin looks away because he doesn't want to forget. He wants to say something about it, but he doesn't get the chance because Todd is suddenly on his feet, striding off after his sneaker, shouting, "I'm getting outta here."

Robin squeezes his hands around his head, trying to compress his thoughts into one good response. This feels just like with Scott, where everything got bad at the end, after the sex part, and he wants to repair it. He catches up with Todd. "I'm sorry. I didn't mean to get you so mad."

"Just forget it, OK? I don't want you to talk about that stuff. It's got nothing to do with you." He rushes angrily through the trees toward the fence. This is another Todd again, neither his usual cool self, nor the person he became while jerking off, but a pissed-off, distressed Todd, unbalanced in a way Robin's never thought him capable. All the way home, Todd drives recklessly, plowing through stop signs and taking corners so fast that Robin has to hold on to the door to keep from landing in his lap. Robin attempts to smooth it over as he clicks open the car door in the Spicers' driveway—"Sorry I got you mad"—but Todd remains silent, almost pouting.

Robin wishes he'd never mentioned New York or the Village. He wishes he could go back to right before then—idling in the cool grass, feeling as if he'd awakened to the place he and Todd were meant to discover together, their private hideaway. He knows—isn't it obvious?—it was his fault the spell had been broken. He should have just kept his mouth shut; he thinks of Jackson saying, "You *ask* for it"; he thinks of Scott saying, "Don't make a big deal about it." Still, he can't shake that image of Todd banging his sneaker against the golf green, flipping out about the *Village,* then stomping away in a rage. That was the most unexpected thing of all, maybe even more unexpected than Todd's mouth on his dick—seeing Todd Spicer completely lose his cool.

Robin takes his seat at the kitchen table in front of a plate of steaming scrambled eggs. Ruby stands at the sink, washing out the last of the pots and pans Clark has used to prepare breakfast. The kitchen is bright with the light of late morning. His mother has put a breezy and plaintive Miles Davis album on the turntable, but the music plays in contrast to her obvious fatigue. She drops herself sluggishly onto a seat at the table, which does not surprise Robin. When he had gotten home from the party, resigned to whatever punishment awaited, his parents were locked in their bedroom arguing strenuously. He wiped grime off himself and brushed his teeth and climbed into Ruby's bed, falling asleep before talking to anyone.

Now his head pounds dully, six chewable orange-flavored aspirin not yet having any effect on the alcohol still sluicing through his bloodstream. *This* is a hangover, he realizes, the *morning after* everyone talks about. He doesn't think he can make himself eat, not only because he feels physically ill but because he's anxiously awaiting an interrogation about why he got home so late, and he's still not sure what made-up story he's going to offer to them.

"Should we say grace?" Ruby asks.

Robin looks over at his mother, who is biting her upper lip, probably trying to keep herself from saying no.

"Sure. Why not?" Clark says cheerfully.

Ruby clasps her hands in front of her and bows her head. "Bless us, oh, Lord, and these Thy gifts we are about to receive through Thy bounty through Christ our Lord. Amen."

"Rub-a-dub-dub, God bless the grub," Robin adds.

"Thank you, *Ruby,*" Clark says. "And, Robin, watch it. That was a little disrespectful."

"Why do you think he said it?" Ruby shoots back.

Robin mutters a halfhearted apology and steps up to the stove to pour himself a cup of coffee.

Dorothy's eyes are on him. "Just decided you needed a little boost, huh?"

Robin sucks in his breath apprehensively. "I've always liked coffee," he says, loading up on milk and sugar.

"It's especially good when you haven't gotten enough sleep," Dorothy retorts, false levity in her voice. "But let's not get into that yet. Let's enjoy this food, shall we?"

He returns to the table, not meeting her eyes, knowing it's only a matter of time before he'll have to answer for last night.

Clark eats hurriedly, forking food into his mouth while still chewing the previous bite. "I wanted to let you two know what's going on," he says with a look at Robin and Ruby.

"About what?" Robin asks.

"About your brother." Clark slurps orange juice. There's an almost antic quality to his speech. "There's some sense from the doctors that Jackson will need to be in the hospital for another month before he'll be well enough to come home."

"That seems far away," Ruby says.

"We should be thankful," Clark says. "Though when he gets home, he's not going to be completely recuperated. He's going to need some time to regain full use of his motor skills."

Clark pauses to think for a moment. Robin senses there is more to this, and he feels dread building up. He looks at his mother, whose face seems very strained.

"The plan is . . ." Clark begins. He spears a piece of bacon on his fork, but it falls off as he lifts it to his mouth. He puts down his fork and wipes his lips. "The plan is to build Jackson his own bedroom. Downstairs. He won't be strong enough, we think, to make it up and down the stairs."

"Build it where?" Robin asks.

"Out from the dining room into the backyard."

Robin looks at Dorothy; the glance she returns reveals to him that she's heard this already, and though she seems unhappy with the idea, Robin can't discern exactly why. His father, on the other hand, is obviously pleased with this plan. "We're going to put a special hospital bed in the room and a treadmill and a couple of other things that he'll need to build his strength back up. Uncle Stan is going to help me find the equipment. He has some leads."

"How are you going to build a room?" Robin asks, remembering the never-finished project of turning the basement into a "family room." They nailed the paneling in but never laid down the floor covering, and once Clark hit a snag rewiring, the entire project was abandoned. The pullout couch now sits on an old brown area rug down there, a shabby reminder of unfinished business.

"The old-fashioned way, Robin," Clark says. "With wood and nails and cement and your basic materials. We'll knock part of the outer wall down to build a special, extra-wide doorway. It's going to be pretty disruptive, but there you go."

"How are we going to pay for that?" Robin asks.

Dorothy speaks up suddenly. "Robin, your father has assured me he'll be working out the details."

"Stan's gonna pitch in a little," Clark answers, tension creeping into his voice.

This must have been what they were fighting about last night, Robin thinks. He doesn't like that he feels so suspicious about the whole thing, that he doubts his father so easily. But there's something desperate about the plan, as if it isn't so much based on sound advice as wishful thinking. The mention of Stan's name also casts a dubious shadow, as if his father has been duped into a half-baked scheme. Robin asks, "Wouldn't it be better to leave him in the hospital until he's totally ready to come home? Like, use the money for that instead?"

Clark shoots an aggravated look to Dorothy. "Don't stare at me," she says defensively. "I didn't tell him to say that."

"Robin, we're just going to figure it out. This is the way I've decided to get Jackson home and back up to speed. You can help me out on weekends and after school. A little more manpower is welcome. And seeing as how you're grounded for the foreseeable future," Clark adds, his voice firm, resolved, "it all works out pretty good for everyone."

Robin's stomach drops. "I'm grounded?"

"As of this morning, buddy boy," Clark says.

The *buddy boy* is a surprise touch; it makes his father sound like Officer Krupke, which makes him feel as if he's already been tried and convicted. Robin slips back in his chair and crosses his arms, outsmarted, dejected. "I didn't even get a chance to explain myself."

Clark slams the table, startling him, and raises his voice. "When did you become such a selfish pain in the ass? That's what I want to know? Huh? When did you become so damn pleased with yourself that you can lie to your parents and get away with it? Or do you just think we're stupid?"

Robin looks over to Ruby, who is staring at her hands, her lips moving ever so slightly, as if whispering to a doll. He looks to his mother for help. She waves her hands in front of her, absolving herself from responsibility. "I have nothing to say."

Robin pushes his chair back and rises. "I'm not hungry. May I be excused?"

"Sit down," Clark commands.

"Don't raise your voice," Dorothy says. "This is obviously difficult for Robin. For all of us."

"Difficult for *Robin?*" Clark mocks.

"You've just given him a very harsh punishment."

"Don't worry, Dottie," Clark snipes. "You can still take him into the city once in a while. Just check with me first."

Dorothy exhales furiously, the tendons in her neck tightening. "Don't speak to me that way. I will not be condescended to."

Robin holds his breath, frightened to find himself in the tightening noose of their anger.

"Why is everybody yelling?" Ruby moans.

"We're not yelling," Dorothy says, her gaze still pinned on Clark. "This is not yelling, Ruby. You don't even know what yelling is."

Ruby begins to sniffle wetly. "Mom—"

"Now she's gonna cry," Robin spits out.

Clark stands up, towering above Robin. "Robin, go to your room. Just go to your room and stay there. And don't come out until I tell you to."

"I *just said* I wanted to go to my room and you said no."

Clark's arm flies up over Robin, his fingers curling tightly together. Robin backs away from him, averting his eyes, stunned by the rage on his father's face.

"Clark, sit down," Dorothy yells.

Ruby's sniffles have grown into sobs.

"Just get the hell upstairs and shut your mouth," Clark says, shaking his fist.

"Whose room am I supposed to go to? Mine or *Ruby's?*"

Dorothy stands now. "Robin, come with me."

"Where are you going?" Clark says.

"I'm taking Robin for a ride so we can talk."

"There's nothing to talk about! I've explained what's going on, and you don't need to baby this kid just because he's too damn full of himself to take what's coming to him."

"*You're* babying him," Dorothy shouts. "You are bellowing like a madman. *Sit down, go to your room, shut the hell up.* What kind of way is that to talk?"

"It's a damn lot better than filling his head with sissy crap like you've been doing for thirteen years."

Robin feels his throat go dry, his ears burning. An image of himself at his mother's side, laughing on a New York sidewalk over some shared joke: sissy crap.

"Go to hell," Dorothy snarls.

"Am I asking too much? Tell me, Dorothy, am I asking too damn much? Am I the only person in this family who cares about Jackson?"

"Don't do this."

"What am I supposed to do?" Clark says. "Tell me what it will take to have a little control of this family?" He reaches out and grabs Robin's shirt in his fist, trying to pull him toward the door.

"Let go!" Robin slides free of Clark's grasp. He darts around the table to stand behind Dorothy. "Mom, make him stop."

He watches as Clark's predatory eyes scan the room—King Kong looking for a pedestrian to scoop up—and land on his plate, which he picks up and hurls at the cabinets on the far side of the room. Clumps of scrambled eggs explode in every direction; ceramic shatters on the pressboard. Ruby shrieks and covers her ears. Dorothy pushes Robin behind her and screams out, "Stop it, stop it, stop it."

Robin makes a move, sprinting through the living room, grabbing his jacket on the way out the front door. On the front lawn, he skids to a

halt: a couple of little kids are playing with toy trucks across
He's never seen them before, they must be cousins of the Kelly
thing, but the effect of them—two boys, one older, one smalle
themselves so easily—leaves him stunned. It's so normal and peaceful—
the whole street is like that: a car rolling slowly by, a leaf blower clearing a lawn, a voice calling from a neighbor's porch. Why is his family so
full of problems? Why is he running out of his house like a criminal? But
then his father is behind him, throwing the screen door open on its
squeaky hinge, calling, "Get back in here," and Robin is dashing alongside the house into the backyard, thinking he'll cut through to the
Spicers, thinking Todd will help him out—a thought that immediately
echoes back as ridiculous: Todd's mad at him, probably won't ever
speak to him again, and besides, his father would just follow him there
and drag him home; this is no solution at all.

His bicycle is leaning against the garage. He throws a leg across,
points the handlebars toward the street, starts pedaling. Both of his parents are in the driveway now, Dorothy with her hand on Clark's arm as
if restraining him. Robin stays to one side, pedals with his eyes closed,
afraid he'll be stopped, afraid they'll stand in the way and he won't be
able to stop, he'll crash into their bodies and knock them down and hurt
them, hurt them just like he hurt Jackson, just like when he couldn't
stop himself and lifted Jackson's legs over the edge of the railing to
throw him into the air, up into the air away from him. *No,* he thinks,
that's not how it happened. He opens his eyes just as his mother is tugging his father out of the path of the bicycle.

When he looks back, Clark has forced Dorothy away from him and
has begun a chase. But he's not close enough. Robin turns down Bergen
Avenue and keeps riding. He cannot pedal fast enough to please himself.

He rides to the center of town and stops at a payphone where a phone
book hangs inside a metal cover. He finds Scott's number. "Hey, it's me,
Robin," he says hopefully.

"Yeah? What do you want?" Scott sounds gruff, but maybe a little
curious, too.

"I want to come over," he says breathlessly. "I'm running away from
home, I think."

"So what am I supposed to do about it?"

"I need somewhere to go. I'm on my bike. My father's probably following me in his car."

"Man, that's lame. You're not supposed to let them *know* you're running away."

Robin wipes sweat off his forehead, checks around for his father. "We had a fight. He threw his plate across the room. I couldn't help it. I always say the wrong thing."

"I have fights with my father every fucking day, man. What's the big deal?"

He stands silently, wishing he hadn't made this call. Even though it was so weird between them at the party, today Scott had seemed like the right person to call, the only person to call, someone who'd understand a house full of commotion.

Robin gets an idea. "Do you have five bucks? I could take a bus to New York."

"I shouldn't even give you the fucking time of day, man."

"Are you mad about last night?" Robin asks. "I tried to find you before I left that party. I wanted to talk to you about stuff."

"I saw what happened," Scott says faintly.

"What do you mean, *what happened?*"

"I saw you walk out with Spicer."

Robin feels instantly panicked. "Scott, we just went for a walk. I was really drunk and had to walk it off."

"Yeah, where'd you go?"

"Just for a walk," he insists. "Can't I go for a walk without getting the third degree? You were the one who ditched me anyway."

Scott clucks his tongue against his teeth, then sighs heavily. "Where are you?"

"In town."

He gives Robin his address and hangs up.

When Robin finally finds Scott's house, his nose is running and he's tired and shaky. He pedals up a cracked asphalt drive alongside a two-story clapboard house that his mother would label "quaint" until she noticed that the curtains were dingy and crookedly hung, the paint was peeling and the bushes were overgrown. Scott walks out to the driveway, sort of nods to him but doesn't get very close.

"Come on inside."

Mr. Schatz is at the kitchen table in a tanktop undershirt, watching a football game on a small-screen black-and-white TV, downing a can of beer. He's as menacing as Robin remembers, his face expressing only hardness. "You're the kid that had to go to the hospital that time—what're ya doing here?"

Scott pulls Robin by the sleeve. "He's my *friend,* Dad. Ever heard of that?"

"Yeah, sure. I got plenty of friends."

"Plenty of losers," Scott mutters.

"Watch your fucking mouth," Mr. Schatz says, tossing an empty can after them.

Robin likes the sound of that: *my friend.* Maybe Scott has forgiven him. Following Scott into his bedroom, he lets himself relax, feeling a little protected at last. Scott's room: a big color poster of David Bowie on the closet door, one of Queen over the bed; a frayed brown rug over a discolored linoleum floor; clothes piled everywhere; albums stacked in the corner next to an elaborate stereo system. The bed sags in the middle, Scooby-Doo sheets crumpled at its baseboard. The one beautiful thing in the whole place is an aquarium containing two dark, delicate angel fish coursing in circles under a soft purple light.

Robin approaches the tank. "They're so pretty," he says, drawing his fingertip along the glass.

Scott tucks a towel along the bottom of the door, then pulls down the shades, sealing the room into darkness. He opens a dresser drawer and pulls out a joint.

Robin looks at him skeptically. "I can't. I gotta get out of here."

"You just got here," Scott says, lighting up.

"I told you, I'm running away."

"You can hang out for a while. They're not going to come looking for you here."

Scott's words make sense, and since he doesn't know what else to do, Robin takes the joint. "Your father won't get mad?"

"He's always mad," Scott says matter-of-factly.

The first puff sends Robin into a minute-long coughing fit. Scott watches him through the whole thing, almost enjoying it, Robin thinks. Then he feels the rush in his head. He knows why they call it stoned: it's like his brain has turned into a weighty rock rolling around inside of his skull. He's just sinking into the high when Scott pulls out a water pistol and starts shooting it at him. Robin tries to dodge and, when he can't, lunges at him, grabbing for the pistol. Scott knocks him onto the bed facedown, then gets on top of him and starts humping Robin's ass through their clothes.

"Cut it out," Robin says, trying to squirm away.

Scott keeps his weight on him and relights the joint. He holds it in front of Robin's mouth until Robin sucks in some more smoke.

"We should play wiener in the bun," Scott says, grinding his boner into Robin's tailbone.

"What's that?" he asks, though he thinks he gets the picture.

"Take your pants off."

"No way."

"Why? You did it for Todd Spicer last night."

Robin tries to fidget out of Scott's hold, dragging himself across the bed on his stomach. Scott leans in and pins him in place by the shoulders. "Scott, what's your *problem?*" he asks, talking quickly. "You're *preoccupied* with Todd Spicer. All we did was go for a walk."

Scott leans more heavily into him. "Who do you think taught me how to play wiener in the bun?"

Robin feels a pit open up in his stomach, feels a lump of lead dropped in there to fill the gulf. Todd and Scott, doing what Todd and he did last night. It makes him jealous, jealous of both of them, of the situation existing before he knew anything about it. He takes a gulp of air and summons enough strength to flip Scott off of him.

From across the bed, Scott looks him in the eye and says teasingly, "Sissy boy."

"Shut up," Robin barks. He gets up to move toward the door. "Takes one to know one."

"That's what *he* called you."

"Who? Todd? When?"

Scott looks away coyly. "Never mind."

Robin takes a step back toward him. He feels his mind dancing between stoned and sober, making it hard to find the right thing to say. "If you have something to tell me . . ."

Scott grabs a pillow and hugs it. He stares into the aquarium, his eyes following the fish as he speaks. "One time me and Todd were at his house, on mushrooms."

"You mean, like *funny* mushrooms?" Robin asks.

"Duh," Scott mocks. "We were totally tripping at his kitchen table, and he looks out the window, and you're sitting on your roof, listening to the radio."

"When was this?"

"I don't know, like a year, year and a half ago." He wipes his nose.

"Doesn't matter. It was back then, when we were still friends. So he sees you from the window, and he's like: *That's Robin MacKenzie. I had a dream about him.*"

"He did?"

Scott nods, his eyes look drowsy now, almost sorrowful. "He said in the dream you were naked and dancing in front of him, or some shit like that, and he was calling you his little sissy boy."

Robin sits down on the bed, dizzy, not sure whether to believe this, though Scott is telling it very calmly, the way secret things sound when they surface. "That's so weird," Robin says. "Are you sure he wasn't just hallucinating on drugs?"

"All I know is, he told me when he woke up from that dream he had come in his pants."

"Oh, my God." Robin rubs his forehead with his fingers. "He had a wet dream about me?" He searches Scott's face for the truth, but Scott just throws his pillow at him.

Robin falls backward onto the bed, feeling somehow dirtied by the story, as if Scott's intention wasn't to reveal something about Todd but to humiliate Robin. He curls into the pillow, in a fetal position. The high is raging through him, truncating his thoughts. He tries to mold questions for Scott but nothing congeals. He suddenly feels very weak.

"Take your pants off, Robin." Robin lets Scott roll him onto his stomach and obediently unclasps his pants, helping Scott slide them down. He hears Scott doing the same.

A warm fleshy thing presses between his butt cheeks. Scott spits into his crack and then rubs his dick back and forth, spreading the wetness around. Each pass across his asshole is like an electric tickle, sending a charge out in waves. Robin's skin goosebumps; he hears himself whimpering, a doll's voice being squeezed out of him. He tries to imagine Scott and Todd doing this—he is Scott and Scott is Todd. He feels like he's at the bottom of some food chain.

Scott moves faster and faster while the bedsprings sing beneath them, finally gasping and holding still. Robin shuts his eyes and waits through a long pause until Scott's goo sprays the small of his back. Scott hops to his feet, grabs a sock off his bed, and wipes Robin clean.

"That's it?" Robin says, still not looking at him. "Do I get to do it to you?"

"No, man, it's over."

He rolls over dejectedly and watches Scott pacing about, acting like he's busy doing something though he's clearly just trying hard to not stand still. "That's not very fair," he mutters. His own dick is wet at the tip, just getting started.

"It's just a game, Robin."

"Oh." He relights the joint, almost burns his hair in the flame. Takes a puff. "So you won and I lost?"

The high feels protective now, soothing him through a situation he isn't very happy with. He spends a moment in complete forgetfulness—unsure what just happened, what he felt about it, why he came here to begin with. Then something breaks through the cloud. "Do you have five dollars now?" Asking the question makes him feel better, like Scott owes him something and he can cash in.

Scott frowns, digs through a drawer. "Here. Here's three dollars and another joint. You can sell it and keep the money."

"Sell a joint?" The idea is perplexing, makes him giggle.

"Just find some kid looking for one and tell him you can hook him up. Then make a meeting place and sell it to him. Go to The Bird."

"Why don't you just give me the money?" he asks, liking this demand, happy to see Scott squirm a little.

"You're the rich one. Why you asking me for money?"

"Yeah, right, like I can just go back home and ask for money."

"You should have planned it better."

Scott's father interrupts their bickering with a loud bang on the door. "I'll kill you kids, smoking that shit in my house."

Scott motions him to the window. Robin follows Scott out onto a small, steep roof, like the one outside his own bedroom. They walk a few steps then climb back into another window, which leads them into a different boy's bedroom, though this one is so clean it looks unlived in. Robin tries to recall if Scott mentioned having a brother, but he hardly has time to consider this before they are dashing down the stairs and past Scott's bellowing father. Robin gets on his bike and Scott gets on his and they race away down the driveway as Mr. Schatz yells his booze-thickened threats from the front door.

Once they are far enough away to be sure Mr. Schatz is not following, they slow down, and their ride drifts into aimlessness. They recount their getaway again and again, each time embellishing the details until what was a quick escape is transformed into a full-fledged romp. Now that they are both running from their fathers, the tension between them has leveled. Scott doesn't mention anything about the party or Todd anymore, and Robin lets himself forget that Scott has been playing hot and cold with him. He still doesn't know whether or not to believe the story about Todd's wet dream, but he puts it out of his thoughts for now and concentrates instead on the sweet pleasure of circling their bikes around each other while they talk the afternoon away.

They ride out to the Ice Pond, where they sit side by side on the rocks throwing stones into the water. "Whoever throws farther gets to make the other one do anything he wants," Scott says.

Robin rolls his eyes, knowing he's going to lose, but agrees anyway. They choose rough gray rocks the same size and weight. "On the count of three."

Scott's rock soars high, but Robin pitches his from the side, sending it straight and fast. It plunks into the brown water more than a foot beyond Scott's.

"Two out of three," Scott says, shuffling away, searching for another rock.

"No way," Robin says. He plants himself in front of Scott. "I won."

"OK. What?" Scott says.

Robin looks around and, finding no one else in sight, grabs Scott's shoulders and pulls his face in for a kiss. Scott is stiff in his grasp, but his mouth remains neutral, neither tightening in resistance nor parting for more. Breath escapes Scott's nose in jittery puffs that land on Robin's upper lip. *He's just waiting for it to be over,* Robin thinks, but when he opens his eyes—he doesn't even remember closing them—Scott's are closed, too. He seems sort of lost in it. Robin adds the slightest pressure to his lips, waits for Scott to respond, for his lips to soften; he does, they do. Little by little, moving in millimeters, the kiss expands. Robin's hands slide to Scott's waist. Scott does the same, pushing his fingers under the waist of Robin's pants, pushing his belly and hips into Robin.

The outside world intrudes—some rumbling sound, just a truck on a nearby road, but it's enough to pull them apart. Nothing is said. Robin fights back the grin that wants to take hold of his face. Scott wipes his lips. They don't meet each other's eyes.

Scott resumes throwing rocks into the pond though there is no more talk of contests. Hours tick by, silent but for the occasional splashes. They sit so that their hips and shoulders touch, close but not too close. Robin is bursting with wanting more, but he lets himself rest on the small victory of kissing Scott. They lean back, curl up against the rocks, and let sleep take over.

When they wake to the setting sun, the spell has worn thin. The night's dropping temperature demands a decision, and Scott, sure that his father is either too drunk to remember what happened or has passed out, decides to go home. Before he leaves, he coaches Robin on what to say to his parents: "I don't know what got into me. I can't explain it. I'm sorry." He says it's the safest bet.

Robin spends the three dollars Scott gave him on food and Asteroids at Jerry's Pizza in town, then nurses a Coke for an hour. He imagines his mother storming in to Jerry's and finding him moping in this red vinyl booth, taking one look and accusing him of feeling sorry for himself. He imagines his father's anger, this new anger that never existed before Jackson's injury, exploding again. Maybe this time he really will get hit. He thinks about sneaking into the house while they are out visiting Jackson, then gets a better idea.

He hops back on his bike and rides to the hospital, arriving before visiting hours are over. As he had hoped, his parents are there. No matter what they say to him, he repeats some version of what Scott advised, and nothing more. It seems to work. He is sternly lectured in the hospital cafeteria and in the car all the way home and again back at the house. His father repeatedly tells him he is selfish, inconsiderate, thoughtless; his mother voices her confusion and disapproval at his rebellion; together they spell out a list of prohibitions: no socializing, no bike rides, no unnecessary phone calls. But the impact is much softer than he suspects it would have been had he not chosen to return to them at Jackson's bedside, where kind-faced nurses were coming and going and the fragile pulse of medical machinery droned eerily all around them.

Chapter Nine

His father has bought the Time-Life home improvement books, and he spends every night after dinner engrossed in them, scrawling notations and inky sketches on a lined pad. Clark's enthusiasm builds each day. Soon all he can talk about is renting equipment and taking measurements and which tools he needs, and how it all has to happen quickly because the weather is getting colder. Robin feels the pressure of the project increasing every day, sees the way it is becoming an obsession. Clark comes into his room at night—Robin is, at last, sleeping in his own bed again—with enthusiastic updates on pricing and specs and the latest details of the schedule. Robin tries to feign interest in the hopes of avoiding conflict for a while, but in the back of his mind he can't shake the idea that it is only a matter of time before something derails this project. He can tell that his mother does not believe in Clark's do-it-yourself project either, but she has not voiced objections. Instead she spends long hours each day at the hospital, making her way through a stack of novels—all her favorites, pulled off dusty shelves. This week it's *Anna Karenina,* which she summarizes for Robin in a dark and brooding manner.

Over the next ten days, their backyard transforms, with bags of cement mix and lumber and supplies piling up under heavy gray tarps. The dining room furniture is carried to the basement, and the carpet is covered with a dropcloth. Finally, one Saturday, Uncle Stan and one of his loping, beer-bellied friends—a so-called contractor—show up with a strange battering tool and proceed to smash away half of the wall.

Robin stands in the living room during the demolition, at the side of his mother, who is sipping whiskey, her face registering shock at the cacophony of breaking plaster and splintering wood. This assault on the senses is worsened by the triumphant hoots of Larry, who has come along to witness the spectacle. Robin is astonished how easy it is to knock down a wall. Don't walls keep everything else in place? As the plaster dust clears, he stares through the hole, half expecting the ceiling to collapse down upon them, the house retaliating against this injury they have inflicted upon it.

The next day, construction comes to an early halt when his father realizes he's ordered too little lumber and must drive across the state line to find a hardware store open on Sunday. Robin, covered in sawdust and perspiration, plops down at the kitchen table with his mother and Aunt Corinne. They're listening to the oldies station, WCBS, humming along with doo-wop and Motown and British Invasion tunes. Corinne was his mother's friend before she married Stan, and every song seems to raise memories of those days before marriage and children. Robin watches Aunt Corinne mouth the words to a Connie Francis song as a large Pisces medallion on a chain bounces between her breasts.

"Oh, God," Dorothy says suddenly, "this song reminds me of Seymour. Remember?"

Corinne rolls her eyes. "How could I forget? It's not like you had any other beaus like him."

"Who's Seymour?" Robin asks.

Corinne looks down as if she's embarrassed. Dorothy says, "Oh, Corinne, for God's sake. It's not such a damn *scandal.*"

"Who's Seymour?" Robin repeats.

"He was very *nice,*" Corinne says. "I always said, Seymour had a very nice way about him."

Dorothy frowns sarcastically and mimics, *"A very nice way about him.* For God's sake, Corinne, that's like a mother describing her ugly daughter as *having a nice personality."*

"Dottie, it is *not.* That's *not* what I meant. I *liked* Seymour."

"When did you go out with him?" Robin asks.

Dorothy gives him a very adult look. "He was my last boyfriend before your father."

"It wasn't very long," Corinne interjects. "Really, Dottie. It was only—what? A month or two?"

"It was seven weeks, to be exact. A very *interesting* seven weeks."

Corinne pours herself some tea. "God, that summer was so hot."

"It was the worst. Ninety percent humidity every day."

"That's the summer we went to Fire Island. Remember, you, me,

Tatjana, Jan, and Sue Benedict. And that was the summer Seymour came to visit."

"And practically moved in," Dorothy says.

"That was a scandal, Dottie. It really was. The way people *talked."*

A nice way about him. Fire Island. Scandal. Robin adds it up: Seymour sounded like a queer. He begins to blurt out the question. "Was Seymour—" and then cuts himself off, not wanting to utter the word, not wanting to meet his mother's eyes with *queer* hanging in the air. Instead he stammers, "Um, was he, um, *black?"*

Dorothy looks at him, surprised. Pleased. Her delighted smile tells him that he's stumbled upon the right answer; she thinks he has been astute. After all the yelling and the chaos that has taken over the house for the past few weeks, he is immensely relieved for this single look of approval. Even if he has impressed her by accident.

"Yes, Robin. He was black, and more than that"—she pauses for dramatic effect—"he was a *bartender."*

Dorothy and Corinne look at each other and then burst into laughter. Corinne gets up and turns down the radio; as she passes Robin and notices his confused look, she brushes him on the head. "That's what your mother said to us—she said, 'I don't know why everybody is in a tizzy about him being black. I can't believe that I'm dating a *bartender.'"* She disappears into the living room. A moment later a Fifth Dimension album starts up on the turntable.

Dorothy takes Robin's hand. "You have to understand, where I grew up, high school boys wound up working as bartenders in the Amherst and Holyoke college bars. It was such a *rouge* thing to me. Of course, I was just being a snob, but it had that resonance to it. Low-life Yankee trash working in small town bars. But *Seymour,* you see, was a bartender at the Hotel Taft. It was very glamorous. His family was in Harlem, and they ran a ladies boutique on 125th Street. He was more middle class than I was."

"So why did you break up with him?"

"Yes, *dear,* it was I who dumped *him,"* she says, offering another smile for his precociousness. "But really, he was a big drinker. Or should I say, I was a big drinker when I was with him. We went out and drank, we stayed at each other's apartments and drank. That month on Fire Island I was tipsy the *entire time* Seymour was visiting, which was about half of that month."

"Why did he make you drink?"

"We just drank together. Neither of us *made* the other drink. It was just . . . part of the way we *were* together." Her voice has a perplexed quality to it, as if she still can't solve the essential puzzle of their relationship.

Corinne has been leaning against the doorframe. She speaks up now. "Robin, you probably don't know this because of your age, but this used to be a much more prejudiced country to live in."

"Still seems pretty prejudiced to me," Robin says. "I mean, all the black kids in lunch sit at a separate table. I have this black friend, George, in my science class, and even though we have the same lunch period and everything, we *never* sit together. He sits with these other black kids—some of them he doesn't even like, and this one girl, Debra, who *nobody* likes. You know what I mean?"

Dorothy frowns, "Forgive me for nagging dear, but please don't end your statements with *you know what I mean*. It's so very *New Jersey*."

"Oh, Mom. Come on. I'm just saying—"

"*I'm just saying,*" Dorothy repeats. She picks at some food on her plate and continues, her voice at once annoyed and regretful. "I remember that day I told Seymour I couldn't see him anymore. It was not one of the lovelier moments of my Single Girl Escapades, let me tell you. He was just crestfallen. But what was I supposed to do? We couldn't get married."

"Did Nana ever meet him? Or Uncle Stan?" Robin asks, wanting the picture filled out, not completely understanding why she wouldn't have married someone she loved, no matter the circumstances.

"No, no, no," Dorothy says quickly. "It was much less *Guess Who's Coming To Dinner?* than it was *Another Country*."

"What's that?"

"A very wonderful, very scandalous novel. Baldwin wrote it—James Baldwin. When you're old enough I'll let you read *that* one."

"Why can't I read it now?"

Dorothy sighs and rubs her temples. "Robin, you may be mature for your age but I don't think you're quite an adult yet. Maybe when you're sixteen or seventeen."

"You always say that."

"I'm your mother, Robin. I'm older than you. Trust me."

"*Trust me,*" Robin repeats sarcastically.

"Ahem," Corinne says. "Time out."

"Sorry," Dorothy says. "Guess I'm still a wee bit tense about it after all these years. About Seymour. I knew I should have seen an analyst when I was twenty-one. A little head shrinking back then and I'm sure I would have had a much more gracious life."

Corinne pats Dorothy's hand. "Well, it all turned out fine, anyway, Dottie, because you met Clark *just* after that, and here we are today."

"Here we are today, indeed," Dorothy says, standing up and busying herself suddenly at the sink. "Here we are," she repeats, bitterly.

Corinne says, "Oh, sweetie, don't be like that. Things are going to work out. It will be a struggle, but it will work out, Dottie. It just will. Whatever happens, it will work out."

Watching his mother scrubbing dishes, Robin is overcome with pity for her, living all these years knowing she could have had another life, a life that she was denied, that she denied herself. He gets up and wraps his arms around her from behind, feels her stop what she's doing and stiffen. She does not turn around, and she does not say anything. He wants her to face him and hug him back, to let him share her memory of lost love, to let it be *their* moment. But when it becomes clear that she won't, he lets go. For the rest of the day, this small denial stays with him, gnawing away the pity he felt for her and replacing it with the stirrings of contempt.

At least once a day since Maggio's party, Robin takes a trip down the corridor where Todd's locker is. A couple of times a week his timing is usually right, and if Todd isn't with anyone else, he says hello to him, and sometimes Todd nods back. Not much more than that ever happens, but Robin keeps at it with the regularity of someone stoking a slow-burning fire.

And then one morning, during a fire drill that empties the student body onto the school's front lawn, he catches sight of him a few yards away. He calls to him excitedly, but Todd continues walking, dragging along a girl whose hand rests in his back pocket.

Robin catches up to them, wanting an acknowledgment at the least. "Hey, Todd, wait up."

"Yo," Todd says.

"Where you going so fast?" Robin asks. "I mean, ha-ha, where's the fire?" He raises his eyebrows, hoping his joke will at least register.

Todd's face remains uninterested. "Debbie's car is over there," he says, pointing toward the parking lot.

Robin stops and lets them pass, feeling foolish. He hears Debbie ask, "Who was that kid?" but he doesn't hear Todd's reply, and it makes him queasy to guess what Todd might be saying.

As he watches them move toward the parking lot, he imagines that he has planted a bomb in Debbie's car and that when the key turns in the ignition the two of them, Todd and this girl he flaunts like a trophy, are blown sky high.

As the construction takes over the house in fits and starts—each evening bringing not only a new addition to the previous day's work but an accompanying new dilemma, which his father, invariably, cannot quite solve—Robin finds himself increasingly on the edge of exploding. When he wakes up in the morning and sees the varnish filings under his fingernails, reminding him that he has been scratching like a cat at his headboard throughout the night, it fills him with such a rage that before he knows it he's punching his fists into his pillow and imagining it's his father, his Uncle Stan, his cousin Larry, the most recent jerk at school to bully him. He wants to hurt someone. *Someone has to pay,* he thinks and then later feels guilty, as if his very thoughts are the problem. One morning when he's punching his pillow he sees his mother's face at the end of his fist, and it frightens him so deeply he freezes like a zombie.

He jerks off every morning, every night, sometimes after school as well if no one is home. He flexes his arms, sucks in his stomach, blanks out his expression in front of the bathroom mirror until he can see the image of a virile young man instead of his own soft body—and then he makes his dick hard and lets his mind travel through its landscape of men and boys, faces and bodies, real and imagined sex, what he has known and what he still wants. He always aims his semen into the bathtub or the sink or the toilet, somewhere to wash away the evidence.

At school he is adrift. Even his favorite subjects—English, social studies—have ceased to interest him at all. One night, after receiving a C on an English test and then getting yelled at by his father while his mother, midway through another wine binge, looked on silently, he sits on the edge of his bed, unable to sleep. The scraped-away spot on his headboard glows in the moonlight—the evidence of his tormented mind leering at him. He goes to the bathroom and instead of jerking off brings a fingernail clipper back to his bed, where he chops at the soft tips of his nails until anything that looks like excess is gone. Then he runs his nails over the board and examines them for spots where the varnish has caught. He cuts at these places, which are clearly not yet trim enough, and then he cuts a little bit more just to be sure, and then tries to make all of them even, including the rough skin at their edges, and then he examines his work again. One nail is tinged at its edge with blood. He snips away at the skin near the cut, wanting to clear the area around the wound, but that just allows it to bleed more freely. He sucks on the blood—he has a dim memory of licking Jackson's blood off his own fingertip when he was with him at the playground right after the fall. Then he snips down on another and another, taking his time. He calmly chops away until most of his fingertips are bleeding, the newly peeled nail beds throbbing from exposure, the fingers themselves almost numb. The pain is small compared to the relief he feels that he will sleep better and that he will now, somehow, be safe from the demons that haunt his dreams.

Robin mixes salad dressing with a fork, watching the red vinegar break into droplets in the golden oil and spin like bubbles trapped in a surf. He pours the combination over a bowl of iceberg lettuce and sliced tomatoes oozing green, larval seeds. He scrapes grated raw carrot on top, followed by cucumber slices and the onion he's minced so small it looks like a mound of wet, crystalline sand. He's sure Ruby won't eat any of his salad but he's gone ahead and made it anyway, simply because he likes putting it together. The two of them are having dinner alone tonight. Clark and Dorothy are at school, meeting with Mr. Cortez. Every time Robin thinks of the three of them sitting in Mr. Cortez's office, his temples throb: at this minute decisions are being made about him. It feels like a lesser version of what he's been doing all the time lately, waiting for news about Jackson. In both cases he only expects to hear something bad.

Ruby lowers her head over her food—Dorothy's leftover meatloaf and roast potatoes—and mouths something reverent with her hands clasped together before picking up her fork. Robin stares at her, half angry at her new piety, half hoping she's praying enough to make up for all the bad stuff he's been doing lately. He shovels a piece of meatloaf into his mouth and chews with difficulty: though it isn't charred, it tastes burned, and though it's dry inside his mouth (in fact it seems to be sucking moisture *out* of his mouth), he can't get over the sensation that it tastes like sweat. He swallows the mouthful with difficulty and gulps down a glass of iced tea made from a powdered mix.

Ruby is watching him intently, chewing her own piece of meat with a similar unpleasant expression on her face.

"This tastes even worse reheated," Robin says, pushing his plate away from him. "I forget what a bad cook Mom is until Nana's around."

Ruby swallows at last, with great effort, and grabs her own drink to wash it down. "I like everything better when Nana's here."

Robin shrugs. Nana gets bossier the longer she's around, which makes his mother more irritated. No matter how much he likes Nana he's usually happy to see her go. "Let's eat the salad," he says.

"I think I'm gonna eat some pudding instead." Ruby gets up from the table and scrapes her food into the garbage.

The sound of their parents' car coming up the driveway interrupts the moment. Ruby quickly crumples a few paper napkins on top of her food in the trash can and gives Robin a pleading glance. "Don't tell," she says and slips quietly out of the kitchen with a cup of pudding.

Clark moves fast and noisily into the house, letting the screen door slam behind him and dropping his heavy coat onto the chair. "What's the story with this Cortez guy?" he demands.

"He's my guidance counselor," Robin says. "He teaches this thing called group guidance where we all sit around and talk about stuff." He pushes his fork through a puddle of dressing separating on his plate. "Where's Mom?"

"I'm coming," Dorothy calls. She enters the house slightly out of breath, sliding a silk scarf off her head, her heels snapping on the tiled floor, her car keys jingling. "Clark, I cannot believe you're this upset."

Clark aims a chunk of meatloaf into his mouth and speaks between bites. "I just want to know since when this school district started hiring hippies! Bad enough they call them *guidance counselors*. Sounds like the kind of person who belongs in a home with a bunch of *slow* people."

Robin looks to his mother, but she's attending to a wine bottle and searching the cupboard for a clean glass. "What, didn't you have a guidance counselor in high school?"

Clark gestures with his fork. "At St. Martin's we had *mentors*. Usually a chaplain or a coach. You know, some guy old enough to be your father, who showed you how to make use of your potential and told you the kind of things you need to know about getting ready for college and—"

Dorothy reaches out and gently grabs Clark's wrist, lowering his arm and the protruding fork to the table. "That's what guidance counselors do, Clark. They just happen to be a little *groovier* these days." She turns her face to Robin. "Did you make this salad? It's lovely."

Robin nods his head but says nothing. Even though his mother is smiling, she looks worn out; he wonders if this is because she's spent the day at Jackson's bedside or because the meeting with Cortez was grueling.

Clark says, "This guy Cortez, what is he, twenty-five, twenty-six years old? Did you see that poster on his wall? He's practically the poster child for the Woodstock Nation."

Dorothy sighs wearily. "Clark, you wouldn't know a hippie if he handed you a flower. Hector Cortez is thirty-three years old, which is four years younger than you." She turns her head to Robin and keeps her eyes focused on him as she sips from her wineglass. "Robin, this entire thing is sounding hysterical, I'm sure. Don't pay any attention to your father. He's just fit to be tied because Mr. Cortez suggested that we might consider putting you in a private high school."

Robin swallows. So this is what's coming, he thinks. Before he can explain that private school wasn't *his* idea, Clark is raising his voice again.

"Not a just private high school—a high school for the arts! An *art* school! Whoever heard of anything except a bunch of screwed-up kids coming out of art school."

"That's ridiculous, Clark. That's an incredibly philistine attitude to take." Dorothy rises from the table and paces to the window. "I knew you were going to act like this."

Art school—Robin isn't sure what that even means. A school where you learn how to paint? He sees a room full of easels, of people in smocks painting straw-covered wine bottles and bowls of fruit and dead birds. The smell of turpentine.

"Dottie, don't give me that. You know I love art as much as the next guy."

"This is New Jersey, Clark. The *next* guy doesn't love art. He watches television."

Clark points a finger into his chest and leans forward. "Listen, lady. I could probably name more famous artists off the top of my head than Hector Cortez, so don't make me out to be some dolt. I have no beef with anyone learning about art. I took art-appreciation classes at St. Martin's. *Classes.*" He zooms his finger to the table for his final word.

"He'll still get a by-the-book education," Dorothy says. "Just without all that ridiculous metal shop and phys. ed. and typing." She swats at the air for emphasis. "The stuff that bores him."

"Maybe if he showed up for a few more classes he wouldn't be so bored."

Robin looks back and forth between them; they are not looking at each other. He clears his throat and says, "I swear, I didn't ask to go to any private school. It was his idea. Mr. Cortez."

Clark looks his way, presses his lips together in an attempted smile. "I believe you, Robin. Don't get me wrong. I'm not saying you're the one coming up with crazy ideas."

Dorothy's voice is steely, her face pinkens as anger pushes the fatigue from her skin. "Clark, it's just a sad statement when a man knows so little about his own son."

"Jesus Christ. Don't you ever let up on me about him?"

Robin feels himself emptying, disappearing from the scene, blood and oxygen being squeezed out of him.

"Don't treat me like a nag," Dorothy says angrily. "I am *not* nagging you. I am looking out for my son's welfare." She stands with her legs apart, her arm outstretched like a fashion model posed to appear more ferocious than beautiful. "I am trying to envision a future for him that would allow him to have a good life, a really good life, not just a predictable one. A life marked by exposure to ideas and worldly experience and, yes, art. These are things I value and that I've taught Robin to value."

Her fury is almost frightening to Robin. He thinks he should be happy that she is fighting for this chance for him—he thinks he should telegraph some gratitude toward her. But mostly he wants to get away from this room; more than that, he wants to slip into the swarming darkness at the back of his skull and emerge as a different boy—unobtrusive, disinterested, normal. Someone not worth an argument.

Clark is saying, "Look, I let you take him to the city every month."

"Hah! You *let* me? I didn't need your *permission.*"

"I gave you my blessing. Give me some credit, for God's sake."

"I fought for even that much. You and I have never seen eye to eye on how best to raise Robin. And you have resisted me every step of the way."

"That's not true," Clark says. "Don't overexaggerate."

Robin opens his mouth to correct his father's diction—*It's exaggerate, not overexaggerate;* the sentence forms reflexively but he stops himself from voicing it, and in the small act of *not* speaking, he feels his first sense of relief during this conversation, as if controlling the small impulses he takes for granted might be the key to becoming that unobtrusive other. He turns his head to the kitchen window, which is casting back a portrait of the three of them in their triangular composition:

Dorothy at the edge, gulping down her wine; Clark across the room, his arms crossed in frustration; and he in the middle, sinking down in his seat like something compressed in a vise.

"Can I be excused?" he asks.

Clark speaks first. "At this point, with your mother putting on airs and name calling, I think it's best that you leave us alone."

"Don't leave the room, Robin," Dorothy says. She walks behind him and rests her hands on his shoulders. "This concerns you."

"I can't take it," Robin says quietly. "The two of you together."

Clark rubs his hand across his face. "Fine, fine. Look, this is all blown out of proportion. OK? I don't like the idea of art school. It has nothing to do with what I do or don't want Robin to become when he grows up. He can become a friggin' artist for all I care. But he's going to get a proper high school education, something that prepares him for college. That's what I have to say about it." He stands, clears his plate into the garbage, bends backward to stretch. "You know, one of the reasons we picked this town was because everyone said it had a good *school* system. The reason we even live here is because we wanted him to go to the very school that he's going to right now."

At this, Robin sits up straight and leans forward. "What do you mean? Who told you Greenlawn was a *good* school?"

"The real estate agent."

Dorothy sits down in her chair, without taking her hand off Robin's shoulder. "A dozen years ago Greenlawn was considered the cream of the suburban crop," she explains. "Not the ritziest, of course, but very solid and stable. It was a new town, with big houses that young couples could still afford. And Corinne and Stan had moved here, and they seemed happy."

Clark jumps in. "And *they* heard the school system was good, too."

"Well, it sure sucks shit now," Robin says.

Dorothy squeezes his arm and admonishes, "There's no reason to be so vulgar."

"Watch your language," Clark commands.

Robin shakes his mother's arm off and pushes his chair back so that he's out of her reach. "Well, excuse my French, but I'm in total *shock* over here. I mean, like, I just found out that the reason we even *live* in this town is because Greenlawn High School is being advertised as a good school to sell people houses. That's just the biggest lie I ever heard." His heart is racing now; his words are picking up speed. "You know, my German teacher falls asleep in class and my science teacher is this gross guy who makes jokes about flat-chested girls or girls with big boobs right in front of them, and my gym teacher is this—I don't know—this *ape,* and everyone in gym except for me and Sco—everyone except me and this one other kid acts like a bully because Pintack sets an example."

"Just because you don't like physical education does not mean you shouldn't go to that school," Clark says in frustration.

"I really think we need to consider art school," Dorothy counters.

Robin feels his mouth getting dry, his eyes getting hot and wet. His voice cracks as he continues. "It's just a big jock school, and if you're not a jock they just make fun of you." He feels something more in his throat wanting to burst out—a cry that would explain to them what is really going on inside his mind—but he fights it back because he knows that they are not listening to him.

Dorothy says, "If I knew fourteen years ago what I know now." She stands and moves to embrace Robin. He sidesteps her, nearly backing into the refrigerator.

Clark puts a finger in his mouth and bites a nail. "Yeah, well, you and me both, Dottie, you and me both." He stands up suddenly. Robin steps aside, expecting to be grabbed or hit, but Clark moves out the kitchen door, waving his arms in a grand gesture of dismissal.

Dorothy wipes the back of her hand across her lips and exhales quietly. She drains the rest of her wine and brushes a lock of hair from her perspiring forehead. "He'll come around," she says with such cool certainty that Robin gets a chill along his spine.

Though he has wanted to flee the room since the start of the conversation, he now feels powerless to even move. He sits, numb, watching his mother get drunk. He is afraid to leave her alone, afraid of how unhinged she seems and how much her love for him seems to be a part of that instability. If he left the room it would be a sign of betrayal. He imagines her unleashing a tirade against him, or collapsing in a fit of wailing, or storming to the car and driving recklessly into an accident.

Finally, to break the silence and bring some animation back to his mother's face, Robin asks, "What would I do in art school? I mean, what kind of art? Paintings?"

"Maybe, and probably some music lessons and literature. All the things you already enjoy."

"But don't you have to audition?"

"For the performing arts, but there are schools for fine arts as well. We'll probably show them a portfolio."

"Like what?"

"Well, I've seen you draw pictures, and you're very good at making up stories. If you wrote some of them down, maybe ten or twenty pages."

"Ten or twenty?"

"Oh, it's nothing. I'll help you with it. And then you could draw some illustrations for the story and you'd have a book. And that would be very impressive for an admissions board."

"I guess so." He thinks of writing assignments for English class, little stories he has written on sheets of paper tucked under his bed. They all seem embarrassing, childish. He asks her, "What would I write about?"

"You could write about one of our trips to New York, where we go and what we see. You'd have to fictionalize the names, of course, to make it literature. And change some of the facts." Her face brightens.

"That seems weird," he says, "to write about you and me." He's wishing that he hadn't raised the subject. Her enthusiasm feels like pressure. "I know—I could take one of the stories that we made up about a stranger and turn it into a short story. I'll think of a lady we saw, and then I'll make up her biography for the book."

She frowns disapprovingly. "You'd have to make it very interesting, make the person really memorable, not just any old ordinary plain Jane on the street."

"I know it's supposed to be interesting, Mom."

"Well, sometimes you're a little pedestrian in your ideas."

"What does that mean?"

"Sometimes, not by any means most of the time, but sometimes, you don't think big enough, Robin." She pauses, as if readying herself to say something difficult. "It's the same part of you that wants to cut school or go to drinking parties." He feels her notice his annoyance, and she quickly adds, "It's just that, for every person you spot on the street whom you imagine to be a spy or a countess or something quite fascinating, there's a person you see whom you decide is merely a housewife from Long Island."

"Some of them *are* housewives from Long Island," he hisses, standing up from the table, anger boiling in his throat. "Like you, Mom. You're a housewife from New Jersey, and you're a very *interesting* person."

She stares at him, stunned. Finally she sputters out, almost plaintively, "I am not a housewife. I have a job. When you're all old enough I'll go full-time at the library."

His words have stung; she clearly doesn't understand why he snapped at her. It is terrible to see her reduced to this, defending herself from his sarcasm. He snatches her glass and the nearly empty wine bottle from the table and dumps them both in the sink. Without meeting her eyes, he mumbles, "I've had enough."

Most days Scott is the only thing he looks forward to, which is ironic because it means looking forward to gym class. Sometimes they get to talk for most of the hour, at the top of the bleachers, above the sounds of bouncing basketballs and sneakers scuffling along the floorboards, ignoring Mr. Pintack's commands to get back in the game. Robin recounts whatever bewildering thing took center stage in his house the day before, like the fight after his parents visited Cortez, or the morning his father's car broke down in the driveway and had to be towed away, or the time Ruby spent the whole day wearing a veil over her face. Always—when they aren't stuck on opposite teams or put through separate drills—Robin talks and Scott listens.

Scott still tries to convince him to ditch, but Robin always refuses and then fills the frustrated silence that follows with updates on Jackson. He always feels better after giving his report. Scott is the only person whose face doesn't scrunch up into pity when Jackson's condition, and what it is doing to his family, is discussed. One day, they stay in the locker room until after everyone leaves and mash faces for about twenty greedy seconds, pulling apart nervously, backing away from each other without saying anything about it. Robin feels his blood thumping in his chest for the next hour.

His mother picks him up after school and drives him to the hospital. Some days she just decides he has to visit. He never asks to go anymore; it's too depressing. Last week there was some talk about how Jackson should get his speech back soon, but as far as Robin can tell Jackson is just as out of it as ever. He's beginning to believe that the doctors are purposefully lying to them, telling them that everything's going to be OK when in fact it's going in the opposite direction.

He approaches Jackson's room with dread, clammy under his clothes, perspiring at the mere notion of his brother's emaciated form. He says hello when he enters, "Hello Jackson," the way he hears people say hello to their pets when they come home at the end of the day. You don't expect a response but you say it just the same. The bones in Jackson's face push against the tightening skin. His nose looks shrunken, as if the softness has been trimmed away, leaving only a sharp ridge. Dorothy sits in a vinyl armchair at Jackson's bedside reading a book, not noticing what Robin says or does. Lately the fire in her has retracted, replaced with a new, false demeanor. She reminds Robin of one of those New York salesladies behind a perfume counter, the kind who ignores you with the greatest of ease and then turns on the superficial charm when you make her stop ignoring you. At some moments Robin finds himself despising her in a way he never before thought possible.

"Mom," he says one afternoon, his eyes on his disappearing brother. *"Mom."*

She looks up from her Tolstoy and flashes her cashier smile. "Yes, dear?"

"I can tell that Jackson isn't getting any better."

The tiny muscles around Dorothy's eyes and lips flinch just ever so slightly, but she freezes her smile. "Don't be a pessimist. The body recuperates at a slow pace. Changes aren't always visible."

"The only change is that he's shriveling away."

"We've been assured by the doctors—"

"Yeah, right," he interrupts. "I feel really reassured looking at him."

She closes the book but leaves her finger holding the page. "Are you having trouble being optimistic, Robin?" she asks tersely.

"Never mind," he says and looks away from her. The worst thing is that he believes she really agrees with him.

Scott hardly ever answers the phone, and Robin finds himself intimidated by Mr. Schatz's gruffness. Sometimes he hangs up without speaking. Even when Scott picks up, his father is often yelling in the background, trying to get Scott off the phone. When Mr. Schatz isn't around, Robin talks for a while, usually about Jackson, and Scott listens. Sometimes while he speaks Robin hears the *slip-click* of a Bic lighter, the sandpaper *whoosh* of Scott taking smoke into his lungs. Sometimes Scott says, "This song is excellent," and holds the phone next to his stereo speakers and Robin listens to all of it. One night Scott props up the receiver while the second side of Patti Smith's "Horses" plays, then goes away. Robin gets nudged off the phone by his mother before Scott comes back. He hangs up on a wild Patti telling the strange sexy story of a boy named Johnny: *An angel looks down on him and says, 'Aw, pretty boy, can't you show me nothing but surrender?'*

Clark has taken Ruby to the hospital. Dorothy has been brooding all day. She blames it on *Anna Karenina:* "the hellish state of that woman's life." She'd shut herself in her darkened bedroom, not even a crack of light under the door, telling him, "It's a fend-for-yourself dinner." Cooking seems like too much work—even a salad is too much. He settles on a bowl piled with his two favorites—vanilla caramel ice cream and rainbow sherbet—and brings it up to his bedroom to enjoy in private.

He leans against the window sill. Todd's bedroom light is on. His window is a yellow rectangle with a silhouette passing across it.

Scott is part of his days now, but it is Todd who has taken over his thoughts. Todd was there first, plus Todd holds the most secrets—it seems that way to Robin: Todd's a pothead but not really a burnout; he's not a jock but he goes to jock parties; he's got this girl Debbie hanging around all the time, but he taught Scott "wiener in the bun" *and put my boner in his mouth*. Todd does whatever he wants, Robin thinks. Todd says whatever he wants. Todd gets all shaken up if you don't say what he wants you to say, so it's good to try to figure out what Todd wants. He likes you better that way.

Robin, nearly in a trance staring at Todd's backlit shadow, throws on a coat and floats downstairs. He leaves a note for his mother claiming that he's studying with Victoria, hoping she doesn't know Victoria has dance class tonight. He ambles across the two backyards with his hands in his front pockets. He's readying himself to give an answer, fantasizing the sudden emergence of an authority figure who steps out of the darkness and demands to know what he is doing. *I'm hanging out with Todd. What's the problem?*

At the Spicers' back door he hears recorded music traveling down from upstairs. When Mrs. Spicer does not answer his knock, he knows only Todd is home. He pushes in.

The spotless kitchen, the dining room and living room, unruffled: Mrs. Spicer is a model of good housekeeping. This is a museum compared to the disorder he lives in. He pokes his head into the den, where the TV sits on a low, varnished table and the cushions on the couch sag from use. The stairs to the bedrooms are carpeted.

There is the feathery smell of pot.

"Todd?" He might still back out, he has not yet been discovered. He raises his voice. "Todd!"

"Who's that?"

"Hi, Todd. It's Robin. Robin MacKenzie." He suddenly thinks Todd won't even remember him—ludicrous, but he thinks it just the same.

Heavy footsteps carry Todd from his attic room, drop him right there in front of Robin. Bare feet, brown corduroy pants pegged high, black Springsteen concert T-shirt, sleeves cut off. Robin takes in so much skin—ankles, arms, neck, and the sliver of his waist that Robin has come to revere above all other flesh. Robin's heartbeat shakes his entire body, rattles his voice as he makes himself speak. "I heard the music and I thought I'd say, um, hi."

Todd shakes his head as if waking from sleep. "Is anyone home?"

"I let myself in." Robin takes a step backward, losing his courage. "I didn't mean to bother you. I can leave. You're probably doing stuff."

Todd pinches a thumb and index finger together and brings an invisible joint to his mouth. "Just the usual," he says.

"Cool," Robin says. He puts his hands in his pockets, brushes the tip of a sneaker on the carpet, averts his eyes from Todd's scrutinizing stare.

Todd is walking back up to his bedroom. Robin makes a split-second decision: Todd did not ask him to leave, so he follows. Closes the attic door behind him. The wooden steps creak under his feet.

The smells of old dust and musty bricks and piles of Todd's unwashed clothes. The ceiling is low. The wallpaper—faded frontier scenes of cowboys on horses pointing guns at Indians with bows drawn—peels at the edges. Patio furniture—a collapsible card table, aluminum-frame chairs crisscrossed by green and yellow nylon—is scattered about. A mattress and boxspring under a tangle of striped sheets are wedged in the corner, where the roof slopes lowest. On the opposite wall is the window that Robin has spied into so many times, surrounded by a collection of bumper stickers. Robin reads one that says, *There is no gravity. The earth just sucks.*

Todd is flipping the record on his turntable. He has not acknowledged Robin's presence within this private chamber. Robin says, "Cool room," to make it clear that he has followed Todd up. Through two enormous wood-paneled speakers, the hiss of the album begins: organ and guitars calling forth a throaty man's voice. Robin has heard it before but can't identify it.

Todd pivots, lifting his arms over his head, stretching one, then the other to the ceiling, muscles and sinew taut. The white-white skin of his armpit, with its shock of black wiry hair, is a secret place exposed. Robin braces his foot flat to the floor to keep his leg from shaking. Todd's languorous stretch lingers on even as he spits out his words. "So why are you hanging around, man?"

In his sneaker is the joint that Scott gave him. He pulls it out—flattened and crooked and a little damp from two weeks in his pocket.

Todd takes a step closer. "Where did you come up with that?"

Robin relaxes; he's scored a point. "From Scott," he says, right away wishing he hadn't.

"Aw, fuck Scott. He's a goddamn faggot," Todd says. "Plus his pot sucks." He kicks at a paperback on the floor, sending it skidding. Robin feels himself slipping down a funnel. The book Todd kicked is *No One Gets Out of Here Alive*—Jim Morrison preens on the scarlet-and-gold cover. This is the music Todd's playing. *Come on come on now touch me babe. Can't you see that I am not afraid?*

Todd takes another step toward Robin. "What does he say about me?"

"Nothing."

"I'll kick his ass if he's talking his bullshit again." Todd lays his palm on Robin's chest.

Todd's touch is a push off a ledge, a blast of heat, a truth serum. "He saw us leave the party together."

Todd is close enough now that his breath lands on Robin's face. "I'm gonna kick his skinny little ass."

Dry mouth, thumping pulse, dizzy skull. "I think he's jealous." Robin's voice, just above a whisper. "Did you . . . do it with him?"

"What?"

"He said you and him—"

"He just can't keep his mouth shut—that's the fucking problem." His hands are clenching inward. "Did he say—" Robin waits for more, but Todd clams up, retreats a step. "Forget it." He turns up the music: *What was that promise that you made?*

Robin clears his throat and takes a deep breath. He wants to say this. "Scott said you taught him this thing called wiener in the bun."

The burning sting skids across his face before he understands it. His balance is gone. He reaches out to brace himself and lands on the bed, his fingers crumpling into the sheets. Throbbing pain across his nose and cheekbone: Todd has just whacked him with the back of his hand.

Todd's voice is half rage, half whine. "That's fucked up! He shouldn't be spreading that shit around!"

Robin scrambles back to where the bed meets the downsloping roof, anticipating another blow. He wipes a drop of blood from his nose.

"What else did he say about me?" Todd demands.

Robin tilts his head back to stop the bloodflow. His eyes are watering. "How should I know what else he says? I don't spend every minute of my life with him."

Todd paces like a creature in a cage. He doesn't meet Robin's eyes—Robin remembers the night on the golf course; his talk of living in the Village rankled Todd so much he turned away from his gaze then, too. Todd says, "I didn't mean to hit you, but you shouldn't repeat the shit Scott Schatz says. Next time you talk to him, you can tell him to go fuck himself." There is a kind of pleading to Todd's voice, which so soon after the explosion surprises Robin.

"You didn't have to hit me." He flashes his palm, smeared scarlet. "Look."

"I'm just mad." The veins in Todd's neck still throb, but he is calming down now. He retrieves a towel from the floor. "Here. Use this."

The terrycloth is rigid, coarse against Robin's nostrils. "Do you have anything cleaner?"

"Oh, shit. That's my sperm towel. Sorry, man." He offers instead a dirt-brown T-shirt streaked with engine grease, then sits next to him on the bed.

Todd's sweat is embedded in the shirt, Robin imagines his blood seeping in and mingling with the sweat, saturating the fibers. Boil the whole thing in water, make Todd-and-Robin tea. He sniffs in; the bones in his face ache. Todd hit him, drew blood—he can't quite believe it. "I feel kind of dizzy now. I should go."

"No!" Todd jumps up from the bed. "You can't leave yet. Your nose is still dripping. I know, let's smoke that doob."

"I can't now," Robin protests.

"It'll be good for you, I swear." A frantic scan of the room—he finds the joint on the floor, where it fell during the impact, and quickly starts it up. "Scott Schatz is a fucking liar, a fucking big-mouth piece of shit scum. I don't know why you hang out with him."

Robin peels the sticky shirt from his nose; the blood has stained the brown cloth black—shades of darkness that remind him of an abstract painting he's seen at MoMA, which brings to mind his mother. *Did she wake up, did she get my note, what if she needs me, wants me to come home? What if she calls over here?*

Todd holds out the joint. He takes it, inhales deeply, painlessly trapping the sweet smoke in his throat. He is amazed how easy smoking has become. Once the high grabs hold he can't help himself—he is talking again about Scott. "Well, I only went over to Scott's because I got in a fight with my father and mother and I was kind of running away. I thought about coming over here, but if I'm gonna run away it should be *to* somewhere, not just my own backyard."

Todd takes the joint back. "It's all the same pile of shit, one street or the next, your street, my street, no big fucking difference. *Except* when you live over by Marble Road, like Scott. That's a fucking ghetto."

Robin slides forward, nearer to Todd, feeling his weight sink into the soft mattress. "Yeah, he seemed really poor. His father was majorly drunk in the kitchen in the middle of the day."

"And his mother's in the fucking loony bin. She tried to kill herself. That's when he got so weird." He falls backward on the bed. "Guess that shit runs in the family: weird mother, weird son."

Robin is considering this information—Scott alluded to it only once— and thinking about his own situation—weird mother/weird son?— when, like an unexpected, abrupt announcement on the P.A. system, Victoria's voice is alive in the room. She is bounding up the stairs, demanding something of Todd—and then, having caught sight of Robin, she falls speechless.

He bolts to his feet and wipes under his nose—blood has clotted like a pebble in his left nostril.

"What are you doing up here?" She slaps at the smoky air. "As if I couldn't figure it out."

Todd answers, "He's just hanging out."

Robin tries to adopt Todd's casual delivery. "You weren't home."

Victoria narrows her eyes at him. "It's Thursday night. I have dance. As if you didn't know."

"No, I knew. I just"—casual, cool—"I thought I'd come over and wait for you to get home."

"And smoke dope?"

Todd smiles. "Like I told Mom, it's incense."

Robin laughs at the lie, but Victoria is not amused. He moves to sit on the bed and then changes his mind; instinctively, it doesn't seem OK to sit so close to Todd at this moment, with Victoria here. He changes direction clumsily and lands in one of the lawn chairs. "I'm sorry. I just got stoned."

Victoria fixes her stare on her brother. "You're such an asshole, Todd."

He shoots up his middle finger. "Sit and spin."

Robin stifles another snicker, palm catching his breath. Victoria's mouth hangs open, incredulous. "I'm going to watch *Mork and Mindy*. Are you coming down?"

"Umm . . ." He looks to Todd, who has flopped back on the bed and splayed his arms over his head—the sexy underskin exposed again. He looks to Victoria, spoil sport disapproval on her face. A tug in either direction: temptation/duty, trouble/familiarity. "I'll be down in a minute," he says. He balls the bloodstained T-shirt into his nose.

"*Fine.* I'm leaving."

Robin listens as her footsteps pound an angry exit. *Fine, I'm leaving.* She could have stayed, he tells himself. She just wanted to be a brat— Todd's bratty younger sister. That's it—Victoria now seems so young to him. Ballet lessons, favorite TV shows. Are they still going to be friends?

Todd calls to her, "Don't tell Mom, man." He hops to his feet and follows her to the bottom of the stairs. She slams the door shut. He turns the lock.

The music drones: *Riders on the storm. Into this house we're born. Into this world we're thrown.* They have sparked up again, sucking from the roach every last wisp of its transformative power. On the last hit—just paper and ash really—Robin burns the tip of his thumb, tries to shake the pain away, licks the tip of his tongue against it, teeth on the nail. He wonders, how does Todd manage to smoke so much, and Scott, too? Every time Robin is high he is aware of a shifting, a forced entry into his perspective; this high world is a threat to the regular, organized state of things. When he stands, the room threatens to slip out from under his feet.

Victoria's presence lingers long after she has removed herself. Robin fears that his disloyalty will anger her, that she will try to balance the scales by telling her mother what he is doing up here. Mrs. Spicer, the upright housewife, would certainly march him back home. And what would *his* mother say? He makes himself stop thinking about it, tells himself that Victoria might disapprove of this, but she wouldn't narc on him. (*Narc*—where did he get that word from? Scott? Todd? Victoria's right—he's becoming like them, a scum.)

He is more afraid that she will figure out the secret longings that coaxed him up here in the first place. Fear, desire, the guy smells of the room, the sultry buzz of the dope—all of it is heightened now. He is no longer alone in the house with Todd, but Todd has bolted them into his fortress; there has been an intrusion, but it has secured their privacy.

What he feels is heat—his ears burning, his throat scorched, the pulse at the tip of his thumb. The accumulation of these little pains makes him think of Jackson—does Jackson feel his injuries? Does he know his body is broken?

"What's up with you, man?" Todd waves his hand past Robin's eyes.

"I can't believe you said Scott's pot sucks. I feel like I'm in a *dream.*"

Todd closes his fingers around his crotch and squeezes. "Maybe you're in a wet dream."

"Scott said you had one"—he tries to make himself stop talking, but the impulse propels the words forward—"about me. He said you said in the dream you were calling me sissy-boy."

"I'm gonna kick his ass. I swear, I'm gonna fucking kill him." Robin snaps from his haze long enough to worry that he will be hit again, but Todd can only work up a sloppy punch to the ceiling angling down over them. He shakes his knuckles and sits on his aching hand. "He made it up anyway."

Robin tries to bring reassurance to his voice. "I know. He was just saying that. I didn't believe him." He makes himself stand up. A queasiness washes through him; he is pissing off Todd and betraying Scott—*cheating* on him is how it feels. *Why can't I just shut up?*

"I'm totally gonna kill him," Todd says, but without much emphasis. "Fuck, I really hurt my hand."

"Don't tell him I told you." He takes a few steps toward the door when Todd's voice calls him back.

"Wait. Look." Todd is unzipping his fly, prying free his semirigid dick. He squeezes it inside his fist and shakes it up and down. "Smoking pot gets me kind of boned up." He rubs it, staring intently at himself as if unable to look away. Robin stares, too: it's the first time he has seen Todd's dick in the light. The skin is dark against Todd's clenched knuckles, and the hair around it curls tightly, a soft, dark moss. He takes a step closer but stops, checking the doorway for Victoria. Todd says, "I bet if I stood in front of my window you could see me from your house."

"Maybe. How would I know?"

"If I jerked off in front of the window you could see me, I bet." Todd raises his lids slowly, unveiling seductive eyes. "That would be funny, if you could see me doing it."

Robin shakes his head, as if in disagreement. He looks away and back, away and back. Hypnotism, a set trap, bait on a line. He doesn't trust the moment, but it doesn't matter. His dick is stiffening in his pants, he finds himself stepping closer.

"Wait," Todd says. He moves his eyes between his dick and Robin's eyes. "Show me yours."

Robin unsnaps the fastener at his waist, pushes down his pants, rolls his underwear to his thighs. He tries to mimic the way Todd is touching himself but it's embarrassing, a show, a display. "What do you want me to do?"

Todd says, "I'll do you, that's all. You don't touch me." He lunges forward. Robin gasps at the smothering warmth of Todd's mouth on his dick, the weird vacuum of it. Then the chill of Todd's cold fingers on his hipbones, rocking him back and forth. His leg bones wobble; he braces himself against Todd's shoulders, wanting to sit down. Todd's face is pure concentration; his back is tense. Robin can count ribs through his T-shirt.

He thinks of Scott, how he probably stood here just like this. He wonders if Scott could know that he is here right now; he imagines him walking in, staring at them in this position. His knees buckle at the idea. Closing his eyes helps—he can control his breath, steady his legs.

The sensations change. He can distinguish Todd's teeth from his tongue from the insides of his cheeks. It gets better from here: an embrace, a tightening, a satisfying tension climbing upward, taking over. He is disappearing, he's still in his skin but also he is flying: a bat flying out from the dark quaking cavern of his body. It expands. Something pulls. His muscles seize up, he hears a whimper as if someone is crying, but it is him, doubling over with the terrific burn of his come emptying into Todd's slick mouth.

Todd pulls off, and Robin watches more of his goop spurt out and drop. The come fascinates him. Another string of it hangs for a moment and then plops onto his sneaker, spreading out like egg white. "Cool. It's still coming out of you," Todd whispers in a voice so mesmerized Robin thinks he is picking it up telepathically. Todd leans back against the bed, pumping on himself until his entire body is rigid except the blur of his right arm and the quivering of his wet lower lip. With an enormous shudder he blasts a pearly string from between his strokes. The look Robin sees on Todd's face is so gentle—Todd weakened, Todd relieved—that for the first time ever he allows himself to relax in Todd's presence. For a short while—thirty seconds, a minute—everything is perfect.

"Do you like me?" Robin asks.

"Pull up your pants. My mother could be home now." Robin feels the protection of the climax crack apart; the old Todd is back. He grabs the crusty towel and hastily wipes himself and the floor, as if it's all been a bother.

Robin gets a whiff of the semen's chlorine stench. He pulls up his pants. "It was just a question, because of that—the blow job you just did."

"Jesus Christ—just cool out about everything." Todd lays himself out on the mattress, a pillow over his face.

Is this something else Scott learned from Todd: no talking about it afterward? His eyes rest on Todd's crotch, asymmetrical curves squeezed into his pants, like a stuffed purse. He wonders suddenly why Todd hasn't let him suck his dick. He doesn't get it at all. "I guess I'll just go now," he says.

"Later."

Downstairs, Victoria takes one look at him and accuses, "Your nose was bleeding."

He turns his face away from her. "What are you talking about?"

"I noticed it before but I didn't say anything." She purses her lips as if she's got something on him. "See what pot does to you?"

"I have them all the time." He begins backing away. "I probably need more vitamins and iron. My mother has some at home in the medicine chest."

Victoria plants her gaze on the TV, her shoulders to Robin. "The show's practically over already."

When Robin steps outside and the cold air hits him, he feels relieved. Three steps into his own yard he feels as if he might cry. He turns around. The light in Todd's room is off.

He goes to bed early, speaking as little as possible to his family. The next morning he skips breakfast and walks to school alone. He isn't thinking anything, or he's forgetting his thoughts as soon as he has them—he isn't sure which. His desires flare up and then disintegrate into disaster: he pictures himself with Todd, driving across America together, broad green fields all around them, Todd's arm across the seat, Jim Morrison on the eight track, Todd singing, *"Come on, touch me babe."* But then Robin says the wrong thing—maybe he just tells Todd how much he likes being with him this way—and Todd gets angry, kicks him out of the car in the middle of a burning red desert, and peels out in a spray of dirt and dust, leaving him to the wolves. He tries to picture Todd and him on Bleecker Street, in the Village, flipping through the record racks at Bleecker Bob's, his hand in Todd's back pocket, right there in the middle of the store . . . but Todd would probably yell at him and smack him in the face or bolt out the door. He'd be stuck in the city all by himself, the drug dealers in the park would sidle up to him, muttering their strange incantations, and the muggers would move in for the kill, knowing he's just a lost kid from New Jersey.

He tries to crush these daydreams, to wrestle himself from their foggy wrap. He thinks more than once that smoking pot must be rotting his brain—that's what they tell you in health class: you can suffer *permanent damage*—but then he decides that he's going crazy, that a poison is leaking into his thoughts and tricking him into acting out all his secret wishes. In social studies they are studying world religions, and that day a question from the Hindu teachings snares his attention: "How can a wise man, knowing the unity of life, seeing all creatures in himself, be deluded or sorrowful?" He cannot make sense of "seeing all creatures in himself," but decides that his problem must be that he just isn't *wise*. He raises his hand and asks his teacher where the Hindus thought wisdom came from. The answer—"Wisdom is found by looking inward"— brings only more confusion; looking inward, he thinks, is where his problems start.

Gym class: no Scott. Passing through the courtyard between classes, no sign of him. Robin is restless with cheater's guilt, full of the need to see Scott, not to confess, but to talk with him about something regular. To make it all OK again. When he gets home from school he dials Scott's number. Scott's father answers—slurring his words as if his mouth is full of toothpaste—and tells Robin Scott can't talk now. Robin leaves a message with the sinking feeling that Mr. Schatz won't deliver it.

At dinnertime his mother questions him about his "silent treatment," and he just says he's got a lot on his mind. Later, after his father knocks another few feet from the old dining room wall; Robin helps by sweeping plaster dust. The house is freezing at night, with only plastic across the hole to the backyard.

He closes his bedroom door and sits in bed in his underwear, reading. The book he's been assigned in English class is *Lord of the Flies,* and by midnight he's still awake and very spooked. He hears the stranded boys chanting in his head like a pulse: *Kill the pig, cut its throat, drink its blood.* He remembers that the ladder his father has been using while building the new room is leaning against the roof outside his bedroom window. A murderer could climb up and slit his throat, drink his blood. He shuts the book and turns off the light and buries himself under the blankets.

He is staring up from his bed at a figure, robed and menacing, long black hair across its brow. He is unable to discern if it is male or female, but knows that the words this person wants to speak are dangerous to him; he knows, too, that he just needs to wake himself up to be rid of it, but his arms have been pinned to the sheets and his mouth is stuffed with a plastic tube that is meant to help him breathe but instead is slowly choking him. He forces the tube out, thrusting it from his throat as if he is vomiting, and bursts back into consciousness, not knowing if he has screamed or not. He listens. No one is stirring in the house. The robed figure is gone, but the room whistles as if a spirit has just rushed through. For a moment he thinks he hears someone calling his name. He looks at the clock. Only thirty minutes have passed since he turned out the light.

When he was younger, the quiet and darkness of night frightened him. His first memories of this house are all set long after sundown. After the noisy brightness he knew from their apartment in the city, where he could fall asleep to the sounds of car horns and the hissing brakes of busses, bedtime here was frightening. His mother had to lull him to sleep reading from *Charlotte's Web* and the *Winnie-the-Pooh* books (which he loved the most, because the boy in them had almost the same name as his). But that was nine years ago, and now he hates it when he gets freaked out at night. Lately he's as bad as Ruby.

He opens his window for air. After the terrible silence of the dream, even the faintest sounds of the night are a comfort: wind disrupting the dried leaves, a motorcycle buzzing its way through empty streets. He pulls a T-shirt on and climbs out onto the roof, happy to get away from his bed, which feels haunted. When his eyes adjust to the light of a half-moon, he feels better. Scattered stars are visible high up, and a single, silent airplane, streaking gold and red light. The roof shingles are gritty, an irritation against the thin cloth of his underwear.

He hears it again: someone calling his name. And footsteps on the ladder, rubber soles squeaking against the aluminum. This is not a dream. He inches back fearfully as the point of a hooded jacket rises over the edge, then a face. *Scott.*

"What are you doing here?" Robin checks over his shoulder, toward his parents' bedroom window.

"Just hanging out, man."

Scott's voice is just above a whisper, but in the empty air it booms. Robin holds his finger in front of his mouth to indicate quiet and motions him closer, where the Spicers' backyard light can't reach them. Scott sits near enough for Robin to smell him. He is giving off heat, as if he's been running.

Scott says, "My Dad was on my case."

"About what?"

"Same old shit. Telling me I'm no good, a piece of shit, the usual."

"He said that to your face?"

"Fuck, what does he care? There's no one around to stop him."

Robin pulls his knees to his chest and stretches his T-shirt down over his legs, embarrassed to be in his underwear, worried his parents will awaken, sensing that something must be very wrong for Scott to be here. He asks, "Did you just sneak out or did you run away from him or what?"

"I just waited till he passed out and then I walked out."

"Passed out from drinking?"

"Sorta." He coughs once, a heavy, phlegmy cough, and spits off the roof. "Then I went to The Bird."

"Really? What's it like at night?"

"It's pitch fucking black inside that birdhouse building. Remember, the one we were in?" Robin only nods; Scott has never since spoken of what happened there between them. "Pretty fucking scary, though. Like, you ever see that movie *The Texas Chainsaw Massacre?*"

"No!" The title alone gives Robin a chill along his shoulders.

Scott shrugs. "My brother snuck me in." His *brother?*—Robin remembers rushing through a bedroom at Scott's house, a very tidy boy's bedroom, as they outran Mr. Schatz that Sunday afternoon a few weeks ago. But before he can ask for details about this never-mentioned brother, Scott says hurriedly, "The Bird wasn't *that* scary, but I started remembering from the movie this scary house with all these teenagers getting stuck on meat hooks, and I was thinking about the psycho guy, Leatherface, sneaking up on me and coming around the corner and—"

Robin cuts him off. "Scott, you're creeping me out."

"Sorry. I got really creeped out at The Bird, but I couldn't go home 'cause I'd knocked my old man out. Actually, I hit him over the head with a frying pan."

Robin stares at him in disbelief.

"Yeah, he was coming after me so I hit him." Scott's voice is now just a whisper, guilty and scared and proud all at once. "He hit me first. And then he chased me around but he tripped on the garbage. And when he fell down I pulled this frying pan off the stove and clobbered him on the side of the head." He unzips his sweatjacket, pulling his T-shirt away from his body to show a stain. "This is some grease from the frying pan that splashed up." He pretends to taste it and fakes a satisfied grin. "Mmm. Fried chicken."

Robin is too startled by the story to notice the attempted humor. "Did he go unconscious?"

"No, he got up, but he was really dizzy, totally out of it. He was already drunk, so I probably just, you know, killed a few more brain cells." He slams a fist into his thigh, twice, and spits out, "Bam, bam!"

"How many times did you hit him?"

"Once, and then I guess one more after that. I would have kept hitting but I thought I'd, like, kill him or something."

Robin tries to picture the scene: the blow to the head, Mr. Schatz's collapse, Scott's second hit, this one from above. He wonders if at that very moment Mr. Schatz is bleeding to death on the kitchen floor.

As if he can read his mind, Scott says, "Nothing happened. Cool out. He just sort of spun around for a minute and then sat down in his chair in the living room." He lowers his head; behind the profile of his hood, only his nose and chin are visible. He mumbles, "I checked to see if he was still breathing. Just in case."

"God, imagine if you killed your father." The comment fades into the night. Robin tightens his arms around his knees, protection from the night's chill, protection from the trouble Scott is in. "What are you gonna do?"

"I don't know. He'll probably black the whole fucking thing out. If not . . . he'll wake up and *really* want to kill me." Robin hears Scott's fear; he knows Scott's been through this kind of thing before, but maybe this is worse than usual. Would Mr. Schatz look here for Scott?

"I don't feel so good, actually," Robin says. "I think I'm getting dizzy up here. I had a nosebleed yesterday and I haven't felt right ever since."

"Should we go inside?" Scott asks, shifting toward Robin.

"*Both* of us?"

"I could crash here for a few hours and then wake up early and split."

Scott's voice is hopeful, though to Robin this sounds like a risky plan. "What if my mother and father wake up? I mean, shouldn't you make sure your father's OK?"

Scott hisses, "You just think I'm a fucking scum, don't you?"

"No!"

"You got no idea what it's like to get slammed in the face."

Robin wants Scott to lower his voice, but Scott's words provoke him. "For your information I got slammed in the face *yesterday.*"

Scott narrows his eyes at him. "By who? Your father? You're bullshitting me. You're trying to act tough."

"I happened to get a bloody nose from someone who you happen to know." Robin turns his head and stares toward the Spicers' house and Todd's darkened window.

Scott follows Robin's sight line. "Right, like *Spicer* hit you in the face. Let me see where."

"You can't *see* anything," Robin says. "He didn't hit me that hard, but I got a nosebleed."

"Shit! What'd you do to him?" Scott now sounds almost proud of him. Robin shrugs. "Nothing."

"Did he only hit you one time, or did he really pound you?"

"Only one time. I got him mad."

"He hit me one time, too," Scott says excitedly. "The only time I ever saw him take a swing at anyone, and it was right at me. I fucking hit him back. He totally wussed out right away, just backed off."

"Wow." Scott's words leave Robin wondering why he himself didn't strike back at Todd—why, in fact, he didn't even think of it. Scott asks, almost shyly, "Did you say something to him, that you *liked* him or something?"

Robin considers his words, then says quietly, "I said something about you."

"Did you tell him stuff I said about him?" Scott asks with alarm in his voice.

"No, I would never!" Suddenly Robin does not want to have this conversation. It's bad enough acting like getting smacked by Todd was a cool thing; now he has to make up a reason why it happened. "I said to him that I'd been hanging out with you, and he said you were a scum, and I said, 'Fuck you,' and he decked me. And then Victoria came in, and I went home."

"I can't believe that," Scott says. He curls tighter, his knees nearly under his chin now, mirroring Robin's own posture. "No, I *can* believe it. He fucking hates my guts."

Robin breathes out slowly, relieved that Scott has bought his lie. He asks carefully, "Todd's weird—don't you think?" Scott does not answer, so he goes on. "He's never what you think he is. First I thought he was really mean, when I was little and he used to call me 'Girly Underwear' all the time and tease me. And then he started being nice to me. He asked me to go to Maggio's party, like he wanted to be friends. Then yesterday . . ." He pantomimes Todd's smack to his face.

"He's a user," Scott says. He shifts closer to Robin so that their hips are touching.

"He's kind of conceited, too," Robin says. "After the party he was talking about how he was going to go cross-country and be a drifter. I could tell he thought he was *so* cool."

"He's full of shit," Scott says.

"Yeah." Robin takes a quick breath and then says something experimental, something he thinks Scott might not be able to handle: "I still think he's cute, though."

Scott says nothing. He clears his throat. Then he says in a soft, uninflected voice, "You're cuter."

Robin is caught off guard. "I am *not.*"

Scott looks off into the darkness, picks a pebble off the roof, and chucks it into the bushes. "I said that to my father tonight."

"You said what?"

"That you were cute. That's why he went after me."

Robin squints through the darkness, trying to read Scott's face, unsure if this is some kind of joke. But Scott has dropped his head between his knees and is sniffling. The curve of his back trembles.

"You really told your father that?"

"It just came out!" Scott lifts his face—his eyes are wet, his voice thick with phlegm. He sucks a gob of snot into his throat and spits, wipes his eyes roughly with the back of his wrist. "I told him I was going out. And he was like, 'You're staying home and gonna help me go through some of the lumber in the shed.' Which was bullshit because he was home all day doing nothing and could-a looked through the fucking lumber *before,* but now suddenly I'm home and we *both* gotta look through the fucking lumber. So the first thing I think of to say is, 'I've already got plans to hang out with Robin.' And he's like, 'Who the fuck is that? Robin from *Batman?*' as if that's really fucking original. And I'm like, 'He's this guy at school. He was here the other day.' And he's like, 'Oh, that fucking wimpy kid.'" The insult jolts Robin; he's forever being called names, but it's worse coming from out of the blue like that, as if at any given moment someone he hardly knows might be slamming him. He shakes the thought away, not wanting to break the momentum of Scott's story: this might be the longest he's heard Scott speak about himself without interruption. "So I'm like, 'Fuck you, Dad, he's not wimpy.' And he's like, 'Sure looked it to me, he looked like a girl.' And I'm like, 'How can you say he looks like a girl, he's practically the cutest guy in the ninth grade.'" He stops abruptly, locking his eyes on Robin's, as if expecting the answer to a question.

Robin's stomach tightens; his face heats up. Even if he could believe that Scott really meant this (but why would Scott lie this way?), he'd also have to imagine Scott saying this to his father. It's too good to be true—*Scott thinks I'm the cutest boy in the ninth grade*—and just plain scary, as if he's found out that he's been implicated in a misdemeanor Scott committed and must now share his fate.

"It just came out without thinking," Scott says, almost pleading. "I don't know. I guess I was just *thinking* that, and then it came out. That you were cute." He slides the bottom of his sneaker on a roof shingle, the noise like sandpaper on wood. "Part of me wanted to say it just to piss him off. So, like, mission accomplished on that one."

In the pause Robin realizes how constant the night's many noises are: the sounds of tires on asphalt, the random call of a night bird, a clunky slam of a windowpane, and the echo of a voice calling a lost pet. And he realizes that he is cold and that he does not want Scott to leave, and that if he is implicated in anything it is exactly what he's wanted all along. In this unexpected moment he understands that Scott has become the person who matters to him most.

"So do you want to come in?" he asks.

Just the sound of Scott's sneakers landing on his rug is enough to accelerate Robin's heartbeat. Terror and excitement. He wants Scott to share his bed rather than getting into Jackson's, but he is too nervous to ask him. Scott glances from one bed to the other and lets his eyes rest on the unmade one: Robin's. An involuntary prayer: *Thank You, God.* Without hesitation Scott unzips his jacket and sits on the bed, kicking off his sneakers, dropping his pants. His colored underwear fades into the dimly lit room; his legs, which Robin has never looked at closely, are pale and thin and bruised on both shins. Robin takes off his own T-shirt. Scott looks at him and after a moment does the same. Robin has always thought of himself as too scrawny but Scott is a rail in comparison: his shoulder blades like bird wings, the concave slope at the center of his chest as bright and delicate as an eggshell. Robin carefully folds his T-shirt and lays it on a chair.

Scott says, "I should be on the outside so I can get out quick in the morning." Robin slides across the bed to the wall and Scott follows.

Robin lies on his back, hearing his every breath and Scott's beside him, out of sync, restless. He shifts his body so that he is touching Scott in random places: their ankles, the curve of their hips, the flat smoothness of their upper arms.

He waits for Scott to get settled, and when Scott rolls away, facing out into the room, Robin lets his body ease slowly toward him. He moves in increments, more nervous than he ever remembers being. First his knees lock behind Scott's; then his stomach presses against Scott's back, and finally his hard-on, cramped in the pouch of his underwear, nestles against Scott's ass.

Scott pulls Robin's arm into his stomach. Robin has been holding his breath; now he exhales. At any moment he expects this to sour, but Scott is different tonight. Unguarded. Robin's other arm has been forced uncomfortably upward, over his head, but he leaves it there, afraid to upset anything. In this too awake state he dreads being caught, dreads everything beyond the shelter of his bedroom. His mind forms images of discovery: his parents, or Scott's father, suddenly banging down the door; Todd Spicer secretly spying on them with binoculars. He imagines Ruby coming into the room, intent on occupying Jackson's bed again.

He is jarred by the disturbing thought that if Jackson hadn't fallen and busted his neck, Jackson would be here right now, and Scott, of course, wouldn't. If the accident had never happened, Robin realizes now, he wouldn't have gone to the hospital on his bike that first night, that night he and Scott first spoke to each other in the Dairy Queen parking lot, when Scott had a bloody nose of his own. If he hadn't met Scott that night, they wouldn't have ditched together, they wouldn't have gotten stoned at The Bird, they would never have had sex. And if he hadn't done all of that with Scott, he wonders, would he have ever agreed to go with Todd to that party, much less leave with him and go to the golf course? For the first time Robin draws this map, this chain of events beginning with Jackson's fall and ending up right here, with Scott in his bed. He keeps himself awake for a very long time, until the map mutates into a tangled, layered web. He falls asleep unsure if he is the spinner of this web or a creature trapped at its heart.

Scott is gone. Robin finds his parents in the kitchen, his mother holding a cold cloth to her head, his father silently studying a sheet of white paper. His father says sternly, "Robin, you have some explaining to do."

Dorothy says, "Clark, let me." She slides the white paper from Clark's hands with a coaxing glance and reads from it: "'Robin, thanks for helping me out. Scott.'"

An instant knot in his stomach. "Where did you find that?"

"On the refrigerator. Under this magnet."

Robin's eyes widen. "How'd it get there?"

Dorothy says, "That's the question I have for you." Her lips press together in a false smile, as if trying to smooth the way for his confession.

"I don't know how it got there." Could Scott have been stupid enough to stick this note to the fridge? He tries to not sound defensive, sets a lie in motion. "This kid Scott wrote it, 'cause I helped him on his English exam."

Clark grabs the note out of Dorothy's hands, snapping the paper crisply in the air. "It's written on my business letterhead!"

"It is?" Maybe Scott wasn't being stupid—maybe this was intentional, some kind of mean trick. His parents are scrutinizing him expectantly. "I mean—yeah, I know it is. Because I gave him a piece."

Clark is stunned. "You *gave* it to him?"

Robin tries to make his explanation sound truthful. "I just had it with me. I took some and put it in my notebook. You know, you leave a pile of it in that drawer, right there." He makes his face sheepish, lays it on thick. "I just thought it was cool that you have your own stationery. I guess I was showing off, Dad."

Clark smiles in spite of himself. "Look, this isn't for show and tell. This is for business purposes and business purposes only. Don't go passing it out like Monopoly money."

"I didn't. I just lent Scott a couple of pieces while we were studying."

Dorothy crosses her arms, suspicion in her eyes despite the placid smile. "I still don't understand how it wound up on the refrigerator."

"I put it there last night." He fears his voice is less convincing now.

"Oh, so now you remember?"

"Yeah, sure. Last night I found it in my notebook and I didn't know where to put it. I guess I just stuck it up there and forgot about it."

"You guess?" she asks.

Clark pushes his chair back and waves his hand. "Who cares when he put it on the fridge? He can put his goddamn birth certificate on the fridge as far as I care. Just don't go handing out my letterhead to your friends. I only get a five hundred sheet allotment per year."

"Sorry, Dad." He turns his back to them both, wipes perspiration from his forehead with his sleeve. What was Scott trying to do, get him in trouble?

Clark stands up, effectively ending the discussion. He gulps down his coffee and straightens his tie. It's the first time he's been in a business suit since Jackson's accident. "I've got to go to the office today for a couple of hours and talk to Steinberg about the Connecticut route, before that shyster tries to reassign my territory to someone else." He leaves without a good-bye, the clinical smell of aftershave lingering behind.

From behind his back, Robin hears the clatter of dishes being cleared, his mother sighing frustratedly before she speaks. "So if I'm not mistaken, this Scott is the boy with whom you went AWOL right after your brother went into the hospital?" He detects the false ring of nonchalance in her question, a breezy layer blanketing her real concern.

"Yeah. So?"

"Should I be concerned that you've continued your friendship with a delinquent?"

He turns around, angrily taking her bait. "I was helping him with some work. That's all."

She picks up the note and places it on the fridge, the magnet tapping into place. "I just can't shake the notion that he was actually *here.*"

"Mom, give me a break." Lately she is fussy when he wants her to leave him alone and distant when he wants access to her. It crosses his mind that she *wants* him to hate her, that she's punishing him for something, but the thought is eerie and poisonous, and he makes it go away. He snatches Scott's note from the refrigerator and crushes it in his fist.

She peers into his face. "The bags under your eyes are big enough to pack a lunch in." All false brightness has left her voice.

"I'm just tired," he says.

"So am I, Robin. Tired of it all." She walks across the room and routs through her purse, surprising him by pulling out her Pall Malls and lighting one up. He's never before seen his mother smoke in the house. Cold air scurries toward them as she slides open a window. He watches smoke coat the glass, meeting the reflection of her exhausted face.

All morning, as he waits to see Scott, static interference courses along Robin's nerves. There is the memory of him and Scott wedged together in his bed, the damp heat of their entangled embrace, the rasp of Scott's breath, vapors settling on his skin. There is also a pit of bitterness at the note left behind, the unnecessary run-in with his parents. And there is his unease about Scott's predicament at home: Mr. Schatz's threats, the violence between them. Where did Scott go when he left his house that morning?

Scott shuffles into phys. ed. late. Robin mouths, "How are you?" across the gymnasium, and Scott pantomimes back, "Stoned." They are assigned to opposing basketball teams, meant to guard each other. The game's momentum carries them back and forth across the court, affording them fragments of conversation.

Robin whispers, "I've been thinking about you."

Scott replies evasively, "Yeah, I was thinking about your room—how come you don't fuck it up at all? It just looked like something from a TV show."

"What are you talking about?"

"Leave some fucking clothes on the floor for one. Just put up some posters and shit. And you could get a black light, or an aquarium like mine, or something cool like that. You just have books and a desk. And all that sports shit in the corner."

"That's Jackson's."

"I thought he's getting his own room."

Robin sighs. Construction has been moving along steadily for a couple of weeks, but in the last few days, Clark has seemed drained of enthusiasm. Robin is wondering if this is the point at which Clark will give up, leave things undone as he has so many times in the past. "I'll believe it when I see it," he says.

Then the basketball shoots toward Robin. He grabs it and stops in his tracks, immediately and totally perplexed as to what should be done with it. Bodies are swarming around him. For a horrible, extended moment, the entire game hinges upon his action. He locates someone he's pretty sure is on his team and hurls it nervously his way. The tidal relief of accomplishment: his teammate is off and running, the ball in his command, the pack trailing behind.

Scott's eyes are closed. He's just been waiting for the interruption to pass.

Robin says, "My parents found that note."

"What note?"

"Don't even pretend . . ." Suddenly the ball is flying toward him again. Robin jitterishly swats it away. It almost lands out of bounds, but a boy on the other team intercepts it. Robin shrinks away as his teammates complain.

Scott says, "I thought your house was gonna be more like Spicer's."

"No way, they're rich. Mr. Spicer's a lawyer. Can't you tell by just looking?"

"Yeah. Well, you still got more money than me."

He tries again. "Scott, why'd you leave that note? I almost got in trouble."

A guy from Robin's team bounds past the two of them in a burst of heat and body odor on his way to a dunk. One of Scott's teammates yells at him for not intervening. Scott flicks him the finger.

The shrill chirp of Mr. Pintack's whistle calls the action to a halt.

Pintack, all bulk and polyester, is striding toward them. "Schatz! MacKenzie!" Robin holds his breath, all eyes are upon them. "Maybe you two should check your schedule," Pintack snarls, pointing toward the door to the girls' gym, "because maybe you're supposed to be on the other side of that wall." He smiles cruelly, looking around at the other boys for confirmation, gathering an alliance.

Robin's usual impulse is to silently look at his feet and blank out his thoughts until moments like this one pass. But there is Scott rolling his eyes, merely bothered and not intimidated by Pintack's braying. Pintack, Robin realizes, is nothing compared to Mr. Schatz. He thinks of Todd Spicer punching him in the face: Pintack can't even go that far. He's all hot air.

"You two want to play ball or you want to stand around gossiping like a couple of chicks?"

Robin looks up into Pintack's infuriating, cocky grin. "Aren't there any other choices?"

Now some of the muffled laughter is *with* him, not *at* him.

The moment of triumph is fleeting, squashed by Pintack choosing another option for him: twenty-five push-ups.

After ten he thinks he will collapse, but he forces himself to continue. His arms inflame, his chest contracts, the heels of his hands cry out for relief. Twelve, thirteen, fourteen—the blood and breath in his head seem to be fighting for space. It's over at fifteen. He is panting, his hot face against the dirty floorboards, the smell of rubber soles enclosing him. Humiliation, as was intended.

He and Scott are sent to opposite benches for the rest of class. Robin spits between a crack in the bleachers. Fifteen push-ups was better than he expected. His muscles throb with a newly discovered assertiveness.

Scott's wearing sweat pants and the same long-sleeve sweatjacket he always has on, and it occurs to Robin that Scott keeps himself covered up to hide the bruises Robin saw last night. In the locker room he asks him, "What are you going to do?"

Scott looks at him blankly. "About what?"

"About your father."

"Next time I'll hit him harder." He forces a laugh, but Robin can't bring himself to smile.

His mother comes into his room at bedtime with ideas about art school, mentioning schools she's heard of, talking as if it's a done deal. She asks for a report on how his story is progressing, and when he tells her that he's having trouble starting, she reminds him of details from various trips they've taken together, events that they've attended, restaurants at which they've eaten, stores where they have shopped. The more she wants to talk about this, the less he wants to listen to her. More than even the completion of Jackson's room, art school has become something he doesn't believe will ever really come to pass.

The next night, after the *Community News* runs a story about a couple of Greenlawn kids busted for selling pot and speed, Dorothy corners him in the bathroom. "I'm going to use this as ammunition," she says, brandishing the paper. "I'm going to tell your father that this kind of thing doesn't happen in art school."

"That's not going to work." He imagines that *everyone* would be doing drugs in art school.

"Of course. I'll *make* it work."

He dreams that night that his father is a priest giving him communion. He is waiting in the aisle at church, waiting to receive the body of Christ, when he realizes that they're at funeral mass for Jackson. The coffin is open. Robin leaves the line to look into the dark box, but the closer he gets, the surer he is that he will not be able to see what lies inside, will not be able to see the image of death. He spits something from his mouth to the floor—an onion, pearly white, smooth. Again and again he tries to pick it up, but it slips from his fingers. He wants to hide it. His mother and father begin arguing over the onion, over who is to blame for it.

Chapter Ten

On his way out of the bathroom—drying his hands on his pajama pants, having just jerked off and cleaned up hastily—Robin hears Ruby crying in her bedroom. He rests his ear against the thin pressboard door. The sobs are muffled, buried beneath her blanket. He steps back, thinking it best to leave her alone; let her cry herself to sleep or let his parents deal with it. But then the thick, phony ruffling of a television laugh track travels up from the living room. He had passed his mother and father on his way upstairs. They were staring at the TV, not conversing, she with her glass of wine and he with his Seagrams. Now, as the insistent canned laughter fights with Ruby's misery for his attention, he realizes how dreary their faces had been and how quickly he has grown accustomed to this. The two of them have been transformed since Jackson's fall: his father's once comfortable detachment has hardened into rage; his mother's irresistible style has been honed to a brittle edge. They have become authorities, decision makers, strangers who argue with each other and stare in confusion, or anger, or some other unreadable agitation, at him and Ruby.

It used to be important, and easy, to play big brother to Ruby. She's always acted young for her age; it's been common for strangers to assume that Jackson was older, that Ruby was the baby of the family. Robin has defended her more than once against taunting from girls who were more mature, more popular. He's helped her with homework, taken her to the movies, brought records home from New Sounds and invited her to listen with him. Just this summer, he'd walked her into town, where they pigged out on candy while he gave her advice about starting middle school. Months have passed since he has asked her how school was going, if classes were hard, if she was making new friends. The accident—that's what changed everything. He can't shake off the anger that it never would have happened if she had simply gotten off the slide when Larry and Jackson were tormenting her. Coming to her rescue was the beginning of the end.

Since then, only Nana has paid any attention to Ruby, but Nana's been away for weeks. Robin takes a deep breath, knocks on her door. The sobs stop quickly, silenced by surprise.

"Ruby?" he whispers. "Can I come in?"

"Why?" Her voice is tentative, choked with phlegm.

He pushes the door open and navigates the darkness. The confectionery smell of the room envelopes him, reminding him of those weeks he spent sleeping here: the talcum powder, the candy-sweet girl's perfume. There is a new smell, too: the spooky aftersmoke of an extinguished candle. He says, "I heard you crying."

She sniffles. Shifts her small body lightly beneath the bedsheets.

He asks, "Are you thinking about Jackson?"

"I'm scared he could—I mean, I had a bad thought. That he could get worse." Her voice is like the shuffling of paper, raspy breaths between words. She inhales wetly. "And then I thought that God was *stupid.*"

Robin reaches into the darkness, his hand landing on the fuzz of her pajama sleeve. "What are you talking about?"

"It's like a broken record in my head," she says. "God is stupid, God is stupid, God is stupid. It won't go away."

He bites his upper lip, glad the darkness hides his struggle not to smile at his sister's blasphemy. He wants to tell her that maybe she's right, that if there is a God He *must* be stupid, because stupid things happen all the time and stupid people are in charge of everything. But her sobs distress him; without her newfound faith she might fall apart. What else does she have right now? "Maybe you just need to go to sleep and ignore the bad voices," he says. "In the morning you'll feel better."

"How can I sleep with this sin in my mind?" she says.

"Hah!" The exclamation jumps from his chest before he can squelch it.

"Don't make fun of me."

"Sorry," he says quickly. "I wasn't laughing at you. I was just thinking, you're so much better than me, Ruby. If you're a sinner, than what am I?"

"What do you mean?" Through the gray light he can see curiosity take hold of her.

Should he explain? He couldn't possibly tell her the details, yet something inside his throat flutters for a moment, the wisp of a need to tell someone, anyone, what his life has become. His secrets fester in the cavity of his body: he could burst open in confession, skin peeling back to reveal fresh sores in need of attention. "Well . . ." he says. "I just mean, you know, I cut school, and I smoke cigarettes and other stuff that's worse than that."

"Like what?" Now she is almost rigid with interest. "Did you steal something?"

"It's just worse than anything you've done—trust me." An uncertain silence descends; he waits for the moment to pass, for the mood to shift—or for it to deepen, for a force to take hold and bind them more tightly together. Robin listens to the warbled TV noises beneath them, their parents separated by only carpet and floorboards. He revisits those moments just before coming in here, when he was in the bathroom spinning fantasies from an underwear ad in his father's *Runner's World* magazine. He thinks too of all the mornings he wakes confused by his dreams and wants to hurt someone and of all the lies he tells instead. A fantasy blooms before him now, of him and Ruby on the slide that horrible evening—except this time they are holding Larry upside down over the edge, each of them clasping an ankle and then letting go. . .

"*I* stole something," Ruby says, snapping him from his reverie.

"What? From where?"

"You can't tell anyone." She shuffles out from under the covers and steps on the rug. He is amazed how light she is on her feet, how skilled at making herself unnoticed. She reaches behind her dresser and pulls out a brass chain with a large pendant on it.

"What is it? Bring it over here," Robin says. He steps to the window, letting it catch streetlight. On the medallion is a sculpted relief of two swimming fish surrounded by planets and stars.

"It's Aunt Corinne's," Ruby says.

He remembers seeing it on his aunt—the Pisces symbol, bobbing between her breasts against a striped blouse; she had it on last time she was here. "It's your sign, too, right? When did you get it?"

"She left it in the bathroom, and I took it. I don't know why she took it off anyway."

"Mom could get you one for yourself."

"I don't really want one. It's kind of ugly." She takes the medallion in her hands and runs her fingers over it. "I think I'm getting possessed. Remember that movie *The Exorcist?*"

"You didn't see that movie."

"So? I *heard* about it. The girl in that got possessed by the devil. So maybe that's it. First I steal this, and then I can't stop thinking that God is stupid."

"Duh, Ruby, you're not possessed. You're practically a *nun*." He takes the medallion back from her, impatient with her ideas. "Do you want me to give it back to Aunt Corinne?"

"No! I don't want anyone to know."

"You could just say you took it out of the bathroom where she left it and then you forgot about it. It hasn't been that long."

She shakes her head vehemently.

He is ready to walk away in frustration when he remembers the resolve that impelled him into the room to begin with. "OK, here's an idea. Why don't we sneak it back? Next time we go over or they come over here?"

"Will you do it? I'm too nervous."

"OK. But you owe me one."

There is a quick rap on the door. It swings open and the overhead light is flashed on—blinding, rude. Clark squints in at them. "What are you two doing? It's almost 11:30."

"Ruby couldn't sleep, so I'm telling her a story." Robin hides the medallion behind his back, slips it down the waistband of his shorts as he speaks, feels it rest between his briefs and the skin of his backside.

Clark softens a bit. "Let's call it a night already. Come on, everyone to bed."

Back in his room, Robin rubs the medallion under his bedsheets. He runs the smooth side of it across his belly and lets the chain drop into his groin, where it tickles until it snags on a hair. He tosses it under his bed. The annoyance at having to undo Ruby's thievery fades as he considers what a relief it is to see a break in her pious mood. The changes that have come over her since the fall are the biggest mystery of all. He thinks it's just as weird that she's going religious as it is that he seems to be going in the opposite direction. Even weirder: Ruby's never shown any signs of being a Holy Roller, but he can remember things about himself going all the way back to first grade. He and his cousin Larry are six and five years old, hiding in the root cellar under Nana's old house; their pants are pushed down and their hands are inside of each other's underwear, wiggling around until they both get stiff. Yeah, he thinks as he falls asleep, this has been going on for a long time.

A brittle morning, everyone on edge: Clark is to meet later in the day with Jackson's doctors to determine when Jackson will be coming home.

Over breakfast Robin asks, "If Jackson comes home this week, where will we put him?" and Clark slams his fists into the table, sending a full cup of coffee crashing to the floor. "Not *if*, Robin. *When. When.*" It has been over three weeks since Clark announced his intention to build Jackson's new room. The room has not been completed. The physical therapy equipment is on hold until they make a payment. Jackson fades and withers like an old newspaper. Robin has expressed what is not meant to be spoken: the fundamental fear that Jackson will not be coming home at all. He repeats to himself his father's command: *Not if, when.* If he can think this way, will it be true?

When he gets to the locker room that day, he finds Scott waiting for him, agitated, grave. "Let's get out of here."

Robin accepts without hesitation, relieved at the notion of escape. They run across the playing fields to the trees that separate the school from nearby houses. The earth, wet from melting frost, squishes under their feet. Watching his breath whiten the air, Robin realizes he hasn't taken his coat along. Maybe this is why Scott is always in his zip-up jacket: he's ready at any moment to make a getaway.

They pass a cigarette back and forth without talking. When he asks Scott what's going on, Scott just says, "A lot," and retreats into his bottled-up agitation.

"Are we going somewhere particular?"

"I don't know. Just keep moving or you'll get cold."

"Do you want to go to The Bird?"

"No."

Robin looks back toward the school, its sand-colored bricks and banks of windows still visible through the leafless trees at the end of the block. It might not be too late to return, to cut himself off from Scott's sullen mood.

He tries once more with Scott. "What do you want from me?"

Scott stops abruptly, crushing the cigarette butt with his sneaker, splaying tobacco on the sidewalk. "I need to maybe crash at your house again. I can sneak in. Is that ladder still out there?"

Robin can't remember if it is or it isn't. He crosses his arms over his chest. "Last time I got in trouble because you left that note."

"I don't remember," he mumbles unconvincingly.

"Come on, Scott. You put it on the fridge." Robin stands still, raising his voice as Scott resumes walking. "My parents could have totally snagged you."

"Maybe that would have helped." Scott coughs up phlegm and spits. He keeps his head lowered, his shoulders curved, his hands in his pockets. "My old man's just going nuts lately."

"Did he hit you again?"

Scott nods and brushes his arm at the point of contact. "We just got this letter from the hospital where my mother is. They're saying she's in there six more months."

"They're making her stay?"

"No one's making her," Scott says, his voice hardening. "She just don't want to leave. But she don't know what it's like for me with him."

They have reached the corner of a busy street. Scott sticks out his thumb. "I'm going there—Bergen Elms. You coming?"

Robin skips ahead to catch up.

The hospital is older and larger than the one in Greenlawn. It looms like a prison, with locked doors, barred windows, and security guards patrolling the grounds. A black woman with straightened hair pulled into a bun sits behind a counter, buzzing people through three separate doorways. She listens to Scott dispassionately, refusing him entrance without an adult. Scott argues with her and then with her supervisor, who tells him to come back with his father. Robin withdraws from the increasing volume of these confrontations, but when Scott finally gains access to an administrator named Dr. Buckley he pulls Robin along with him.

Dr. Buckley is a pink-faced, white-haired man in a three-piece suit. He looks to Robin like he should be on Channel 13 introducing *Masterpiece Theater*. He shakes Scott's hand as they enter his office.

"Scott Schatz? I'm Dr. Buckley. Head of client relations." He turns his gaze to Robin, meeting his eyes for just a moment. "And you are?"

"Robin MacKenzie."

"He's my buddy," Scott says quickly.

The doctor frowns. "I really can't discuss your mother's case with anyone outside of the family."

· Scott grabs Robin by the arm. "Just stay. This guy can't make you leave."

"Actually, Mr. Schatz, I can," he says officiously. "I can make you both leave, so why don't you just cooperate?"

Scott, still curling his fingers around Robin's wrist, steps toward the doctor's big desk. "Look, I'm not stupid. You can say anything you want and I don't have any rights. But at least if I got a friend here I got a witness."

The doctor's face lightens with amusement. Robin hates the condescension he sees there and resolves to stay by Scott's side. "Very well. Why don't you both have a seat?" He motions them to chairs: leather upholstered, chocolate brown, and very deep. The toes of Robin's sneakers just barely graze the plush beige carpet.

Scott's face is pure determination. "We got this letter saying that my mother wants to stick around here another six months and I want to know what the deal is."

"Well, the *deal* is . . ." Dr. Buckley's voice trails off. He consults a file through a pair of reading glasses at the end of his nose. "You can read the diagnosis here, son. She's clinically depressed and could still potentially do herself and others harm." He slides the folder across his desk.

"She's been here over a year and you can't make her not want to hurt herself?" Scott peers into the folder, his eyes darting frantically across a stack of white and pink and goldenrod-colored pages, forms and charts thick with medical lingo. To Robin, Scott looks like a lost traveler, incapable of reading the only map he has.

Robin clears his throat. "May I look?"

"Out of the question," Dr. Buckley declares, but Scott hands Robin the folder anyway. Robin scans the top page; he only manages to make out "mg" a number of times before Dr. Buckley snatches it back.

"They've got her on a lot of drugs," Robin tells Scott.

The doctor shuts the file and crosses his hands on top of it. "Of course she's being given medication. That's standard procedure."

Scott leans in toward the desk, his neck tense with anger. "What are you doping her up with?"

Dr. Buckley takes off his glasses. His sober face seems to Robin to be the picture of insincerity. "Scott, this is a perfectly reputable hospital, one of the best in the state. Your mother isn't being harmed. Quite the contrary."

"Bullshit," Scott scowls. Robin looks past Dr. Buckley's desk to the half dozen diplomas and certificates on the wall. He's amazed at Scott's ability to call a man with so many official documents a liar. He wonders if his parents are being jerked around by Jackson's doctors. With a stab of guilt he remembers his father's meeting scheduled for today. Will there be any good news tonight?

Dr. Buckley drones on, unruffled by Scott's distrust. "Any other information specifically about her treatment will require the presence of your father, I'm afraid." He motions grandly to the phone. "Shall we call him now? I assume he knows you're here and not in school."

Scott sinks back into the voluminous leather cushions. Robin senses their loss as the battle winds down.

"I've said all I can say. Your mother has asked for an extended schedule of recuperation, and I'm sure it's in her best interest that you support that decision."

Scott's voice tightens in desperation. "If she knew I wanted her to come home I bet she'd get out. If she knew what Dad's like. I'll be the next one in here if I have to stay alone with that guy for much longer."

Dr. Buckley leans forward on his elbows. "Is there trouble at home, Scott?" Scott averts his eyes and says nothing.

Dr. Buckley scribbles on a pad in front of him, then passes this to Robin, whose seat is closer. "Your *buddy* might want to hold on to this," the doctor says to Robin. "It's the number of our twenty-four-hour referral line, especially helpful for the families of clients." Robin hands it to Scott, who crumples the paper into his pocket and charges from the room.

Scott is not waiting for him in the corridor. Robin checks the bathrooms and the stairwells, verging on panic. He locates him at last in the parking lot, tearing his way down a row of cars by leaping furiously from one hood to the next. He could be an escaped inmate, arms flapping like busted wings, face irate, his landings heavy and clumsy. Robin takes off after him, calling for him to stop. He watches as Scott jumps off the last car and bounds to a chain link fence at the perimeter, curling his fingers through the crisscrossed steel and lashing against it with all his strength. Through the hiss of parkway traffic Robin can hear Scott howling like an abandoned dog. When Robin gets to his side, he slides to the ground, suddenly out of breath, lifeless.

Cautiously, not sure the gesture won't be rejected, he puts his hand on top of Scott's. "I'm sorry about your mom."

"I'm sorry I don't have a grenade to lob into that asshole's office."

"Maybe you need a lawyer."

"I need another fucking life," Scott spits back.

Robin bites his lower lip to keep it from quivering. "Six months isn't that long, really."

"Easy for you to say." Scott pulls his hand out from Robin's grip and turns away from him.

At the other end of the lot, a security car swerves toward them. Robin hops to his feet and grabs Scott's jacket in his fist. "Come on. The cops are coming."

202 / K.M. Soehnlein

Scott snaps into alertness and takes off running, so fast Robin is left behind still thinking about it. The security car moves toward him. He forces
his legs to move, chasing Scott across the lot, through rows of cars, past a
bank of shuttle vans marked with the hospital seal. Shielded from view,
they scramble behind a dumpster and along a wall to the rear of the building. A concrete ramp slants up to the loading dock. Out of sight of the
parking lot, they stop to catch their breath, leaning their palms on their
knees. Their eyes dart from where they have just been to where they must
still move, coming to rest for a moment upon each other. Robin hacks up
a sour gob from the back of his throat, spits forcefully. They watch it splat,
a slimy green daisy on the asphalt. "Fucking cigarettes," Robin says.

"You're getting *tough*, man."

Robin looks away from Scott's eyes, which are telegraphing too much
strange admiration for him to understand. "Am not." He bites his lip to
fight a nervous smile. At his feet is a Burger King bag, crumpled and
stuffed. He scoops it up and pulls out a half-eaten burger and a half-
filled strawberry shake. "Hey, look," he says to Scott. "Leftovers."

Scott grabs the burger and pitches it at the hospital, as if this is the
grenade he had fantasized about. It peels apart in midair and sails into a
pane of glass; the meat sticks to the surface for a few seconds and leaves
behind a red-and-green condiment smear. Just then the security car rolls
into view.

Robin runs a few feet forward and hurls the milkshake forcefully, forgetting for the moment all the times he's been told he throws like a girl.
It sails high and far, spraying pink liquid and landing with a satisfying
splat on the hood of the car. Scott calls out his name and cheers, then
takes off running again, past the rear parking gate, through a humming
industrial lot and out to the road. Robin follows, so unexpectedly happy
that his legs no longer feel any strain at all.

They are crouching at the edge of the Garden State Parkway under the
big green sign for exit 165. Traffic is continuous, with few breaks. On
the other side, across eight lanes and a grassy divider, is a pulloff, where
a handful of people are waiting at a bus shelter. Robin has made a decision for them both: they're getting on the next Red and Tan bus that
pulls up. If his calculations are right, that should be in about five minutes, and the sign above the driver's window should read: *Port
Authority Bus Terminal, New York City.*

A deep voice shouts from the top of the embankment slope. Two security guards glare down at them.

"Come on," Scott says. He leaps up and onto the highway. The first two lanes are clear and he waits at the edge of a third for a car to pass. Its horn blasts in alarm as it whizzes by. When he reaches the fourth lane a screech of brakes cuts through the air and another horn sounds. Scott collapses on the grassy divider. Robin feels his mouth go dry.

The guards are yelling behind him. There is no time to waste. He runs into one lane . . . more brakes . . . voices yelling . . . another lane, the third . . . more squealing tires. He gasps for air as his feet land on the grass. Now they just have to do it again.

Thirty minutes later Robin is cursing his impulsiveness. The skyline has just come into view over the Meadowlands—his favorite part of the trip, the point in the journey where his heart begins to beat faster and his body tenses in anticipation of the city—but Scott is asleep next to him. Or perhaps just pretending to sleep; Robin isn't sure. Ten minutes ago Scott told him to shut up and then leaned his head back and closed his eyes. Robin had apparently been talking too much. Scott knows so little about the city, Robin had realized, and he was compelled to give him some pointers: don't gawk at people who look strange to you, or you'll wind up looking like the real outsider. Don't stop and talk to guys mumbling in your direction in the park—they're trying to sell you hard drugs. You need exact change to take a city bus; the driver won't break a bill for you. He wanted to take Scott to a museum but Scott wasn't interested. He was just outlining the best way to hail a cab when Scott cut him off. "Stop acting like a fucking know-it-all, man." Now he's feeling foolish. How could Scott understand what it meant to him to go to New York? Worse than that, he realizes with a weighty clarity, he has once again blatantly disobeyed his parents, this time beyond any rationalization or apology, and now, as the bus approaches the tunnel, there is literally no turning back.

The Port Authority Bus Terminal sprawls across four square blocks in the center of Manhattan. From the street it is nearly impossible to get a complete view of the structure. Its tunnels and overhead walkways give the illusion that it continues into everything around it, a cocoon at the center of a spiderweb. North on Eighth Avenue and west on Forty-Second Street, signs in red and yellow and blue and black advertise only sex and fast food. Even in daylight, lights flash and neon hums.

Descending down a narrow escalator from the bus gate, Robin watches Scott looking around in quiet awe. People crowd every corridor, even in the middle of the day. Scott buys an Orange Julius and a pretzel. Robin spends five dollars on a knit hat emblazoned with a New York Yankees logo like the one on Scott's baseball cap. He had hoped to buy a jacket or sweatshirt but he only had a ten dollar bill on him. Scott announces that he has to pee.

"Me, too," Robin says, beginning to feel the pain of holding it in for so long. "Just wait and we'll go to a restaurant."

"Why?"

"The bathrooms here are scary."

"Mr. Big Shot City Boy is afraid to take a piss?"

"*Fine.*"

The doorway to the men's room is like the mouth of an open ammonia bottle. A slightly stooped worker arcs a long mop back and forth, glazing the mustard yellow tiles in his path. A black man in filthy clothing has flipped up one of the dryer nozzles on the wall and wobbles drunkenly within the warm blast, the bottoms of his pants soaking up the floor. Scott pinches his nose, talks in an exaggerated muffle. "It smells April fresh in here." He unzips his fly at a urinal.

Robin stands at the one next to him and looks down at a well of stinky piss around an eroding green deodorant disk.

"What does the sign say in a Polish bathroom?" Scott asks. "*Don't eat the mints.*"

"My grandmother is Polish, asshole." Robin flushes the silver arm and water gushes down with such force it sprays back at him. He jumps away, just barely avoiding getting doused. Scott laughs as he watches the fizz rise.

Robin moves down to the next one, also not yet cleaned. He breathes through his mouth.

The door swings open. A man in a suit steps up to the broken urinal between them, resting his briefcase next to Robin's ankle. Robin checks out his profile: skin rough from ancient acne, hair styled and wavy, wide neck pushing out of his starched collar. The guy looks at Robin, his chin almost touching the shoulder pad of his blue blazer. Robin turns away from the penetrating gaze, stares down at the urinal; when he looks up again the guy is still staring, his eyes commanding, his neck tense. He is shaking his arm as if trying to get every last drop out of his dick. Even though his bladder is full, Robin can't make himself pee; he flushes and zips up, wishing he hadn't let Scott bring them in here.

At the sink, cold water on his face breaks the spell of the ammonia fumes and the intensity of the man's eyes. He swishes water in his mouth, spits out tiny flecks of food dislodged from his teeth, hacks up a glob of tobacco-stained mucus. He wants to wipe his armpits, looks around for paper towels but finds only blow dryers attached to the walls. The custodian's mop is almost licking at his heels, the vapors intensifying.

In the mirror he sees the suit has fixed his gaze on Scott; his arm is still pumping. Scott is looking back at this guy, at this guy's face and down into his crotch. The man steps back a couple of inches, revealing his fist sliding to and fro along a stiff pink penis. Robin's eyes widen. What does this guy want? Is he going to do something to Scott? Scott is shaking his own dick, but not very hard—still, he doesn't move away. Why is Scott staying there? A queasiness seeps through Robin's gut as he watches Scott watch this guy beat off. The way the guy towers over Scott, his buttocks clenched inside his creased pants, his dick visible in glimpses between his fingers—it's creepy but Robin finds himself captivated. His own cock is cramped in the folds of his underwear, threatening to get hard.

The dryer quiets suddenly. A tiny gasp rises from the guy at the urinal and fades into the easy-listening music. He's getting carried away—on top of everything else, Robin thinks, there's something ridiculous about this. Robin doesn't know if he's mad or upset or excited that Scott hasn't moved away—maybe a little of all three—but then Scott turns and catches his eye in the mirror. His mouth is twisted in a smile as if he might bust out laughing and his eyes are bright with mischief—it dawns on Robin that Scott's hatching a plan.

The bum in the dirty clothes smacks the blow dryer and it begins its mechanical hum again.

The man in the suit is jerking faster on himself, his face red with pressure, his eyes squeezed tight. Scott carefully zips up his fly and then pauses, shifting his stance as if ready to pounce. The suit is on a runaway train, his body freezing, his hips thrusting forward, his breath groaning out of him, getting louder. At the very moment he hits his peak with a guttural grunt, Scott reaches across and slams the flusher. The rush of water cascades down and splashes back up into the guy's crotch, on his hand and dick and the fabric of his pants. Scott is already running out of the bathroom, whooping in delight. Robin gets one last look in the mirror—the man has stepped back, his ecstasy dissolving into confusion, then anger. "What the hell?" he shouts, looking down at his soaked trousers. Robin gets a last look at the guy's swollen dick—already deflating from the shock—and then he takes off, too, past the custodian, who looks up without much interest, and out the swinging doors. The air in the corridor is cool and clean.

He spots Scott down the hall, waving him on. "That was *excellent,*" Scott is yelling.

"You're an asshole," Robin yells back. "You'll get us both in trouble." He gets to Scott's side and punches him in the arm.

Scott pushes him away, annoyed. "Yeah, right. Like some queer jerking the turkey is gonna have *us* arrested."

"You're not in New Jersey now. The rules are different here." He looks back over his shoulder, but the suit has yet to emerge from the bathroom. Still, he feels anxious and wants to move on. He's suddenly aware of the bustle of people all around them, the beehive of activity. "Let's get out of here."

"Oh, come on, Robin. Lighten up. It was funny."

"I didn't know what you were doing!" Robin shouts.

"What, did you think I was really gonna whack off with that guy?" Scott says this in a way that sinks Robin into shame. He tries to explain. "From where I was standing, you just looked like you were *into* it."

Scott sticks his finger down his throat. "Right, like that asshole was some big turn-on."

"How would I know what turns you on?" Robin spits out and dashes off toward the Eighth Avenue subway, pushing through the crowd fast enough to leave Scott behind. He positions himself behind the big newsstand near the subway entrance, watching as Scott spins around, trying to locate him in the rush of people. Robin savors the moment—Scott disoriented, helpless. Who's in charge now? When he's satisfied that he's gained the upper hand, he calls Scott's name, ready for an argument.

Scott runs to his side, his voice contrite. "I didn't mean to freak you out," he says. "Don't be mad."

Robin takes Scott to Washington Square Park and points through the arch to a building he and his mother have spun many stories about: One Fifth Avenue. "That's where I'm going to live one day."

Scott laughs. "In your dreams."

"What do you know about any of it?"

Scott holds out his hands in a sign of surrender. "OK, OK, sorry. You're really Mr. Touchy today—you know that?"

"I just wish you'd give me a break every once in a while."

They plant themselves on a park bench to people-watch. A woman and her teenage son catch Robin's eye. The boy is about their age, his hair slicked back, his neck wrapped in a scratchy-looking scarf, his coat and pants stiff, almost dandified. He carries a clarinet case.

"Check out the band fag," Scott says.

Robin and the boy lock eyes; the boy looks away and then back. His mother is talking animatedly and doesn't notice her son isn't paying attention. Robin sees a curiosity, a longing, in the boy's eyes that he knows reflects from his own stare. He wonders what that boy and his mother talk about. He imagines the boy saying to her, "Who is that guy and what is he up to?" What kind of story would they make up about him? About him and Scott?

Since leaving behind the antic pace of the Port Authority, Scott has eased into the city just fine, is even becoming adventurous. Scott wanders around the park on his own for a few minutes. When he returns, he asks Robin to give him a dollar and follow him. Robin watches fearfully, heart pounding, as Scott buys a joint off of a scary guy with wild eyes and ashy skin who had approached them muttering, "Sense, sense."

Scott drags him to a set of steps leading down to a basement apartment and lights up. They smoke in quick puffs, passing the joint back and forth to each other as if afraid to hold on to it too long. "Keep a look out for the fuzz," Scott tells him.

Flying, floaty, warming up in the afternoon sun. The park shifts into a glazed newness for Robin; it's a fairground, a picture book, a board game. Candyland. Scott walks to the large circular fountain in the center of the park—the water's never on anymore, Robin realizes—and hops up on the fountain's outer wall, scissoring his arms as he walks, trying to keep balanced. Robin hangs back on his bench, studying him. The moment stretches, brightens, removes itself from time: Scott on display, Robin watching, his tangle of feelings for Scott loosening, unfolding, softening. *Scott.* He whispers, *Hey, Scott. Hey, I really like you. This is so cool, being here with you. I wish you would really let me do stuff with you.* He thinks about how he wants to really taste Scott's skin. He wants to kiss him for a long time and stick his nose in his armpit and really smell him and hold one of his butt cheeks in each of his hands. He grins at the picture: kissing Scott with his hands on his butt. Thoughts tumble forth, each new idea pushing out the next as if he's opened up an overstuffed cupboard and the contents are showering down.

Scott looks over and smiles, coptering his arms as he wobbles on the ledge. When he rights himself at last, his face goofs up at Robin. Robin waves back. The distance between them becomes clear again. He reminds himself, *Scott has no idea what I'm thinking, and he's not standing there thinking the same thing. How could I ever say what I want to say to him?*

They wander aimlessly, first south and then west and then north and west again. Past Sixth Avenue the city's orderly grid unravels. Fourth Street and Tenth Street meet at an intersection; Bleecker actually crosses itself. On Christopher, there are more gay guys than he's ever seen before. His mother has never taken him this deep into the Village. It's as though they've wandered into an outrageous homosexual labyrinth: men on the corner, men sitting on stoops, men laughing in doorways of stores. Leather pants bulging at the crotch, bushy mustaches, flannel shirts with the sleeves cut off, even in this cold weather. Disco music trumpets from a window above: *You make me feel mighty real.* He catches snippets of conversation where "Mary" and "Louise" and "honey" and "sister" fly between men who look too mean and masculine to be talking that way. Some of the men are sexy—one of them looks like Mr. Cortez, with dark curly hair and tight polyester dress pants—but most of them seem dangerous, alien. Scott is quieter than he's been all day; Robin can tell he's checking out the scene. He'll watch a particular character walk by, then chuckle or mutter something inaudible, and then move on without a word to Robin.

They stop when they can go no farther, at the edge of the Hudson, looking out onto New Jersey: drab, industrial, impersonal, the waterfront landscape a buffer between the tidy suburbs beyond it and this strange corner of the city. If you measured it, yard by yard, it wouldn't be so far away—which is the strangest thing of all because he feels like he's traveled an odyssey to get here. How many hours have passed? Neither he nor Scott has a watch, and the piers don't offer a time and temperature display like on the bank in the center of Greenlawn. His head spins just thinking about what awaits him when he gets home, and yet he can't bring himself to go back, to smash the glass around this day in the city with Scott.

They finish off the joint they'd started earlier, and Robin feels himself flooded again with a need for Scott. This time, he speaks his mind. "I want to do . . . more stuff with you."

"What kind of stuff?"

"Sex stuff."

"I don't know." After a silent moment Scott runs a few feet, picks up an empty beer can, and throws it into the river. It lands in the gray water with a faint *splat*. He finds one thing after another to throw in the water: a sliced-off stretch of tire, a chunk of asphalt, a newspaper that he crumples into a wad. The whole display is so unhinged and jittery that Robin decides to ask again.

"So you don't think we should?"

"I said I don't know. I don't really know if I like it that much."

"Um, which part don't you like?"

"I don't know. I mean, sometimes I like it. Better than beating off, anyway. I mean, it's not like I do it that much."

"You think I do? I never did it with anyone before you."

"I don't want to talk about this," Scott says, his voice nearly whining. "Why do you always have to talk so much about everything? You're like a girl that way."

"You drive me crazy, Scott. One minute you're nice and the next minute you're an asshole. Just like Todd."

"Shut up!" Scott shouts. "Just shut your mouth! You don't know anything about me. And you don't know anything about Spicer, either. Before that time his father beat him up, he used to be a really great person. He used to treat me nice, not like you, always acting like you're better than me or something. I don't even care if you're *doing* it with him, because he's just a totally different person now."

If Scott's accusations didn't sound so untrue, Robin might feel stung by them. He might feel jealous, listening to Scott describe this special bond he once shared with Todd. Instead he's just skeptical. He's known Todd for most of his life, and Todd has never been *nice*. "Why don't you ever tell me about what happened with you and him?" he says, lowering his voice. "You act like I know what happened, and I don't."

"Nothing happened."

It is one of life's great injustices, Robin thinks, that he doesn't have a way into other people's thoughts. He wishes he had ESP to take him to where he is prohibited, to see where he cannot go, to understand what hasn't been explained. He wants to know what other people think all the time, but it's impossible because, even if they tell you, you can't be sure it's true. Does anybody *not* lie? People lie to avoid getting in trouble, to stop other people from reacting badly, to get what they want (or not get what they don't want), to not hurt your feelings. Even when you think that someone is being totally up front with you, in the back of your mind you still wonder if they are lying. What part of what they're saying isn't true?

There are more reasons to lie, Robin has come to realize, than to tell the truth. Sometimes, when people believe they're being honest with you, you actually know better than they do, so what they're saying turns out to be a lie anyway. You can knowingly tell someone a lie and then convince yourself it's true. So what's the truth, anyway? You make it up as you go along.

He's sure Scott liked *doing* it with him, but Scott now says he didn't, so either Scott is lying outright and knows it, or he thinks he's telling Robin the truth and nothing Robin says to him will persuade him otherwise. Neither of those possibilities offer much hope in this moment.

Darkness and cold settle early upon them. They are arguing at the top of the stairs to the Number 1 train—neither of them sure exactly what to do next—when a pale, skinny guy with wild eyes approaches them. He's more heavily dressed then they are, but his body shivers feverishly. He says furtively, "Ludes?"

Robin says, "No," not exactly sure what kind of a drug a lude is— but Scott, in the same breath, says, "Maybe."

The guy waves Scott into a doorway. Robin tries to protest but follows a few steps away. "Just be cool," Scott says, looking back over his shoulder.

The guy pulls out a Sucrets box full of little white pills, each with a line cut down its diameter. "This isn't real," Scott says, fingering one. "It's supposed to have 714 on it."

Robin is surprised by Scott's knowledge, but he keeps quiet, narrowing his eyes at the dealer, pretending he's also suspicious about the pill's quality.

"They're Mexican," the guy says. "Very strong."

The guy wants ten dollars. Robin reluctantly hands over his last couple of bucks to Scott, and between them, they scrape up six, which turns out to be enough. Watching their last money disappear into the guy's pocket, Robin blurts out nervously, "Wait. We shouldn't do this. How are we going to get home?"

"We won't care after we split this," Scott says.

Robin asks the dealer, "What happens to you when you take it?"

"Oh, man, I don't take this shit. I just sell it—then I buy the good stuff."

As the guy walks away, Robin sees that he's just a teenager, though his bedraggled appearance made him look much older.

"*The good stuff*—I bet he was talking about acid," Robin says.

"He was a junkie," Scott says.

"Exactly."

Scott laughs. "*Exactly*," he mimics. "Don't you know the difference between a junkie and an acid head?"

Robin looks away, embarrassed. "So how do you know so much, anyway?"

Scott steps into Seventh Avenue as the light turns green. "You know what your problem is, Robin? You never had an older brother. You got no one to show you anything about the world." He darts into the little park at Sheridan Square.

Robin runs to catch up with him. "I know *plenty* about the world."

"Yeah, but Danny—he was the one who showed me everything."

"Your brother?"

"Yeah, he was cool. He was a lot older than me. Like ten years." Scott sits on a park bench, stuffing his hands in his pockets.

Robin steps closer, curious. He asks tentatively, "He died, right?"

"Yeah, like two years ago. He had a heart attack. He was only nineteen. That's why my mother went nuts."

"You can't get a heart attack when you're nineteen!" Scott shoots him a look, daring him to doubt this story. Robin quickly adds, "I mean, I've never heard of that."

"He took a punch in a bar fight, supposedly a big, mother-fucking punch," Scott says, shaking his head as if unable to make sense of it. "*A blow to the chest*—that's what they told me. It was a freak thing."

"Maybe his heart was weak," Robin offers.

Scott shrugs. "Maybe. What do I know? He used to do a lot of drugs. Too many of these."

Scott snaps the Quaalude along its seam, pops half in his mouth, pinches his nose and swallows. He offers the other half to Robin, but Robin waves it away. Scott is doing his best to act nonchalant about Danny's death, but two years doesn't seem long enough for the hurt to go away. Robin wonders if after Danny took that blow to the chest he was hospitalized for a while, like Jackson; he wonders if Scott visited every day or if he avoided it like Robin has. He's amazed that Scott has spoken of this at all, and he wants to ask him more about it, but Scott is suddenly on his feet again.

"I got an idea," Scott says. "Let's just ask someone for bread."

212 / K.M. Soehnlein

"You mean beg?" Robin takes a look around. Who would they ask? The only other people in Sheridan Square are a couple of old bums and a few homos.

"All we need is a few bucks for some food and the bus, right?"

"You shouldn't have bought that lude."

Scott again offers him the remaining half, but when Robin again refuses, he swallows it as well.

"All right," Robin says, heaving a sigh. "Let's get some money. If you're going to have a heart attack, we better do it fast."

The guy's apartment is dark and run-down and curiously empty—"It's mostly a weekend place," he tells them as they enter. Thick leaves of paint peel from the kitchen walls; a cupboard door that won't shut reveals only bare shelves behind it; the toilet, in a tiny closet at one end of the kitchen, hisses without stopping. A shower stall, dingy curtain exposed, stands next to it. The living room walls are bare. A chenille couch, a cracked glass coffee table, a lightbulb glowing green under a lampshade scarred with cigarette burns.

Robin hadn't really believed anyone would give them money, but this guy was more than willing, as long as they came here, to his apartment. He was clean and dressed well enough to seem harmless, and he lived only a couple of blocks away. They agreed without consulting each other, just followed along, listening to him tell a sort-of-funny story about an elderly couple arguing on the subway.

His name is Vincent. Late twenties, Robin guesses. Italian or Greek— a thick, low hairline, a prominent forehead, a long face and wide chin. He's not quite handsome: his eyes are deeply set, his skin sallow. He got them stoned almost as soon as they walked in the door, and now he's playing classical music and serving Pepsi. Scott is about to drop off to sleep on the couch, and Robin is worried that it's going to be hard to get out of here. Why did he trust this guy? Because it was cold out, and he was worried that Scott was spacing out from the lude.

Vincent walks over to Scott and pushes his shoulder. He waves the pot pipe in front of Scott's face and whispers, "Scott, we saved some for you."

Robin giggles. "So then we ran across the highway and left those guys in the dust," he says. He had begun this story a while ago and has just remembered to finish it. The pot is either stronger than he's used to or it's laced with something. The numbness is disconcerting.

"So you're wanted criminals in New Jersey. For assaulting a cop car with a milkshake."

"We're not *wanted*." Robin takes the pipe from Vincent and sucks in harder.

"Sure you're wanted," Vincent says. He lays a hand on Robin's shoulder, lets it drop down his back. "I want you."

Smoke explodes from Robin's throat, his chest constricting. He steps away from Vincent's touch. "I hope Scott wakes up soon. We gotta get going. Do you mind giving me that money now?"

Vincent walks into another room. "This way." Robin moves toward his voice tentatively. "The view from over here is spectacular," Vincent says.

Robin steps into the doorway. Vincent is sitting on the edge of a big, unmade bed. His gaze is fixed out a bank of windows at the deep blue night sky, orange lights glowing all the way down Seventh Avenue to the Twin Towers. The entire view is repeated in a mirror above the bed. He crooks his finger, beckoning. Robin takes another step in.

Vincent pulls a wallet out of his back pocket, lays it on the bed, and pats it twice. Robin hesitates, waiting for some other invitation, but Vincent remains transfixed on the view. After a moment Robin picks up the wallet and opens it. There's about sixty dollars inside, all in tens and twenties. He pulls out a ten.

Vincent's hand slaps down on top of his. "Hey!" he yells. "What do you think you're doing?"

Robin drops the wallet and the money. "Oh, I'm sorry. I thought I could take—actually, five bucks would be enough."

"Are you trying to steal from me?"

"No, you said—" He cuts himself off, uncertain what has just happened. Vincent grabs Robin under each arm and holds him in place. The tightness of his grip is a shock; he is unable to move. "I'm sorry. Really."

Vincent leans his face close enough for Robin to smell his breath, which has a sour tinge to it. "I guess I'll believe you. You're young, and you probably don't know any better. You just haven't learned your manners yet. I'm doing you a favor and you seem very unappreciative." He squeezes his fingertips into Robin's rib cage.

"No, I'm very appreciative," Robin says. "I'm just stoned. I don't know what I'm doing."

"Besides, you're not in a rush, are you, Robin? We hardly even got to know each other."

Vincent loosens his grasp and runs his hands firmly along Robin's back. He hooks his thumbs into the waist of Robin's jeans. Robin thinks of fleeing, but Scott remains sleeping in the next room, most likely still unwakable. He knows he couldn't get them both out of here quickly. Vincent moves one of his hands to his own zipper and tugs it down. He fumbles inside the crotch of his jeans like he's fishing for something at the bottom of an aquarium; his fingers emerge, wrapped around an already swollen penis. Robin looks and then looks away. Vincent is bigger down there than anyone he's seen before. "You've done this before, right, Robin?"

"I guess so."

Vincent grabs one of Robin's hands and moves it onto his cock. It feels hot and damp; he tries to pull away, but Vincent won't let him. With his other hand he is shuffling his pants down. "Why don't you do the same?"

"I don't want to," Robins says quietly.

"Don't be so shy," Vincent says. His voice is no longer angry, but Robin is still afraid. He unclasps his jeans, pulls down the zipper. Vincent tugs them down.

"Take off your shoes and pants," Vincent commands.

Robin follows his orders, first relieved to be free of Vincent's touch, and then stupefied to find himself standing in his underwear and socks while Vincent strokes himself. What if Scott wakes up and sees him like this? He couldn't explain himself.

"Can we close the door?"

"Leave it open," Vincent says firmly. "If Scott wakes up, he can join us. You'd like that, wouldn't you?"

Robin doesn't answer. He doesn't know what he wants. Maybe Scott will wake up and help him get the fuck out of here. "Sit over here," Vincent commands. Robin lets his body be swept onto Vincent's lap, neither helping nor hindering him. His legs straddle Vincent's. He closes his eyes so he doesn't have to look at Vincent's face.

The penis is like a warm roll under his ass. Vincent slides back and forth and Robin remembers all those "Here we go on the Bumpity Road" games from years ago, getting passed from aunt to uncle, from lap to lap. He is suddenly very sad, ready to cry.

Vincent squeezes some goo from a tube, reaches underneath Robin and wipes it along his crack. Robin bucks up. "That's cold!" he protests, but Vincent just shushes him and wipes the rest of the lubricant on Robin's dick. Robin pushes away from him, wanting at least for

Vincent's hand to stop making him hard, but Vincent does not let up. He is petrified at the idea that Vincent, sliding beneath him, is going to try to stick it up his butt. He can feel the head prodding his asshole. He opens his eyes and says, "Let's stop." Vincent pulls the head away from his hole but keeps grinding, sliding back and forth, and Robin can tell from Vincent's eyes, so transfixed on him, that there will be no stopping until Vincent comes.

Vincent grinds away, his breath getting heavier, his fingers pressing deeper into Robin's ribs. His face reminds Robin of the guy at the urinal this morning, lost in his own world, which reminds him again of Scott on the couch. Robin tries to will his erection away but the sensations take over until he finally stops squirming and just lets Vincent finish him off. Ploop, onto Vincent's shirt.

Vincent groans, "Oh, yeah, baby," and slams up from his hips. Again, then again. Robin winces as a jet of stickiness hits his asshole and balls. Vincent slides it around his thighs, the sound increasingly gummy, their flesh adhering to each other. Vincent's pubic hair is covered in milky foam.

"Do you have a towel?" Robin asks. He looks back to the doorway, afraid Scott is standing there.

Vincent traces his fingers along Robin's face. "You're one hot number—you know that? You got me off so *fast*. You got so *into* it."

Robin feels his insides clench in confusion. Maybe he *was* into it and only trying to convince himself otherwise. Maybe Vincent saw something in his expression or body language. He shouldn't have taken his pants off; he shouldn't have let himself come. He pulls on his clothes and hurries past the couch, where Scott is still zonked out.

In the mirror over the kitchen sink, he sees a zombie face—tense, deadened, lost—that he hardly recognizes as his own. He splashes cold water on his forehead and eyes and scrubs his hands with a cracked chip of soap.

Vincent's face appears in the mirror; he places one hand on Robin's neck, stroking his hair, and stuffs the other in his back pocket. "You feel good?"

"Yeah, sure," Robin says, squirming away. "I'm just worried about Scott."

"He's your boyfriend?"

"I don't know." Robin avoids Vincent's stare. How is he going to get them out of here?

"We don't have to tell him about us. We don't have to tell anyone."

"Sure."

"I like you."

"Thank you. I mean, I like you, too." The longer this gets dragged out, the dirtier he feels. "So what about the money?"

Vincent pats his ass. "Right there."

Robin pulls two ten dollar bills from his back pocket. He hurries past Vincent to the couch where Scott lies, caught in a vivid dream, his eyes dancing under his lids. Spit hangs from the corner of his lips.

He repeats Scott's name over and over, shaking him forcefully. "We got the money. We're going." He's sure he cannot keep himself from crying if Scott doesn't wake up.

At last Scott's eyes open, though he doesn't respond or even seem to comprehend where they are.

"What time is it?" Scott mumbles.

"Time to send you guys back into the world." This is Vincent, carrying two glasses of Pepsi. He stands above them, his crotch at Robin's eye level. Robin turns away, disgusted. Vincent's fly is only partially zipped.

Robin shivers with only his knit cap to protect him from the cold. The city buzzes in the glow of headlights, streetlights, and the fluorescent illumination pouring from the cigar store on Sheridan Square. Scott stumbles along at his side.

"Vincent gave me more money than I said we needed. We could even take a cab to the Port Authority."

"What'd you have to do? Give him a blow job?"

Robin turns, furious, and points a finger at him. "Fuck you. I never blew anybody."

"How much did he give you?"

"Ten," he lies. *If Scott wants to be an asshole, I'm going to keep most of the money for myself. I earned it,* he thinks bitterly.

"Give me five."

"No way. I got it from him. I'll pay your bus fare and that's it."

"You *did* blow him."

Robin grabs Scott's arm and spins him around. "If it wasn't for me you'd still be passed out on his couch and who knows *what* that guy could have done." Robin knows he's just a spit away from telling Scott about what happened with Vincent, but he can't figure out how to describe it in a way that would sound like it wasn't his own fault. Should he just come out and say, "That sex maniac made me play wiener in the bun?"

"You're acting weird," Scott says, looking away from his cold stare. At the corner, Robin puts all his coins into a pay phone.

"Hello?"

"Victoria, it's Robin. I need to ask you a favor."

"Where are you?" She sounds worried.

"I can't really say."

"Well, they practically called the cops about you."

"I'm in New York with Scott."

"Oh my God. You are *so* in trouble."

"If my mother calls you, tell her I told you I'm studying for science with George Lincoln."

"She already called me."

He leans the receiver into his leg and curses again. From the opposite corner, Scott shoots him a wary glance. "OK," he says at last. "If she calls again, don't tell her I called you."

"She's supposed to call me again in, like, ten minutes. You know she's a major worrier."

He makes a collect call.

"Where are you?" To his relief, his mother, and not his father, has answered.

"Don't worry. I'm fine."

"Tell me where you are."

He tries to stall but she forces it out of him, and next thing he knows she's crying. He almost never hears her cry, but this is instantaneous.

"Mom, don't worry. I'm *fine.*"

She sniffles. "I don't think you're ready to be in New York without me, Robin."

He can't sort out what he's feeling: guilty, angry, overpowered by mental exhaustion. He tries to sound relaxed, though his voice is quavering. "Mom, don't freak out. I know my way around. I just wanted to tell you I'll be home soon."

His father grabs the phone. "Are you in trouble? Have you gotten yourself into trouble?"

He holds the receiver in the air until he hears his mother's sniffling voice again. "Please, just reassure me that you're in no harm," she says.

"Yeah, I'm fine." He thinks of Vincent's hands squeezing his ribs and adds nervously, "Nothing I couldn't handle, ha ha."

"I'm just stunned, Robin. I really don't know what to say." Her voice falls into a helpless silence.

His father again: "I'm coming in to get you."

"No. We have bus money."

"Who are you with?"

"A friend."

"What friend?"

"Dad, we'll take the bus. I've done it a million times."

"No fucking way. You're not going through the Port Authority at this time of night."

"Yes, I am," he says, irritated. "OK?"

His mother again, excited by an idea: "I want you to go to my friend Tatjana's, on Columbus Avenue. Remember, we had lunch there last year? We can drive in and meet you there."

"Mom, I don't want to see Tatjana right now. We'll just get on the bus and come home."

"Who are you with? What's-his-name—*Scott?* It's always that name."

He looks to Scott, who is watching him intently.

"Mom, just let us come home without making a big production out of it."

"Don't mouth off to me!" He is surprised by her sudden shrieking. "In case you are wondering at all, your brother is not doing well. The doctors said today that he's taken on a new infection. We needed to be at the hospital tonight, but we've spent the whole day trying to figure out where you are! Are you completely oblivious to what's going on?"

"No, I'm not. I'm just . . ." He bites on his tongue, holding back tears again. He had forgotten all about Jackson. His father is right—he is selfish and inconsiderate, and he causes harm to everyone. "I don't know how to explain it," he says and hangs up, pressing his palms into his wet eyes.

Scott is at his side, his voice gentle. "Just ignore them, man. Just ignore their bogus shit." Scott drops an arm across his shoulders. Robin curls into his chest and lets a couple of tears spill out, and after a few moments, Scott wraps his other arm around and holds him while he shakes.

They stand like that for a minute, maybe two, until Robin forms an image of himself as lost in the center of an enormous steel maze. He pushes away from Scott, and the city's clamor roars up. He does not want to cry on the street. After what happened with Vincent he thinks he hasn't the slightest idea how to make his way through this city and all of its traps. Scott's face questions him, almost tenderly; he guesses that Scott is scared, too. He remembers Scott this morning, in that doctor's office, in that enormous hospital with his mother stowed somewhere inside, unreachable.

He makes himself stop crying. This isn't some romantic movie. He's not Natalie Wood on the fire escape. He has to get them both back to New Jersey.

The inside of the bus is shadow on shadow, only the filmiest orange light seeping in from the road outside. Scott has insisted that Robin wear his zip-up sweatjacket to stay warm, and Robin returns the favor by pulling Scott close to him, coaxing him into sleep. Robin's arm has gone numb, but he does not shake Scott's head from his shoulder. Along the highway, New Jersey presents a series of spooky landscapes: the barren, swampy Meadowlands; the concrete bunker clothing outlets; the vast sports complex rising up from acres of parking lots. Last year his father took him and Jackson to a Cosmos soccer game at Giants Stadium. He brought his transistor radio and spent most of the game roaming the stadium's corridors listening to the Top 40 Countdown on WNBC. For a while he sat outside the men's room, watching them come and go, all the dads and sons, the single guys tucking in their shirts and the loud guys—buddies together—laughing; all of them in some strange cycle of drinking beer in and pissing it out, buying more beer and rushing back to join the cheering crowd. Robin sees himself there, sitting on the cool concrete floor, radio pressed to his ear, singing along with Donna Summer: *Last dance, last chance for love.* Jackson had mocked him that night for his lack of interest in the game, and they wound up in a name-calling argument so mean-spirited that Robin spent the next few days dreaming up ways to ambush his brother and beat him to a pulp. Maybe, Robin thinks now, Jackson will be a new, nicer person when he wakes from his coma. Or maybe the struggle of learning to use his body again will transform him; instead of the hyperactive kid he's always been, he'll be a considerate person, grateful for a new chance in the world. Maybe his body will never be quite right again and he'll have to develop his mind; maybe they'll one day be friends. Robin cuts off his daydream—deriding himself for this wishful thinking. None of them even knows what's going to happen tomorrow, much less in the far-off future. He can't even be sure what will happen when he gets home.

The bus passes through industrial sprawl and the towns he's never stopped in, where the houses are so close they're almost attached; then the new malls along Route 4, the car dealerships and the fourplex movie theater that is now a tenplex; and finally the quiet, orderly towns winding along Kinderkamack Road, where thick, twisted oaks line the side-walks. After this strange day in New York, he sees it all anew; he feels the weighty pressure of *returning* inside of him, like the prodigal son going back to a family that cannot imagine the life he's been leading while away from them. He manufactures a lie to tell his parents—*We were trying to find Scott's aunt in the city to ask if he could move in with her*—but the effort of concocting a story that they won't believe just ex-hausts him more. What if I tell them the truth? *I ditched school, hitched a ride to Bergen Elms, where Scott and I made a scene and were chased across the Garden State Parkway by security guards, went to the city with hardly any money in my pocket (not even wearing a coat!), bought drugs on the street, hung out at the piers. Went to a strange guy's apart-ment and . . .* Robin lets out a "Ha!" that sounds kind of deranged. If I told my parents that, he thinks, they'd probably put *me* in Bergen Elms. He wants to tell someone, though. Victoria? She couldn't handle it. Ruby? Ridiculous. Todd? He'd throw a fit because Scott was involved. Robin realizes with a pang in his stomach that the person he'd like to tell is Jackson; he wouldn't tell him everything (he certainly wouldn't mention what happened with Vincent). But he wants Jackson to know he's not a wimp or a mama's boy anymore. What did his mother mean, Jackson has a new infection? Was she just trying to lay a guilt trip on him, or is it really *bad?* Robin squeezes his eyes shut, wanting the ques-tions to stop, wanting, for once, some answers.

He sees his father leaning on the car next to the bus shelter before they even get off. Arms crossed, chin raised, eyes searching the bus windows. Scott wakes up as they pull to a stop.

Robin watches his breath curl like mist as he steps to the sidewalk, surprised how much colder it is here than in the city. It's the last unfet-tered thought he has before everything erupts around him. His mother is rushing out of the car, shouting in a voice straining between relief and anger, "Let me look at you before I slap you;" his father steps forward and lays a hand on his shoulder, his stony expression a portent of the punishment ahead; the bus groans and takes off again, bellowing fumes. His numb arm awakes in a dance of pins and needles.

He turns around to say good-bye to Scott, but it's too late. An explo-sion, an implosion, the night splits open: Mr. Schatz is there, one meaty fist already clamped around Scott's bony arm. Robin opens his mouth to protest but no words come out.

"In the car," Robin's father commands, guiding him toward his mother. She tries to embrace him, but he wriggles away, stepping back toward Scott, who is trying to shake himself free of his father.

"Robin, let's go."

"No!" Robin shouts. "Scott should come with us."

Mr. Schatz is already tugging Scott toward the van. "Let go. You're hurting me," Scott begs.

"Don't even try it," Mr. Schatz says. He pauses long enough to make eye contact with Clark and Dorothy. "Thanks for the call. Sorry you got dragged into this."

"Sure. If there's anything we can do . . ." Clark's voice trails off.

Robin looks in disbelief at his father. "You called him?" he whispers in horror.

His mother speaks through a balloon of cigarette smoke. "Robin, we've been worried to death all day."

He steps away from his parents again and shouts to Scott, "Call me later!"

As Mr. Schatz's van pulls away, Robin looks at his mother and father and yells, "I can't believe you called his father! You assholes!"

His mother charges at him, shakes him by the shoulders, her cigarette breath spews into his face. "What is happening to you?" she cries hysterically.

"Don't touch me," he growls. All he can see when he meets her eyes is the face of a betrayer.

His father pulls him to the car. "Not another word out of you. Not a word."

He searches through the back window, praying that Scott has jumped from the van and is now running back toward him.

They move from the center of town to the dark streets of his neighborhood. His father watches him in the rearview mirror, his eyes glowing with contempt. "In case you happen to give a shit, your brother isn't coming home anytime soon."

"Lucky him," Robin growls.

Dorothy spins around. "Robin, that boy is a *runaway*, for crying out loud."

"He's not a runaway! His father beats the shit out of him all the time." He pauses, waiting for either of them to show some sign of concern for Scott.

"You don't know what's going on in that family," his mother says, her voice exasperated. "And it's really not any of our business."

"I know more about it than you! Why do you think we had to go to New York? We were trying to find one of his relatives so he could live with them."

His father cuts him off. "Enough!"

His mother stares straight ahead and says softly, "Robin, we had *no idea* where you were."

"I couldn't tell you; it was an emergency. You don't understand, his father could *kill* him!" His heart is beating so fast he is sure they must be able to hear it. "Scott's father is a *major* drinker, and he takes it out on Scott. Plus his mother's in Bergen Elms; she's been there for like a year, because his brother died—" He stops. They aren't listening. He is looking up at them from the bottom of a deep, narrow well, his voice dissolving before it reaches their ears. "It's all just fucked up. That's why we went into the city. He's probably getting the shit beat out of him right now."

"I don't—I don't understand why you're getting involved with this boy's troubles," his mother says, her voice straining to sound reasonable. "You shouldn't be in New York without me." She reaches back across the seat as if she would caress his face, but he swats her away.

"Hey!" His father pivots, raising his hand as if he would strike—but the move jerks the steering wheel, throwing Robin and Dorothy into their doors. A car horn blares from the road and tires squeal as oncoming headlights arc across their faces. Clark shouts and spins the wheel to regain control. They careen down Bergen Avenue, unscathed but shaken.

"Clark, please. Everyone just stay composed. *Please.*" Dorothy's voice quavers. She grips the dashboard and rights herself.

Clark speaks through gritted teeth. "Robin, just think about your own family for a while. Think about what the hell is going on with your *own* goddamn family."

Robin replays the near collision, imagining that his father had spun the wheel just a moment later, that the car he had cut off was just a few feet closer. He imagines the massive force of the impact and the scream of shattered glass. He is trapped beneath twisted metal, the life being squeezed out of him, his parents just on the other side of the seat, eyes open, mouths bloody, breathing their last breaths.

Chapter Eleven

Scott is not in school the next day, or the next. By the third day with no sign of him, Robin is frantic: Scott has been beaten to death by his father; Scott has finally struck back hard enough to kill his father; Mr. Schatz has had him arrested or locked up in Bergen Elms. Robin waits for the phone to ring late at night, for word from Scott on the run from the cops. On the fourth night, after dinner, Dorothy answers a call on the first ring and finds no voice on the other end; Robin, convinced it was Scott trying to get through, spends the next few days waiting for another call, which never comes.

His parents have forbidden him from using the phone, even to reach Victoria. He finally just stops speaking to any of them, even to Nana Rena, who has come back for another visit. The house suffocates in silence. Nana watches television with the volume so low he is sure she can't hear it. His mother and father exchange wordless, weary stares with each other. Ruby and he stay in their rooms as much as possible. He wears Scott's hooded jacket every day, afraid that to not wear it will jinx his chances of finding him.

For a full week he signs in to central detention. He does his homework and talks to no one. His mother picks him up at four o'clock and takes him to the hospital for an hour, where he completes his assignments in a chair outside Jackson's room. He can't look at Jackson without feeling like he himself wants to curl up and die. Jackson is hardly recognizable: bony, wet-breathed, weaker than the machines that sustain him. He has been fighting off a respiratory infection, and the increased strain on his breathing has transformed his body into something tense and fragile, like the unbroken surface of water. Robin finds himself wondering if the sight of Jackson's deterioration has been chosen by his parents as his punishment.

When they had arrived home, that last night he saw Scott, his mother kissed him good night and then turned to his father, saying, "Don't overdo it, Clark." Watching her climb the stairs without a look back, clutching a wine bottle and a glass, Robin realized that a plan had already been arranged. His mother had wanted to stay and his father made her promise she wouldn't interfere—or perhaps she had simply absolved herself of any responsibility, no longer convinced she could talk sense to him. Alone with his father in the kitchen that night, Robin felt nothing: no fear, no remorse, no allegiance to anyone but Scott.

"Aren't you supposed to say, 'This is going to hurt me more than it hurts you?'" he had asked.

His father downed a shot of whiskey, took a deep breath. "Are you doing drugs?"

Robin said, "No," and his father slammed him across the face with the back of his hand. "This is to make sure you don't get any ideas about it," he said, then slammed the other side of his face, knuckles crunching against Robin's cheekbone like a bag of gravel. Robin stumbled backward from the impact, balancing himself against the smooth, cold surface of the refrigerator.

He shut his eyes, waiting for the next blow, but his father said, "OK, that's it—I'm not a violent man," as if he were negotiating the punishment with some invisible third party who wanted him to continue hitting.

His father rubbed one hand soothingly with the other. He sat at the kitchen table, sipping whiskey and badgering him about responsibility. Robin remained standing, concentrating on the pain in his face in the hopes of easing it. Counting to himself each hot pulse of blood to his cheeks, he obliterated his father's voice.

Now, a week later, just a single passage from the hour-long harangue has stuck: "You want to have it both ways. You want special treatment, for us to send you to some private school, *and* you want to be able to cut school and take off for the day with some little pothead." He thinks about it: Victoria gave them Scott's last name, and they called Scott's father. Scott's father told them that Scott was a pothead, which was all they needed to know.

When Nana admonishes him that his *silent treatment* isn't helping the situation, he says to her, "It's not the silent treatment. I just have nothing to say." She stares at him as if she too is convinced that he is on drugs.

* * *

One night, while waiting for sleep to overtake him, he remembers this moment: looking into the kitchen mirror at Vincent's apartment, Vincent behind him, a heavy hand on his ass, asking, "Is Scott your boyfriend?" Robin can't remember what he answered; he thinks he said yes. How did Vincent know? He and Scott weren't acting like boyfriends, were they? And how, he asks himself, did Vincent know that I would do sex with him? Was it just that he was sure I could be scared into it? Or did he see something in me that made him think it would be easy? He stays awake for hours, horrified at the idea that he might *look gay*, that he was somehow prey to gay sex maniacs, the kind of Village queers Todd had warned him about.

He takes a science test and surprises everyone by acing it. At dinner that night, his father proclaims the new disciplinary measures a success.

That night Robin sticks his face in his pillow and lets sobbing overtake him: just a week since Scott disappeared from his sights and already his memories of that day are fading into dreams that he can only half conjure. Just one piece of that night still shakes his bones like an electric jolt: the terrible shock of Mr. Schatz—the fury his presence stirred from the air, the twisting of Scott's body as he tried in vain to pull away from his father's imprisoning grasp. When he pictures this, he thinks that he will never see Scott again, that Scott must have been seriously injured that night, maybe he's even dead, his body stuffed in a plastic bag by his father and left at the town dump. It would be his fault, like Jackson's being in the hospital is his fault, like Vincent getting him to do sex was his fault, too. He pulls on his hair and screams from the back of his throat into his pillow. The muscles in his face ache from crying; he chokes on snot and saliva. When he hears his mother's worried footsteps hurrying up the stairs, he runs into the bathroom, locking himself in, running the water, flushing the toilet again and again. He does not answer her, he does not shout out at her, he cannot break the spell of his wailing. He will not talk to her or to any of them—they are as much to blame as he is. They made him into who he is: his mother with her stuck-up attitudes and her pride in all his weakest qualities; his father never listening to him, never caring about him. He has become a dangerous person because of them; he has come to hate himself along with them.

Only when he realizes that this is the first time since Jackson's fall that he has been able to cry uncontrollably does it begin to subside. When he leaves the bathroom he lets his mother embrace him, and he does not protest when she leads him back to his bed. As she strokes his hair, he thinks of how it would feel to take so many pills that you didn't wake up, or to jump from a high place and die on impact with the ground. A rope around his neck, the chair beneath kicked away. His father's razor blades across his wrists, blood bubbling out. A bottle of Drano—he could pinch his nose and make himself swallow. Shove his face in the bathtub and hold it there until he passed out. A gun, a bullet in his temple. Something so quick he wouldn't feel the pain.

In the cafeteria he asks the lunch lady to give him ten dimes for a dollar, and between every class, he goes to the payphone and dials Scott's number. Day after day he does this with no answer, until his calls are no longer hopeful, just a habit. And then one day Mr. Schatz answers, and Robin is so startled that he instantly hangs up.

His first thought is that if Mr. Schatz is alive then Scott really is dead, and he feels the tears welling up, feels his imagination already transporting him to the police station where he reports the crime, then on to the morgue where he identifies Scott's battered body. He sees the coffin wheeled up to the altar at St. Bart's, the crowded church murmuring in collective grief. He sees himself in the courtroom, where he points the finger from the witness stand and testifies, with perfect composure, to the bruises and scars on Scott's body, the dried blood under his nose and the stories of his father's beatings that Scott had passed on to him. "Hearsay!" Mr. Schatz's lawyers will shout, but his testimony will have been so compelling that the judge will quickly overrule. Robin will continue, more determined than ever to bring justice to Scott's memory.

He makes himself dial again. This time, after Mr. Schatz grunts a hello, Robin blurts out, "Is Scott there?"

"No." The voice is almost defiant.

"Do you know where he is?"

"Who wants to know?" Mr. Schatz slurs his words into one drunken, mush-mouthed phrase: *Whowanshoono?*

"Oh, I'm just . . . an acquaintance of your son."

"Are you that kid? What's the name . . . MacKenzie?" *Muh-gen-zhi.*

Robin deepens his voice and says, "No, sir. Actually, this is Mr. Cortez from Greenlawn High. I'm a guidance counselor, and I'm wondering if Scott has been home sick this week?"

"How come you just said you were a friend?"

"I said I was an acquaintance, Mr. Schatz." Robin fakes a chummy laugh. "Ha-ha-ha, no matter. You see, sir, actually, it's our policy to not reveal who we are at first. Sometimes we catch truants that way, you know, by saying we're an acquaintance. Reverse psychology. It works on those juvenile delinquents." Robin clears his throat and tries to maintain a deep, even-toned delivery. "Sir, we're just trying to locate your son. He hasn't been at school. Has there been trouble at home? Is there anything you want to tell us?"

"Who the fuck is this?"

"Perhaps I could come by the house for a visit. Sometimes we do that with problem cases."

"Look, kid, I don't know what kind of asshole you think I am, but I got news for you: I don't know where Scott is. He took off a week ago. How do you like that? And another thing: if you see him, tell him to stay the fuck away. I got no more patience for his shit." There's a shattering of glass in the background, Mr. Schatz striking out in fury. Robin slams down the receiver. His knuckles are white.

Now he doesn't know what to believe. If Scott ran away, wouldn't he have called by now? Maybe he is mad at Robin because his parents brought Mr. Schatz to the bus that night. He might have saved a little money from selling pot, but probably not even enough to last him a week. Whom would he have asked for money? Robin thinks about it and the name Todd Spicer comes back at him like a shout from the end of a tunnel.

He corners Victoria between classes. "Do you know if your brother has heard from Scott Schatz lately?"

"No."

"I think he ran away, but he doesn't have any money."

"Robin, I told you not to hang out with him. He's such a megaloser."

"I bet Todd knows where he is."

"Yeah, right. They're not even friends. You're so *mental* about this."

He feels himself snap. "Shut up, Victoria. Just shut your mouth. You don't know anything! You're just some stuck-up bitch who acts like she's better than everybody else." Without any effort, his voice is at hysterical pitch.

Victoria backs away, checking over her shoulder for someone level-headed to intervene. "Grow up, Robin," she says, her voice shaky. "Why don't you ask someone who cares?"

"I thought you were my friend," he accuses.

"I was your friend before you turned into Sibyl."

He slams his fist into a locker, and she jumps back. She stares for a moment, stunned by his aggression. And then her face hardens. She gives him the finger and walks away.

He stands at the edge of the courtyard between classes, trying to work up the nerve to ask Todd directly, but he can't get near him without navigating the circle of burnouts who surround him. That girl Debbie is always there, laughing at Todd's jokes, slipping her hand into his back pocket.

Instead, he waits for the second bell to ring and the halls to clear of students and teachers; then he retreats to a quiet stairwell behind the stage of the school auditorium. From the other end of the hall he can hear the school choir, the few students with any talent fighting to be heard over the off-key masses. He recognizes the tune, "Getting to Know You." His mother and he stayed up late one night watching *The King and I* on the midnight movie, and he had cried at the part where the princess and her lover met secretly, singing "We Kiss in the Shadows." The next day, he went to New Sounds and purchased the soundtrack. He spent days sketching pictures of Deborah Kerr's pale blue ballgown, trying to get it just right. He finds himself humming along—and then makes himself stop. An angry chill runs up his spine. The song is foolish; the whole film, he thinks now, is such a corny fantasy. Life isn't about winning the favor of strangers with your good manners and charming perseverance. In real life, Anna's strong-mindedness would probably get her thrown into prison and tortured by the King of Siam's henchmen. In real life, if you broke out into song, you wouldn't make new friends—you'd get your ass kicked. Why do movies try to convince you happiness is only a song away? Next time he goes to New Sounds he's going to buy the Patti Smith record Scott played for him.

"Something bad happened to Scott."

His parents look at each other. His father sighs, annoyed. "Not during dinner, Robin."

"Who's Scott?" Ruby asks.

"He's not at school. All week. What do you think that means?"

He is frustrated by their silence, each of them looking as if they are trying to *prepare* something to say, something other than the truth. "I called his father and he sounded really suspicious, and it made me think that maybe something's wrong."

Clark is clearly unhappy with this news. "You shouldn't be bothering the guy."

"I wasn't *bothering* him. I was asking where Scott was, which is pretty normal for a friend to do." He slides his plate away, exasperated that they can't see the urgency of the situation.

His mother lays down her knife and fork. She speaks each word carefully, deliberately. "Robin, I know Scott is your friend, and I'm sure he'd be happy to know that you're concerned about him." He doesn't like the way this is starting—it sounds like she's ready to preach—but he waits before interrupting, hoping maybe she might still possess the capacity to understand him. "I know you've spent time with him and had some adventures together, but the fact is that you don't know him very well. Now, your father and I spoke to Mr. Cortez about him." She shoots out her hand to silence him, seeing that he has opened his mouth in surprise. "Wait. Don't say anything. When we met with Hector we just asked him what we should know about this new friend of yours, and he told us that Scott has a history of running away. He's been caught selling marijuana to kids at school. He's been left back a year."

She pauses for a sip of wine, and Robin interjects. "But all that's just because—well, he has reasons!"

"His home life is very *difficult,* it's true. And God knows your father and I have a lot of sympathy for the fact that he's lost his brother. . . ." Her attention drifts away for just an instant—a pause heavy enough for Robin to register the ever present specter of Jackson's mortality.

"Who's Scott?" Ruby repeats, her eyes shifting awkwardly between her hardly touched London broil dinner and the faces around the table.

"This is a boy who goes to school with Robin—"

Robin interrupts defiantly. "He's my new best friend."

"He had an older brother who died a violent death. It's not at all the same situation that Jackson is in, so we don't need to be thinking bad thoughts. Don't let any of this upset you, Ruby."

Ruby remains expressionless. "I'm not upset."

Clark reaches out and pats her shoulder. "You're excused from the table, if you don't want to stay."

Robin is surprised when she doesn't leave, and he reads this as a display of solidarity. "You know, Mom, just 'cause Scott's a little bit of a burnout doesn't mean . . ."

She shakes her head; she isn't going to budge. "I'm telling you what Mr. Cortez told us. You know Mr. Cortez, Robin. He's got your best interests in mind."

Robin's leg shakes under the table, rippling the surface of his water glass. His mother is so sure, so calm, that he thinks maybe he should listen to her. Scott has never revealed very much about himself, after all.

The fact that he hasn't called Robin might be proof that he never cared for him—and if Scott doesn't care for him, Robin thinks, maybe he's been lying to him, too. Maybe things aren't so bad at home. Maybe Scott himself is the problem. . . But that doesn't make sense either. He has seen the bruises, seen Mr. Schatz in action. Why is his mother making him doubt what is true? "All I know is, I think something really bad happened to him."

"Your mother's right. It's not your concern." Clark has relief written all over his face; Dorothy's speech has spared him having to make one himself.

Robin slams his hands on the table. "Forget it, just forget it!" He raises his voice in sarcasm, gesturing exaggeratedly as he stomps from the kitchen. "We'll just *forget* about the fact that this kid who gets beaten up by his father every day has not been seen by anyone for a whole *week,* and we'll just act like everything's *normal.* Even though he's my only friend in the whole world, I'll just stop worrying." From the top of the stairs he yells out once more. "Everything's normal! Just perfectly normal!"

He dashes to his parents' bedroom and dials Scott's number. He won't hang up until he gets an answer. Until he finds Scott. He lies on the floor with the receiver a foot away from him. His breath slows down, keeping rhythm with the unanswered mechanical ring. The operator interrupts—*Please hang up and try again.* His eyes shut heavily.

He snaps awake at the sound of the phone being put back on the receiver. Ruby stands above him. "I'll pray for Scott."

"Don't pray for him. Just help me."

"What can I do?"

"I don't know," he says, his voice cracking. "I have to figure something out. I *have* to."

Ruby drops down on the rug next to him and takes his hands in hers. Her touch is warm, her grip sturdy. He searches her face, expecting to see pity, a glazed, angelic smile meant to smooth away his worries. Instead, her gaze is concentrated, her jaw set in fierce determination. "You'll figure it out," she insists. "You're smart, Robin. And you're strong. You just have to believe."

Believe? He repeats the word in his head, and it sounds like a question. *Believe in what?* But her fingers tighten around his, and he understands that *she* believes in him, in this mysterious notion of his strength, and for the moment it is enough, and he is thankful for it. He squeezes back to let her know he is willing to try.

* * *

No one speaks of being thankful at the Thanksgiving table. Robin feels
Jackson's absence as palpably as the winter drafts that hiss through the
exposed, unfinished room, chilling the dining room table where they eat
their holiday feast and struggle to make conversation. Nana keeps their
plates full while Dorothy gets looped on wine.

Stan takes advantage of the moody silences around the table, filling in
empty space with his opinions on the state of the world. His particular
fixation this day: San Francisco, which has been all over the news lately.
First came reports of the San Franciscans who followed a guy named
Reverend Jim Jones to Guyana and committed mass suicide under his
direction. Robin saw the gruesome photos in *Time:* a metal basin, the
kind you use in bobbing for apples, filled with poisoned grape Kool-Aid;
a field of twisted corpses facedown all around. Then there was the city
supervisor who gunned down the mayor of San Francisco and another
supervisor; this second victim, Robin had been surprised to learn, was a
homosexual. He tries to picture this guy in San Francisco's City Hall.
Was he like one of those muscular, mustached men from Christopher
Street, but sitting behind a desk signing official documents? It doesn't
make any sense. How did he even get into office? Who would vote for a
gay?

Stan uses this fact as proof of the city's absurdity. "So you got them
electing a fag *and* an assassin. No wonder they're all running off to Guyana and killing themselves. I always said, San Francisco is like a breakfast cereal—fruits, nuts, and flakes!"

"Dad, you heard that on Johnny Carson," Larry says, unimpressed.

"It was probably funny when *he* told it," Robin mutters.

"Guess I gotta work on my delivery," Stan says, his smile fading.

Robin is struck by the notion that Scott might have run away to San
Francisco. Maybe he had heard Todd talk about hitting the road, heading out to northern California with its fields of pot plants. Maybe he figured it was the place to go if you didn't have anywhere else.

The fact that their house is in tatters still catches Robin by surprise. The
dining room carpet ends in a pile of fine sawdust, and at night, the bare,
unfinished wood planks disappear into the darkness of two-by-fours
and tarpaulin. When you talk inside the new room your voice reverber-
ates like breath blown into a bottle.

Even with Jackson's return postponed indefinitely, construction of the
room must be finished. Stan and Larry stay the night, and the next

morning everyone rises early. They work for hours, Stan supervising, Clark and Larry looking to him for leads. All morning long, as Sheetrock goes up and Spackle is smeared, Robin hovers at the edges, fetching tools and doing as he is told, maintaining a resentful silence. He is aware of the role he is playing: Jackson's role, youngest boy among the men of the family, the acolyte learning the ropes. A portent of the future, he thinks with a shiver—Robin forced to be the boy that Jackson was.

Nana makes them turkey-and-stuffing sandwiches. Robin takes his outside, in the cold, to eat alone. He looks at the house, at the exterior of the room they have been building. Plastic window coverings strain against the wind, snapping like wings that have been pinned down. The bare pine looks as though it has burst from the gray siding like an alien growth with a plan of its own. The roof now connects to the roof outside of his bedroom window; if Ruby climbed out her window they could meet in the middle. He has lost his private balcony.

Larry sits down next to him on the back stoop. Robin turns away from him and takes a bite of his sandwich. "What's your problem?" Larry asks. "What, are you mad at me?"

"I'm not interested enough in you to be mad at you," Robin says.

"Well, *excuse me*," Larry says. He treads across the lawn, kicking dead leaves from his path. Robin watches Larry's cocky strut—he has it all down: how to get through the world with every step an assertion of power. No one ever accused Larry of walking with too much of a sway.

The slam of a car door carries from across the back hedge. In the Spicers' yard a hostile exchange of voices erupts. Robin stands to get a better look. Todd is sitting behind the wheel of his car; his father is shouting at him through the window. Though he can't discern the words, Robin recognizes in Mr. Spicer's gestures and vocal tones a frustration so similar to his own father's when he struggles to make himself heard by Robin. The comparison is unsettling. Mr. Spicer looms large in his mind, a serious, traditional man whose rare bursts of rage are almost legendary; both Victoria and Scott have referred to the severe beating he gave Todd. Just a few months ago, the idea of his own father hitting him across the face was alien to Robin. Now he wonders if it was inevitable, if it is something that sooner or later happens to teenage boys: their fathers' frustrations uncoil in one mad snap.

The shouting is overpowered by the car's ignition. Todd guns the engine a couple of times, then reverses in a cloud of singed rubber. Mr. Spicer stomps back in the house.

"Who was that?" Larry asks him.

"Todd Spicer," Robin says, as if Larry should know all about him. "'69 Camaro. Very cool."

"He's a friend of mine."

"Yeah, right. Tell me another one."

Robin shrugs—he can't be bothered trying to convince Larry. He turns around to see Ruby at the back door. "What was all that noise?" she asks.

"*Todd Spicer,*" Larry says, faking breathless adoration.

"He just drove off in his new car. His father was yelling at him."

"I bet I know why," Ruby says, lowering her voice with the promise of gossip. She looks around, making sure no one is eavesdropping. "Cathy Delatore said that Todd got Debbie Staley pregnant."

Robin isn't sure he's heard her right. Debbie? The girl who hangs all over Todd at school? Even though Robin has seen them together, he's never believed that they were having sex. If Todd was doing it with this girl, why would he want to do stuff with Robin? "Todd didn't get any girl pregnant."

"How would you know?" Ruby challenges. "They wouldn't just announce it to the whole world."

Larry puffs up his chest. "Well, she's just gonna have to get an abortion."

Ruby's jaw drops in shock. "That's disgusting."

"You mean to tell me you wouldn't get rid of it if it was you?"

Robin can see Larry bullying in on Ruby. "Stop bothering her, Larry. She's not getting pregnant anytime soon."

Ruby crosses her arms. "I don't believe in sex before marriage. It's against God."

"Everyone does it anyway." Larry loops his thumbs in his waistband and leans in closer to them both. "I got a girlfriend now, and we're gonna do it."

"I don't care," Ruby says.

"What about you, Robin? You gonna *do it* before you get married?" His face is smug, his voice facetious.

Robin reaches out and gives Larry a little shove. "Maybe I already have. I certainly wouldn't tell you."

"Bullshit."

"It's not bullshit."

Ruby is telegraphing her confusion to Robin. Their father has instructed them that sex before marriage is prohibited, and at St. Bart's the priest has lectured many times about resisting such temptation.

Ruby might be titillated by gossip about Todd Spicer, but she does not want to hear Robin hint that he, too, has transgressed. Larry's egged him on this far, but now Robin wants this conversation to end.

"This is stupid," he says impatiently, trying to use his sense of superiority to get the better of Larry. "Because, for one thing, Todd's not even doing it with that girl—he would have told me, or Victoria would have told me. And another thing, Larry, you're just a big talker and a bully and all the rest of it."

Ruby, relieved that Robin has asserted some control, pipes in, "And not *everybody* does it before marriage. Catholic people don't."

Larry locks his meanest smile in place. "Your *mother* did."

Ruby's jaw drops again. Robin sees in her eyes that Larry's words have stung. When your mother is insulted, he knows, you're supposed to rise up in defense. But there's no time. Larry's on a roll. "My father told me. She was pregnant when they got married. That's *why* they got married." He turns to Robin. "When's your birthday?"

"December 15th."

"And when did they get married?"

"At the end of May." He looks at Ruby, already counting to seven. "But that doesn't mean anything, because for your information I was born almost two months premature." This is what he was told by his father when he was very young, what he's always believed without question.

"You're just lucky you weren't an abortion."

"You better shut your fucking mouth," Robin yells.

"Make me."

Ruby verges on bursting into tears. She turns to run back in the house just as Dorothy is opening the door, announcing, "Last call for lunch." Ruby rushes past her, obviously upset.

"What in God's name? Ruby!" Dorothy looks to Robin for an explanation.

His face burns in rage and confusion. "How much did I weigh when I was born?"

"Ten pounds or so. You were a big baby." Dorothy looks puzzled, even alarmed.

"That's not what Dad told me." He casts a sidelong glance to Larry, who looks away, as if all of this has nothing to do with him. Robin hates his cousin more than ever, hates the way Larry is capable of only one thing: hurting anyone he thinks of as weak. "You should go talk to Ruby," he instructs his mother coolly. "She's upset."

"Oh, for God's sake, what brought this on?" The screen door slams behind her.

Watching her slip away, knowing she did not understand what he was really asking her—not only about the circumstances of his birth but about the lies told to him through the years—Robin clenches his jaw, steeling himself against the disappointment that consumes him.

"Told you," Larry says.

Robin reaches out, entwines his fingers in Larry's hair and pulls. With his other hand he digs into Larry's exposed Adam's apple, catching him completely off guard. Words rush out like lethal gas. "I am going to kill you one day, Larry. I swear, one day, I am going to figure out how to kill you."

Larry manages to push him off. "You couldn't hurt a fucking two-year-old," he wails—but his cherry-red skin and the ambushed shock in his eyes tell Robin otherwise.

He is on his bicycle, heading down the driveway. For days he has been thinking about how he might sneak out of the house, and now the opportunity has presented itself without announcement. He just walked past Larry to the garage. Pedaling fast down Bergen Avenue, the cold wind bringing tears to his eyes, he is freer than he has been in days, in weeks. Maybe ever. It's not happiness: at this speed, sadness and freedom seem like the same thing.

His mother and father, married because of him. Once they had been young, almost as young as Todd and Debbie, just doing it for the hell of it, because it felt good. Then there must have been a conversation, a decision to go ahead and get married. Maybe they had been planning it already; or maybe they hadn't really loved each other. Maybe that's why they fight so much now, because from the start they weren't in love. They married because he came along.

But why has he never been told of this?

His mother keeping such a big secret from him—that's what thrashes inside his skull, sours in his throat. As if she was ashamed. As if *he* were something to be ashamed of. He's glad he is keeping secrets from her now; he could keep secrets for the rest of his life and it would still not be enough pay her back. He throws his weight into his legs, emboldened by injustice. Familiar houses come slowly into view and then quickly out again—it seems to him that he is discarding them, dismissing everything in sight as useless, unworthy.

He considers going to Scott's and demanding Scott's whereabouts from Mr. Schatz. A fantasy takes hold: he finds Scott's hiding place, rescues him, takes him away. They could hitchhike cross country, go all the way to San Francisco and live in peace with the flakes and fruits and nuts. He might find Scott at The Bird, holed up in the abandoned aviary, living off stolen food, bathing in the stream at night. Waiting.

The Bird. Anxiety rises up, a pocket of air in his throat. Without Scott, he must fight back the old fears: he is too young, too weak, not cool enough for this place. He has to ride past half a dozen parked cars, and the kids hanging out, to get to the bike rack at the entrance to the woods. He slows his pace, thinking that haste will reveal his discomfort. And then he sees a car that he recognizes: a '69 Camaro.

Todd, leaning against the trunk. Faded denim jacket and black T-shirt. Beer can tilted back. Ethan and Tully and a couple of others circle around. At his side, under the protective reach of his arm, is Debbie Staley. Robin scans her body for signs of pregnancy. No big belly, no swollen breasts—just a smiling, skinny, flat-chested girl sucking on a roach.

Ethan sees him first. "Hey, Spicer, there's your little friend."

Todd nods at him, no sign of welcome on his face. He clutches Debbie tighter—the smallest of gestures, but one that Robin takes personally. Todd is off-limits.

"I want to ask you something," Robin calls out to Todd. He hears the timidity in his voice and wants to stomp it out. "Have you heard from Scott lately?"

Todd swigs his beer. "Scott who?"

Robin spins his pedals backward, a wobbly tension holding him in place. "I think he ran away. He hasn't been in school and his father's been really rough on him lately, so I was worried—"

Todd looks away, annoyed. "Look, man, I don't know anything about it."

"Do you know where I could look?"

"Yeah, why don't you look under a rock?" He pauses, looks coolly into Robin's eyes. *Girly Underwear.*"

Robin drops back, stunned.

Todd adds, "Why don't you just get lost, *Girly Underwear?*"

Only when Debbie starts laughing, burying her head into Todd's chest as if this insult, this dismissal, is a private joke they share, does Robin feel the violent pounding of his pulse. He calls out, "So I heard this rumor today, about you, Todd. And you—" He indicates Debbie. "Yeah, I heard that you got her pregnant."

"Whoa—" The crowd around Todd is shocked, maybe even impressed, by Robin's nerve. Debbie's mouth widens. Todd steps forward angrily, his face reddening.

"But I said it couldn't be true," Robin continues, amazed at the composure he hears in his voice.

"Is that so?" Todd says, his angry glare warning that Robin is treading on thin ice.

"Yeah, I said there's no way you could get her pregnant. Because you're such a fag."

Todd just stares, breath seized in his chest. In the dead brown of Todd's eyes Robin reads that they are now enemies, that he has defaulted on everything Todd had let him in on, has renounced the access he had gained, has disallowed the closeness he might have wished for the future. Whatever it was that connected him to Todd, whatever it was that made Todd want to do sex things with him, is now history. Todd has not done or said anything in response, and even though Robin knows that Todd must soon do or say something to gain back the upper hand, and that it will only get worse from this point on, he cannot stop himself from inflaming the situation further. He wants the freedom to be as mean as everyone has ever been to him. He hates Todd Spicer. He hates him more than he could hate his parents for lying to him, he hates him the way he hates Larry or Uncle Stan or Mr. Schatz. He hates the meanness, hates it so much that he wants only to reflect it back. He inches the bike forward and hisses, "Cocksucker."

Todd leaps toward him. Robin speeds into the parking lot, pointing his bike toward the exit—and puts himself into the path of a moving car. He swerves to avoid it and his front tire slips on loose gravel. The bike skids out from under him, sending him tumbling into a pile of dead leaves. The car passes, horn honking.

He is pinned under the greasy gears of his bike, his knee throbbing, his jeans streaked with dirt. Todd stands above him, beer can in hand.

"Where'd you learn to ride this spiffy bike, Girly Underwear?" He kicks one of his workboots into the wheel, sending it whizzing on its axis.

Robin pulls his leg out from under the frame and scoots back. Todd moves with him, straddling his body, a leg on either side. Robin watches Todd's hand wrap tighter around the beer can, callused fingertips denting the aluminum.

Todd licks his lips. "I think you owe me a fucking apology, Girly Underwear. Maybe that way I won't have to bust up your face." He lowers his voice. "I've done it before. I'll do it again."

"I never did anything to you!" His voice quavers; his throat has gone dry. His smallness exposes itself it in so many ways—he wants to stamp it all out. "I'll hit you back this time," he says angrily.

"Oh, you're so fucking tough," Todd mocks. Robin is ready for the beer to come pouring down, but instead Todd drops to a squat, still straddling Robin's body, and tips the can back, drinking greedily.

Todd's body, so close to him. The familiar smells: cigarettes and beer, vinyl car interior, sweat-stained clothes. Robin can't help himself: he watches Todd's throat ripple, catches the caress of hair against Todd's neck, feels himself dissolving at the edges. His hatred for Todd has only subdued this longing, not obliterated it—and Todd knows this. Todd smiles an unreadable, close-lipped smile, and then without warning thrusts his head forward, splattering a mouthful of beer across Robin's face.

The shock of it: skin icy, eyes stinging, cheeks heavy with foam. He shakes his head to be free of it. Todd's lips are parted now, buttered with beer and spit. He inches closer.

Robin hisses through gritted teeth. "What do you want from me?"

"Dust," Todd says in a hush.

"What?"

"That's all you are to me, Robin," he whispers. "A pile of fucking dust." He fires a needle of breath at Robin's face, extinguishing a candle. "And that goes for Scott Schatz, too. Jesus, I can't believe you're wearing his smelly old jacket." With one last contemptuous glare, he pushes himself to his feet.

Robin remains on the ground, stunned. *Is it over?* Todd struts back to the car, exaggerating his triumph: his arms cast wide, his voice bellowing, "Gotta teach these punks some respect."

"What did you say to him?" Debbie asks.

"I made him eat his words," Todd growls, peeling open a victory beer.

"You should have creamed him," Ethan complains.

Robin concentrates on Todd, surrounded again by his fan club, all of them evaluating the show. *I'm supposed to run off crying now so he can gloat in it. No way.* He wipes his face and sucks snot up his nose, spits a gob from the back of his throat. Standing up, he takes his time wiping off, checking the frame for damage, inspecting the chain. It's a test: how long can he linger, knowing that Todd might still come back over and beat him up? But Todd does not even look his way—leaving Robin wondering whether this failure to make eye contact is a further insult or, on the other hand, a failure of Todd's will.

He pedals slowly toward the exit. The air flutters against his damp skin. Free of Todd's overwhelming physical closeness, he allows himself the experience of relief: *I didn't eat my words. Fag. Cocksucker.* Todd couldn't deny it.

He pedals through Greenlawn, feeling at one moment completely abandoned; at the next, completely set free. Going toward something or moving away—he can't tell the difference. He just rides.

A song enters his head, a song from *Saturday Night Fever,* and he sings aloud, his voice alternately pained and defiant. *I'm going nowhere, somebody help me, somebody help me, yeah. I'm stayin' alive.*

And then he remembers; he knows where he must go next.

Jackson is curled on his side, folding into himself, a fetus. Robin strokes his hair, it is oily, flattened to the skull. He listens to the horrible raspy breaths. This half-alive creature is the same person as his wild brother. Just a couple of months ago Jackson was streaking through the house naked; now Jackson doesn't even have the strength to wake.

"Goddamn it," he pleads. "Come on, Jackson. Enough of this shit already. Enough of this playing around. Just come home, would you? You'll get your own room and everything. It's gonna be different now. You won't believe how much everything's changed. You won't believe how much *I've* changed."

On past visits, he's looked at Jackson's decrepit form and felt hatred, as if Jackson was willfully doing this, an act of vengeance. Now, such an idea is ridiculous. Now, battered by the day's betrayals—first his mother, then Todd—Robin wants to go back home and beat Larry into a stupor, as if that might release Jackson. A trade-off, one casualty for another.

An hour, two hours. The bedside chair offers comfort, so he stays there, a blanked-out sentinel, oblivious to time. The nurses smile sympathetically, bring him orange juice and animal crackers.

One of them calls his mother. She whooshes in—sunglasses, head scarf, raincoat, smudged scarlet lipstick—a movie star hiding in public. "Visiting hours are over," she says dryly.

She smells of wine and cigarettes; will she smell the beer soaked into him?

She drives them through streets already flashy with Christmas kitsch. Santa's sleigh and two token reindeer nailed to a roof; dwarf-sized, plastic Nativity sets glowing eerily from front lawns; houses smothered in schizophrenic blinking bulbs. He does not account for his hours missing, lets her believe he was at the hospital the entire time. She chainsmokes and does not say where they are going.

Eastward for half an hour, a steady grade uphill until they are in a parking lot atop the Palisades, overlooking the Hudson River, the George Washington Bridge, the New York City skyline. The engine stills. They stare through the windshield.

The city looks entirely different from inside out, he thinks. From here, at this distance, it is only beautiful, an island fortress with candles in every window. Now that he's been there without his mother, without money, without even a coat, he wonders if that beauty is just one more lie. He recalls the dim, shabby terror of Vincent's apartment and, afterward, the way the streets seemed unnavigable, the peril endless. Has he been fooled into trusting New York because he was protected from really knowing it?

"Not so long ago, we could never get you to shut up," Dorothy says. "Lately, you're so quiet."

"Lately life sucks."

"Yes, well . . ."

Silence envelops them. Each of her smoky exhalations is like wind in a tunnel.

"Can I have one?" he asks, taking her Pall Malls from the dashboard.

"Don't be difficult." She eases the pack from his hand.

He watches her try to start speaking, the way her face reveals the formation and discarding of possible opening lines. She rubs her temples. "I have such a headache all the time. The TV is on so much these days—"

"That's because of Nana and Uncle Stan."

"Yes, well, I never wanted my children to watch television. We didn't have a TV when I was growing up. And when I finally saw what television was, when I started living at Smith, I couldn't believe it. I had always thought a TV would bring theater and opera into your home—but when I turned on television, it was nothing but bad jokes. Milton Berle, for God's sake!"

She is suddenly animated. Robin manages a brief, encouraging smile despite his impatience. He wants her to address what Larry told him today, but it is a small comfort to hear in her voice the rhythm and en- thusiasm of the private talks they have shared together in the past.

"Oh, I know I sound like a complete snob, but I was such a romantic. I fancied myself an intellectual. I read Mary McCarthy. I went to Smith—even if it was only because my mother worked there." She pauses and smiles sheepishly, amused by her own pretension. "Actually, I was more of a snob before I even got to Smith than anyone from my background had a right to be! Every year of my life I saw them, like an endless parade of princesses. All the rich girls shopping in town over the holidays. The expensive cars driven from New York and Boston. It *shaped* me. When I began attending classes at Smith, I was still living at home, but I managed to make friends with two suite mates—they were Philadelphia Irish, nouveau riche, a couple of Grace Kellys. After an ini- tial period of enchantment I realized they were vacuous. Their parents bought them televisions, which were always on. *I* wanted to write po- etry and study the history of painting and sculpture, and they would hang around drugstores reading *True Confessions*. I vowed I would never buy a television, and I vowed when Clark moved his in that I would keep you three away from it as much as possible. I think I've done a pretty good job protecting you from the banality of the boob tube."

She looks to him for more encouragement, but he cannot keep it up. He has heard this story before, its details always slightly rearranged. (Last time the suite mates were from New Haven, "a couple of Katherine Hepburns.") Usually this inconsistency is part of the fun of her stories, but now it is just a frustrating diversion.

He takes a deep breath and blurts out, "Why didn't you ever tell me about how you and Dad got married? Did you want to protect me from that, too?"

She stubs her cigarette out in the ashtray, defeat in her eyes. "I'm get- ting there, I'm getting there. God, I despise confessions." She lets herself out of the car and indicates that he should follow.

He takes a Pall Mall from the pack on the dashboard and grabs the matchbook. The coldness of the night is abrasive, and his knee aches from the skid he took today on his bike. He winces as he jumps up on the hood.

"Are you hurt?" she asks.

"It's nothing."

"Your cousin didn't hurt you, did he?"

"No." He remembers the threat he made to Larry during lunch. He can still taste a hunger for violence in his throat. "Not physically."

Sitting beside him on the warm hood, Dorothy links her arm in his. "If it's of any help in redeeming my virtue, I'll just start off by saying that I never liked sex that much. I liked it now and then, but not all the time and not with someone I hardly knew. I was scared to death of getting pregnant—that's partially why—but also I just loathed feeling cheap. I had made it to New York City; sex just reminded me of the girls I went to high school with, who were all married and pregnant by age twenty. I thought, 'There but for the grace of God go I, and damn if I'm going to let some flashy stud have his way with me.'"

"So are you trying to tell me that Dad was one of these user guys who just wanted you for sex?" He sees Todd Spicer crouching above him at The Bird, smug in the knowledge of how sexy he looked to Robin, even as he tormented him.

"Clark was the only one who *never* tried to lay me. He always stopped at the actual intercourse. 'We should wait,' he would say, and then he'd roll away and say, 'Phew!' and wipe his brow as if the restraint was exhausting him. And I thought, 'No man has ever exalted me like that,' and I stopped dating other men and decided I would stick with Clark. And after Seymour, he was just so *easy*. No one didn't like Clark back then. He was just a heck of a nice guy."

Deep inhale. Awkward silence.

"The irony of course was that with Clark I got pregnant. We finally did do it—about three months after we met, we started doing it every night of the week. I practically just moved in with him. He had a little place on West Twenty-Third Street, over a Chinese restaurant—"

"I know. You've showed me."

"Of course, of course. We had only been going at it for about five weeks when I suddenly knew I was pregnant. I sensed it before I knew it. I just didn't feel right, physically, *chemically*. I was unable to keep my guard up, unable to project confidence. One day I was crossing Herald Square and someone brushed past me rather roughly, as happens every five minutes in the city, and I immediately wanted to cry. By the time I made it to the other side of the street, I thought, 'This is what it feels like to be pregnant.'"

"It's like you were psychic!" he says, impressed by this part of the story.

She waves her hand dismissively. "Oh, perhaps I'm exaggerating with hindsight. We talked about *not* getting married, or rather I talked about it, but Clark was so convincing that next thing I knew it was my wedding day. I missed my career, and I hated being home all day, but you were a gorgeous baby, Robin, and a genuine charmer and clearly very smart from the beginning. You were easy to like. So, as they say these days, *I went with it.*"

"Can I ask a question?" He waits to find the right word. She is looking away. He brings the cigarette he has been holding to his lips and strikes a match, asking his question through clenched lips. "Did you ever resent me?"

"I felt so many things, and I guess some of them weren't very nice." She frowns as he takes a drag, her eyes registering not so much disapproval as surprise; he realizes his smoking must look rather skilled to her, which provides him a taste of rebellious pride. "Resentment? I suppose that came later, years later, in New Jersey." Her voice softens. "One day it finally hit me—I had spent the last four or five years pregnant. Really, I just fell ill. I thought, 'Dorothy, my God, this has got to stop. Stop having children. Three is at least one too many!' That's why I'm so sick lately, Robin, because I remember this so clearly—it was one of the watershed moments of my life. Jackson was in the crib and Ruby was crying every night still—she was the noisiest of the three of you—and you were a handful of curious energy, and it just hit me. I thought, 'I shouldn't have had this last one.' Jackson."

She is trembling at his side. He thinks he is like an older brother to her in this moment. She says, "I feel so responsible. For all of it."

She slides off the hood and totters toward the stone wall at the edge of the parking lot. Robin watches her enter the landscape, wondering if she's stumbling because she's emotionally overwrought or just intoxicated. A stream of her words rushes into the air plaintively. "And your father is falling apart, he's really becoming so much like *his* father, just petty and unflinching. He was always so bumbling and sweet—who knew that in his grief he would harden like this? And Ruby's gone Catholic on us, for which I blame my mother, though I have no right to complain. I'm a lousy mother for Ruby. I have no idea how to raise a girl. I've always said that I wouldn't raise her like my mother raised me, which has basically meant that I haven't raised her at all." She wraps her arms around herself. "I've made a mess of everything, and I feel incapable of being any other way. Sometimes all I can come up with is that I just want out, that I just don't want this to be my life."

He stands up, wanting to reach out to her, to offer a tonic to this sad-

244 / K.M. Soehnlein

ness, but she unexpectedly spins around, and her voice is full of accusation. "And what do *you* want from me, Robin?" She marches back to him, takes the cigarette from his fingers, and finishes it off.

"What do you mean?"

"You've become the household juvenile delinquent, and I'm completely beside myself about it. I didn't raise you to be like this, so I know it's not natural behavior for you. I assume you are crying out for attention. This is why I brought you out here tonight."

Where did her vulnerability go? Why is she suddenly so cold? He feels like he's been slapped and he wants to slap back. "You just don't understand me."

"No one understands you as well as I do. And no one loves you as much either."

He hears no uncertainty in her voice and wants to argue with her, to offer contradictory evidence, but the headrush from the cigarette and her abrupt mood swing have fuzzed his thoughts. And then she is speaking again, more quietly this time, as if tapping away at his shell with a small, sharp chisel.

"I remember when I discovered that you were buying teen magazines, those tacky, mass-produced things with pictures of tacky little TV stars. *Tiger Beat.* You were six, seven years old. You used to take the money Grampa Leo gave you and buy yourself a copy of *Tiger Beat* on the way home from school. My God, you were a six-year-old boy with the obsessions of a ten- or twelve-year-old girl."

He glares at her, distrustful. He remembers sneaking those magazines into his room, staring at David Cassidy and Leif Garret, then sliding them under his bed. What ever happened to them? Did she throw them out? And why is she bringing this up now? He tries to pull his arm out from hers, but she senses his intent and clamps down. "I thought you wanted to talk about you, not about me," he says defensively.

"I *am* talking about me. At least I'm trying to. After I found your *Tiger Beat* stash, I started looking, really looking, at other boys your age. I would study them while I talked with their mothers on the sidewalk after school. And it was very clear. I thought, 'Robin is not like any of those other boys.' I couldn't even describe the difference. I mean, I could, but it would sound cliché. *He was gentle. He was emotional. He was sensitive.* You know what it was? You were *flirty.* You were this delicate blond boy who knew that people were attracted to his looks. Boys and girls, and mothers, and teachers. You flirted with them all. A first grader, batting your eyelashes at other boys and saying, 'I'll tell you a se-cret.' There was no other boy at your school, or anywhere that I looked, who had this quality."

"Mom, I think you're exaggerating," he says, but he's not sure she is. He remembers saying, *I'll tell you a secret,* to Jimmy Woods in second grade; he doesn't remember what the secret was but he knows that he and Jimmy had their pants down together one day in the woods behind the playground and showed each other their boners, and he knows that afterward Jimmy Woods never looked him in the eye again. It was like that time with Larry in Nana's cellar, and there were others, too, back then: boys he convinced to show him their boners. He remembers these things like rides he once took at an amusement park: there's the blur of sensation—the thrill and the terror mixed up together—but no real be-ginning, middle, or end. His mother is organizing the memories into something with a *point*. She's never spoken like this before, about him, *to* him, and he doesn't like it.

"I'm not exaggerating. I remember it very clearly. Realizing you were different was disturbing, with a life's worth of implications—and God knows I'll be dealing with the implications for my entire life. We both will. But oddly enough, and most importantly, it was actually the thing that made me love you more than ever before. I concluded that your particular qualities made you extremely *special*. I thought you were . . . oh, I don't know . . . I thought you were a *prize*. It was very selfish, re-ally. I thought, if my firstborn is special, then I must be special, too. I sort of consoled myself by saying, 'I have a special child.'"

"Great. I'm so fucking *special*," he growls sarcastically. "Why didn't you put me in *special* education?"

She lights another cigarette, showing no sign of having heard this re-mark. She is faraway, trying to make sense of something. "I spoke to my mother once about all this, but she just looked confused and said, 'Of course Robin's special. He's your son,' and I changed the subject. I cer-tainly didn't speak to Clark about it—it would have made him very ner-vous. Unable to concentrate."

"Because I wasn't normal?" he asks. Again, she doesn't answer. He feels himself growing angry at her. "You know, Mom, you're saying some pretty heavy shit."

She stares him down. "This is not *heavy shit*, Robin. This is life. Let me tell you something: life is going to be hard. It's going to be hard *every day*. That's what life *is*. You get up, it's another day, you don't know what is going to land in your lap, but you can bet your last nickel that some of it is going to be difficult. I've tried to protect you from this basic fact, but there's no reason to anymore. Just get used to it."

"I don't want to get used to it! I want things to get better, to change." In his voice he hears the unfiltered mess of his thoughts: rage and fear, determination and pleading. He adds softly, "I don't know if you've noticed, but I'm actually kind of depressed."

She takes hold of his chin, her long fingers on his jaw. She searches his eyes as if she might see "depression" written there, then lets go, unsatisfied. "Well, I asked you what you want from me, Robin. Tell me, what shall I do?"

He slides off the hood of the car and walks toward the edge of the embankment. The city beckons like a campfire, twinkling orange and blue, filling the sky with light, the river with jewels. Is that where Scott went? Did he take the bus on his own? Is he burrowing through the alleys by night? Robin shivers at the idea of it: Scott lost in the vastness, no one to turn to, preyed on by sex maniacs. He turns back to his mother. "OK, OK, I know what you can do for me. Will you call Mr. Cortez on Monday and ask him if he knows where Scott is?"

She drops the cigarette and stamps it out violently. "Scott, Scott, Scott. Robin, why does it have to be this boy?"

"Do you think I'm not so special anymore?" he asks venomously.

"Don't push your luck. You know, you're very bright Robin, but still impressionable. Be careful who influences you." He senses her resolve fading. Her shoulders have slumped; her hands are on her forehead again, circling away a headache. "I used to think I had a picture of what your life would be like, but now I have no idea."

He has no desire to ask her about that picture, doesn't want to hear anyone else's version of his life anymore, especially his mother's. His head is already too full of other people's ideas, of information he did not ask for but which sticks to him stubbornly nonetheless. "Please do me that one favor, Mom. I'm not asking that much."

"Oh, all right." Her voice cracks. She drags herself back into the car.

He can't tell if she is being sincere or just mollifying him. But he has her agreement, and he will make her stick to it. He slides into the seat next to her, relieved to be leaving this place and the tension they've brought here.

She grips the wheel as she pumps the gas. "This is the part where I drive us both off the cliff." She lets out a witchy laugh—an eerie, shrill sound that, syllable by syllable, translates itself into a wail.

He puts his hand on her shoulder and tries to soothe. Her sobs pick up force, fall into a rhythm, transform her face into a pained, tear-streaked mask. He pulls her to him, cradling her against his chest. It embarrasses him to see her like this; at the same time he feels very grown-up, very sober.

"Robin, make me a promise. If Clark and I ever divorce, you'll stay with me, won't you?"

He shushes her. "It's not going to happen, so don't talk about it."

She pulls out of his arms and touches her lips to his. "Promise me."

"Of course, Mom. Of course." He gently guides her back behind the wheel, wanting to be free of the intensity of her need.

She studies herself in the rearview mirror, gazing with pity upon her image. He waits for her to start the car, but she is strangely unable to move.

Minutes go by. "Mom?"

She stares at the dashboard as if she can't make any sense of it. He instructs her calmly: "Put the key in the ignition." She starts the engine, but remains impassive, her face blank.

"Mom, put the car in reverse." She nods, as if revisiting something long forgotten. "Check your blind spots. Watch out for cars. The traffic's heavy on the Palisades. Just take it slowly."

She follows his instructions, a zombie taking orders, and in this way, turn by turn, he guides them home.

Chapter Twelve

He begins to visit Jackson by himself after school, after his mother has left and before his father, with Ruby in tow, shows up in the evening. He thinks about these visits all day long, preparing the stories he will tell his brother.

Every day he relates to Jackson another piece of what life has been like without him: Clark and Dorothy's increased hostility toward each other, Ruby's new religion, his own rebelliousness. These stories are unlike any he has ever fabricated with his mother. Now, he keeps his language precise and as rational as he can, trying to preempt the reactions he knows Jackson would display—confusion, protest, mockery. The tales are a stream of words flowing from one visit to the next, returned to over a week's time. I will make him understand, he thinks. I am his big brother, and it's my job to make him trust me.

Slowly, over the course of days, he spells out his new understanding of their family: their parents have never really loved each other; once his mother got pregnant, the thrill wore off. The marriage was probably a mistake—Robin's birth was probably a mistake—but it's too late to change that. His mother thinks he's special, his father thinks he's an embarrassment, and somewhere in between is the fact of his almost fourteen years of life. He offers his explanation to Jackson's inert body. "The way Mom and Dad live, it's like once upon a time they called a truce. Somewhere around the time you were born Mom freaked out. Maybe she threatened to leave; maybe she just turned into a bitch. I'm not sure. But they made some kind of agreement, maybe not a *spoken* agreement, but, you know . . . something like this: Mom got me, and Dad got you, and they kind of share Ruby or just ignore her. But now with you kind of out of it, Dad's mad. He wants me to be more like you, and Mom wants me to be more like—I don't know—like *her*. Everything might fall apart if you don't get better."

As he's speaking, he visualizes a reel-to-reel tape imbedded in Jackson's brain, recording his words; he imagines Jackson waking from his coma, opening his mouth and spouting back everything Robin's been saying. So when he talks about Scott or Todd, about his adventures with them, he censors himself. He stops the story about going to the golf course with Todd at the point where they were splashing around skinny-dipping; he describes the night Scott slept over in his bed, but makes it sound as if they just have a particularly intense friendship. He says, "There's other stuff, but I'll tell you when you're older. You're not mature enough yet." Or, "I can't say anything more because I think the nurses might hear."

Some days he just talks about something that he read in a book or saw on TV, because the family stuff, the Scott stuff and the what's-going-on-in-my-head stuff, even in the unloading of it, is a burden. Some days he just wants someone to talk with about the unimportant things. Jackson's never been the right person for that, but lately there's no one else.

He corners his mother one night in the kitchen, where she sits with her glass of wine, sorting through a pile of bills. More than a week has passed since she took him to the Palisades. "Did you ask Mr. Cortez about Scott?"

She nods without taking her eyes from her paperwork.

"Why didn't you tell me?" he asks in astonishment. "What did he say?"

"He said that Scott was living with relatives in another town."

"What relatives? What other town?" His eyes widen in amazement at the information, at her nonchalance in revealing it.

"He wouldn't give me details."

"Why not? Did you tell him I've been trying to find Scott?"

She shuffles through a pile of mail, pulling a few envelopes from it. "I wrote away for literature on prep schools, and I'd like you to look this over."

"Mom, I'm asking you about Scott."

"I've said it before, Robin. I'll say it again: I don't think it's any of our—"

He cuts her off, infuriated. "It is my business—it *is*—and I can't believe you won't help. You promised me."

She finally raises her head. Her voice is unyielding. "Robin, I've never, ever said this to you in your entire life, but I'm going to say it now because I am at my wit's end: I'm your mother, and you must listen to me. It's that simple. No more questions. Just do as you're told and stop asking about Scott."

She thrusts the school brochures at him, but he backs away empty handed, hissing out a threat. "Fine, if that's the way you want it. You know, I made a promise to you that night, but I guess I'll just take that one back, too."

A few days later, Dorothy asks him what he wants for his birthday.

"I don't want anything anyone can give me wrapped in a box."

"That's very noble, Robin, but if I were to get you something, what would you like it to be?"

He tells her he wants a camera, which is something he hasn't thought about since he learned that photography was *not* part of freshman art. He had a camera when he was younger, an Instamatic that didn't keep anything in focus. The colors of the pictures disappointed him: skies always nearly white, trees and lawns lurid and shiny as Astroturf. Faces were flat and bright from the flash or hidden by shadows. He finally put the camera away, thinking one day he'd have a Canon like his father's, only he'd use it more often, not just on the one vacation they took every year. He wanted to take photos like the reproductions his mother had framed around the house—Cartier-Bresson, Stieglitz, Doisneau; people in the city, in their homes; the emotion of fleeting moments perfectly preserved—not the boring shots of monuments and nature glimpsed through a car window that his father favored. When he hears himself asking his mother for a camera for his birthday it seems like a long-standing wish suddenly voicing itself. Later, his father tells him out of the blue, "Don't expect a lot for your birthday, Robin. It's just not a good year."

He gives up on the camera after that, even as part of him holds fast to the idea. He makes a list of the things he wants to photograph and recites it to Jackson at the hospital: "Strangers on the street in New York City who catch my eye, like the crazy guy with the dogs in the wheelchair on Eighth Street, and the woman with the leopard-print pants, who I definitely think was a model. Kids at school when they're not looking, especially the kids I don't like doing gross things in the cafeteria, like Seth Carter stuffing a disgusting sloppy joe in his mouth, or Danielle Louis mixing her mashed potatoes and wax beans. If you look close you'll see the grossest things people do while they're eating. Victoria sometimes eats butter on a fork! And last but not least, I would like to take pictures of Scott, in his room or in the courtyard at school or at The Bird."

He thinks to himself that he would also want to take pictures of Jackson in the hospital, to show to him when he was out and feeling better.

December 15. Robin's birthday. Nana has made a chocolate cake from scratch, and Ruby has spread white frosting from a can and pressed M&Ms into the surface in the shape of the letter "R." Fifteen candles— one for each year and one for good luck—lie in a pile on the counter. Dorothy has insisted on a celebration, although Robin had no one to call now that Scott was gone and Victoria is no longer speaking to him. It will just be his parents and Ruby, Nana, Uncle Stan, Aunt Corinne, and Larry. Dorothy has recruited Clark to help her blow up a bag of white balloons. Clark criticizes the color, but Dorothy brushes him off. "White in winter is perfect. And for a birthday, it's absolutely the right choice." She piles the shiny white balloons in corners around the house, like enormous spilled pearls.

For Robin, a roomful of balloons is a room brimming with tension— a room waiting to explode. The sound of popping balloons is one of his least favorite sounds. No matter how prepared he is for a balloon's eruption, the noise still shocks him. He doesn't protest his mother's white balloons, though, because maybe, without Jackson, their presence will be bearable. Jackson with balloons was a monster. He carried balloons behind people and popped them without warning, and if anyone protested, he'd stomp on one or two right in the middle of the floor. He'd spear them on his silverware and hold them close to candles (which is why they've never used helium). Robin believes that some of Jackson's happiest moments were when he popped four or five balloons in a row, working the room into an uproar.

The lights are turned out. The song begins. Dorothy waltzes the cake into the room, candles blazing. Make a wish, they say. Robin presses his eyes together and holds his breath and thinks, *Please bring Scott back,* but in the split second before he blows out the candles, Larry speaks up, saying, "I wish Jackson was here," and the words hit him like a blow to the gut. As he exhales, his eyes meet Larry's, and he cannot help but feel that Larry knows he made the wrong wish. Robin remembers Larry on the slide that day, taunting Ruby, taunting him, too; he remembers the horrible sound of Jackson's bones cracking as Larry turned him over, and he thinks, *It's your fault.*

From his father, Hemingway's *The Old Man and the Sea;* from Ruby, a Miss Piggy coffee cup that reads, "This mug belongs to *moi;*" from his mother, a blank journal with a violet cloth cover, which he likes more than he lets on. Aunt Corinne gives him a boring argyle sweater that he doesn't think he'll wear, though Dorothy grandly announces that it will be perfect for his new school. Then she presents another box. "It's from all of us," she says, but from the look on his father's face, Robin is sure that she bought it without telling him.

The camera is heavy in his hands. Its black-and-silver metal gleams like a gun. The weight and texture of it proclaim the seriousness of its purpose. There is a zoom lens encircled with tiny numbers. There are settings for things he doesn't know how to use and a separate flash unit that slides onto the top. Holding it up to his face, he feels like an adult. People react when he points it at them: Nana backs away; Aunt Corinne adjusts her hair; Larry pushes up the tip of his nose and grunts like a pig. He likes this power to rouse people from their passivity; he likes this injection of control. It feels natural.

"Everyone stand together," he says. "On the count of three." Through the viewfinder they look posed and stiff, false in their snug harmony. He gets an idea: "Oh, wait, something's wrong." Everyone relaxes for a moment, allowing him to adjust. He waits until the composition unravels—his mother's smile faded, his father's posture loosened, Ruby's and Larry's eyes gazing elsewhere—and then snaps the image without announcement. A chorus of protests follows, but he ignores it. This image of his family in disarray has been preserved.

Later, while the adults are playing cards around the table, Ruby pulls him aside. "What about what you promised?"

He takes the stolen Pisces medallion from under his bed and carries it to his parents' room, where the coats and purses have been dropped onto the bed. He finds Aunt Corinne's purse and shoves the medallion inside, burying it at the bottom so that she might think she had overlooked it there.

He is startled by the ringing of the phone. The purse slips from his hands. As he is gathering up the spilled contents, Larry pushes open the bedroom door.

"Hey—that's my mother's!"

"It is? I just noticed it fell off the bed and I'm cleaning it up." He stuffs everything back in and snaps it shut, the medallion now tangled up with the rest of it. He curses Ruby under his breath, curses himself for agreeing to help her.

"You're stealing from my mother." Larry moves closer, thrilled to be catching Robin red-handed.

"I wasn't stealing, I was just looking at it. It's a nice purse."

"What? Do you want one of your own?"

"Shut up, Larry."

"I bet you were going to put on her makeup." Larry jumps behind him, reaching beneath the waistline of his jeans and tugging upward on his underwear. "Wedgie!"

Robin is twisting out of Larry's grip when the bedroom door slams open again. His mother braces herself against the doorframe, her face pale and horrified. Robin has never seen her look so ghostly. "Get off me," he says to Larry, pushing him away and adjusting his pants.

Larry turns to Dorothy. "Robin was stealing from my mother."

Dorothy opens her mouth but does not speak. A tremor races outward from her chest, along her limbs, up to her face. Her teeth are nearly chattering.

Robin jumps to his own defense, "I wasn't stealing. I was going to put something back—"

"I caught him!"

"Damn it, Larry," Dorothy shouts, her eyes wild. "Go downstairs!"

Larry slides through the doorway past Dorothy, avoiding contact with her as if her unhinged behavior were contagious.

Robin tries again to explain. "I swear I wasn't stealing. Aunt Corinne's purse just spilled."

"No, no, no, no . . ." She is walking toward him, arms outstretched as if to brace herself for a fall.

"Mom?"

From downstairs he hears muffled commotion, someone sobbing, heavy footsteps out the door. The screech of his father's car speeding into the street. What he sees in his mother's face has nothing to do with finding him and Larry fighting. It is a reflection of something much larger, much more terrible. Some news that has just come in over the phone.

When she says it he has already figured it out: "Jackson is dead."

She falls toward him as she says the words. He steadies her, guiding her to the bed, where she curls up in spasms. Her cries are the sound of physical injury, breath screaming out against pain. He stretches his arms wide, as if sheltering a shivering child with a cloak, and presses down against her, afraid that in her shock she might die, too. He is aware of his own trembling moving from inside out, but he forces himself to ignore it, to hold tighter to her. There is nothing else to do. He has no other thoughts in his head. Her grief is the only real thing.

What happens now? He is caught in a daze of incomprehension. He cannot remember from one moment to the next where his thoughts have been. He is dissolving.

Four in the morning, wide awake, he crawls downstairs with his new camera. He skims the instruction booklet and then sits on the floor in the dining room, pointing the lens toward the unfinished room. He removes the shade from an end table lamp and shines the bulb on the plastic windows. He focuses on the pale grain of the two-by-fours overhead. He zooms in on nailheads and Sheetrock seams and dust piled in the corners. He doesn't stop to question what he is doing. When he runs out of film, he realizes he has been keeping a running commentary throughout, an explanation, to accompany the photos, for his next visit to Jackson.

He feels stupid, unprepared, witless. He rips the film from the camera, stomps his heel on the canister, runs it under water in the sink, buries it in the trash can.

Nothing is harder to grasp than this: there will be no more hospital visits. No more watching and waiting, no more tallying of days, no further deterioration. It is over. They lost.

In the morning, his mother wakes him up from a deep, disturbing sleep and announces that he and Ruby are to come shopping with her. She buys clothes for each of them. Robin gets a black three-piece suit and a pair of pleated black trousers and a black sweater. She buys Ruby two black dresses and a black skirt and sweater. Ruby complains that the sweater is itchy, but Dorothy says she must wear it anyway. Ruby begins to cry. Dorothy walks her to the car and tells her to wait there while she and Robin continue on, but Robin steps to her defense.

"I'm not leaving Ruby here," he says, seething at his mother's cruelty.

Dorothy looks exasperated, beleaguered. "Fine. Fine. But no more arguing from either of you. Not today. Just do what I say—no more questions."

She buys herself two black dresses, a pantsuit, a trench coat, new black pumps, and a black leather purse. Robin is awed by the beauty of it all. When Dorothy is satisfied, they throw everything in the trunk and proceed to a hair salon. He gets his hair shampooed by a teenage girl whose breasts dangle loosely in her shirt just in front of his face; he is surprised to feel himself getting hard under the white smock they've made him wear. His mother stands next to the stylist, delivering clipped instructions. Despite Robin's objections she orders that his hair be cut short. Wet locks flutter to the floor, lightening as they lose their moisture. He finds himself saying good-bye to his long-haired self, which is sadder than he allows himself to admit. When finished, he has a side part and short bangs smoothed to the side. In the mirror his ears look enormous. He tells the hairdresser that it's fine, though he is obviously lying, and she looks as unhappy as he is. Ruby surprises him with a whispered encouragement: "It'll grow back. Don't worry. You let it grow long like you had it. It was so pretty that way." Ruby also gets a few inches cut off, though the change is much less dramatic.

Together, they thumb through fashion magazines in the waiting area, trying to guess what Dorothy's hair will look like when her turn is through. An hour later she emerges: her hair is parted down the center and dyed ink black except for two white-blond streaks, thick as ribbons, that frame her face dramatically. The streaks are cut shorter than the rest, which has been straightened to hang below her shoulders. The first thing Robin thinks is that she looks like Morticia Addams.

"Tell me you like it," Dorothy commands, seeing their shocked faces, "and then we'll go home."

Clark is passed out on the couch. Nana is in the kitchen, refilling ice trays. An empty bottle of Seagrams rests at the bottom of the trash can.

Robin hangs up his new clothes and sits at his desk. He pulls out a pencil and his new journal and he writes at the top of the page: "A Day in the City." He writes a sentence: "Bobby McDonald and his mother decided to go into New York City, which is the most exciting city in the world according to Mrs. McDonald." He reads it over and decides it sounds phony. He erases the sentence and tries again. "Bobby McDonald was very excited to be going into the city with his mother." He sits with his elbow on the desk, his forehead resting on his hand. He doesn't like the name he has given the boy. He tries another: "John Maxwell." Then: "Max Johnson." Then: "Max Jackson." He crosses out the word "Jackson" so hard he rips the paper; then he rips the page from the book, crumpling it into a tight ball, squeezing until his knuckles turn white.

The house is very quiet and very warm. He opens the window and sits on his bed with his knees at his chest and lets the cold air in. He can see Todd's window, but it is without meaning to him; not a tinge of desire or anger or longing or excitement makes itself felt. He has not yet called Victoria and told her what happened, so he's sure that Todd does not know either. He finds this comforting. It seems a very long distance between that window and this one, the distance between the living and the dead.

People outside the family say they are proud of him: the model of composure, his mother's strength through these long weeks. He knows what they are seeing: the old him, the Robin from before the fall who did not disobey, did not surprise anyone with bad behavior, did not refuse to account for himself. They are deceived by the new black clothes and the prep school hair cut. For two nights, while Jackson's body is on view inside a dark wood coffin at Ryan's Funeral Home in Greenlawn, Robin sits quietly in his chair, his hands clasped in his lap, his eyes lowered. Guests enter the room and walk directly to his parents. He stands to shake hands with his father's business associates and the parents of kids in the neighborhood and his mother's friends from the city who have made their way to New Jersey to pay their respects. The funeral parlor is crowded, and the crowd is thick with sadness at the death of someone so young. Still, there is much conversation and even occasional laughter, especially in the back of the room and the hallway, where guests are coming and going. This is the most surprising thing of all—more surprising even than the sight of his brother's dead body inside the casket: that people are able to talk to each other with ease, that there are things to be said that have nothing at all to do with Jackson.

The Spicers arrive early the second evening. Todd wears a wool suit jacket, a button-down shirt, and blue jeans; he shifts his shoulders against the jacket's confinement and keeps one hand in his pocket at all times. Robin's stomach twists into knots, but he holds his breath and tries not to show how surprised he is. Victoria crosses the room and hugs Robin and cries onto his shoulder. She talks through a runny nose and a stream of tears, saying over and over that she can't believe it. Holding her like this, stroking her hair and whispering comforting words to her, he understands that even as he has been accusing himself of not thinking enough about Jackson over these past months, Jackson's imminent death has never *not* been lodged in his mind. For Victoria, the funeral is something yet to be grasped; the very idea of Jackson's death is new. He looks around the room at the crowd and thinks that he may be more prepared for this than any of them. He was there when it started.

Todd stays away from him until just before his parents are ready to leave, and then he sits in the empty seat to Robin's side. "I'm really sorry about your brother. It really fucking sucks."

Robin thanks him without meeting his eyes.

"I guess it's pretty hard for you," Todd says.

Robin looks at Todd's face for some hint that Todd has ever cared for him at all. This face withholds so much: it does not want to be read. Robin thinks that what he always understood as Todd's sexy strength was perhaps nothing more than a mask for secrets.

"Yes, it's hard," Robin says to him. "But I'm strong."

Todd nods. He bites his lower lip. He looks up toward the casket. "So about what happened, that time, at The Bird—"

"Forget it," Robin says resolutely. "*I* have."

After a minute of awkward silence, Todd walks away, and Robin places his hand on the empty seat. A trace of warmth meets his palm. He gets one more look at Todd, from behind. Robin can hardly match up this Todd, stiff with nervousness, being led out the door by his mother and father, with Todd at The Bird, towering above him, his every motion a threat. *That* Todd had been terrifying, commanding, unshakable. In that moment, the two of them, and the anger that ran between them like an electric current, filled the whole world. Now it seems as though such an explosive moment did not happen, that it *could not* have happened. It was part of some game, some play on a stage, a dream that is crisp and sensual upon waking but a few hours later is less than nothing. This Todd, here tonight, proves it.

When people pay him compliments, when they say he is strong, he knows better than to believe them. They are really saying that he is a good boy, a model son, which is not true. When he tells Todd Spicer that he is strong, he is saying that he is dangerous, that he is capable of great selfishness and indifference and hatred. He knows that when he keeps his head down and his hands clasped while the priest concludes the wake with prayers, anyone who is watching him must think he is praying for Jackson's soul. But he is not; he is praying for his own.

He believes himself to be capable of anything, now that he has contributed to the death of his brother. He is not certain he will go unpunished, but he does not think there is any greater punishment than living through this now. Or rather, he knows that everything that follows will be a punishment, because he will always know what he really is: a killer. The proof is indisputable: Jackson died on his birthday.

At the funeral mass, he walks down the aisle with his family and sits in the front row. The tears have not yet come to him—he has lain awake for three nights, willing himself to cry, waiting for tears as a sign that he is not cold and unfeeling, that his brother's death is affecting him as it should. The more he thinks about it, the more impossible it becomes to cry, the more empty of life he feels.

Exhaustion claws at him. He falls asleep for five minutes on the way to the burial, then wakes to find spit drooling onto his shoulder. He is embarrassed; they are in a limousine and he feels as if he should be as alert and dignified as his mother. She sits across from him, staring out the window, unreadable behind her big sunglasses. She looks both stricken and chic, he thinks, like Jackie Onassis.

The cemetery is an anticlimax. He wanted to see the coffin go into the ground. He wanted to throw flowers into the hole. He imagined someone—his mother? Ruby? his *father?*—collapsing in a fit of grief. But there were simply more prayers to be said, more of God's word to be heard, and then they climbed back into the limo and left Jackson's body in a box to be buried by strangers.

The food is impressive; the caterers have outdone themselves. The dining room table is covered to the edges with silver trays of hors d'oeuvres, each with its own cup of toothpicks and dipping sauce, and platters of fresh vegetables and fancy crackers, and baskets of bread, and cheeses Robin has never before tasted. Friends have brought food; Aunt Corinne has made his favorite Jell-O cake. The guests crowd around, filling their plates, gulping down cocktails. Men gather in the unfinished room, talking about construction. Everyone says something brief and sympathetic to him and Ruby. The muscles of his face hurt from being polite.

He finally pulls himself from the living room and slips upstairs to his bedroom, relieved for the chance to be alone.

Larry is sitting on Jackson's bed. His gaze is lowered; he is biting a nail, a finger in his mouth. To his side, votive candles flicker on the dresser, where Ruby has renovated her altar to Jackson.

"What are you doing?" Robin demands.

Larry looks up, startled. "It's a free country. I can sit here."

"This is my room," Robin says, "and I don't want you up here."

Larry stares at him angrily, hands curling into fists. "It's still *Jackson's* room, too."

Robin locks his eyes onto Larry's. "No, it's just *my* room now."

Larry plants himself in front of Robin and pokes his chest. "You can't tell me what to do."

"Fine. Be that way. I'm not staying in here with you." Robin throws open the window and climbs out onto the roof.

The cold air envelopes him—and he's instantly fuming that Larry drove him from his own bedroom. He stamps his feet on the shingles and screams, "Fuck!" over and over. Larry, Todd Spicer, Uncle Stan, his father, his mother. Everyone thinks they can push him around. He turns over in his head what he should have said to Larry, how he should have knocked Larry against the wall and then picked him up and tossed him out the door. "FUCK!" The word is like fuel. He paces to where the shingles end and the exposed wood of the new roof begins. He stomps and kicks, trembling the wood beneath his weight. The more he thinks about it, the angrier he gets, blood pumping into his neck, burning his ears, cresting like a wave in his skull.

The back door slams below; his father stands in the backyard, looking up for the source of the disturbance. Before Robin even registers this, Larry is climbing through the window to the roof. "What are you throwing such a conniption for?" he says in the tough-guy voice that Robin has come to hate so much.

"Don't talk to me like that!"

"Yeah? Make me."

Robin grits his teeth. That day on the slide, tormenting Ruby, Larry had spoken in that same voice, as if Robin was so easily bullied. It was that voice that had such an influence on Jackson, that made his own brother think of him as a fag, the way everyone else did. And, as much as anything else, it was that voice—telling him to shut up—that made Robin climb up the slide to confront them both.

Everything Larry has ever said to him, every moment Robin has ever spent in his mocking company, now rises up in front of Robin, a wall of bricks trapping him in some unwanted, submissive space, a space he no longer can bear. Without thinking, he runs across the shingles, mouth open, unleashing guttural fury he cannot control. He batters his head and shoulder into Larry's chest, knocking him down, pinning him. Larry's freckled cheeks flush and he gulps for air. He tries to speak, but

Robin wraps his hands around Larry's throat and squeezes. He lifts Larry's head with his hands and smashes it back down.

"I hate you!" Robin screams. "I hate you! I hate your fucking guts!"

He hears his name shouted from the yard, a faint, distant bell which he ignores. All there is for him is Larry's skin, bright red under his grip, Larry's lips turning blue. Larry lands punches on Robin's back, his body struggling for life, but Robin does not loosen his grip. He feels Larry thrash against him, feels Larry's hipbones in his crotch, feels his own dick getting hard from the friction of the struggle. Larry is trying to make him stop but Robin will not, *cannot*; every ounce of Larry's resistance increases his rage. He lunges forward, dragging Larry underneath him like trapped roadkill. He tightens his knuckles, the softness of Larry's flesh collapsing under his fingertips. "I hate you!" He squeezes and drags, he bangs into Larry with his crotch. He sees the edge of the roof, and the dead grass below, and the piled plywood and the cracked concrete. He wants to get to the edge—that is all he wants: to pull Larry to the edge. A voice from below orders him to stop. At the periphery of his vision people are gathering and calling to him. The sound of fear.

He will not stop.

Violence surges through his bones, his muscles, the raw hot yell raging from his throat. The machinery of his body gone mad. He wants to rise, to rise up from his body, for the violence to set him free. He wants to be in the air, with this boy, this normal boy whom he must destroy, in his grip. His claws want the puncture of skin, a bath of hot blood. His wings want to take him out over the yard; he wants to drop his hated prey to a bone-cracking death. And then he looks into Larry's eyes and sees fear, sees that Larry is terribly, deathly afraid of him; he knows that Larry's blood and breath are exploding, that Larry feels the empty, airy chill behind his head like the slope of a cliff and the domineering slams against his body like the beating it is. Robin's vision clears for a moment: he is on the roof, strangling Larry, thrusting into him, screaming words that his own ears cannot really hear, and he understands that he is *not* a bird of prey; he understands, too, that still he is lethal, in his own body, with his own hands. He looks into Larry's eyes and knows that Larry believes this, too. Larry's eyes scream for mercy.

Strong hands grab him around the middle, wrench him away from Larry. Someone is tossing him aside. His mother. Robin struggles from her grip, and his father, suddenly there, too, knocks him onto his ass, yelling "Jesus Christ, what are you doing? What are you doing?"

Robin hears his own voice at last, screaming, "He did it! He killed

Jackson! When Jackson was on the ground he turned him over and cracked his neck. It was his fault. He did it. It's not my fault! It's not my fault!"

His mother's hand slaps hard and flat against his face, silencing him. Robin gasps as if he's been sucked into a vacuum. He looks to his mother for help but sees only fear and confusion. She is afraid of him, too.

Larry is curled into Uncle Stan's chest, sobbing helplessly; Stan runs his hand across Larry's head as if he were ironing away the trauma. The crowd in the backyard stares up in rapt fascination. Robin finds Ruby: in the wide wonderment of her eyes, he senses her approval. She removes her hands from her mouth; her lips form a single phrase: "I love you."

A burning inside his chest, shooting upward into his skull like a flaming arrow. He shuts his eyes, his face contorts, he bites his lower lip until he pierces his own flesh. Tears run from his eyes like blood from a wound; he cannot stop the flow, nor can he see or feel beyond it. For hours, after the guests leave and the party is cleared from the house, he lies in his bed weeping. His mother sits with him, clenching his hand as if holding him back from the pull of an undertow.

He is home sick for days, half conscious from a sudden flu. He drinks soup and tea and eats only buttered white toast. He feels the pains inside his body—first from eating after so long with no food, and then from hunger after waiting too long again—in a cycle that never brings relief. A headache pounds and does not abate; his throat is raw; his ears hum with a faraway whistle. The house is quiet as a hospital room. He hears no arguing, no talking back, no reprimands. He fantasizes that he'll die here on this couch in the living room with his mother and his sister tending him, the surrounding silence expanding until it simply swallows him up.

In his dreams now he is always killing, and he is always in danger as well. He is the one stalking in darkness with a gleaming silver blade in his hand, and he is the screaming victim falling in fear. He has woken up shaking with fright every day for a week. When he looks at his face in the bathroom mirror, his eyes are dark and secretive: he sees himself going mad.

He stumbles from the couch, the fire in his throat impelling him toward a glass of water. As his eyes search the darkness beyond the TV's fluttering, he picks up his mother's voice. She is in the kitchen, on the phone. He hears her speak his name; he stops to listen. Her voice is tense, insistent: "Robin was beside himself—can't you see that? . . . No, I don't think . . . Yes, it was very upsetting . . . Mother, of course I understand that . . . I told you—I don't want to know what Larry said . . . He's very sick right now, very weak. I am not going to make him apologize . . . No, no, I do not want . . . I'll talk to Corinne myself . . . No, not Stan— I don't care what Clark says . . . Mother, *I am not going to argue with you.*"

It returns as a wave, crashing from the back of Robin's brain. A violent collision in close-up: the grit of the roof, Larry's pink skin, his own white knuckles tightening, his bones pressing down. At the center of it all, the guiding force, is a powerful, focused fury: the belief that he was balancing the scales. Only now, listening to his mother and envisioning Nana on the other end of the call, does he grasp something very basic about what happened on the roof: everyone saw it. What felt like a personal mission, private and fated, a long time coming, was actually a public event, an older boy attacking a younger boy, a seemingly random assault. It didn't look like justice—it looked like cruelty. He thinks about how quiet the house has been since the funeral. Are people staying away from them? Are they whispering about the tragic, messed-up MacKenzie family: one son dead, the other a violent mental case?

His throat is still stinging, begging for water; just swallowing spit feels abrasive, a Brillo pad on his vocal chords. The pain has been constant since that afternoon, when his accusations about Larry burst forth. He wonders, *Did anyone believe me?*

He moves to the kitchen door, and Dorothy quickly gets off the phone. She clenches her jaw, her face contorted defensively.

"Who was that?" he asks.

"That was your grandmother. We had some words." Her eyes meet his, wondering, he is sure, how much he overheard. He gives no indication.

"Is everything OK?" he asks.

"I told her it was best that we have a quiet Christmas this year."

Christmas—it must be only days away. He'd completely forgotten. Every year they ate Christmas dinner at Aunt Corinne's. This year, it seems, would be different.

He moves to the sink, fills a glass from the tap. For years he's imagined beating up Larry, has contemplated the sweet victory of it. But now he sees Larry at home, traumatized in the arms of Aunt Corinne, perhaps tormented by nightmares of his own, and he takes no comfort in it. He considers making an offering, explaining his actions—though some part of him immediately rebels against the notion, not wanting to give up the ground he has fought for. He guzzles the water, wipes his mouth on his pajama sleeve. "It really hurts to talk right now."

Her eyes study him closely and gradually her gaze softens. "There's no need for you to talk," she says very gently. "You just concentrate on getting better."

He offers her a smile, thankful for the protection she is extending, and returns to the comfort of the couch. He curls up beneath his blanket, closing himself off from the world around him.

The skeleton of a Christmas celebration: a minimally decorated tree, hauled into the house by Clark on Christmas Eve; Barbra Streisand on the turntable; a handful of presents for Robin and Ruby. One box contains a zippered sweatjacket, meant to replace the tattered one he got from Scott; he musters up enough enthusiasm to thank his parents, but lays it aside without trying it on. Dorothy cooks a simple dinner, which they eat in almost torturous silence.

Robin's favorite gift is a copy of Salinger's *Franny and Zooey*. He spends the afternoon reading it, enraptured with the young hero, Zooey Glass, wanting to *be* Zooey Glass: a handsome, intelligent actor living in a roomy New York apartment, solving the problems of his colorful family with the help of an older, wiser brother. Dorothy sits next to him on the couch, sipping brandy for hours, listening to a Mahler symphony on the stereo, her eyes unfocused, her thoughts unknowable.

A car enters their driveway, its headlights filling the living room windows. Ruby peers through the glass, then turns around in surprise. "It's Uncle Stan," she says.

Clark jumps up from his armchair, where he has been reading the newspaper. Robin looks to his mother, who is staring wide-eyed at her husband. "I asked him to drop by," Clark explains.

"Oh, Clark, you didn't."

"We've got to get this settled, Dottie," he says, hands extended wide as if measuring something enormous. "He's your brother, and he's going to be around. I still need him to help finish the room. We're leaking heat every day."

"Absolutely not," Dorothy says, rising to her feet and passing Clark on the way to the door. "Not now."

"Aw, Dottie, for the love of Christ—"

She heads outside in her stockings, her steps unsteady but determined. Clark follows her, instructing Robin and Ruby to stay put and slamming the door behind him.

Robin rushes to Ruby's side at the window. "He looks drunk," Ruby says.

So does she, Robin thinks, but remains silent as an argument erupts. Within moments, all three adults are shouting. Robin hears his name mentioned, and Larry's and Jackson's, in the midst of sentences that he can't make out, though each moment bristles with anger. "They're talking about the funeral," he says to Ruby.

She nods back at him knowingly, whispering, "I was wondering if this was going to happen." Her voice sounds wiser than he thought possible.

Clark is jockeying for position between Dorothy and Stan, attempting to arbitrate, but it soon becomes clear that they are talking past him, firing their accusations at each other, and gradually he backs out of sight. Robin is caught between wanting Dorothy to win this fight, to see Stan slump away, humiliated, and an equally powerful urge to rush to her side and say something, anything, that might bring this to a close. Perhaps Ruby senses his turmoil—she grabs his hand and holds tight, keeping him at her side, behind the safety of the window.

"Get away from there," Clark commands, suddenly behind them. Robin turns around, sees his father's agonized frustration, his hands balled into fists. "It's none of your business."

"It's about me, right? About me and Larry?"

Clark squeezes his eyes shut, as if unable to answer. "It's about a lot of things. A lifetime."

His father looks so unhappy, embarrassed, shaken up. It's painful to see. "I'll go out there," Robin insists. "I'll say something, whatever you want."

"You can't make it right. It's bigger than you. And on top of it, they're *inebriated.*"

Ruby speaks up, urgency and authority in her delicate voice. "Robin was telling the truth, Dad. About Larry and Jackson, on the playground. That's how it happened."

Robin sucks in his breath. Ruby's eyes are alive with righteousness. Clark looks from one to the other, opens his mouth to speak, then clamps his lips together. His eyes water. Finally, in a hush, he says, "It doesn't change anything. It can't bring back my son."

He leaves them alone. Robin looks at Ruby, marveling at her performance. He mouths the words, *Thank you.*

"I owed you a favor. Remember?"

Outside a car door slams. Rubber on cement, the squeal of acceleration. Stan is gone. Their mother stands on the front lawn teetering on trembling legs, her head in her hands.

"Come on," Robin says to Ruby, "Let's bring her back in."

In the week that follows, the temperature drops and Clark makes a decision: he brings in a team of builders, three men who make fast work of finishing off the construction of Jackson's room. Robin still thinks of it that way—*Jackson's room*—because it has yet to be given another purpose, though no one ever refers to it as anything but "the room." Just a couple of weeks ago, it seemed as though his father and Stan would be bumbling through the project forever. Stan is not part of this now; he hasn't returned since Christmas night. Even Clark's involvement is minimal. He's gone back to work, getting up early, eating breakfast to the newsradio and catching the commuter train. Dorothy has returned to work as well, picking up day shifts at the library. In their absence, the house trembles with alien activity, as if it has been handed over to strangers. When his parents return at night, they have very little to say to each other.

Robin often spends the night in the living room, avoiding the eerie emptiness of his bedroom. All of Jackson's belongings remain, inescapable reminders of everything that has transpired, everything that has fallen apart, his own unresolved guilt. Even the votive candles on the dresser are coated in dust; Ruby no longer tends the altar she had assembled. Some days, when he enters the room to pick out his clothes, he sits on Jackson's bed and tries to talk to him, the way he did at the hospital. He begins a story, an update on their family, but he finds it hard to continue. His mind drifts somewhere else—to the dread of returning to school in the New Year, or to Scott, who has yet to surface. Catching himself off track, Robin simply runs his fingers along Jackson's superhero sheets, whispers an apology, asks him to come back.

Asleep on the couch. He wakes before he opens his eyes, stirred by hushed, strained voices on the verge of argument. His mother sits on the arm, her back to him.

"Why aren't you coming to bed?" his father is asking.

"I'm just paying Robin some mind."

Robin keeps his eyes closed, pretending.

"He's asleep. Tuck him in and come to bed."

"I'm not tired, Clark."

"Are you going to stay up all night?"

Robin hears her shift uncomfortably, letting out a chilly sigh.

"Dottie, I'm asking you to . . . join me."

"Not tonight."

"Why do you do that? You make me feel bad that I want to be close to you."

"Keep your voice down. He's sleeping." Her hand falls to Robin's hair. He sucks in his breath, remains still.

"Then let him sleep. I want to be with you tonight."

She does not respond.

Almost pleading: "It's been so long, Dottie. I want to be inside of you."

"Well, I'm sorry, but my own needs right now are not so . . . *acute.*"

His voice swells. "You make me feel like shit—you know that?"

"And you make me feel like a receptacle. So we're even."

Clark's footsteps travel away, his wounded words trailing behind: "You don't have to act like you have it so bad. I'm still a decent-looking guy. I'm still your husband."

Stroking Robin's head, still believing him to be asleep, she murmurs, "Yes, Clark, you're my husband. For a while, you're still my husband."

He feels himself tighten inside, steeling himself up against all that is yet to come.

Chapter Thirteen

He returns to school on a January day of startling clarity. The sun is large and low in a pale blue sky; broad, blinding swathes of light reflect off banks of white, white snow. He has refused a ride from his mother and now plods through ice and slush, sweating under the weight of his winter clothes. He is no longer ill but is aware of the limits of his physical strength; even breathing takes effort. Time stretches as he anticipates his return, as he tries to imagine what he will say to anyone who asks where he's been. Or does everyone already know what has happened, and will they greet him with awkward silence? He has spoken very few words to Victoria since the funeral, and none to anyone else beyond his family. Mr. Cortez called once to check in, but Robin wouldn't speak with him, full of resentment because Cortez had denied his mother's request about Scott.

Today he'll visit Mr. Cortez to arrange a schedule of meetings with Dr. Gottlieb, the school district's psychiatrist. Robin had refused to partake in these sessions when his parents first raised the idea; he consented only after they told him he would visit Dr. Gottlieb instead of going to phys. ed. He might as well be going to confession at St. Bart's: he's afraid what he will reveal, what will be found out about him, what the consequences will be. He has never seen Dr. Gottlieb, but he imagines him to look like the actor who played the police chief in *Rebel Without A Cause,* who wants to be helpful but in the end just isn't there when he's needed.

His goal: to be solitary, unobtrusive, invisible. He wants to avoid the minefield of explanation, isn't sure he could even come up with adequate small talk about Jackson's death. His head aches with disturbing knowledge about himself and the way the world works. His mother used to tell him he was one of a kind among his peers, more sophisticated and worldly because she had shown him the city and promised him the secret wisdom that it held. But only now does he truly think of himself as different from the others: most people go along as if life is basically good even though bad things happen every now and then. But Robin believes he has figured out the truth, a truth larger than anything his mother ever taught him—that life is mostly bad because people are capable of terrible things. Most people think that life offers you endless opportunities to get what you want, but Robin thinks there are endless possibilities for it all to be taken away.

His English teacher welcomes him back in front of the entire class, but he does not look up for fear his eyes will telegraph some terrible truth about himself. In social studies his long absence is not acknowledged at all, which is worse because he spends the entire class anxiously expecting the spotlight to be turned on him again, avoiding the stares of curious classmates. During third period he struggles in vain to get up to speed on his German lessons, the day's dialogue far surpassing his knowledge. After three hours he's actually looking forward to seeing Mr. Cortez.

On his way into the guidance office, he catches sight of Todd Spicer striding down the hall with Ethan and Tully, laughing and faking a punch into Ethan's chest. The image is timeless; he could have seen Todd like this on any day since he's been in high school. Nothing that has happened in the last few months has had the power to alter this basic fact about Todd: every day, between classes, he can be spotted with his pals in the hallway, laughing and faking punches. The familiarity of the moment is remarkable to Robin. How can it be that everything has changed inside of him when all around everything seems to be the same as ever?

Todd's eyes rest on him for a moment, then willfully, casually look away without recognition. Robin remembers Todd delivering that same studied avoidance once before: to Scott, in the cafeteria, passing him by as if he wasn't there. He thinks, *So this is what it feels like.*

"Good morning, Robin."

"Nothing good about it so far."

Mr. Cortez expresses his sympathy about Jackson, surprising Robin by pulling him into a sturdy embrace. "Having trouble coping with it all?" Mr. Cortez asks.

"If I wasn't, we wouldn't be sending me to a head shrinker, would we?" Robin hears the sarcasm in his own voice, traces it back to the anger he is harboring toward Cortez.

Mr. Cortez says, "You're not crazy, Robin. That's not what this is about. You've been put under a great deal of stress, and we need to get to the bottom of it."

Mr. Cortez speaks all the right words, but it feels like a trap is being laid. "Yeah, well just don't expect me to spill my guts to some stranger," Robin says.

There's a new photograph framed on Mr. Cortez's desk. It's the same woman from the other picture, only now she looks less like a hippie and more like someone who gets up and goes to work. In this picture she's older, and her hair is shorter and permed, and she's wearing a pantsuit and high heels. Mr. Cortez has his arm around her waist, a big grin on his face, as if just being at her side is enough to make him proud.

Cortez sees Robin looking at the photo and smiles. "You want to know a secret? She's pregnant."

"Your wife?" Cortez nods. Robin studies her thin figure. "She's not pregnant in this picture, is she?"

"Yeah, Jenny had just gotten the test back, and she said, 'You better take a picture before I get big because my body will never be the same again.' You know, *women.*"

Robin puts the picture back on the desk. He is thinking of his mother, of what that must have been like. *Getting the test back:* passing meant failing. "Was it an accident?"

Cortez picks up the frame, studies it as if the answer to Robin's question lies coded in the image. "You want to know the truth? We weren't going to have kids. We decided we didn't want to bring another kid into the world, what with overpopulation and nuclear meltdowns and all the rest of it. Like racism. I mean, this kid's gonna be half Puerto Rican and half Irish. Maybe he'll have a tough time of it."

"So then why are you doing it?"

"You can't always think philosophically about these things. Sometimes you just go with your gut instinct instead of what you think you *should* do."

Cortez smiles—Robin sees contentment there, expectation, joy. He can't discern any hidden agenda. Without warning, his own eyes water up. He lowers his head and sucks in his breath to keep tears from spilling, but Cortez notices and pats his shoulder empathetically.

Robin slinks back from the touch, remembering his stored-up anger. He wipes his eyes and blurts, "Do you have a number where I can find

Scott Schatz?" Cortez's expression momentarily hardens, which Robin takes as the prelude to a refusal. "Forget it," he says, rising to his feet. "I shouldn't have asked. My mother said you wouldn't tell her."

Mr. Cortez holds out his hands as if deflecting an onrush. "Whoa, wait a minute. I'm not the heavy here, Robin. I told your mom where Scott is now, and I said I'd leave it up to her to decide whether or not to tell you."

"Really?" Robin lowers himself back to his seat, bewildered. Who's lying—Mr. Cortez or his mother?

"Look, Robin. Scott's fine. He's living with his brother's wife for a while. Waiting for his mother's release."

"His brother's *wife?*"

"Do you know about his brother?"

"Duh, he's *dead.*" The thought sprints through him that he and Scott now have this in common. It's so obvious—he can't believe he hadn't yet made the connection. All along, Scott has been living with this reality: to be the one left behind after a brother dies. *That's why he always listened when I talked about Jackson—he knew what was coming.*

Cortez is explaining. "Daniel Schatz married a girl named Gail a few months before he died. And she lives—" He stops himself. "Well, she lives nearby."

"Where?"

"In Bergen County—that's all I'll say."

"You really told my mother? She said you wouldn't tell her." Robin still isn't sure what to believe.

"I guess she has her reasons for keeping it to herself." Cortez rubs his fingers against his brow. "Robin, you know, every year I tend to get in a little over my head with one student—I guess you're the lucky candidate this time. But I can only go so far. Your parents have final say."

Leaving the office, clutching a schedule of appointments with Dr. Gottlieb, Robin turns one more time to look at Mr. Cortez, with the vague notion that he's left something important behind. Cortez's back is to him as he stands leafing through a file cabinet. Robin takes in the curve of his shoulders, the shifting of his torso as he raises his arm, the vertical stripes of a button-down shirt disappearing behind his belt. Mr. Cortez looks like he has been poured into a compact body mold—not fat or skinny, not bulky or pudgy or bony. He looks solid. Robin takes this in with a yearning that is less about desire than about a need for an answer: what does a man—a man he might even trust—look like? *Maybe that's all I need. Just be more like Mr. Cortez. Less like my*

THE WORLD OF NORMAL BOYS / 271

*mother and more like Mr. Cortez: Go with your gut instinct, not what
you think you should do.*

Finding Scott now seems more urgent than ever.

When you call Information, you are first asked the town of the listing
you are looking for, which is of course the one thing Robin doesn't
know. He checks out a reference book on New Jersey from the school library that lists every town in Bergen County, and he pulls a chair up to
the payphone outside the cafeteria.

"What city please?"

"Allendale."

"Yes?"

"Gail Schatz?" He spells it for her.

"I'm sorry. I have no listing under that name."

"How about Daniel Schatz?"

When he figures out that the call is free—that he doesn't have to
worry about running out of dimes—he grows elated. There are seventy
towns in Bergen County. It can't take that long.

It takes until Palisades Park.

"Is Scott home?"

"Yeah, hold on." She shouts the name. Robin holds his breath, astonished that this moment is finally here. Through the phone, the
woman shushes a baby's cries. She says into his ear, "Sorry, hon, I gotta
drop you," and lets the receiver clunk against a wall. He waits nervously, trying to plan what to say. *Hi, Scott. It's Robin. Remember me?*

Suddenly back on the line, she says breathlessly, "I *thought* he was
here. Want to leave a message?"

He hangs up without another word, unwilling to leave his name,
afraid that this woman—Gail—would not pass the message on to Scott.
She might have the same attitude as Dorothy: she might be determined
to keep Scott and him separated.

Maybe it was a fluke. Maybe it wasn't the right number. Maybe it
was another Scott. He calls again.

"May I speak with Scott Schatz?"

"He's not home right now. Who's this?"

He hangs up, reeling at the sudden turn of events.

After the third call she recognizes his voice. "Oh, it's you again," she
says. "The kid with no name." She almost sounds amused.

Every time he tries to reach Scott over the next few days, Gail answers the phone. He never speaks, just hangs up at the sound of her voice.

The only thing to do is to go there. For days he makes the plan. He gets the street address from the operator, buys a county map at the Getty gas station in town, checks and rechecks the bus schedule.

He gets Ruby to cover for him. "I'm going to walk you to church Saturday morning, but I'm not going inside. When you get home, just tell Mom I needed to be by myself for a while."

She hesitates at first, not wanting to be part of a lie, but then he gives in and tells her that he's found Scott. "You told me to believe," he reminds her, and she agrees to his plan.

He has always wondered about the passengers who get on the bus at one stop in New Jersey and get off at another. For Robin, there has only ever been one destination: New York City. Why weren't these people going all the way? His mother once pointed out to him that not everyone had a car, that some people relied on the Red and Tan Lines to get around. But he never liked the idea of it; it seemed sad to him, as if these people were doomed to never get out of New Jersey. Now he finds himself disembarking at an intersection in Palisades Park that he has passed through dozens of times before.

10 A.M. A Saturday in January, 1979. From the street the town does not look half as sad or strange as it does through the tinted windows of the bus. It's just another town, with cars parking in front of stores and a bank at the corner displaying an American flag and an enormous digital clock. Robin knows Scott doesn't get up early on Saturday mornings, and he has planned to be here at a time when he thinks he will find him in. He calls from a payphone at the corner. "Is Scott there?"

"Oh, my God," Gail shrieks. "You actually called when he's *home.* Scott!"

The phone changes hands. "Hello?" Scott's voice in his ear, clear as can be.

Robin suddenly understands why people say "your heart skips a beat," because that's what his does at that moment. He has to force the words from his throat. "Hi, Scott. It's Robin. Robin MacKenzie?"

"I knew it was you," Scott says. "Why didn't you tell her your name?"

"I don't know." Robin can't tell if Scott is happy to hear from him or not.

"Man, you were driving Gail mental. She was like, 'You little druggie, what kind of enemies you got out there?'" Scott laughs, and just as Robin is wondering if Gail is still within earshot, Scott calls, "Right, Gail? Isn't that what you said?"

Robin hears Gail ask, "So who is it?"

"It's Robin," Scott says. "Remember? I told you about him. Who I went to the city with? Whose *parents . . .*"

"Oh, yeah. That one."

"What did you say about me?" Robin asks, unsure if he should be pleased that Scott's been talking about him or full of dread at what has been said.

"I just told her about going to the city, and how your parents busted me—"

"Busted *us,*" Robin interrupts. "You have no idea what kind of things have been happening to me."

"Whatever," Scott says, his voice cooling off. A car horn blares in the street behind Robin. "Where are you, anyway?"

Robin forces a light laugh. "Oh, you know, in your town."

"You're in Pal Park? Right now at this fucking moment?"

"I got your address, so I figured—"

"Well, I can't just leave the house."

Robin is startled at Scott's curtness. "Why not? Are you grounded?"

"I mean, I just woke up and I can't just leave because *you* suddenly show up."

Scott's words sting. Robin pushes down the hurt and lets himself make a demand. "Give me one good reason why you can't see me right now."

Scott says, "OK," but offers nothing. Robin feels him backing down and feels his own determination increasing. He's not going to let Scott, of all people, try to brush him off. Scott is all he's got left, and he wants to make that clear.

"I'm not trying to be a pain, Scott. I just thought you would want to see me. I mean, I want to see you. So what's your problem?"

Scott's voice is an angry hush. "I don't have a fucking *problem.*"

The playground is the new kind: the equipment built from old truck tires strung on chains between wooden beams. The tire holes are all filled with snow, white on black, like enormous Oreos. Robin looks at the slide. It isn't very tall, and its chute corkscrews in wide arcs to a deep snowbank that probably covers a sandbox. To get to the top, you climb

big wooden blocks, not a steep steel ladder. Robin intones a deep, om-
nipotent voice, like Orson Welles on the wine commercials: "No children will be killed on *this* playground."

Robin is wearing the zippered sweatjacket—the original, not his
Christmas gift—under his own quilted down vest. It's not really heavy
enough for the weather, but he's hardly let a day go by where he hasn't
worn it, or curled up with it under his blanket, or sniffed the arm pits
for a lingering trace of Scott's body. He doesn't even think of it as
"Scott's jacket" anymore; it's "the jacket Scott gave me." But when
Scott comes through the chain link fence of the playground where he's
told Robin to meet him, he does not seem to notice the jacket, which,
Robin thinks, is a bad omen.

Scott is wearing sunglasses and an old army trenchcoat several sizes
too big for him. The hem of it sweeps against the snow. Robin can see
black lace-up boots kicking out from under Scott's jeans as Scott takes
long strides across the icy playground.

"Nice buzz," Scott says as he gets closer, puffing breath into the air.

Robin pulls off his cap and turns his head. "It's dorky, isn't it?"

"You should get rid of that side part and clip it really short," Scott
says. He pulls out a pack of cigarettes, pops two up. Robin takes one.
"Mine is all coming off soon. As soon as I can convince Gail. It's gonna
be cool, really punk."

Robin lights his cigarette, hands trembling. He and Scott exhale at
the same time, the twin jets of smoke crashing in the air between them.
He says, "I can't believe I'm really talking to you! I've been trying to
find you for so long!"

"I've been here. I'm living with Gail. She's kind of my sister." His
voice sounds deliberately obscure.

"She's your sister-in-law," Robin says eagerly. "I finally got the scoop
from Cortez. I had to get the phone number from Information. I called
the operator like fifty times!" Robin tries to decipher Scott's silence,
wishing he could see Scott's eyes behind his sunglasses. "I was worried,
you know, because of that night after we were in New York."

"Nothing to worry about now."

"So everything's OK with your father?"

"He's there, I'm here. That's good."

"I'm so sorry about my parents calling him." Scott does not respond.
Robin is growing alarmed by Scott's silence; surely it can not be a good
sign. "I was so pissed at them—you have no idea."

"It doesn't matter, because here I am now." A cold gust of wind rustles some bare branches above them. "Gail's cool, and she's got this kid I never knew about—Jake—so I'm kind of an uncle. 'Uncle Scotty.' Man, what do you think about that?" A hint of satisfaction colors his voice.

"Your brother had a kid, and you never knew it?" Robin is still having trouble understanding how Scott wound up living here.

"No," Scott says, impatiently. "It's a newer baby than that. From another guy."

"She got married again?"

"No, she just *had a baby*." Robin imagines Scott's eyes rolling disdainfully behind his dark glasses, annoyed at how slow on the uptake he is. Scott hops around on his feet suddenly. "Fucking cold out here." He lands in the path of the sun so that Robin can only see him in silhouette as he speaks. "Only thing is, she won't let me sell weed anymore, but I guess that's cool. She says, if I sell, I'm back to the old man. So that settled that. It's decent though, 'cause I'm gonna get my shit together."

"What do you mean?" Robin says, shielding his eyes.

"I don't ditch school anymore. Try to do some homework. I'm gonna get a job. There's a record store near here I put an application in for. I told them I was eighteen. I'm gonna turn over a new leaf, etcetera, etcetera, etcetera. Good riddance to Greenlawn—that's about all I can say."

"That's really good," Robin says. The air is cold and brittle, and he feels it against his body like a punishment. The conversation stalls until he gets up the courage to ask, "Do you want to hang out anymore? I could take the bus. That's what I did today."

"You don't need to do that. I mean, if it's too much trouble, just forget it."

"It's no trouble. I had to sneak away but Ruby's gonna tell them—"

Scott interrupts. "I've got this new life now, you know? I don't think I can just . . ." He looks away. "Don't make a big deal out of it."

Robin feels the approaching dead end of this conversation and wants to switch tracks. He doesn't want Scott to turn this against him; next thing he'll either accuse him of acting like a girl or will fall into silence and not budge. He clears his throat in desperation and announces, "My brother died."

Scott's cool crumbles. He removes his sunglasses and takes a step closer. "Oh, shit. That sucks."

Robin feels a tingle of shame, using Jackson's death to lure Scott back in, but it's worth it just to get a look at Scott's eyes, which are much more vulnerable than his tough stance had let on. "I just don't know what to do," he says. "About Jackson."

"Do? What 'do?' He's dead, man. I mean, not to be an asshole about it, but there's nothing to *do*." Scott flicks his cigarette to his feet and stomps it out under one of his heavy boots. "Just don't let anyone lay any trips on you."

"I hate getting out of bed in the morning. Half the time I just can't even get my brain to work right."

The sun has swum behind a cloud, casting everything around them into a shadowless gray. "My advice is, just keep your mouth shut. When Danny died, I didn't talk to anyone for a month. Everyone was full of shit." He faces Robin. "I still talk to him, try to get him to come back. 'Yo, Dan-my-man. Just come on back. We'll forget about the whole thing.' I been saying that one for years."

"But you didn't *make* Danny die."

"You didn't make Jackson die, either. You told me it was an accident."

"But I *wanted* it to happen," he says, revealing for the first time to anyone the burden of his ill wishes. He remembers, as if it was just yesterday, praying to God: *Make something bad happen to Jackson.* And it happened: his petition was granted. He doesn't know whether to whisper in shame or shout loud enough for its severity to be understood. He says it again, his voice cracking: "I *wanted* it."

"Look. It wasn't, you know, premeditated. There's a big difference between wanting something to happen and making it happen. So what? You told him once 'I hate you' or 'I wish you were dead.' Even if you told him that ten times the week of the accident, so what? My brother used to tell me I was the biggest pain in his ass on the face of the earth, and you think that means anything? He was my brother. Jackson was your brother. That's what means something."

Scott turns and walks away from him, toward the exit of the playground. "Come on, man. It's too cold out here."

Robin stands, momentarily stunned by Scott's words. Is it that simple? He asked for it, but he didn't really *want* it. He didn't cause it. It's never been completely clear what happened that day on the slide, but now, in the light of Scott's certainty, he comes to an understanding. Whatever happened just before Jackson tumbled to the pavement didn't start with his wish for Jackson's death. He says the words to himself, listens to them, lets them sink in: *I didn't want him to die.*

Up ahead, Scott waves him on. It takes Robin a moment to catch up.

* * *

Scott's bedroom was once the dining room of the little house that Gail rents. Picture windows, covered with dark, tacked-up curtains, line one wall. On the other side of the room, sliding doors block off the kitchen. A couple of bedsheets hang between the living room and Scott's sleeping area, bunching up sloppily on the tramped-down olive green carpet. Gail and the baby are out, but the evidence of their life here can't be missed. Toys and books and piles of clothes clutter the floor and the furniture, even in Scott's room. The only thing familiar is Scott's aquarium, dotted with purple fish.

They are sitting on Scott's bed, passing a roach back and forth. Scott is rolling a fresh joint on a Cars album. The record on the turntable spins out an anxious male voice: *I don't mind you coming here, and wasting all my time.*

"I thought we couldn't smoke," Robin says.

"She doesn't care if I smoke it, as long as I don't sell it." Scott pinches the roach between his fingers. "You know, Spicer used to tell me, 'You shouldn't *do* more than you *deal*,' but Gail actually has the opposite philosophy. A little smoking never hurt anyone, but dealing makes you paranoid." He takes another puff. "The biggest bummer is that I have to buy it from these kids at my new school, and their pot *sucks*. I'm like the biggest hardass customer, too, because I know quality."

"I guess I might buy some of my own," Robin says, thinking of this for the first time. "Not that I know how."

"You know how. We did it in New York."

"In New York, *they* ask *you*." He remembers their stoned afternoon in the Village, watching the homosexuals parade around in the falling sun. He remembers revealing to Scott that he wanted to do more sex stuff together. He remembers Scott's resistance. Has this changed, too, along with all the other changes in Scott's life?

"Go to Socks," Scott says. "Barry Sokowitz. That's who I used to buy my dope from."

Robin has seen this guy: a hairy, acne-scarred ox in a Judas Priest T-shirt hanging out in the courtyard. Trying to set up a drug purchase with him seems preposterous. Robin recites a line from a lesson in health class: "Marijuana kills brain cells."

"And lowers your sperm count." Scott rolls next to him and inserts the joint backward between his lips. The ember disappears inside his mouth. He thrusts the outward-pointing tip into Robin's face. Through clenched lips he instructs, "Shotgun."

"I could burn you," Robin says, but Scott's eyes urge him on. He moves close enough to Scott to feel breath puffing from his nose, and sucks in on the roach. A delicate shock of static electricity flicks between their lips. The pungent resin cuts at his throat.

A rush to his skull, like heat from an open oven.

Scott widens his lips to show Robin a wisp of smoke inside his own mouth. He gulps it down his throat. "It worked."

Robin hasn't been high since before Jackson died. He sinks eagerly into it, as if smoking could bring him back to those days, when the worst had not yet happened. He visualizes the sweet smoke wrapping around his brain stem, blanketing worries and troubles. A word emerges from the fog. "Painkiller."

"You got that right," Scott says, flopping back on the bed. "My mom's got her drugs and I've got mine."

The kissing is the best part. When their tongues are swirling around each other, it's like a magic spell, stirring a cauldron together, something new rising up. He feels better about Scott while kissing him than at any other time. He likes the smells of it, too, smells you only get when you are up close to someone: cool and smoky in the damp under his arms; like lemon or mustard in the warmth between his thighs; inside his mouth, where he smells like a baby. Compared to the kissing, the humping is more like work—he worries that Scott will come first and then end it abruptly. But this time it didn't happen that way. This time Robin lay on top of Scott; this time, he sucked on Scott's neck so hard he left a little bruise behind; this time, unlike any other time with Scott, Robin shot first. When he was done, he put his mouth around Scott's dick, staring up at him, watching the pleasure in his face. He understood what Todd liked so much about sucking. It was like dessert in the middle of the day.

Now, their clothes are back on, the come towel is crumpled up on the floor and Scott is shuffling around the bed, lost to the jitters that overtake him whenever they've finished having sex. Robin lets himself lie back down, his arms gathering a pillow under his head. He finds himself inside a peacefulness so deep and rare it is hued with sadness. "Can I just ask you a question?"

Scott studies him from above. "I know you're thinking something, I can see it. You have that it's-hard-being-Robin look on your face."

Robin smiles in spite of himself, then takes a breath to ask his question. "How come I never hear from you anymore? You could have called."

"Are you mental? No way was I going to call and have to talk to your parents."

Robin's shoulders tense up guiltily, feeling the weight of his parents' decision to contact Scott's father that night. He wants to shake off this burden—he wants Scott to stop blaming him for this. "You know something?" he says, sitting up forcefully. "You're a liar, Scott. You could have figured out some other way to get in touch with me."

"Talk about a liar—the whole time, you were talking one pile of shit to me and then running off and doing it with Todd fucking Spicer."

Scott says this without looking at him, but Robin hears the hurt and betrayal in Scott's voice. *It's true, it's true,* he thinks. *I did tell Todd things you told me, and then told you I didn't tell him. But it's not that simple.* He tries to sort it out, at last willing himself to protest aloud: "You never told me anything about what went on with you and him. I asked, but you never told me."

Scott kicks a ball of clothing across the rug. "Look, Spicer played a lot of head games with me. He promised me shit and didn't do it. He'd fuck with my head in front of his friends and slap me around and shit. OK? I don't want to talk about it."

Robin stands up, approaches him. He lowers his voice. "I just want to know one thing. Why were you making fun of me? Huh? Why were you telling me I was cute and stuff? Were you just playing head games with *me*? You're the one who started all of this. At The Bird, that was *you*. I would never have even tried to be your friend if you didn't act like you liked me. And I would have never *done it* with Todd if you hadn't acted like you'd *stopped* liking me."

"Robin, in my whole life, I never met anyone who had to *talk* about everything so much. Why you gotta fucking *talk* about everything?"

Scott spins on his toes and stomps out of the room, into the kitchen, leaving Robin surrounded by his accusation, shouting after him, "Why won't you talk about *any* of it?"

He finds Scott standing on a small porch overlooking the backyard. This house, and the entire neighborhood, rests atop a ridge that slopes gradually down to the Palisades. Beyond rows of peaked rooftops, New York's skyscrapers mirror slivers of pale sunlight against the flat gray haze. Between where Robin stands and where the city beckons on the horizon is a dense, cluttered grid of narrow streets, crisscrossing phone lines, uniformly drab houses and parked cars. This ridge is the same one he can see from the bus, the one that slowly reveals the skyline behind it the nearer you get. He thought this place would have been right at the edge of the cliffs; he is surprised this sense of closeness was just an illusion.

Scott says, "Every time we, you know, *fool around,* I swear to myself I'm never gonna do it again."

"Why?"

"Because it's not right."

Robin bristles—this sounds like something coming from a Catholic sermon, not from Scott. "So? Neither is cutting school but you keep on doing *that.*"

"Cutting school isn't the same thing. Cutting school is, like, getting away from fucked-up things. Fooling around—that's like getting deeper into them." He turns to Robin, wanting his agreement. "We can be friends. That's all. Just friends. I mean no more fooling around."

"I *know* what you mean."

"Good. So everything's cool?"

Robin throws his arms wide in exasperation and shouts, "How can you say that? Fifteen minutes ago we were *doing it.*" Scott shushes him, scanning the yards below for possible eavesdroppers, but Robin cannot hold back. "I'm not saying you have to announce it over the loud-speaker before the Pledge of Allegiance every morning, but give me a break, Scott. You could at least admit it to me."

"I'm just trying to make things normal in my life. Is there something wrong with that?"

"Yes!" Robin exclaims. "When people who aren't normal try to make their lives normal it doesn't work. It's like my mother. When she got pregnant, she thought she could have this normal life with my father and leave the city and be a housewife—but she's not normal, so it isn't working. She's turning into a drunk because of it and making the rest of us miserable. Especially my father, who really *could* be normal." The words spill forth quickly and without effort, but when he is finished he is shaking.

Scott stares at him, tugging agitatedly on his T-shirt. "All I know is that the more normal my life gets, the sooner my mother's going to want to come home."

Robin catches a glimpse of the hickey at the base of Scott's neck. He remembers sucking the skin there, mesmerized by the thin rope of muscle between his teeth; he remembers Scott gasping his name while he did it; he said, "Robin," just once, sounding full of wonder, entranced, grateful. That moment stands so sharply in contrast with this one now that Robin feels no confusion at all: he understands, perhaps for the first time, that Scott is not of one mind when it comes to him. He makes Robin feel like the greatest comfort he's ever known and then, later, like the source of all his pain, just another problem in his fucked-up life.

"I'm gonna go," Robin says.

Scott looks both alarmed and relieved. "You can stay a little while more, if you want. Gail probably won't care." He attempts a light-hearted laugh and rubs his collarbone. "I'll just be keeping this covered up for a while."

"I'm going now," Robin repeats, determined to get outside where he can be free of Scott's mixed signals. He walks back into the house, with its stink of diapers and marijuana and greasy plastic toys, and points himself toward the front door.

As he speeds through the rooms, the details are vivid, as if frozen by the flash of a camera. He doubts that he will ever be here again, which only makes him sure he will remember it forever. He got one thing he came here for—another chance to see Scott—but that was all. He let himself believe for a few minutes while they were kissing and lying together that Scott might love him, but he understands now that even if that were true, Scott would not admit it.

He thinks back to that first day, hitchhiking with Scott, riding in the convertible, imagining himself on a magic carpet, making an escape. It was truer than he could have known—he feels so very far away from the person he was that day: the first day he ditched school, the first day he got stoned, the first day he kissed a boy. He has become this new person because of Scott; they've been together on that ride all along. But now? They need different things; they fear different outcomes. The voyage means something different to him than it does to Scott, and once those different meanings are in place, how much is left of what was shared together?

The winter air slaps against him. Blinding sunlight blooms through the clouds. Behind him, Scott's footsteps rush to follow. "Later," Scott calls.

"No," Robin says, summoning up his exit line. "I don't have that much time." But he is not as strong as he has learned to act: when he commands himself not to look back, it is no easy thing.

THE WORLD OF NORMAL BOYS

K.M. SOEHNLEIN

ABOUT THIS GUIDE

The suggested questions are intended to enhance your
group's reading of K.M. Soehnlein's *The World of Normal Boys*.
In this stunning debut, K.M. Soehnlein captures the spirit of a
generation in the haunting, unstoppable voice of thirteen-year-old
Robin MacKenzie, a modern-day Holden Caulfield, whose
struggle for a place in the world is as ferocious as it is real.

DISCUSSION QUESTIONS

1. *The World of Normal Boys* has been called a "coming of age novel." Yet Robin MacKenzie only ages from 13 to 14, and by the end of the book much is still uncertain about his future. How would you describe Robin's journey? What awareness or insight into life does he gain? What does he lose?

2. Robin's closest relationship has always been with his mother, Dorothy, but over the course of the novel they grow apart. What is the cause of this distance? Locate the specific places in the novel where Robin begins to question and re-evaluate their relationship.

3. The story is set in suburban New Jersey in 1978. How does the author use the artifacts and attitudes of the era to develop the characters and move the plot forward? How are the time and place reflected in the characters' behavior and dialogue? How would this story be different if it was set today?

4. At the beginning of the novel, Robin is experiencing the very first explorations of his sexuality (his first wet dream, his first time masturbating). By the end of the novel—just a few months later—he's quite sexually experienced. How do you explain this accleration? What role do Jackson's injuries and hospitalization play in Robin's sexual development, if any?

5. Jackson's fall from the slide affects every member of the MacKenzie family differently. Describe how Ruby, Dorothy and Clark all change as a consequence of the accident. How do their relationships to each other change? What did you find most surprising about the way the family begins to unravel?

6. Robin blames himself for Jackson's fall. Talk about the role of guilt as a motivating factor for him. How does his reaction to the incident on the slide differ from Ruby's and Larry's? How does this play out for all three of them in the final climax on the roof after the funeral?

7. Robin and Scott are very different types of boys, from different backgrounds, and yet they manage to become friends. What draws them to each other? What keeps them involved with each other, despite their frequent arguments? Do you imagine

that they will be able to sustain some kind of friendship beyond the end of the novel?

8. Todd Spicer is an object of fascination for Robin, and also a source of great confusion. He is sometimes friendly to Robin and sometimes bullies him. He pursues sexual encounters with Robin, and had a past relationship with Scott, but also seems to be involved with Debbie. How do you explain Todd?

9. As Robin gets more deeply involved with Todd and Scott, he winds up lying to each of them about his relationship with the other. Why do you think he does this? What did you think of his behavior?

10. Although Robin comes to recognize that his sexual desires are toward boys, he never gets to the point of labeling himself as "gay." How does he come to understand his sexuality? How does that differ from what Todd and Scott each think about his own sexuality? How much do you think Dorothy recognizes or understands this part of Robin?

11. From the beginning of the novel, Robin fantasizes a future life in New York City. How does this fantasy compare to the reality he experiences when he and Scott go to the city together? How does Robin's perception of the city change?

12. Throughout the book, tension between Dorothy and Stan is obvious but never explained. What do you imagine is at the root of their conflict? Why do you think the author keeps it mysterious? How does the conflict between Dorothy and Stan trickle down to their children?

13. When Robin first meets Scott, Mr. Schatz has just given Scott a bloody nose. Robin recalls that he hasn't been hit by his father since a spanking when he was very young. But Clark grows increasingly angry and violent toward Robin over the course of the novel. What are the implications of this rage on Robin? What does it say about the way the novel depicts relationships between fathers and sons?

14. Many of Robin's dreams are described throughout the novel. What do these dreams tell you about him? What effect do they have on the overall feel of the way the novel is written?

15. Even though so many difficult events and significant milestones are packed into a very short period of Robin's life, the novel

never feels unrealistic. How does the author make such extreme events seem convincing and believable?

16. What do you think the title means? Robin says in Chapter Two that he doesn't understand "this whole world of normal boys." In Chapter Eleven, arguing with his parents, he shouts sarcastically, "Everything's normal, just perfectly normal." In the final scene with Scott, Robin concludes that he, and his mother, are not normal—though he says this with some degree of acceptance. What do you think the novel says about the idea of normalcy, especially as it relates to boyhood, sexuality and family dynamics?